"WHAT ARE YOU DOING? WHY . . ."

"It should be obvious what I'm doing."

" 'Tis broad daylight! I have work to do. Duties . . ."

"Your duties lie here with me. Did you think I wanted you for just one night?"

Her breath caught in her throat as the heat in his eyes caught her full force. "Yes. I thought . . ."

He kissed her again, and this time she was past resisting. The feel of his mouth on hers was inescapably right, as if it were something she'd been awaiting all her life.

HIGH PRAISE FOR EMILY BRADSHAW AND HER PREVIOUS NOVELS

MIDNIGHT DANCER

"With a splendid blend of humor, action, adventure and poignancy, Emily Bradshaw draws readers into a wild Western romance that is a true winner."
—*Romantic Times*

"*Midnight Dancer* is a great retelling of the classic Eliza Doolittle–Henry Higgins story with a Western twist. The lead characters and secondary players are top rate. . . . George Bernard Shaw would have been proud to have written this Emily Bradshaw classic." —*Affaire de Coeur*

HALFWAY TO PARADISE

"Emily Bradshaw writes an incredible novel that makes it easy to read about a nation and its people in conflict. *Halfway to Paradise* is rich with historical accuracy, two excellent lead characters and a tremendous plot." —*Affaire de Coeur*

"Emily Bradshaw presents the reader with another extraordinary story of life. Her wonderful characters . . . and adventurous events that lead to marriage and happiness will keep you riveted to these pages leading all the way to Paradise. A great story!"
—*Rendezvous*

HEART'S JOURNEY

"RIVETING . . . filled with poignant details and trials." —*Affaire de Coeur*

"Brims with poignancy and humor . . . a love story you can't forget. Emily Bradshaw combines historical details with a cast of endearing characters, and adds a dash of exhilarating adventure and a heavy dose of sensuality to come up with a winner!"
—*Romantic Times*

CACTUS BLOSSOM

"This is a fast, enjoyable read with dashes of humor, adventure and romance. . . . Read this one for the pure enjoyment of it." —*Rendezvous*

"Maxie is a heroine you'll never forget. Hunter is a hero with all the right ingredients . . . including a wild streak that makes a walk on the wild side seem mighty appealing." —*Affaire de Coeur*

Also by Emily Bradshaw:

MIDNIGHT DANCER
HALFWAY TO PARADISE
HEART'S JOURNEY
CACTUS BLOSSOM

SWEET SORCERY

EMILY BRADSHAW

A DELL BOOK

Published by
Dell Publishing
a division of
Bantam Doubleday Dell Publishing Group, Inc.
1540 Broadway
New York, New York 10036

If you purchased this book without a cover you should be aware that this book is stolen property. It was reported as "unsold and destroyed" to the publisher and neither the author nor the publisher has received any payment for this "stripped book."

Copyright © 1995 by Emily Krokosz

All rights reserved. No part of this book may be reproduced or transmitted in any form or by any means, electronic or mechanical, including photocopying, recording, or by any information storage and retrieval system, without the written permission of the Publisher, except where permitted by law.

The trademark Dell® is registered in the U.S. Patent and Trademark Office.

ISBN: 0-440-22134-X

Printed in the United States of America

Published simultaneously in Canada

November 1995

10 9 8 7 6 5 4 3 2 1

RAD

One

The pool was hidden deep in the forest. Fringed by ferns and swathed in steam, the water's surface mirrored the canopy above and blended its earthy green with the rich emerald of mysterious depths. Not a ripple marred its perfection, as if the breeze dared not intrude upon its peace.

The pool was not a secret. Fisherfolk in their huts by the cold northern sea sometimes spoke of it in whispered tones. Ploughmen's wives might frighten their children into good behavior with threats of leaving them among the dripping ferns at the pond's edge. Everyone knew that mortals dared not trespass there—only fairies, witches, gnomes, demons and other creatures of magic or evil.

Therefore no intruding eyes saw the nude girl as she stepped from the embrace of the forest onto the grassy bank. Almost reverently, she entered the warm, welcoming water. Steam swirled gently upward from the surface, clothing her in a misty veil, wrapping long legs, slender arms, and feminine curves in wisps of white that stirred and curled with every movement.

The girl knelt as if in prayer. Water lapped at her narrow waist; droplets from the steam graced her hair and lashes with sparkling dewdrop jewels. She murmured a few words fit only for fairies' ears, then slid quietly beneath the water. When she emerged, a sleek wet cloak of golden hair covered her shoulders and back. Water ran in sheets over smooth flesh as she stood and raised her arms as if in benediction.

Suddenly, the quiet reverence blossomed into a pixieish smile. She dove, cleaving the dark green surface in nearly soundless grace. The steam cavorted with her when she burst forth in a fountain of sparkling droplets. Like a pale golden otter she played, and the pool seemed to play with her. Silvery warm laughter rippled through the silence and set the leaves of the forest canopy shivering in delighted response—until finally she propped herself against a pillow of moss, stilled her movements and allowed the glade to settle into silence once again.

For a moment Gisela of Ardun lay perfectly still in the warm water, enjoying the absolute peace. The only sound was the soft patter of the pool spilling over its mineral-coated lip into a tiny stream that disappeared into the greenery. The silence was a blessing to her ears, the soft greens and browns soothing to her eyes. All that morning she had labored in the weaving house. Her ears ached from the clatter of looms and female voices; her eyes ached from focusing on the array of threads and straining to detect flaws in the weave. No sufferer of congested chest or sour stomach had summoned her to her little infirmary to prepare a potion of relief. No boils called to be lanced, no bones to be set, no monthly cramps to be dosed. This day, it seemed, Ardun enjoyed remarkable health. Therefore, Gisela had to make herself useful at the distaffs and looms. Worse, if someone didn't do her the mercy of needing a healer by midafternoon, she would find herself laboring in the hot kitchen.

But for now, at least, she had escaped. The pool was not so far from the stronghold of Ardun—only a short walk if one didn't dawdle. This place was holy, or cursed, depending upon one's point of view, and no one dared intrude upon the spirits that frequented the pool. Only Gisela. She came here to relax, to escape the tiresome routine of her days, and to talk with her mother—beautiful Gersvinda, dead for eight years, yet living still in the magic of the forest.

"Mother." Gisela leaned her head back onto the pillow of moss and closed her eyes. "My mother, you are still in my heart."

The breeze whispered through the leaves in what might have been an answer. Gisela opened her eyes. Mischief colored her smile.

"I suppose you know that Lord Ercangar is dead. I hope at each sunrise he is required to wash your feet and at each sunset serve you honeyed mead."

She doubted that spirits had feet to wash, and death no doubt dimmed one's taste for honeyed mead, but Gisela thought spiritual equivalents must exist. The dead Saxon lord of Ardun deserved to wait upon Gersvinda hand and foot to atone for the way he'd treated her in life. Not that he'd treated anyone else much better. Even in dying he'd left the people of Ardun a twisted legacy.

"Trouble is coming," she told her mother with a sigh. "I can feel it stalking us. Close. Soon."

The water of the pool seemed to ripple reassurance. Trouble, yes, but not here, not now. Here and now was the sweet sorcery of the fairy pond, pure and warm, like the magic in the vast blue vault of the sky, a meadow of wildflowers, the deep, cool shadows of the forest. All this magic Gersvinda had taught her daughter to see. All this magic Gersvinda had been able to use with a word, a chant, a flick of her fingers. Sadly, however, Gisela wasn't the witch that her mother had been.

The people hereabouts didn't know that, though. This past week the stablemaster's wife had spread the story of how Gisela had removed a demon's curse from her son. The poultice of chickweed leaves Gisela had applied to the boy's skin rash was scarcely a magic spell, but when the ailment had disappeared, the goodwife was convinced that witchcraft had restored her son to health. Gisela had been a much better student of Gersvinda's herbwifery than of her sorcery.

The warm water seemed to seep into Gisela's pores and set free the tensions she'd been holding inside. She should be getting back to the stronghold and to her duties. Ermentrude would miss her in the kitchen as the dinner hour approached, and she'd be lucky to escape a tongue-lashing if the cook found out she'd been dawdling in the woods while someone else turned the spit or shelled the hazelnuts. Something had called her here this day, however. Perhaps Gersvinda's spirit. Perhaps the magic of the pond. The glade held a strange expectation. Gisela could almost see the leaves above her shiver with it.

Expectation of what? If she had Gersvinda's skill, she might have read the knowledge that hung just beyond seeing, just beyond hearing. But she was merely a servant and herbwife—and a witch who couldn't cast a simple circle without getting the spell backward.

Gisela closed her eyes for a last moment of peace before returning to the stronghold and Ermentrude's scolding. Silence stole over her. She could feel herself relaxing, inch by inch. The twinge of the muscle she had pulled carrying the slops to the hogs that morning faded. Fingers that ached from hours spent at the loom relaxed. Her body seemed to lighten and float weightlessly in the warm water.

Then, in the midst of comfort, she was transported.

Sunlight flashed from polished iron armor. A sword swung and slashed, red with gore. Two men hacked at each other. The clash of their weapons was a mad cacophony above the raucous shouts of the crowd. Dressed in costly white raiment such as she had never worn, Gisela sat alone at one end of the field, raised above the battle, watching. The odors of blood and sweat filled her nostrils. Distant as she was, she heard the warriors' labored breathing, choked on the dryness in their throats. Fear and bitter despair sat like bile in her mouth. The crowd's clamor became the roar of blood in her ears. One of the warriors turned her way. His stare pierced like an iron lance. Tall, straight, and proud, he raised his sword high and brought it down until it pointed toward her. Gisela felt life and hope run out of her, as a cracked cup might spill its contents onto the sand.

Then came fire, consuming everything but the horror. The world was reduced to shimmering red and orange. Heat scorched her skin and hair. Even her soul was ablaze.

Gisela gasped and floundered in the water. Her cry of terror died in her throat when she opened her eyes to see only the green and misty glade, the ferns dripping with condensed droplets of steam, the pool's surface, agitated by her panicked stirring, still shadowed from the summer sun by the tangled vault of leafy branches over her head. She sank down again into the water, shivering now where she had been burning only a moment before. Her heart pounded against her ribs as if it sought escape.

The vision was always the same. It came to her in dreams and at odd moments when her mind drifted. Sunlight on armor, two men fighting, and then the consuming fire. The first time she'd experienced the terror had been the night of Ercangar's death. Three times since that night she had endured it, panicking, burning, only to open her eyes and find that the nightmare wasn't real.

It was real, however, or at least it would be, Gisela feared; for the one bit of sorcery Gersvinda had passed undiluted to her daughter was the curse of envisioning the future.

A soft growl took Gisela's attention away from her distress. She blinked the water from her eyes, then smiled at the creature that emerged cautiously from the dense forest greenery.

"Silver!"

The silver-gray wolf sat down on the bank of the pool, its head cocked inquisitively at the sound of Gisela's voice.

"Welcome, my friend. I need to see a friendly face."

Silver's jaws opened in a tongue-lolling smile.

"You've grown since I last saw you. Not a pup anymore, are you, you beautiful creature?"

As if to deny her statement, the wolf stood, rooed out a puppyish howl, and bowed in an invitation to play—front legs flat on the ground and rump in the air.

"Where's your dignity?" Gisela demanded with a laugh. She sent a fountain of water spurting in the wolf's direction. In a flash of quicksilver, the creature dodged and pranced along the bank, tongue lolling and amber eyes glowing.

"I'm not going to chase you through the woods today, you sprite. If you want to play, you're going to have to get wet."

Silver looked at Gisela longingly.

"Come on in, goosebrain. A little water won't hurt you."

The wolf pawed at the surface of the pond, then snatched back his wet foot as though it had been burned.

"Come in, little silver princeling, and I'll teach you how to swim."

Ears pinned close to its head, the wolf placed one paw in the water, then another.

"That's right, my love."

All four legs in the water now, Silver gave the pond's surface a suspicious sniff.

"It's not going to eat you."

Silver expressed his doubt in a soft growl, but took the plunge anyway. The wake of his abrupt entrance washed over Gisela and left her sputtering. She wiped the water from her eyes to find Silver happily circling her in a strong dog paddle.

"Ah. Mother Earth already taught you how to swim."

Suddenly Silver's head swung around, ears pricked. A very unpuppyish growl rumbled from his throat as he lunged for dry land. In a flash of silver-tipped gray, he disappeared into the forest.

Alarmed, Gisela turned full circle to survey the glade. No one dared to come here except her. Yet she heard a rustling, then the faint clank of something striking metal. Someone was indeed coming.

Gisela's heart jumped into her throat, but before she could flee, two men pushed through the leafy forest screen into the glade.

"What ho, Edgar the Disbeliever! I told you I smelled water, and here it is!"

"Aye, Notker, and something besides," Edgar said in an awed voice.

Gisela felt both men's eyes fasten on her with the same intensity that Silver might regard a juicy rabbit. She sank into the pond to her shoulders, acutely aware of her nakedness. Her eating knife—the only weapon she carried—hung with her clothing on a chokeberry thicket ten steps from the pond, but it might have been hung on the moon for all the good it would do her.

"A water sprite, no less!" the man called Edgar chortled. "I knew this land would have something to make it worth taking back from the heathens."

These were no wanderers from Ardun. Their words were so heavily accented that Gisela scarcely understood half of what they said. Their clothing and armor were of far finer quality than any worn by the fighting men of Ardun. Leather cuirasses covered with overlapping metal plates—like the scales of a snake—covered their chests. Loose woollen trousers were cross-gartered to their legs with leather thongs. One wore heavy-soled sandals on his feet, the other a fine pair of stiffened hide boots.

The man called Notker leered at her with an unpleasant smile. "My grandsire used to tell me a story of how he once trapped a water sprite. Three days and nights serving him was the price he put on her freedom, and he said when the three days and nights were over, his cock was limp as a fish and worn nearly raw. 'Twas a good many days before he could get it stiff again. But worth it, he told me."

"We don't have three days and nights," Edgar said.

"We have an hour or so. That's better than nothing."

"We're late back already."

"Then what matters an hour later?"

Almost numb with horror, Gisela began to back toward the far bank, wondering if she could possibly get to her knife in time.

"Nay, water sprite," Notker chided. "You must pay the price before you go free." He motioned for Edgar to circle around the pond in the direction of her retreat. "We're two likely lads. Better than some you've had, I'll vow. Show us a fine time and there'll be no harm come to you."

"Come to me, my pretty," Edgar entreated from the bank behind her.

"She's going to be stubborn," Notker decided with a hint of relish in his voice. "Take some persuading, she will." He took off his pointed helm, shrugged laboriously out of his cuirass, and all but ripped off his shirt. The speed with which he unwound the leather cross garters that held his leggings bore witness that he had ample practice in hasty undressings. Naked, he was just as intimidating as he was in armor. His stocky, barrel-like body was a solid block of muscle. Abundant body hair was matted to his skin by sweat.

He waded irreverently into the pond and splashed toward her. Gisela was surprised the pond didn't spit him out, or swallow him whole for the sacrilege of polluting its clean water with his presence.

"Leave some for me, Notker," Edgar warned.

"There's plenty for both, from the looks of it."

"Get away from me!"

"Hah!" Notker exclaimed. "It talks!"

"I warn you! I . . . I . . ."

"You what?" He grabbed her wrist. "You've been waiting for a man just like me?"

"How dare you lay a finger on me, you overgrown, warty boar!"

"It growls like a she-bitch!"

Notker seemed delighted. He pulled her toward the shore, eyes feasting on the flesh that was revealed as she emerged from the water. Gisela kicked, twisted, and fought. When that didn't work, she screamed.

"Shut her up!" Edgar warned. "We don't want— *yiiii*!" Edgar's scream was louder than Gisela's as a hundred pounds of fur-covered muscle launched itself for his throat, teeth flashing. "Notker!"

Notker had his own hands full as Gisela took advantage of her assailant's diverted attention to bring her knee up into his unprotected groin. She wished she could remember one of her mother's more dire curses to bring down upon the villain's head, but crushed ballocks would do well enough, judging by his howl. Gisela lunged for the bank. Her feet hit dry land at a dead run. Silver was a gray streak at her side as she dove into the welcoming green tangle of the forest.

* * *

Rutgar of Belthane plowed his way through the tangled greenery of the forest in the direction of the shouts and screams that had just fallen ominously silent. Hand on the hilt of his sword, blood running high for a fight, he burst onto the banks of a peaceful pond, only to find no enemy to use his blade upon. His two tardy scouts were alone at the spring. Rutgar's quick scrutiny revealed no one else in sight.

"What in Christ's holy name is going on here?" he demanded.

Notker, hunched over in the pool, merely groaned, his hands clutched between his beefy, naked legs. On the opposite bank, Edgar cradled one arm.

"My lord!" Edgar croaked.

Rutgar detected the smear of crimson on Edgar's tunic. His eyes narrowed, and his blood began to heat again. "You were set upon?"

"Aye, my lord!"

"Saxons?"

"Aye," Notker managed to grunt. "Devils!"

"They had a monstrous beast with them," Edgar complained. "Fangs like daggers."

"Ah, saints!" Notker groaned. "My ballocks'll never be the same."

"We drove them back into the forest," Edgar assured Rutgar. "They'll not be back, my lord."

Rutgar cursed. "Witless fools. They'll not be back indeed! They run to warn the rebels who hold Ardun! Which direction?"

Edgar and Notker exchanged a pained look, and reluctantly, Notker pointed. "That way."

Rutgar plunged into the forest, muttering a litany of imprecations against the scouts who tarried about their return until their commander was forced to search them out, who stupidly let themselves be discovered by the enemy they sought to surprise, who stood and moaned about their hurts while that enemy escaped. His vexation climbed as brambles and prickly hedges poked and scratched, branches seemed to sweep out to block his path, weeds and vines wrapped themselves around his ankles. The forest itself seemed to plot against him.

Nevertheless he found the enemy, the dread Saxon and monstrous beast, in a clearing only a few minutes trot from the pond. At first he stared in disbelief. Then he sheathed his sword and laughed.

In a quick flurry of silver gray, the beast was gone. The girl gave a shriek and leapt from the log where she'd sat picking thorns from her foot. She fled only a few steps before she yelped in pain and tumbled to the ground. There was absolutely nothing hiding the girl's abundant charms. She was comely, long-legged and golden-haired, with a face and body designed to lure men from their duties.

"A Saxon devil indeed!" Rutgar chuckled, shaking his head. "Those two will not live this down anytime soon."

"Stay away from me!" the maid warned. "Touch me and I'll make you sorry you were born!"

"And how will you do that, pray tell?"

"I will manage, believe me." The maid lifted her pointed little chin and glared at him from wide amber eyes. Her tight-lipped, determined dignity—maintained in spite of being sprawled on her backside in the dirt, made Rutgar want to smile. He didn't smile, though. It wouldn't do to fall into the same trap that had snared the hapless Edgar and Notker.

"What I believe, little maid, is that you are a kink in some very carefully laid plans. I fear that something must be done about you."

* * *

Gisela dug her fingers into the dirt, wondering if she might be able to spring away if she blinded the man with a spray of dirt. Her foot throbbed, reminding her that springing was not a possibility right now, and neither was running. She silently cursed the treacherous thorns that still pierced the ball of her foot.

The man cocked his head and regarded her as he might a troublesome wart. His eyes burned over her body, making her want to scramble for the cover of the brush. Something in the poised readiness of his stance told her that movement would be unwise, however, so she stayed frozen, feeling like a rabbit held in the gaze of a wolf. This man was not like the others at the pool. They were careless and strutting. This man did not appear to be one who was ever careless, nor did he have need to strut his power; it surrounded him like an aura. His shoulder-length black hair caught a gust of the breeze and switched over a face that was lean and sun-bronzed. The obdurate lines of his jaw, the straight, narrow nose, and the dark slash of his brows inspired an odd flash of recognition in Gisela's mind. The eerie sense of knowing him, coupled with the certainty she had never seen him before, sent a shiver down her spine.

He unfastened the scarlet cloak that covered him from shoulder to midcalf. Sun winked off the polished iron scales of the armor that guarded his chest and thighs. "Put this on. Unless, of course, you prefer to remain naked."

Gisela caught the cloak and gratefully wrapped it around her.

"Now, maid, are you going to come without a fuss?"

"I'm no threat to you. Why don't you leave me be?"

The man laughed. The sound was soft and deep. It made the leaves shiver; it made Gisela shiver.

"I'll be more trouble than I'm worth," she promised with desperate bravado. "I guarantee it."

"You'd be wise to be no trouble at all. I'm not a man known for patience."

A stout stick lay within her reach. She wondered if she could use it as the weapon. The man's sword was sheathed. If she was fast enough . . .

For so big a man, he was incredibly fast. Gisela almost didn't have time to flinch before he had her in his grasp. "Has no one ever taught you the wisdom of surrender in the face of impossible odds?" The sun gleamed on the knife in his hand. Gisela gasped and redoubled her effort to be free.

"Be still, wench! This is for your foot. I've no mind to carry you if you can walk."

She wasn't convinced. Arms flailing, feet kicking, she waited for the bite of his blade as he cursed. Strong arms lifted and subdued her, and despite her struggle, she found herself trussed in his cloak like a swaddled babe and dumped on the ground with her feet in his lap.

"Christ's holy bones! If all Saxon maids are as troublesome as you, 'tis no wonder Saxon warriors are such mean-tempered devils!"

"Yowch!" she cried when he took the knife to the thorns.

"Not only sweet-tempered, but brave as well. Hold still, you little fiend, or you'll lose your foot."

"Ow! Ouch! Ham-handed oaf! Release me!"

"Ham-handed am I? In some circles, my bare-assed lady, I'm counted quite an expert with a blade of any kind. You should be grateful. If I were a less tolerant fellow, I'd be using it on something other than your foot. Now, I think I've wasted enough time on your behalf. Let's be on our way."

Gisela had little choice but to submit to being prodded back toward the pond.

Rutgar spared his erring scouts no part of the embarrassment that they'd earned when he arrived with his captive at the pond. "*This* is the Saxon devil who managed to lay you both low?" he taunted. "Perhaps we should recruit our fighting forces from amongst the Saxon maidens of Ardun."

"Aye," Edgar mumbled. Notker merely gave the girl a look of sullen lust, which she returned with a defiant glare.

Edgar muttered, "Keep a sharp eye, my lord. The hellbitch had a mad wolf with her."

"The beast fled. There appear to be all sorts of strange creatures in these Saxon woods," Rutgar observed wryly. His stiff-backed prisoner shot him a look worthy of an offended queen.

A few moments walk brought them to the spot where Rutgar had tethered his horse near Notker's and Edgar's—the woods around the pond were too dense to let a horse pass with ease.

Once they were mounted, the cloak that wrapped the girl afforded Rutgar no protection from the warmth of firm buttocks tucked against his groin or the long feminine legs resting against his thighs. When they arrived back at the encampment, Rutgar's braes were strained to the limit, and he was in no humor to be charitable to the creature who was the cause of his discomfort and inconvenience. The attention she immediately attracted from his men, who should have been seeing to their weapons and armor, didn't improve his mood.

Rutgar summoned his servant Odo with an impatient wave. "Take the girl to my tent. Make sure she can't get away, or we'll have the whole garrison at Ardun awaiting us tomorrow."

"Who is she?"

"She's trouble. My only concern with her is that she doesn't get to Ardun before we do. Make sure of it, Odo. And find some clothes to cover her. I want my cloak back."

The girl cast an uncertain look back at him as old Odo led her away. Rutgar cursed under his breath. With those bewitching gold eyes of hers, she'd have the whole camp panting after her if she was anywhere in sight. He went to the water bucket and emptied it over his head, but even the shock of cold water did little to ease the ache in his groin.

That was where Etich, his lieutenant, found him, dripping and cursing the fact that men were so vulnerable to the charms of women.

"I see you found them," Etich rumbled. He was known as the Bear to the men who fought beside him. Big as his namesake and almost as hairy, the giant had been Rutgar's friend since before Rutgar had reached manhood.

"I did—at a pond where they stopped to dally with a local wench. Their lust was more important to them than reporting their reconnaissance of Ardun."

"Fools," the giant grunted.

"The wench gave them what they deserved." Rutgar grinned. "And more."

Etich's eyes narrowed in his broad face. "And then ran off to warn Ardun?"

"Nay. She's in my tent, and there she'll stay."

An ursine brow twitched. "Convenient."

"If you want her in your tent, be my guest, but guard your ballocks. She's a little demon."

"In that case, my lord, she's all yours."

Rutgar grunted. "Get Aldwin and Leo and meet me back here to talk about Notker and Edgar's report. If things go wrong tomorrow, this could become a drawn-out siege, and that's exactly what I don't want. So let's not let things go wrong."

Etich chuckled. "That would be my choice."

"Don't underestimate this Aelrhane fellow. I've fought the Saxons before. They're a worthy enemy. The sight of their own blood only makes them fight harder. He's got a strong palisade with guard towers all around, and according to Notker's observations over the last three days, the guards don't let down their vigilance much—except sometimes in the very early dawn when a man's most likely to nod off to sleep. We need to get in there before they know we're on them or we're likely to have a fight on our hands that will leave the place scarcely worth having. I don't want to be lord of a domain with burned-out storehouses and starving serfs."

"If they have a brain among them, they'll surrender."

Rutgar grinned wolfishly. "They will fight, Bear. They're Saxons."

Etich left to fetch the other senior commanders, and Rutgar squatted to draw a rough diagram of Ardun's defenses in the dirt—a square with four watchtowers and one heavily guarded, barred gate. Earthen ramparts and a deep dry ditch surrounded a log palisade twice as high as the Bear stood. Rutgar pondered the stronghold's obvious weak points— the west log palisade, which Notker had reported under repair, the gate, which no matter how heavily guarded, was always a weakness, and along one of the palisades, probably the one closest to the encroaching forest, a bolt-hole. Every holding had one—a hidden way out in case of conquest, and a way in to the attacker lucky enough or smart enough to find it.

Tomorrow he would take Ardun, as King Charles had ordered. He had spent most of his life fighting for the Frankish king, from the Spanish march to Lombardy to Bavaria, in hopes that this opportunity would someday be granted him—land of his own to rule, to nuture, to make into a home. Finally he had it within his grasp. He would be lord of Ardun, vassal of the greatest king in Christendom, defender of the Saxon March.

Ardun would be his, and God help anyone who stood in his way.

Two

Gisela couldn't decide if she was more terrified or indignant. Dressed in dirty tunic and braes borrowed from some filthy man who apparently was twice her size, she sat on the rush mats that covered the tent floor. The old man had made very sure she could not escape, for not only were her hands tied, but she was chained to the centerpole like a dog.

No man at Ardun would have dared treat her in such a manner. He would have feared that his ballocks would shrivel on the spot or his next born would sport two heads. Not that Gisela had the talent for such powerful magic, nor would she have sought revenge in such a low manner, but all at Ardun knew that sorcery was her birthright. Lord and servant, freeman and serf, all showed the same caution with the witch Gersvinda's daughter that they would accord a poison-tipped lance.

These men, however, were not from Ardun. Gisela knew the face of every man and woman who lived on the estate—every warrior, stableboy, cook, ironsmith, farmwife, and ploughman. She could name every one of the fighting men that Aelrhane had brought to Ardun when old Ercangar had ceded to him on his deathbed. The men of Stringau, also, were familiar to her, though that estate was a day's ride north. The men gathered in the encampment were strangers to her and to the land. Invaders.

The word settled like a stone on her heart. Invaders meant war, and war meant corpses staining Mother Earth with their blood, children starving, disease stalking through stronghold and villages, ravaging like a hungry wolf. For so many years her home had drowned in the blood of its people along with the blood of those who sought to rule them. Now blood would flow again.

The afternoon stretched miserably on. Gisela leaned against the centerpole and thought about the great guardian oaks that ringed the camp. Her mother had told her that the great trees were holy. They stood sentry against the evil that continually threatened to upset the balance of the world. If Gersvinda had been right, then why were these allowing bringers of doom to camp peacefully in their shade? Gisela thought about the unsuspecting innocents at Ardun. Luitgard —eleven years old and possessed of a winsome beauty that would make her natural prey for warriors seeking sport. Blind Drada, who ruled in the weaving house: her old hands could find any flaw in the cloth that came off the looms, and she could tell by touch if the weave was tight and finely done. Her old heart might not endure the terror of the fray to come. Ermentrude: queen of the kitchen. For all that her scoldings could be sharp, she was always one to slip a pastry or sweetmeat to the children who plagued her kitchen like a swarm of little bees.

Men and their wars! The children and women and aged suffered for the warriors' blood sport. Aelrhane would no doubt welcome the prospect of fighting. He strutted about in his new role as lord of the domain, but counting cattle and sheep and arbitrating the problems of stewards, tenants, and serfs only made him yawn. This afternoon he probably was in the hall, planning a hunt with Eric and Einmar—not suspecting that beyond sight of the watchtowers were camped stalkers who regarded *him* as prey.

In hopeless frustration, Gisela tested the bonds that held her. The chain had no flaws to exploit, and the rope was securely tied. She stood and yanked at the chain where it was fastened around the post, but the iron lock held fast. A deep chuckle behind her made her start and whirl around. As if punishing her for her earlier abuse, the chain yanked her back. Overbalanced, she sat down hard on the rush mats.

Her captor looked down at her, hands on hips, mouth curving in an amused smile. "I see Odo took me at my word. You're trussed more securely than a dog who's been at the chickens."

Gisela glared up indignantly. She seemed continually in a position where she had to look up at this oaf, and she didn't like it one bit. She was accustomed to a bit more respect. "Lout! Abuser of innocent maids!

May your sword arm wither and your hair fall out." She lashed out with her foot, intending to vent her anger on his shin, but he nimbly jumped out of the way.

"Still have some sting left in you, I see. Watch who you bite, little buglet, or you might get swatted like a mosquito." He smacked his hands together as if swatting an insect. "Now, behave yourself, or I'll hand you over to the commander, who is known far and wide as a swine who eats tender maids for his supper."

Gisela glanced out the opening of the tent to where a giant of a man talked with several others. He pounded a fist the size of a ham into his other hand and gestured for one of the men to do something. Taller, broader, and hairier than any man Gisela had ever seen, he stumped out of the narrow range of her view. She imagined the earth shaking and the guardian oaks quaking at his every stride. Her eyes grew round.

Her captor's gaze had followed hers. Seeing her wide-eyed reaction to the giant, he grinned and nodded. "Pull in your stinger, buglet, and I'll shirk my duty to tell the warlord of my little prisoner."

"That . . . that creature is your warlord?"

"Fierce-looking, isn't he?" the Frank commented. He went to the bucket in the corner of the tent and offered her a dipper of water. She drank deeply and gratefully. When she handed the dipper back, he regarded her with something that could have been regret.

"What am I to do with you?"

"Let me go," she suggested.

He chuckled, and a smile momentarily creased his sun-browned face and softened his eyes. Gisela noted that his mouth, when it softened, was sculpted in curves almost too beautiful to be part of a warrior's face.

"If you had been tending to your tasks as a maid should, you'd now be safe in your hut or sheltered behind the walls of Ardun."

"And how is that safe, with your army waiting to pounce? Who are you that sneaks through the forest in a land where you don't belong?"

"We belong here, woman. 'Tis the rebels who hide behind the walls of Ardun who tread where they shouldn't."

"They are Saxons on Saxon land."

"This is not Saxon land; it is King Charles's land. He rules from Saxony to Spain, from the sea in the west to the land of the Avars in the east, and he'll give up no part of his kingdom to rebels."

Gisela took a deep, startled breath. These men did not ride for some minor Frankish warlord who sought to expand his holdings, they hied from the greatest warlord of all: the Frankish king who claimed to be king of the Saxons as well.

"Less blood will be spilled if a certain impertinent maid is prevented from carrying warning to her friends."

Gisela flinched as his hand reached out to a deep scratch that marred the skin of her cheek. His touch was gentle, but the cut smarted.

"Did Edgar or Notker give you this?"

"Nay. Those goatish louts were not fast enough to lay a hand on me. 'Twas a branch in the forest when I fled."

"How has such an impertinent serf survived to ripen to womanhood? I hope Aelrhane is as lax in his discipline of Ardun's fighters. If so, we will have no trouble taking the prize tomorrow."

"You have no right to destroy our peace!"

"Blame not me, little maid. Your lord Ercangar asked for war when he surrendered Ardun to Saxon rebels. Now, do you know what meek silence is? If so, I suggest you practice it, for if I weary of sharing this tent with you, I will put you out for the giant to deal with."

She opened her mouth for a caustic reply, then snapped it shut. How she wished that she could truly call some devilish curse down upon these Frankish invaders. But as wary as Ardun was of her witchery, she probably couldn't successfully summon one bee to sting the giant warlord's backside, much less have the earth open to swallow his whole troop. Just in case they might work, however, she muttered the requisite words under her breath while the servant came in and helped her captor remove his cuirass. When the task was finished, the servant squatted in one corner of the tent, drawing a whetstone along the blade of a sword and looking at her with round eyes, like a child wistfully gawking at honey treats.

"You, too, Odo?"

"Eh?"

"Watch yourself, old man. Edgar and Notker have learned of her sting already. I thought you were old enough to know better."

The servant chuckled. "E'en a white-haired ancient appreciates the sight of a comely maid, especially when the eyes have been denied the sight for days at a time."

The master growled. "Fetch the wench bread and cheese."

When Odo had gone, the Frank unfastened the chain and untied her hands so that the blood could flow to her fingers. "I'll have no more trouble from you, buglet. Brandish your stinger again and I'll swat you so that you stay swatted."

Gisela couldn't resist. They were alone, and she was untied. She lunged for the tent opening, only to be painfully yanked back by the trailing banner of her hair.

"*Yowch!* Let me go!"

"You do not learn quickly, do you?"

She clawed at his eyes. He grabbed her wrists, pinning both togther in the vise of one of his large hands. For a moment their eyes locked. Once again she experienced a jolt of recognition. Some other time, some other place, she had looked up into those iron-gray eyes, felt his hand upon her, seen her name formed by the sculpted lips. The tent suddenly seemed very crowded. There was too little air to breathe.

Then the tent flap was brushed aside and old Odo came in bearing a small loaf of bread and round of cheese. The warrior let her go and shook his head, like a dog shaking off water, and the intensity that had gripped him was gone. "You try my patience, maid. Eat, then sleep. I want to hear no more from you."

Gisela turned away and tried to catch her breath. Odo shoved the bread and cheese into her hands, and she forced herself to eat. When she was finished, the Frank ordered Odo to tie her hands and feet.

"Wait." Gisela pushed away the rope as the servant attempted to do his master's bidding. "Must I pass the night bound like a pig bound for the spit?"

" 'Twill remind you that any attempt to escape will have unpleasant consequences." He plucked a leaf from her hair and released it to float past her eyes—a reminder of their little tussle in the forest. "Sleep well, maid. And quietly."

The Frank followed his own advice. In a few moments his shallow breathing showed him to be peacefully asleep on the pallet across the tent. Gisela wondered at such confidence that would allow him to sleep so well the night before he might be killed in battle. Perhaps he believed that his giant warlord was so fierce he could overwhelm Aelrhane without a fight. If so, he didn't know much about Aelrhane.

She tested her bonds. They were secure. Not tight enough to cut off the flow of blood, but certainly sufficient to keep her from squirming free. She prayed silently—a prayer to the old gods that had been worshiped by her people since the dawn of time, and a plea to the Christian God as well. She didn't want to ignore any possible source of help. But the rope that bound her stayed in place.

She sighed wearily. The Frank continued to sleep quietly on his pallet. The rhythm of his breathing lulled her reluctantly into a fitful doze. . . .

Gisela woke with a start, but some instinct warned her to silence. The sound that had awakened her came again. A brush against the tent wall behind her. A low whine.

Heart thumping, Gisela turned her head as far as she could—to glimpse a wet, black nose push under the tent wall. She gave thanks to whichever god had answered her prayers. Quietly she scooted against the wall. Silver's warm tongue caressed her chafed hands and wrists, then his strong teeth went to work on her bonds.

Gisela halted, panting. Ahead, looming up out of the darkness, she could just make out the log stockade that crowned the rise ahead. Ardun. Finally. The night remained thick and black, and Gisela had no sense of how closely dawn might lurk below the horizon. It seemed she had run for hours. Her bare feet were cut and bruised, her hair interwoven with brambles, and every exposed section of skin scratched and scraped. She had run with no pause to rest, imagining with every step that the Franks pursued, fearing all the while she would lose her way in the dark.

Now that she had finally stopped, her lungs refused to be satisfied with the amount of air she could draw in. Spots swam before her eyes like fireflies in the gloom.

Silver gave her hip a nudge. She laid a hand on the softly furred head.

"Thank you, friend." Another few deep breaths, and her wind began to return. "Go now. There are those at Ardun who wouldn't be properly appreciative. And don't let those Franks catch you. I don't want to see that silver pelt of yours keeping the ogre of a Frankish warlord warm."

A wet tongue swiped her hand, and the next moment the wolf disappeared into the forest. A faint sound made her glance back along the path in alarm, but no pursuers jumped out at her. She chided herself for being so goosey. Neither her captor nor his servant could have awakened yet from the blows she had given them. Not that the blows had been that great—a mere tap with the back of the Frank's war axe to ensure that he and his servant didn't awaken to find her gone. The knot their heads would boast when they woke was certainly less of an injury than Aelrhane would deal them when they braved the stronghold.

The sentries who paced the camp's perimeter had been a bit harder to deal with. One had almost discovered her when a branch had whipped back from her passage with a swish that was all too audible in the quiet night. She had frozen to absolute stillness for what had seemed an eternity, and finally the guard had moved on in his rounds. The sentries were looking for enemies from without, not within, and so she had managed to slip by them undetected.

Gisela began to run again. No hail or challenge greeted her at Ardun's gate, and she cursed Aelrhane for his complacency. Did he take his people's safety so lightly?

She shouted up to the gatehouse tower. After a moment had passed, a sleepy "Who begs entrance?" answered her. She recognized the voice of Galt, who liked his mead far too much to be useful as a sentry.

" 'Tis Gisela. Let me in."

"Who?"

"Gisela. Quickly! I have urgent news."

She heard Galt muttering all the way down the tower ladder. When the gate swung open, he peered out at her suspiciously.

"Gisela? Is it you?"

"Galt, you've known me since I had but ten years. Don't you recognize me?"

"Uh . . ."

As he raised his torch she squeezed through the small span he'd allowed the gate to open. Galt backed away, his expression mingling fear and awe, clearly believing that only demons, fairies, and witches dared be abroad in the woods at night.

"Close the gate and bar it well."

Galt obeyed with alacrity. Any other woman he would have told to mind her spinning and let him mind the gate. Any other woman he would have interrogated as to the reason she was roaming the woods in the dark. The questions were in his eyes, but Gisela knew that he dared not voice them.

Gisela opened her mouth to explain, but then realized if she told Galt that the Franks were on the march, he would only panic and infect the entire stronghold with his hysteria. Aelrhane was the man to warn, but a mere serving girl—even Gisela—would have difficulty gaining access to the lord of Ardun in the wee hours of the morning. Lothar, then, was her next choice. He would be sleeping in the barracks, or if not there, in the large hall of the stone manor that stood in the center of the stronghold.

"Galt, how long before dawn?"

The guard shrugged. "An hour. Perhaps less."

"Do you know where Lothar is?"

"Asleep?"

Gisela sighed and turned toward the barracks, a long log building that housed warriors and some of the male servants. She prayed Lothar was sleeping there instead of the manor.

Lothar saved her the trouble of searching for him by choosing that moment to walk out of the small chapel that huddled against the west palisade. Gisela ran toward him. She should have known he'd be in the chapel when all others still slept.

"Gisela! What are you doing up at this time of morning?"

Suddenly the events of the night overwhelmed her, and she lost the control that she'd clung to so desperately. She threw her arms around Lothar's neck and buried her face in his shoulder.

"Hold now! What's this?"

"I was bathing in the fairy pond and was taken by King Charles's men. They are here, Lothar! Just over an hour's ride away, and they mean to attack with the dawn to take Ardun back for their master!"

"Charles's men! God protect us! Are you certain?"

"I had it from the mouth of one of the warriors."

"How many men?"

"I counted about thirty-five—maybe a few more. Plus servants and lackeys with the supply wagons. The warlord who leads them is a giant. He looks more beast than man."

Lothar drew her against his chest in comfort. In the years since her mother had died, only Lothar had ever offered solace for her grief over Gersvinda or comfort during the other trials of growing up. Gentle Lothar. While others at Ardun knew of Gisela's connection to Ercangar, their dead lord, Lothar openly acknowledged her birth as his father had not. While others alternately revered her as holy and feared her as an unpredictable evil, naming her sorceress out of her hearing, Lothar simply gave her his affection and named her sister.

"My father was a fool to give Ardun over to Aelrhane. Now these Franks come to exact the king's revenge."

"Perhaps if we didn't fight, this Frank would rule us peaceably."

"Aelrhane will fight. The man's life is fighting." He set Gisela back from him and regarded her with a wry smile. "You look as though you've been wrestling with trolls. Did the Franks harm you, Sister?"

"My dignity is all they injured."

"Go wash yourself while I find Aelrhane. If our fate comes with the dawn, we have little time to prepare."

Relieved to have the burden of warning shift from her shoulders, Gisela hastened to the women's quarters. Her entrance woke Drada, who muttered at the noise at such an early hour.

"Wake up, old mother. We've work to do."

Drada grunted.

"The Frankish king's men are here. They'll be at our walls with the sun's rising."

Drada's thin lips compressed into a line, and the seamed face sagged away from eyeless sockets. Her sixty years on this earth had been laced with war, and she knew the ways of battle better than she wanted to. She rolled heavily from her pallet and pushed herself to her feet. "We'll need bandages, water from the well, a fire to heat the irons for cauterizing wounds. Wake the others, girl, and then see to your medicinals."

The other women roused reluctantly, but when they heard what danger the morning brought, they went about preparing for the wounded with brisk if resigned efficiency. They, too, had spent much of their lives watching their men kill each other for land, supremacy, or sometimes nothing but male pride. With Drada's consent, Gisela sent Luitgard to the village with a warning of what was to come. The comely child would be far safer in the village, where the forest offered a thousand hiding places, than within the stockade where she could be trapped by lusty Franks celebrating their victory. Once Gisela had seen Luitgard slip safely out the gate, she went to the little infirmary at one end of the women's quarters. There she inventoried her supply of herbs and remedies. She was short on slippery elm and meadowsweet, but those remedies for bilious stomachs were not likely to be needed in the aftermath of battle. She had enough slippery elm powder to serve as a binder in poultices. Her shelves held plenty of garlic and myrrh to fight suppuration of wounds, knitbone to speed healing, and white willow for fever. The tincture of poplar buds had been soaking only a week instead of the two or three it required to reach full strength, but what she had would have to do.

"Maid Gisela."

Gisela looked up to see Drada's grandson Guntar at the door of the infirmary. His face looked pale against the shock of his bright red hair.

"Yes, Guntar?"

"Lord Aelrhane sent me to find you. He would speak to you in the hall."

"I'll be right there." She put the crockery jar that held the tincture back on its shelf, regretting suddenly that she hadn't thought to change into a kirtle and tunic and decently cover her hair with a headcloth. She was still barefoot and dressed in the dirty clothing borrowed from the Franks. Now she had no time to make herself presentable.

"Maid Gisela? Are we all going to die?" The boy danced a childish hop beside her as she headed for the stone manor that sat in the center of the compound.

"No, Guntar." Gisela hoped she didn't lie. She couldn't imagine her captor slaughtering children. She could only hope that his beast of a commander was not as fearsome as he appeared. "No, Guntar. I hope you will live to see a few more years."

"The Christian priest says we'll all be killed and go to hell. He says because Lord Ercangar defied the king of the Franks that God is angry and sent these men to hack us to pieces."

"You shouldn't be frightened by anything Father Gaunt says. God does not really speak to him, and if He did, I doubt Father Gaunt would listen."

"Why does Aelrhane let him stay? I don't like him."

"Father Gaunt stays because Lord Ercangar wished it. Ercangar believed in the Christian God."

"Do you believe in the Christian God, Gisela?"

"Yes."

"But my mother says you follow the old gods. She says you're a witch."

"The God I believe in has many names and can be worshiped in many ways. And He doesn't send warriors to kill children."

Guntar sighed. "I guess we'll find out who's right, huh?"

"I suppose we will." The manor loomed before them. "Go help the women fetch water from the well, Guntar, and stay with your grandmother when the Franks come. Do you hear? She will need your protection."

"I will," he promised, scampering away.

Aelrhane and Lothar awaited her in the hall, which smelled of tallow lamps, stale rushes, and woodsmoke. Seated beside the cold hearth like a queen on a throne, Ercangar's mother Adalinde presided in calm dignity. She nodded a regal welcome to Gisela.

Aelrhane didn't bother to greet her. "Are you sure these are Charles's men, girl?"

"One of their warriors himself declared it to me. He looked to be a nobleman, so I trust he should know for whom he fights."

Aelrhane cursed and slammed his fist against the planks of the table. "He's left us alone for years. I'd hoped he'd forgotten Ardun existed."

"The interloper let us be as long as my son paid his tribute of produce and sent our young men to fight his wars. Now that Ardun is ruled by those who don't bow to the invader, the monster is once again roused."

"Gisela!" Aelrhane entreated urgently. "What do you see?"

He asked for a vision. All of Ardun knew that Gisela had the sight, but only rarely was she asked to reveal what came to her. In this world, one was better off not knowing the future.

"I have vision of men fighting—but only two men, in a terrible duel. I see the sun glinting off iron armor, blood flowing, and at the end—fire. I don't know if this vision is the battle with the Franks, my lord, but I do know that the enemy that comes tomorrow is a fearsome one. With my own eyes this night I saw a company of hardened warriors led by a warlord who is a monstrous giant. The warrior who held me considers the defenders of Ardun so little danger that he falls asleep like an untroubled babe the night before battle. When I was taken into the camp, I saw swords honed to razor edges, lances sharpened until the iron points will pierce muscle and bone like a needle punctures silk, armor polished until it reflects every ray of the sun. The men spoke the Frankish tongue among themselves, and said the word Saxon as if it were a curse."

"The king's men." Aelrhane kneaded his forehead with his hands and sighed. "Our warriors are eager to fight, but the stockade is still weak in several places. The west palisade especially. We can't defend the village or farms . . ."

"I sent Luitgard to the village with warning. They will hide."

Lothar warned, "If the Franks can't get through our walls, they'll burn the fields and slaughter the stock. 'Tis best to surrender and swear fealty to this lord the king has sent."

"Traitor!" Adalinde spat. "This is Saxon land, ruled by Saxons. You would give it to these invaders just as your father did."

"Grandmother, for eight years the king of the Franks has claimed Ardun; it was surrendered willingly by my father in return for peace and protection. He was mad with death's shadow when he gave it over to a man who refuses the king's claim."

"You think yourself cheated by your father! That is why you mouth such seditious advice."

"My father knew I had no wish to rule here."

"Then you are a fool. Land is power. And Saxon land should be Saxon power."

"Aelrhane," Lothar pleaded, "resist and you will force us into a battle we cannot win. Think of the lives that will be wasted."

"We will defend Ardun," Adalinde declared. "We will defend it to the last drop of blood in the last man of Ardun, if necessary."

Gisela thought that Adalinde was being a bit generous with other people's blood, and from the expression that suddenly twisted Aelrhane's ruddy face, she guessed that he felt the same as she.

"Dying in battle serves no purpose but to give poets fodder for their songs. We will fight, but if the battle goes against us, we will take to the forest and harry the Franks until Ardun is back in our hands—as we did before."

Gisela felt a chill as she imagined more years of raiding and death, where no man, woman, child, cow, or goat was safe from the warrior wolves who tore the land between them. As if drawn by the hand of doom, she looked up to the high window that let morning's first gray light into the hall.

Dawn was at hand.

Three

The sun crested the rise to the east in a blood-red, incandescent sliver that set fire to the dark warriors who waited there. Gisela squinted into the blinding light, her face pressed against the palisade to see better through the small space between the logs.

"Are they coming?" Guntar asked in a breathless voice. He crowded Gisela on one side; old Drada pressed against her on the other. Beside them Fredelin the cook's girl, Rolf the stable lad, Gillan and Atruda the fire tenders, all had one eye pressed against knotholes and openings between the rough logs.

"They come," Gisela confirmed.

They came indeed, holding their banner before them—a small boar's head streaming a length of brightly colored hose that caught the breeze and waved aloft in coruscating challenge. Like fiends emerging from the fires of hell they rode out of the scorching glow of the sun. Their outlines wavered in the burning crimson light. Red sparks shot from iron armor and glanced from iron-tipped lances, razor-edged war axes, polished round shields. Warriors of iron—iron armor, iron weapons, iron shields, iron souls. Hard, unyielding, crushing iron.

Gisela couldn't breathe. She felt the weight of all that iron pressing down upon her. The smell of blood clogged her nostrils, and cries rang in her ears—screams of terror, shouts of anger. The world tilted from the violence of her vision, and she clung to the rough logs to stay upright.

"Maid Gisela! Are you all right?"

Guntar's voice drew her back. Gisela opened her eyes to see his anxious face looking up at her. His hand clutched at her arm.

"Maid Gisela?"

"I'm all right, Guntar."

"Can I look?" His voice wavered between excitement and fear.

"Look your fill, lad."

Drada fumbled for Gisela's hand, squeezing it tight when Gisela put it in her grasp.

"They come," the old blind woman said, not a question, but a statement spoken in resigned certainty. "The peace is over."

"Aye, old mother. They ride slowly, letting us look

full well at them and see their power. They know I carried warning, so they try to conquer us with intimidation rather than surprise."

Drada nodded. "Do they succeed?"

"They're a fearful sight," Gisela told her with a sigh. "Their horses are big as dragons and the warriors sit astride them like iron gods bent on destruction."

"Holy Christ be our shield, then."

"They're big!" Guntar exclaimed. "Look at those horses! They've all got horses!"

"Horses can't jump the ditch or climb our stout log palisade," Rolf the stable lad reminded him. "Aelrhane could beat any one of those Franks with one hand."

"Look at the giant!" Guntar breathed in awe. "He's big as Thor!"

"And broad as mighty Woden," Gillan the fire tender joined in. "And the one beside him rides tall as a god." Her voice trembled between apprehension and admiration.

"Aelrhane will take them down a size or two," Rolf insisted.

Atruda scoffed. "They make Aelrhane's warriors look like scrawny roosters."

"The enemy always appear as monsters," Drada commented. "But they bleed like men."

"I wish I could fight!" Guntar declared.

Gisela battled a sick feeling. "Time enough in your life to fight, Guntar. Let yourself grow to manhood first."

"I'm almost a man."

"What's this?" A wiry, dark-bearded warrior clad in a leather byrnie scrambled down the ladder that led to the platform above. "Don't ye know there be a battle coming, fools? What're ye doing here?"

"I want to watch!" Guntar begged. "I'm almost old enough to fight."

"If the Frankish devils break through the wall, even babes like you will be fighting for your lives. Now be a good lad and take these females and young ones to the stone house for safekeeping."

The men on the wall were beginning to shoot arrows and verbal insults at the enemy. As she hurried with the little group toward the the shelter of the stone manor, Gisela flinched at the sound of a well remembered Frankish voice demanding Aelrhane's surrender to his rightful lord. Laughter greeted the demand, and the twang of bows once again started their inimical song. She remembered the foretaste of blood and terror that had set her reeling at the wall—likely Saxon blood and Saxon screams. If the Frankish warlord broke through the palisade, no place would afford shelter to those who defied him.

The mood in the audience hall of the manor was drawn even tighter than the strain Gisela had sensed on the palisade. Warriors at least could release their tension in fighting. They had some control over their destinies. Those who huddled behind the stone walls of the manor could only wait—a harder task than fighting.

Gisela went at once to check on the supplies she had brought earlier from her infirmary, for the wounded would be brought to the manor for treatment. The stronghold's only stone building—in peacetime the residence of the lord and the officers of his personal guard—was the last line of defense during an attack.

"You brought your herbs and potions, I see." Adalinde paused in her restless pacing long enough to notice Gisela. "Good. We'll have need of them before the hour's out, you can be sure. You are . . . you are a good girl, Gisela." She laid an age-spotted hand on Gisela's arm and for a moment looked as though she would say something else. Her thin lips tightened around silence, however, and with a scowl she resumed her pacing.

Gisela allowed herself a brief little smile. Not often did Adalinde relax her stern dignity. The momentary affection that had softened the creased, wintry face testified to the strain the old lady suffered. Never had she acknowledged Gisela as granddaughter, though in numerous small ways—a thin smile, an absent pat on the arm, a searching look—she recognized the blood bond between them.

While Adalinde paced, the women clustered around the hearth, or dashed to and from the kitchen, where bread was rising and several pots of stew simmered. Even during a battle people must eat. Others sat in frightened silence, or followed their mistress's example and paced in restless frustration. Old men gazed longingly at the barred door, their eyes locked onto memories of other battles, deeds of heroism or bloody terror, their own days and nights of battle lust, fear, desperation, triumph. Children sat on the benches and rush-covered floor playing games, building forts out of the dirty rushes, or sleeping. The tension that shivered between their mothers and aunts and old grandfathers made them quieter than usual, but they didn't really understand why the day was not going forward with the usual chores—why the cows in the byre next to the stable hadn't been turned out into the pasture outside the palisade, why the smithy didn't ring with the sound of metal hammering metal, why the lord Aelrhane wasn't hailing his comrades, as he did most mornings, to be out chasing the stag and the boar, why their aunts and mothers weren't boiling the laundry, tending the garden, searching the poultry yard for eggs, or sitting at the looms and spinning wheels. They didn't understand that war had come with the morning light, and the adults didn't try to make them understand. There would be time enough when the battle was won or lost to teach them what was at stake this day.

Guntar, no longer a child but not yet a warrior, was delegated by Adalinde to scamper periodically to the palisade and report back on the progress of the fighting. Midmorning he reported that the Frankish archers were so accurate in their firing over the walls that several Saxon defenders had been wounded, and in fact two warriors followed on Guntar's heels, one with an arrow in his thigh and another carrying a comrade whose shoulder spouted crimson. Father Gaunt, who had been muttering quiet prayers all morning, folded his hands and earnestly cried to God for protection.

As the sun reached its zenith, the women prepared to send bowls of stew out to the palisade. Guntar came in with the news that some of the more agile Franks had managed to scale the rough logs of the palisade, and fighting had erupted inside the walls. Other Franks were battering at the weakened west palisade, and might break through at any moment. Aelrhane's warriors fought valiantly, he insisted, but his voice held a tremor of fear.

The women abandoned the idea of sending food to their defenders. Adalinde ordered the manor door solidly barred and opened only to admit the wounded, who began to stumble, crawl, or be carried into the hall in frightening numbers. Lothar was one of them. Gisela noted his arrival out of the corner of her eye as she wrapped a poultice of knitbone and yarrow over a bloody axe wound. Her heart sank. Lothar was carried past her on a litter, one pale hand hanging limply over the side, fingers dripping a trail of blood. The rest of him she couldn't see. She rushed to his side as he was set down among the other wounded.

"A sword opened his side," explained one of the men who had carried him in. "And another stroke caught his arm."

The carrier himself looked in little better condition than Lothar, but he wouldn't sit when Gisela bade him. "I caught just a nick here and there," he said. "See to Lothar, maid Gisela. We can't have the old lord's son cut down by mangy Franks."

Gisela carefully lifted Lothar's bloody tunic from the gaping slash over his ribs.

"Can you mend him, lady?"

"If God is merciful." Gisela tried to keep her voice and hands steady, though her stomach clenched at the sight of Lothar's wound. She saw a spark of sympathy in the bearer's eyes. All of Ardun knew old Ercangar's son was her brother, though none dared acknowledge it.

"If you've magic enough to protect us, maid, now would be the time to use it." Without waiting for her answer, the man turned to leave.

Lothar mercifully remained unconscious while Gisela cleaned and stitched his wounds. He didn't awaken until she wrapped his arm and side in poultices that would speed the healing and ward off suppuration.

"The sting of healing is worse than the sword stroke," he complained with a smile.

"You're lucky you've life left to feel the sting. If the blade had cut more to the left, we would be burying you instead of listening to your complaining."

"We may all be buried soon enough. The leader is a warlord even I have heard of. His name is Rutgar, and he fights like hell's own champion. His men as well."

"Was it this Rutgar who laid you low?"

"Aye. The Frankish commander himself was first inside the walls. My sword arm is no match for his."

"We are losing, then?"

"We're being cut to shreds. The west palisade has fallen, and now the devils are pushing steadily inward. I saw Aelrhane himself backed up against the stable wall fighting for his life. Ercangar in his death madness has killed us all, unless Holy Christ will extend the hand of mercy. Only He can save us now."

Adalinde stopped her pacing and impaled Lothar on a contemptuous gaze. "You pray to the wrong god, grandson. Why do you entreat the very god who attacks us, whose warriors burned our holy tree Irminsul and who has sent his armies to destroy us?" Her voice was sour with with the bile of hatred. "The Franks win converts with fire and sword. Their Christian God crushes any who won't grovel before Him and His fat bishops and abbots. Yet you would look to this very God to save you from his own minions?"

Lothar grimaced. "Grandmother . . ."

"Better we should pray to the old gods for deliverance from this Rutgar and his hellhounds. The old ways will save us still." Her eyes turned on Gisela in a penetrating stare. "We have our own magic."

Gisela felt a chill blow over her flesh like a icy wind. She feared the light in her grandmother's eyes more than she feared the battle that raged outside the manor walls.

A fierce pounding on the stout wooden door ended the tense silence that encompassed the room after Adalinde's speech.

"Unbar the doors!" came Aelrhane's hoarse shout.

Adalinde herself rushed to lift the bar. Aelrhane stumbled in, followed by a handful of warriors streaming with sweat and blood.

"The day is lost!" Aelrhane declared. "We must flee."

"You will leave us to the mercy of the Franks?" one woman wailed.

"The Franks will not soil their blades on such as you, woman. My warriors must survive to wrest back what is ours."

"You will continue the fight!" Adalinde declared triumphantly.

The light in Aelrhane's eyes matched Adalinde's. One would not know, Gisela thought dismally, that the day had cost them their home and so many Saxon lives.

"My lord," Gisela entreated Aelrhane quietly, "would you continue this terror yet longer? Have your people and this land not run with enough blood?"

"The battle is not lost until we are all dead," Aelrhane replied grimly. "And the battle will not be lost. We will harry the Franks until they learn that Saxon land is not worth the amount of blood they must spill to keep it."

"Our blood or theirs?" Gisela asked caustically.

Aelrhane pinned her with burning eyes. "Theirs, if I have aught to say about it."

"Aye! Their blood will flow!" Adalinde proclaimed. "The Franks will gain their small victory only to learn once and for all that Saxon land can only be ruled by Saxons. Our triumph begins here! One day our people will regain all that is rightfully ours."

"That day will come," Aelrhane agreed. "If we must spend more blood to bring it, then that is what we'll do." He looked at Adalinde expectantly.

"Go without me," she told him. "My place is here, to harass the enemy from within their stolen stronghold."

"So be it," he assented. "A small troop of men have volunteered to stay and cover our escape. The wounded who can walk should come with me, and we need a few women to do the camp's work and see to our warriors' needs. Who will come?"

Two young kitchen girls—Gruda and Frieda—stepped forward. Aelrhane leveled a narrow-eyed stare at the others. Hesitantly, one more woman stepped forward: Matrude, whose husband had just died of his wounds only moments before.

"You will come with us also," Aelrhane commanded Gisela. "We have need of your talents."

"No!" Gisela shook her head. "I am no fighter who can make Frankish blood run."

"You can fight in other ways, witch. The old gods favor you. Your dreams will keep us from danger and your spells will be our shield against Frankish power."

Gisela could have cried out, as her heart urged, that her loyalty was with Ardun and its people. She cared little whether Aelrhane or this Rutgar ruled, as long as they ruled wisely and in peace. But she knew her protest would be useless. Gersvinda at the height of her power might have stood against Aelrhane; Gisela could not.

"Lothar . . ." Gisela laid a despairing hand on Lothar's pale brow.

"I will care for my grandson," Adalinde promised.

"Come!" Aelrhane ordered.

Some frantic minutes later, scraped and bruised from the rough passage through the bolt-hole tunnel, Gisela turned at the edge of the forest and drank in what she believed would be her last look at Ardun. A few fires sent black smoke billowing up into a sullen gray sky, but the sounds of fighting had died. Now would be the time for a vision, but no vision came. She closed her eyes to blot out the sad sight and concentrated on sending any magic that might reside in her soul toward those left behind. She wished them mercy, life, and though the outlook was bleak—happiness. For herself and her companions, however, she could muster very little hope.

Rutgar surveyed the last remnants of the Saxon defenders who crouched in a dispirited huddle under the watchful eyes of Odo and the footsoldier Gaston. It was difficult to believe that this sorry crew was all who remained of the company that had defended the stronghold. The fighting had been hard, but not so hard that so many should have been killed. No piles of bodies indicated such wholesale slaughter.

He addressed a Saxon who was scarcely more than a boy. "How many held this stronghold, lad?"

The boy regarded him with angry eyes.

Gaston prodded the boy with his longsword. "Answer him, Saxon whelp."

The boy smiled, then spat on the ground a bare inch from Rutgar's boots.

Gaston cursed and raised his sword.

"Hold!" Rutgar commanded. "If we split the skull of every Saxon who offers us insult here, we'll have to work the land ourselves—cook and weave as well, I suspect."

"They need to learn some manners, I'd say," Gaston replied.

"Aye. And they'll learn. But if you knock the donkey over the head to teach him not to balk, then you'll find you have no more donkey to bear your burdens."

Gaston merely growled.

"Who among you can tell me where Aelrhane is?" Rutgar asked.

One Saxon lifted his lip like a cur dog about to bite. Others gazed at the ground.

"The Saxon scum is probably hiding with the women and children," Etich the Bear sneered as he walked up to the group. "The place is ours, Rutgar. The fire that some fool set to the grain storage is out. No other man lifts a sword. These are all that are left —these and whoever is in there."

Rutgar looked at the stone building Etich indicated. Square and squat, it was more a residence than a fortress, probably built from the ruins of an old Roman villa. No battlements or watchtowers guarded the approaches. The shuttered windows were large enough to allow entrance of an enemy, and the portico flanked double wooden doors that didn't look as though they could stand more than a few well-delivered blows from a ram.

Rutgar motioned two of his men to stay behind with the prisoners and motioned several others to follow him up the worn stone steps leading to the manor's entrance.

"Etich, my friend. Use your bear's paw against the door and let those inside know that the master of Ardun demands entrance."

"That I will!" Etich bared his teeth in a wicked grin.

The door shook under the Bear's hammerlike blows. "Saxons of Ardun, your defenders have fallen. If you expect mercy of your new master, surrender yourselves!"

Only silence answered.

"Get the ram," Rutgar commanded. "We will not

waste time begging compliance from these stubborn Saxons."

The entrance withstood but one blow from the ram. On the second the bar splintered and the doors crashed inward. Shield raised and sword at ready for possible resistance, Rutgar swept in at the head of his men. Frightened faces greeted them, anxious eyes, a few wavering cries. Women clutched babes to their breasts as if the Franks might snatch them away to be roasted for supper. Older children peeked from the folds of the women's skirts, their eyes large and round with fear. A few old men brandished clubs of firewood. One ancient fellow held a pitted sword that had seen better days. With both hands gripping the butt, he attempted to keep it aloft and pointing toward the invaders, though his wasted arms trembled with the effort.

The only Saxons who might have put up a fight lay on bloody pallets and benches, some unconscious, some staring with hostile eyes at the invading Franks. At least one stared sightlessly at Death's gate. All were beyond fighting, for now at least.

Rutgar lowered his sword. There was no danger here.

"Welcome, warlord Rutgar." A woman spoke from her seat on the dais at the far end of the hearth. The somber colors of her clothing blended with the gloom of the hall. Precious stones, blood-red and equally somber, studded her girdle, and gold embroidery decorated the edges of her dark kirtle and tunic. The creases of her face and steel gray hair that peeked from beneath her headrail revealed her age.

"You are mistress here?" Rutgar demanded.

"Until you came I was."

"Tell your people to set aside their weapons."

She motioned for the geriatric warriors to obey. "Do clubs and rusty swords vex you, noble Frank?"

Rutgar almost smiled at the crackle of spirit in the old woman's voice. "Any resistance vexes me. Your people should bear that in mind. Where is the man called Aelrhane?"

"Aelrhane and the best of his men have fled to the forest, leaving us here to face your mercy." Adalinde rose with queenly dignity. "I am Adalinde, mother of Ercangar, who was lord here for thirty-five years."

"For the last eight years, Ercanger was lord here only by the grace of Charles, king of the Franks and the Saxons as well. I come to reclaim this domain in the name of its rightful king."

Adalinde nodded her head in acquiescence. "So be it. Perhaps the question of who should rule Ardun is a matter you should discuss with Ercangar's son Lothar."

She pointed a long, bony finger at a young man who sat slumped against the wall. The stone behind him and the pallet beneath him were both stained with blood. As all eyes turned toward him, the Saxon attempted to rise, then grimaced in humiliation as the weakness of his body betrayed him and sent him slumping once again to the floor. Rutgar could see that the man didn't lack nerve or pride.

"You've seen your share of the fighting today," Rutgar said, squatting down beside the bloodied warrior.

"This fight was not of my making."

"The son must drink the brew the father stirs." Rutgar took his dagger, the scramasax, from his belt and tested its balance in his hand. "Does your granddam tell the truth about Aelrhane?"

"Aye," Lothar said in a hoarse voice. "He is in the forest, where you'll not find him. He means to pick away at Ardun from the outside until there is nothing left for the Franks to rule."

"So." Rutgar tried to read the downed warrior who lay at his feet. Somehow he did not have the look of a fighting man about him, though he'd given a good enough account of himself in battle. Rutgar himself had delivered the blow that brought the Saxon down, if memory served rightly. "Aelrhane will pick from the outside, and the dispossessed heir pick from within."

In a swift, smooth motion Rutgar brought his knife blade to lie against Lothar's throat. A few feminine gasps punctuated the sudden tension. Neither Rutgar nor Lothar moved.

"Give me a reason not to kill you here and now, boy. I'll not be looking over my shoulder every day for Saxon discontents who would put you in your father's place."

Lothar's eyes didn't waver as he looked up into Rutgar's face. "No Saxon rebels will rally around me as their champion," he said steadily. "All here know that I honor Charles as king. I fought to defend my home and my people, and I will fight again, if need be, against Aelrhane, or against you, or whoever threatens the peace of Ardun. If that is reason to kill me, then be done with it."

Someone started to weep, and a child whined. Rutgar's eyes held Lothar's as he tried to see the truth or the lie in the man's words.

"I wouldn't worry so much about Lothar," Adalinde advised contemptuously. "He's much better at praying than fighting."

Rutgar held the knife steady. "Would you swear an oath of loyalty to me personally—to become my vassal?"

A muscle in Lothar's jaw jumped. A tiny drop of blood bloomed from the tip of the knife.

"An oath is sacred. Mine belongs to God and to my people."

For a moment Rutgar's hand tightened on the butt of the knife. Finally he ground out a curse and sheathed the blade, motioning Etich over to him. "Lock up this 'servant of God and his people' until I make up my mind what to do with him. And make sure his wounds are tended. I don't want him to die before I decide whether or not to kill him. I don't like having my mind made up for me."

As Etich carefully slung Lothar over his broad shoulder, Rutgar turned to scrutinize Adalinde.

"Lothar is not the one you should fear," she said calmly.

"Do I seem to fear him?"

"Nay. But you would be wise to fear Aelrhane and his band. All I wish for is peace, noble warlord. I feel obligated to warn you that these men will never surrender. They have a talisman of good fortune that gives them faith in their ultimate victory."

"And what is this magic talisman?" he asked irritably. The headache that had plagued him from before dawn when he'd awakened with a goose egg on his skull was not improving his temper or tolerance.

"Aelrhane has a sorceress to guide him," Adalinde confided. "She is favored of the old Saxon gods and would like to see Saxon ways return to Ardun. Unless your sword can defeat magic, warlord, you would be wise to return to your king and tell him you want nothing to do with Ardun."

Rutgar chuckled. "Woman, save your tales to scare your great-grandchildren. Witches do not frighten me."

"Perhaps they should."

"Should I confine you with your grandson? Or are you willing to keep your place and see to the needs of your people and my men?"

Adalinde lowered her eyes. "I am but a woman, noble warlord. Born to serve, not to fight. I am yours to command."

"See that you are, lady. I do not tolerate treachery, and I will not withhold the hand of punishment, even for a woman." Rutgar put a hand to his aching head. "Speaking of women—Odo, search the stronghold for the little maid who was our guest in camp last night." He gave the servant a grim smile. "My head still aches from her attention. I am glad that one was not on the walls defending Ardun, or we'd still be fighting."

Four

Gisela added a handful of wild onions to the vegetables simmering in the big iron kettle. A few feet away, a second cooking fire sputtered and steamed as a spitted piglet dripped juices into the flames. The warm late afternoon air was heavy with the aroma of roasting pork and the sharp tang of the wild onions Gisela had gathered that morning.

In the week since she had fled Ardun with Aelrhane, Gisela had spent the hour after dawn each morning searching the forest for herbs and medicinals to augment the few supplies she had brought with her from the stronghold. The forest was especially beautiful with the early morning dew still clinging to leaves and hanging in rows of sparkling drops from the needles of pine and fir. Silver always joined her, romping with puppyish glee or playing games of stalk and pounce with the local rodents while Gisela hunted her plants. The birds serenaded her from the branches, even on the two mornings that it rained.

That precious hour of peace and solitude every day had kept Gisela from absolute despair, for the forest's awesome grandeur was a reminder that nature's splendor would continue: the rivers would still run to the sea, the great guardian oaks that had stood for centuries would still hold their leafy boughs aloft to capture the rays of the sun, the otters would still play on the riverbank, and the deer still graze in the meadows. Despite what foolish madness man perpetuated upon himself, the world would continue.

Gruda walked up and tapped Gisela on the shoulder, bringing her back to her present surroundings—the cluttered Saxon camp that reeked of pork, turnips, and the odor of an inadequately dug latrine.

"Are you sure that wolf of yours isn't waiting to tear somebody's throat out the minute one of us lets our guard down?"

Gisela looked at Silver, who was just visible lying in the thick brush that guarded the camp. Most days he appeared two or three times, sat or lay down for a few minutes, then disappeared into the forest once he understood that Gisela was not going to join him to play wolf games among the trees and ferns.

"If you leave him alone," Gisela assured the girl, "he'll leave you alone."

"Aye, well, 'tis a bit of a fright seeing him lying there with those yellow eyes watching and watching, but if he's one o' yours, I suppose I won't fret." She took a long sniff. "Those turnips and onions smell passing good. Where did you find them?"

"On the other side of the ridge."

"In Dark Hollow? I hear there's dwarves and trolls live there." She cast a dubious look at the simmering pot, as though the vegetables might jump out at her.

Gisela had no time to answer, for just then Aelrhane trotted out of the tangle of brush, followed by his men. Simultaneously, Silver disappeared as though he'd faded into the air itself. Gisela didn't blame the wolf, for the Saxon warriors were a frightening sight. Bloodied swords swung at their sides. A few of the warriors sported gashes and bruises, but they were grinning and laughing, drunk with the exhilaration of the fight. They groped playfully at Gruda and Frieda and poured themselves tankards of the mead that was cooling in the creek.

"I thought you were hunting this day." Gisela flinched as Aelrhane stuck a blood-caked sword into the dirt by the fire.

"Aye, we hunted well."

"Is that Frankish blood on your blade?"

"Nay. Not yet."

Aelrhane's lieutenant, a broad, red-haired man by the name of Griff, sliced himself a portion of the sizzling pig and gave Gisela a boyish grin. "We paid a visit to the village of Verhonne."

Gisela gasped. "Verhonne? What madness is this? Verhonne is Saxon! The village belongs to Ardun!"

"Aye!" Aelrhane answered. "And that's why we attacked it." His mouth twitched in the beginning of a grin. "Now don't give me the hex like you're doing, Gisela. We slaughtered the livestock, not the villagers. We're not anxious to spill Saxon blood, even though the men of Verhonne have accepted the Frank like sheep embracing a wolf as their shepherd. Hah!" He laughed at his clever comparison. "If I were not such a fine fighting man, I could be a jongleur."

"How dare you laugh at what you have done!" Gisela took Aelrhane's arm and pulled him away from the group of men around the cook fires. "How will our people eat if you kill the livestock and burn the crops? I suppose you intend to destroy the crops as well!"

"Cease your harangue, Gisela! How I war is not your affair! Your place here is to tend the sick and give our men heart—and to use your magic to give us victory."

"You didn't answer my question," she said sharply. "How will our people eat?"

"You know nothing of war, woman! Ardun depends upon grain and meat from the villages and farms. If their source of supplies is gutted, Ardun will fall."

"And you will rule a starving people! You will kill the villagers and farmers slowly instead of with the clean slice of a sword."

"That is war!" Aelrhane shrugged. "People have starved before and Ardun is still here."

"Those are your own people you are depriving. Who will follow you after they have turned against you?"

"They will follow whoever rules at Ardun, as they always have—as you always have. 'Tis not your place to tell me what to do. Witch you may be, but still a mere woman, and a badly born woman at that!"

"Men!" Gisela exploded. "You think with your bloody sword arms, as if God never gave you a heart or a brain!"

She stalked away, unable to bear the sight of his complacent satisfaction.

"Our sword arms are not what we think with!" he

called after her, a hint of mirth in his voice. "At least not according to most women!"

Gisela snorted in disgust as she marched toward her own little shelter of interwoven pine branches. Her flight was interrupted by Einmar, a grizzled veteran who had served Ercangar since long before Gisela first came to the stronghold.

"Maid Gisela . . ." He held out a hand as if to stop her by force, then withdrew it hastily. "Lady . . . We'd not have you think that we would hurt the villagers, our own people."

Gisela sighed. "Oh, Einmar! Did you not think that your raid was harm?"

He regarded her fearfully. No doubt, Gisela thought, he believed she would shrivel his sword arm or make him lose his hair before the sun rose again.

"Don't look at me so, Einmar. I'm not angry with you, or Griff, or Hugo—or even Aelrhane. I'm simply angry that the world is what it is, and that all men feel they must draw blood before they are truly men."

He gave her a puzzled look. "Aye?"

He didn't understand, Gisela knew. There was no room for gentleness or mercy in a man's world.

That night, as Gisela unrolled her blankets to prepare her bed, a light tap on the deerhide that covered the doorway announced a visitor. When she pushed aside the covering, Aelrhane sketched a little bow to her.

"Come talk with me, maid Gisela, and let me make my apology to you."

She looked at him askance.

"Truly," he insisted.

Gisela set down her blankets and silently allowed him to lead her into the shadows at one end of the clearing where they made their camp.

"I'm sorry what I said this afternoon about your being lowborn. I didn't mean it."

" 'Twas naught but the truth, Aelrhane. I'm well aware of the circumstances of my birth."

"That does not excuse my insult. I was angry, and when I'm angry, I often lose control of my tongue."

The moon illuminated his guileless smile, white teeth flashing in the bush of his forked beard. Gisela eyed him distrustfully. She knew that smile of his.

"You didn't bring me out here just to apologize, did you, Aelrhane?"

"Truly you see into men's hearts." For a moment his eyes seemed to catch the moonlight as they searched her face. "Have you seen aught, Gisela?"

She sighed and sat down on a mossy log. "I dream again and again of a great duel and raging fire. The vision overpowers whatever else the Gift shows me."

"Who fights in your sorcerous duel?"

"I cannot see the faces, but the vision is so strong that I must believe it has more to do with my own fate than anyone else's. For our own sorry band, I see nothing distinct. But I am plagued with uneasiness for us all, Aelrhane."

"Is that your magical sight speaking, or your own heart?"

"I don't know." She sighed. "I truly don't know."

Aelrhane paced for a moment, his figure moving in and out of moonlight and shadow like a dark and uneasy spirit. Finally he stopped.

"It matters not so much what you see, I suppose. Your being here heartens the men. They believe associating with a witch makes them invulnerable."

"You shouldn't let them believe that, Aelrhane. I am a very inept witch. I don't have the power my mother had."

Aelrhane shrugged. "I think you don't know your own power." Grinning, he sat down beside her and took her hand. "You should try casting a spell to harry our enemy the Franks."

She shook her head. "To conjure evil risks that evil becoming a part of your soul."

"Every soul must have some evil in it. Elsewise the world would hold no interest."

He leaned toward her, his hands moving smoothly under the sleeves of her tunic and up her arms. Through the thin, tight sleeves of her threadbare kirtle Gisela could feel the heat of his flesh. "Life could be more interesting for both of us, Gisela."

She flinched away as his mouth sought hers.

He drew back. "Am I such a troll that you refuse me?"

"Nay, Aelrhane. You are not a troll. But I am not a woman given to lying with every man who would have me."

His fingers lightly skimmed her face, brushing back the the errant locks that had escaped her braid. "I am not just any man, Gisela. I will rule here."

"Leave me be."

"And if I say no?"

"You do not truly want me, Aelrhane. You would take me only to make your men hold you in awe. You want to claim my power for your own."

Aelrhane smiled. His arm snaked around her waist. She pulled away, but he held her tight. "You are indeed a witch to see so clearly into a man's soul. But don't think I wouldn't enjoy claiming you for my own. Your mother served Ercangar in such a way when he was lord of Ardun. It seems right that you should serve me."

"Not in that way!" She cuffed him, but he merely laughed.

"Aelrhane, I warn you! I will shrivel your prideful horn to the size of a worm if it so much as touches me, and your hands to palsied stumps!"

"You will not want to do such damage once I've shown you what pleasure is."

"Arrogant cur!"

His mouth came down upon hers, and his tongue thrust inside, a wet, unwelcome invader. The taste of sour mead and cheese, the acrid odor of sweat and blood, overwhelmed her. Using all her strength, Gisela pushed him off and jumped to her feet. Aelrhane cursed and came after her. Agile as a deer, she danced out of reach. She didn't fear the look of angry frustration on his face, for she knew that Aelrhane had enough belief in her magic that he would not dare actually force her.

"Leave me be, Aelrhane. Go to Matrude to spend your lust. She will welcome you."

"Cursed insolent woman! Come back here!" He stood, legs apart, fists planted firmly on his hips, scowling mightily. "By Freya's mighty tits, woman! I'm not going to hurt you. I want to pleasure you!"

A menacing growl interrupted his declaration. At the edge of the clearing, moonlight glinted off silvery fur. A pair of slanted amber eyes seem to glow with unearthly light.

Aelrhane exhaled a long, shaky breath, then cursed. "Woman, you make life very difficult for a man."

"Nay, Aelrhane. You make life difficult for yourself." While Aerhane glared balefully, she moved to stand beside the wolf and ran her hand through the thick pelt. Silver's eyes never wavered from the Saxon leader.

"That cursed wolf of yours should go back to the forest where he belongs," Aelrhane complained, his voice thick with frustration.

"Silver is where he belongs," Gisela replied quietly. "We are the ones who are not."

Next morning, Aelrhane expressed his vexation by ordering Gisela about like a slave. She refused his petty tasks and went about her own business. The self-styled Saxon savior could stew in his own ire for all she cared. She was not about to let him seduce her just so he could gain power from the magic he imagined her to possess. She had managed to keep her maidenhead to the ripe age of nineteen, thanks to most men's skittishness about her magic. She had no intention of yielding to Aelrhane or any man who saw her only as a means to power.

Later in the morning, as the sun climbed toward its zenith and the air grew hot and still, Gisela laid out dandelion leaves and hawthorne flowers to dry. Gruda helped her. A withered hand gave the girl an interest in healing, and though Gisela knew no infusion or poultice that could regenerate the wasted flesh, she was happy to pass on her knowledge. Einmar, who had been left behind that morning to guard the camp, also took an interest in leaves and flower petals.

"Could ye brew me up a potion to rid me of the boils beneath me arm, lady?"

"I could make a poultice," Gisela offered. "Though you'd have to let me cut them to release the pus before the poultice would be of much help."

"Cut?"

"As I've told you before." Gisela smiled and wondered how men who launched themselves joyfully into a melee of blades and lances without flinching could without fail break into a cold sweat when she approached them with a needle to stitch their wounds or a knife to lance a boil.

Einmar grimaced. "Cut, eh? Well . . ."

He was saved from his decision when Aelrhane cantered into camp on a lathered black horse. He reined the horse in sharply, setting the beast on its hindquarters and stirring up a cloud of dust. Close behind him, panting to keep up on foot, the other ten who had accompanied him broke into the clearing with whoops of triumph.

With a savage howl, he tossed a limp body from where it rode on the horse's withers. It landed face down upon the ground, coming to rest with a meaty thump. Gisela looked at the body and tried to keep a shudder from her voice.

"Who is he?"

"A Frank." Aelrhane pronounced the word as if it were a curse. Then he grinned. "He was kind enough to offer me this fine horse."

"What happened?"

"We were coming up to the farm by Blackwater Spring when three of the devils rode into the forest so close we could have hit them with spit. We dropped down upon them from the trees. This one's horse fell. The others escaped. When they saw our numbers, they decided to leave this one to us."

Gareth strutted over to the body and nudged it with his foot. "He put up a good fight for a Frank, but I bested him in the end." He spat contemptuously.

If he'd been a cock, Gisela thought, he'd be preening his feathers and crowing. She knelt beside the body and examined the crust of blood matting the hair on the back of the Frank's head. "I see you bested him from behind, mighty Gareth."

The warrior's inflated chest collapsed just a bit.

"How many of you did it take to bring him down?"

No one answered. A slight movement of the man on the ground caught Gisela's attention.

"He's still alive."

"Aye," Aelrhane said. "For now. The clean thrust of a sword is too good for a Frank. I have a better use for the scum." With his foot, he turned the body over. The face was streaked with blood, sweat, and dirt. His armor, if he'd worn any, had been stripped from him, and his linen shirt was spotted with blood. "You were in the Franks' camp, Gisela. Do you recognize this one?"

Gisela gazed down into the face of her former captor, arrogant even beneath its mask of blood and grime. "I know him," she said.

Rutgar slowly swam up from a vortex of blackness. Memory flashed across his awareness in distorted images—the ground coming up to meet him, two Saxon blades swinging in his direction, then white-hot lightning cutting into his head, which throbbed now with each pulse of blood through his veins. Some pig of a Saxon had attacked him from behind.

Eyes closed, motionless, Rutgar tested the feel and sounds of his environment. He lay on something soft, and his hands were tethered above his head. The smell of venison tickled his nose and teased his stomach. A slight breeze on his face was cool. That and the lack of birdsong told him the sun was down. Some distance away, voices talked and laughed—both men and women. Nearby was only silence, however. No footfalls. No breathing. No rustle of clothing, rattle of armor, or scrape of sword or dagger.

Rutgar opened his eyes to darkness. He lay in a

shelter of some kind—branches and brush propped against a tree trunk and covered with hides. A few open spaces admitted a dim glow of firelight from outside. He was alone on a bed of branches, naked but for a blanket that covered him from the waist down, and whoever had tied him had meant him to stay tied, for his bonds didn't budge when he tested them.

The flap of the shelter lifted and for a moment a slight feminine figure was silhouetted against the firelight of the outside.

"Awake, I see," she said softly.

"You!" Rutgar recognized her voice and her form even before she lit the tallow lamp. The soft light confirmed his suspicion, shimmering in the waves of her pale hair and gleaming in amber eyes. "Christ's blood! I should have known you were mixed up in this somewhere."

"Indeed, noble sir? Why is that?"

"Whenever you are around, something begins to hurt. You left me with a lump the size of an egg when you took your leave of my hospitality."

She knelt beside him and peered at the bandage that crossed his chest. "Did you expect me to remain trussed in your tent simply because it was your pleasure?" Slender, tapered fingers brushed lightly over the linen wrapped around his head. Gentle as it was, her touch ignited a burst of pain.

He grimaced, and immediately regretted it. Lightning seemed to shoot through his head. "Is this your revenge, woman?"

"Nay. None of this is my doing. If I'd wanted to split your head thusly, I'd have used the other side of your war axe when I took my leave of you."

He gave her a dire look. She merely smiled. The maid really did know how to humiliate a man.

"With good fortune, the bandage will hold and keep the rocks in your head from falling out. What possessed you to ride through our Saxon forest with only two companions? And those cowards who leave their comrade to his fate?

"Should I let mangy outlaws dictate what I do and where I ride?" he growled. "I think not. And those you call cowards will be back with a larger force to sweep this forest clean."

"Perhaps you underestimate the danger from those you call outlaws."

He grunted his contempt.

The lamplight shot gold sparks from her hair as she turned to fetch a bowl from the ground beside her. Slight, with delicate features, a long slender neck, narrow, tapered hands, and arms that looked as if they would break with one twist of Rutgar's hand, Gisela didn't fit his image of a woman who would lurk in the forest with Saxon renegades. Neither did she look as though she could escape a camp of armed Franks, disposing of one of the king's most noted fighting men as though he were the helpless woman instead of she.

"How did you escape my camp?" he asked.

She smiled with infuriating aplomb. "Magic."

"Magic?" Rutgar snorted with disbelief.

"As I said. Magic. Can you eat a bit? Food might make you feel better."

"You're the witch Adalinde warned me about. The sorceress who supposedly calls down the wrath of the old Saxon gods on the wicked minions of King Charles."

"Some call me witch," she admitted. "Will you eat?"

"I'd be foolish to take anything from your hand."

" 'Tis not poisoned." She took a sip from the bowl. "You see? Eat, my lord. You will need your strength."

She sighed, set the bowl down, and sat down beside him. "I must warn you that Aelrhane plans an unpleasant fate for you. He bade me bring you to your senses only so he can take you to a spot within the hearing of Ardun and torture you to death. Your screams will let your comrades know that a horrible death awaits them behind every tree and in every thicket of our Saxon forest. Put fear into a man and you've halfway defeated him, Aelrhane says."

"Now that's news designed to give me an appetite indeed!"

She gave him a wry smile. "You needn't let your stomach curdle. I plan to see that you're well away from here before Aelrhane can carry out his plans."

He shot her an incredulous look. "Why?"

"I am a healer. I dislike seeing a man skewered, burned, and ripped apart solely for the entertainment of hearing him scream. I doubt you are a man of such fearsome importance that the future of my countrymen turns upon your fate."

Rutgar cocked one brow and smiled. "Indeed, I've been told often enough I've little importance at all. Glad I am to hear a Saxon serf confirm it."

"Would you rather add your blood to the scarlet rivers that have already covered this land?"

"By all means not."

"Then eat. You will need your strength."

"Cut me loose, woman, so I can eat with my own hands. I'll not be fed like a babe." When she appeared uncertain, he laughed softly. "Do you plan for me to leave here with my hands still tied? I'll not attack you. There's no need, is there, since you say you will aid me?"

Gingerly, she cut him free.

Rutgar sat up and rubbed his wrists to restore circulation. "Did they bring my horse along to the camp?"

"Yes, but . . ."

"Is he sound after the fall he took?"

"I don't know, but you can't think to take the horse with you."

"Doomsayer is a valuable animal. I'm not leaving him with Saxon outlaws."

"You should be grateful that you're not leaving most of your body parts with Saxon outlaws."

"I will take the horse with me." He gulped the stew she offered while she glared at him.

"You're going to get yourself killed! And probably me as well. You can't sneak away from camp on a horse! In fact, I still haven't quite thought of how I'm to get you away. There's a guard posted only ten steps from my shelter."

The stew settled warmly on Rutgar's stomach. Already he felt better. "I should think you'd be an expert at escape. You did well enough in my encampment."

"That was different."

"Just conjure up a little of that magic of yours."

She tilted her head and gave him a faraway smile, as if she were doing just that. He was amazed that such a delicate-looking little wench could hold such audacious spirit in her soul. She'd had the courage to conk him over the head and elude his sentries, and now she was apparently hatching a similar scheme to visit upon Aelrhane. He could almost feel sorry for the man.

"Call the guard in here," he suggested. "If we take care of that problem, we can then see to my horse."

"You cannot simply stroll up to the animal as though . . ."

"Have faith, maid. We will manage."

The guard came trustingly to Gisela's summons, and guilt clouded her face. The maid was softhearted, Rutgar concluded. Too softhearted for this violent land. He, fortunately, was not plagued with that problem. The guard had no time to call out when he saw that Rutgar was awake, unbound, and on his feet. Rutgar curled his arms neatly around the man's throat and dragged him the rest of the way into the shelter.

"Don't kill him!" Gisela gasped.

"As you will," Rutgar conceded reluctantly. It went against his fighting instinct to leave anything but dead enemies at his back, but in this case he would bow to the maid's squeamishness. As the man slumped from the pressure on his throat, Rutgar gave him a sharp clout to the head with his fist and dropped him to the floor. The girl was at the guard's side immediately, feeling for a pulse.

"You hit him very hard."

"I don't want him to wake up for a while. Help me strip him."

"But why . . . ?"

"You left me with no clothes."

Her eyes darted toward him, then quickly shied away. A crimson flush crawled up her cheeks. The blanket that had covered him had fallen away when he stood, and his nakedness was amply revealed. "Your . . . uh . . . your clothes were blood-soaked."

"These will do well enough. I can cover my head and face with the headwrap. Do you know where my sword is?"

"I believe it is with your horse." Her eyes narrowed. "You must vow that you will not use it in this camp. I won't have you shed the blood of any Saxons this night."

He lifted one brow. "Do you fear one man can overpower your valiant Saxon warriors?"

"Certainly not. But you'd no doubt do damage to one or two. Give me your vow, or I call Aelrhane this moment."

"You're a stubborn little maid."

"So I've been told. I'll have your vow, Frank."

Rutgar sighed. "You have it—until I am away from this camp."

She nodded. Poking her head out the deerhide flap, she motioned that all was safe. "This is madness," she muttered as they left the shelter. "With the guard unconscious, you can simply slip into the forest and none will be the wiser."

"Not without my horse."

"You'll not have much use for a horse if Aelrhane discovers us."

No one stopped them, however, as Rutgar and Gisela crossed the clearing to where Doomsayer was tethered. The women were busy cleaning up after the evening meal, and Aelrhane and his warriors were laughing, boasting, and arguing over their cups of mead, no doubt anticipating great entertainment in his tortured demise. Rutgar couldn't blame Aelrhane too much; his plan was grisly, but tactically sound.

Much to Rutgar's relief, Doomsayer was sound also. The fall had done much less damage to the horse than to the rider.

"Now what?" Gisela asked irritably. "You can hardly mount in full view of Aelrhane and trot away."

Rutgar glanced toward Gisela's shelter, which was at the edge of the trees. "No, but your lean-to will hide me if I lead the horse into the forest behind it."

"I suppose we just casually lead the horse over there?"

"You do. Do you not treat beasts as well as people, as most healers do?"

"Yes, but . . ."

"Say you're testing him for lameness, or whatever lie comes to your mind. I doubt Aelrhane suspects such a loyal Saxon sorceress would turn against him."

"I *haven't* turned against him!" she whispered vehemently.

"As you say. I'll meet you at your shelter."

Rutgar walked away, standing straight and walking boldly, as if he had every right to be striding around a camp of Saxon rebels. His head pounded at every step, and the burning of lesser cuts and bruises attacked him like a swarm of bees. Out of the corner of his eye, he saw the witch bend down to examine one of Doomsayer's hocks. The warhorse, normally nasty to anyone other than himself, looked like a friendly hound lapping up her attention. She untied him and led him toward the trees on the opposite side of the clearing.

"What are you doing, maid?" one fellow by the fire asked.

"Your prize has a swollen fetlock, Gareth. I go to soak his leg in the stream."

"I didn't notice any swelling earlier."

" 'Tis not bad. I'll apply a poultice if need be. He should be sound in a day or so."

"He's a worthy beast. Treat him with care."

Gisela and Doomsayer disappeared into the dark forest. A few moments later, Rutgar saw them dimly outlined by moonlight in the woods just beyond her shelter. He checked the guard, who was still unconscious, then he slipped Gisela's knife into his belt, and quietly moved to meet her.

"Be cautious," Gisela warned as she handed him the

reins. "There are two sentries patrolling." Her gaze dropped, and her mouth, a graceful curve of rosepetal pink, drew into an anxious line. "Don't punish the people of Ardun for what Aelrhane has done."

"You can scold me if I become too harsh with them." At her look of surprise, he grinned. "Did you think I would leave you here to aid the rebels, witch?"

Five

Gisela's eyes widened in alarm, but before she could protest, the Frank had her in his grip. He twisted her so that her back was pressed against him while one of his large, callused hands stifled her cries.

"Don't fight me, maid. You've saved my life this night, and I'm grateful. But since your rebels believe their pet witch gives them such a fighting edge, I would be foolish to leave you here."

Keeping one hand across her mouth, he quickly unwound the Saxon guard's head-piece from around his head and fastened it over her mouth. Then he easily lifted her onto Doomsayer and vaulted to the horse's back behind her.

Gisela grew angrier by the moment as they silently rode away from Aelrhane's camp. She kicked at the shins that rode behind her feet and flailed blindly to the rear, hoping to hit something either sensitive or essential, but her captor responded by pinning her wrists with one large hand. She felt surrounded by him—helpless, and the total loss of control was infuriating. She could feel the flexing of his powerful thighs beneath hers. At her back, his chest buttressed her like a stone wall. What a fool she was to set loose such a devil and expect to control him.

A good distance from camp, they met a party of Franks who were combing the woods for him, just as he had predicted they would. He pulled the filthy gag from Gisela's mouth. She gasped for fresh air.

"You're alive, I see." The fearsome giant himself—the man whom her captor had said was the warlord Rutgar—greeted them. A smile split his broad hairy face and made it a bit less terrifying.

"Aye. By the skin of my teeth and the assistance of a maid who dislikes the sight of blood."

"Lord Rutgar!" said one of the Franks. "Shall we ride forward and take the Saxon camp?"

"Not this night, Antonius." Her captor gave Gisela's waist a gentle squeeze. "I made a vow not to kill any Saxons this night. We will dispatch a party from the stronghold tomorrow."

"They will move their camp."

"Aye, unless they're stupider than I believe. But once given, an oath must be honored."

Gisela followed the conversation with momentary confusion. Her eyes flew to the giant, who sat in silence. He was not the warlord Rutgar. The man who held her before him on his horse, the man she'd conked on the head with his own war axe, the man she'd teased and insulted, the man she'd helped escaped—*he* was the infamous Rutgar.

"You! You swine!" She twisted to throw the scathing insult full at his face. "You let me believe that he"—she waved a hand in the giant's direction—"that you . . . you falsehearted knave! You liar!"

She was a fool, a dupe, and a brainless idiot. How could she have been so easily gulled?

Rutgar merely grinned. The pig found her ire very amusing. His men also, judging by their smiles. She longed to turned every last one of them into snakes. Especially their arrogant lord. It would be an expression of his true character.

"I didn't lie," the villain had the nerve to deny. "Rutgar is an ogre who eats tender maids for supper, or so his reputation would have the world believe."

Gisela ground her teeth. "I hope Aelrhane has you for supper, you blackhearted wart toad!" A furious twist of her body unexpectedly won a moment's freedom from Rutgar's grasp. Instinctively, she threw herself from the horse. The moment her feet hit the ground, she bolted. She dared a glance over her shoulder and saw Rutgar knock aside a lance that one of his men prepared to launch in her direction. "Nay! I will take care of the wench. Stay and wait."

At first she rejoiced, thinking she could easily outrun him, injured as he was, but he followed at an easy trot, close enough to keep sight of her in the dark forest, but not really trying to catch her.

She urged more speed from her legs. If she could lose him in the dark, even for a moment, perhaps he would not find her again. But no matter how fast she ran or how twisted was her path, he ran with her—

easily, seemingly without effort. What for her was a desperate sprint seemed for him to be an easy jog. How could he run so easily with his scalp held together with a dirty rag and a dozen lesser wounds slicing his body? The man simply wasn't human!

The more exhausted Gisela became, the angrier she got. She ran until her breath came in painful gasps and her legs burned in protest. A tree root caught her toe, and she stumbled. She got to her feet, only to stumble again.

"Tired yet?" came an amused inquiry from the darkness several paces away.

"No!" She got up and started running, but was jerked abruptly back by a hand that reached for her out of the darkness. Gisela twisted, lost her balance, and fell. The breath whooshed out of her lungs as Rutgar rolled on top of her.

Rutgar braced himself on his arms. His hard body tangled with hers in disturbing intimacy.

"I'd advise surrender," he said calmly.

Gisela didn't have enough breath to answer. His face hovered so closely above hers that she could see his faint smile and the moonlit gleam of mocking eyes.

"I'm a man of limited patience. Next time you try to run from me I'll simply bind you hand and foot and teach you the humility serfs owe their masters. 'Tis a lesson you've failed to learn in the past, I think."

"Get off me!" Gisela managed to choke out.

He moved his leg, which rested between hers. The contact of hard muscle against the softness between her thighs inspired an uncomfortably erotic ache in her body. There beat within her a perverse urge to surrender—not to his power, but to the smile that was for some reason no longer arrogant and the gleam in eyes that no longer mocked.

"I find this a quite comfortable place to rest after you ran me so mercilessly," he said with a wicked grin. "I'm a wounded man, you know."

Gisela summoned all her indignation. "You'll regret this, you lackwit cur!"

"Really?" He brushed a twig from her hair in a gesture that was almost tender. "I'm not regretting it yet. Are you?"

"I regret being foolish enough to take pity on you!"

"I don't think I've shown you sufficient gratitude for that act of mercy."

She read the intent in his eyes, along with the foolish awakening of a yearning within her own breast. "I warn you," she threatened desperately. "Make me angry enough and I'll shrivel your ballocks to the size of pebbles."

He dared to laugh when any other man of her acquaintance would have cringed. "You are a witch, aren't you? I'll have to pay special attention to my ballocks this night to ensure they keep their present size." His eyes gleamed like polished steel in the darkness. "You're also quite an extraordinary woman."

Slowly, his mouth lowered toward hers. Pinned by the weight of his muscular body, Gisela couldn't move. His lips brushed over hers, gently caressing. She frantically tried to move her head away, but his mouth followed, sealing possessively over hers. Her resistance faltered, and his tongue charmed its way inside, exploring in a way that sent streaks of fire arrowing toward the juncture of her thighs. She could not fight the sensation that overwhelmed her; primitive instinct made her arch up against the male body that covered her. Her breasts swelled as they rubbed against the hard muscle of his chest; the moist warmth between her legs became a burning ache as she pressed hard against his thigh. She drowned in a whirlpool of sensation, emotion and eros eddying together into an irresistible maelstrom. Her heart and mind still spun when he finally gave her back her mouth.

"I don't feel the least shriveled, buglet. Is the sting of your curses so weak?"

Embarrassment at her own response turned to fury. "You want curses, you Frankish pig? I'll show you curses!" Words poured out of her in the old Saxon tongue—incantations, pleas to the Saxon gods, the Christian God, and any other god who might be listening in. She cursed Rutgar, his sire and dam, his children, his friends and comrades, and anyone who felt a charitable thought toward him. Then she started on the sword he fought with; the shield that protected him, the armor that safeguarded his body, and the horse that carried him into battle. May they all fail at once. She cursed his dreams, his desires, his ambitions, and the hard masculine arousal that pressed into the softness of her hip as a reminder of her own traitorous weakness.

Unaffected by her rage, Rutgar rolled off her and, before she could dart away, lifted her to her feet. "Would you care to translate that incantation of gibberish?"

She thrust out her chin in pugnacious challenge. "I called down a curse that will turn your heart to stone and your life's dreams to dust—among other things."

"Is that all?" His wry smile showed not a flicker of the dread that should have met such a pronouncement. "You're wide of the target, lady witch. Any number of women can tell you that my heart is already stone, and I build my ambitions not upon dreams, but on the strength of my arm."

"I threw something in for that, also," she assured him in a miffed voice.

"Ah. In that case, we should make haste back to my men before my strength fades."

She flinched away from his touch as he took her arm.

He shook his head and smiled. "Don't hold a grudge, little maid. You've done your duty by your friends and tried to strike fear into my heart. There was just one thing you didn't take into account—I don't believe in witches."

Gisela kicked at the husk of some unidentified vegetable that had been removed when the cellar had been cleared to serve as her prison. The air was cold in her little underground cell—good for vegetables, uncomfortable for prisoners. Her clothing afforded little warmth. The loose tunic, dirty and torn from her rough journey through the forest the night before, was strictly a summer weave of wool, and the kirtle beneath was threadbare from the day Atruda had given it to her because it no longer fit her plumper frame.

Gisela quit torturing the vegetable debris and slumped back against the dirt wall. A hard wooden bench had been moved into the cellar for her to sit and sleep on. Other furnishings included a single lamp, two blankets, a jar for waste, and a bucket of water. She could cross the length of the cell in four paces or the width in three—if her steps were small.

Many serfs at Ardun had less comfortable quarters, Gisela knew. The difference was that they could leave theirs. She couldn't. No doubt Rutgar intended her to rot of boredom, if he had intentions toward her at all. Likely she was forgotten the moment he handed her over to his mountainous lackey. That one—the same bearlike nightmare whom the deceitful Rutgar had led her to believe was the warlord—had not been nearly as fierce as his appearance would suggest.

"Don't fret overmuch," the giant had advised her with a grin that made him look even more like a bear. "Rutgar hasn't eaten a maid for supper in the last year or so, that I know of. He's lost the taste, I think."

Had she appeared that frightened when he'd escorted her to her cell? Gisela wondered. In truth, she wasn't frightened as much as embarrassed and angry. A kind deed had earned her the fate of being dragged through the forest, assaulted, then dumped into a cold vegetable cellar. She should learn to curtail her kind impulses. Letting Rutgar writhe on the point of Aelrhane's lance would have been far wiser.

Just her luck that of all the men at Ardun, Rutgar was the one who saw through her act to the woman beneath: he merely laughed at her threats and curses. The memory of his kiss made her fume anew. She had never felt so out of control, so exposed, vulnerable, powerless over her own emotions. Worse, the monster had felt her response, for how could she hide such a thing from his knowing senses? How foolish and naive he must believe her!

Gisela kicked at the dirt floor. Callous, unfeeling hegoat! It would serve the knave right if she cast a love spell that would have him groveling at her feet and begging her favor. Gisela had to laugh at the picture. She would be fortunate not to miss her aim and find a pig infatuated with her instead of a Frankish warlord.

Gisela had no way of counting the hours or days she spent in her prison. Now and then Odo brought her a meal of thin soup or coarse bread and cheese. Once a boy she'd never before seen came to change the bucket of water and carry out the waste jar. Neither one spoke to her. Odo merely gave her a chastising glare, and the youngster acted as though she might bite him if he so much as looked at her.

What seemed to be hours might have been mere minutes, and days might really have been hours. She slept often. The oblivion of dreams was more entertaining than staring at the dirt walls of her little cell— until she had a visitor.

Father Gaunt was a rotund little man who was as devoted to the banquet table as he was to the holy altar. His girth gave him the appearance of good humor, but the unfailingly grim set of his mouth reminded all within his sight that sin was a very serious business. The day Gersvinda had died, he'd had her hut in the village burned and declared that the witch had returned to Satan, her master. Gisela had always suspected that the priest thought she was in the hut when he set it afire. He and his plump wife, Hilde, had taken every opportunity since that day to remind all who would listen of the devil-tainted blood that ran through her veins.

As he came down the steps into her cell, the priest smiled beatifically—his best sacramental smile.

"So, witch, your sorcery did not save you from the good Christian warrior that our most righteous king sent to punish the heathens of this barbarian place."

Gisela sighed. She sensed a long sermon in the making. Being locked in a cell was bad enough without the dour priest to make it worse.

" 'Tis a lesson that pagans are always slow to learn, but learn they must, by fire and sword if sweet reason will not move them. God will not be denied. His will must be done, or vengeance is swift."

God was surely taking vengeance on pagan and Christian alike by letting Father Gaunt into their midst, Gisela reflected. "Do you have a reason for your visit, Father?" She looked around the empty cell with a smile. "I'm quite occupied, as you can see, and have little time for this chatter."

Father Gaunt's face grew red. "Insolent girl. I am extending the hand of charity, and you meet me with insult. I have come to hear your confession, to help you shed the iniquity of your heritage and bring you into holy obedience."

Gisela reflected for a moment on the nature of holy obedience. She couldn't afford to pay a coin or give an hour's labor to the priest and his wife to buy intercession for her imagined sins. Nor could she pay for Gaunt's muttered prayers over the bones of some long dead saint or a sliver of wood supposedly from the holy cross—methods he used to treat the few at Ardun who took their ailments to the Church rather than the herbwife—herself.

"I'm sorry to disappoint you, Father, but I have nothing to confess."

His brows crashed down in a mighty frown designed to scare the devil himself. "Pride and arrogance. Trade with the devil. Luring the weak from the arms of the Church with your false and sinful potions and incantations. What do you call those deeds if not sins, girl?"

"My potions merely cure stomach pains and chest congestions. They have nothing to do with the Church."

"Only God can take away the ills He visits upon the sinful."

"Then perhaps God works through me, and not you, Father. My potions seem to have a much higher cure rate than your holy bones."

"Blasphemy as well as witchcraft! Woman, I have tried to be merciful, but I can see that you are unrepentant and determined to be damned. I shall recommend to Lord Rutgar that you be kept down here until you rot, along with the other recalcitrant Saxons who share this miserable hole."

"What other recalcitrant Saxons?"

The priest's eyes lit at her show of concern. "Two cells down is a young man whose back was opened by the lash. Lord Rutgar knows how to handle those miscreants who would defy their king. In the very next cell languishes old Ercangar's impertinent son, who fancies himself called by God but still defends the pagans with his sword."

Gisela's heart jumped at mention of her brother. "Lothar has not been cared for as an honorable warrior should?"

"Honorable? To fight against one's king and then refuse oath to one's rightful lord? Lothar simply reaps the fruits of his stubbornness."

Lothar in the very next cell, his wounds festering and uncared for? Ardun's people whipped? In a flare of temper, Gisela suddenly didn't care that her tormentor was a supposed holy man. He was sadistic, and she didn't hesitate to turn the tables on him.

"You listen to me, Father, and listen well, for I want you to carry a message to your precious Lord Rutgar."

"How dare you presume to order me!"

"I presume whatever I want. You tell Rutgar that I want to see him. Do you understand, you disgusting little smirch on all that is holy?"

The priest's eyes grew wide, his face glowed red.

"Tell Rutgar I wish to see him now, and convince him to come, or that cow you have in the byre will give you a two-headed calf in a few weeks, and her milk will turn sour as bile."

Gisela didn't hesitate to threaten the priest with sorcery, for he believed in magic every bit as much as she. His rituals were full of it under the name of holiness and miracles. It did the man good to be reminded that he did not have a monopoly on magic at Ardun.

"Foul witch! I'll fetch you Rutgar indeed, and hope he comes down here to pronounce sentence upon your head. If he listens to the advice of God's spokesman, he will!"

Rutgar had about reached the end of his patience, which under the best of circumstances was not a long journey. Every face in the hall, Frank and Saxon alike, turned toward the dais expectantly, waiting for his decision. They were like children—all of them. Sullen, squabbling, quarrelsome children, and his Franks were no better than the Saxons. Truth to tell, they were worse.

"Why did you strike the boy, Ulrich?"

Standing slump-shouldered before the master's chair, Ulrich fastened his gaze on the toes of Rutgar's boots.

"Well, man? Speak out."

"The boy was a sluggard, lord. He needed a few blows to teach him his duties."

"Was there some specific reason that you raised your hand to him?"

"He stabled my horse while the beast was still damp with sweat, lord. It could have congested his lungs or settled in his joints. That horse cost me ten solidi."

"The boy's life will cost you much more," Rutgar

said grimly. "By killing my serf, you have robbed me of my property, which I deem worth one hundred solidi."

The man's head snapped up. "But lord, I have not had so much in all my life! I am but a simple freeholder doing my bounden service to the king, not a wealthy magnate such as you."

"A period of ten years service will suffice to pay the fine."

"But lord!"

"Be grateful I don't demand your service for the rest of your life, Ulrich. But I warn you, if ever again you are caught doing violence to one under my protection, be it serf or freeborn, man, woman, or child, you'll hang."

"Aye, lord."

"Remember that when you are next tempted to strike someone weaker than yourself."

The throng in the hall parted to make a path for Ulrich to leave. The silence that followed the man's sentence was broken by a woman's weeping. The dead stableboy's grandmother, an old serf woman, dared to fasten Rutgar with reddened, resentful eyes.

Rutgar motioned to Etich, who bent near. "See that the boy's family is granted freedom and a piece of good land to work."

"The boy had only the grandmother."

"Then give the old woman some land and some sturdy serfs to work it for her."

"Aye, Rutgar. But don't you think that's a bit generous for the life of a mere serf child?"

"A bit of generosity here and there might do to win me the loyalty of these people. I will need it if I'm to keep this land."

"Aye," Etich replied with a sigh. "Give me a good,

straightforward battle any day over trying to woo a gaggle of serfs and peasants."

"What is the next matter?" Rutgar tried to conceal his distaste, but in his heart he agreed with Etich. He was a fighting man, not a diplomat. He had no talent for sitting in judgment or politicking to sway the mood of a people.

"A freeman who works one of the outlying farms claims two Franks raped his daughter. He has pointed out Theodoric and Alared as the men."

Rutgar wanted nothing more than to leave the crowded hall, mount Doomsayer, and gallop until the fresh wind had washed all this human squalor from his mind. "Call them," he said grimly.

Alared and Theodoric admitted their crime with little remorse. The girl had invited their attentions, they claimed.

"Is the girl of childbearing age?"

"Yes, my lord," the father answered. "Gert's a good girl. She wouldn't have lain willingly with this scum."

Rutgar had little doubt of that. He himself had been on the receiving end of a Saxon maid's ire—and that for only a token kiss. He smiled. Along that path lay a wealth of distraction from the matter at hand. Rutgar wrenched his mind back to where it belonged.

"Bring the girl," he commanded.

She was slight, with dull brown hair and pocked skin. Tears streamed down her face and dampened the lank strands of her hair. The purple and greenish bruises on her cheek and neck didn't help her appearance.

Rutgar fixed the two accused men with a level, deadly stare. "I've not yet seen a willing maid who rose from the sport with such marks."

The two accused looked at the floor. Rutgar turned

his attention to the wronged farmer, whose sad eyes rested upon the girl; they were full of pain and loss. Where was his fury? Rutgar wondered. Was the man so accustomed to being downtrodden that he could not feel ire at such an outrage? Through Rutgar's mind flashed a hint of the white-hot anger he would feel if a woman of his—daughter or wife—were so abused. Gisela's face swam into his mind's view. He flinched visibly that his imagination should make such an unwise choice.

"Rutgar?"

Etich's voice called him back. He cleared his throat. "I was considering," he said, only half truthfully.

Etich raised the single continuous brow that roofed his eyes.

Rutgar fixed the abject father with a serious gaze. "What is your name, old man?"

"Frederic, my lord."

"Frederic, the punishment for rape is usually death, but that would compensate you little. I give you a choice. You may see these men hang or have them as your slaves to do with as you will."

"I'll take them as slaves, lord. And if they touch my girl again they'll be eunuchs."

"So be it, then."

The Saxons in the hall murmured approval. A good number of the Frankish contingent nodded as well. Others frowned at the rushes on the floor or hid their feelings behind stony faces.

"Is that the last?" Rutgar asked Etich hopefully.

"For today."

Rutgar grunted in disgust. "I want an assembly of the men at the beginning of the evening watch. Why is it they can't understand that they're here to protect these people, not cut a swath through the population like wolves raiding a sheepfold?"

Etich's answer was drowned out by an imperious demand. "Lord Rutgar, I must see you!" Ardun's priest thundered into the hall in a holy fury.

Rutgar closed his eyes and sighed. All he needed to top off the afternoon was a dose of Gaunt's offended righteousness. He opened them to the sight of the priest's purple face and brimstone eyes. "What is it, good Father?"

"The witch has threatened me. She ordered me to summon you to her cell and promised unholy retribution if I didn't."

"Did she now? Are your ballocks in danger of shrinkage, Father?"

The priest became an even darker purple.

"Sorry, Father. 'Tis not the first time I've crossed words and more with your witch."

"She's not my witch; she's an unholy blight on this stronghold. She should be punished for her mischief. Punished more strongly than being shut up in a comfortable cell."

Rutgar's frustration neared the boiling point, and the troublesome little talisman of Saxon power seemed as good a target as any, seeing that she herself had invited him into her presence. Her honest disdain and uncalculating courage might be refreshing after an afternoon spent among the placating and whining.

"I will deal with the girl, Father. You see to God's problems and I will see to the witch's."

Six

Rutgar's shoulders brushed both sides of the passage as he stalked toward the witch's cell. He unbarred the cell door and flung it violently open. The maid jumped in alarm, then straightened her spine and smoothed her dirty gown. She was like a graceful flame in the cell's dim gloom. After three days in this hole, her hair was still bright, her skin still impossibly fair. Beneath her dirty, threadbare clothing, the feminine lines of her body curved and beckoned at her every move. She looked up at him with a composure that was infuriating and enticing at the same time. He wondered what it would take to douse her spirit and discovered a reluctance to find out.

The cell floor was several steps lower than the passageway. Rutgar took the steps slowly, expecting her to back away from his advance. As he should have known she would, the witch held her ground.

"I see you received my message," she said calmly. A man who believed in witches and suchlike nonsense might imagine that the burning of her amber eyes was more than the mere reflection of the cell's one meager lamp.

Rutgar tried to summon the anger and frustration that had driven him to her cell. It had cooled considerably. "I received your summons, witch. Good Father Gaunt is a bit upset with you. What threat did you use to make him foam at the mouth so?"

"Father Gaunt foams at the mouth at every opportunity. It did not require a very creative threat. I assure you, my lord, that my threats to the priest were not so gruesome as your actions toward the people of Ardun."

Three long days of solitude and imprisonment apparently had taught her nothing of the wisdom of submission, for she faced him with a brazenness that would have done credit to a warrior. "Conquest always involves a certain amount of unpleasantness. 'Tis the way of the world."

"What did the boy two cells down do to deserve to be whipped?"

"The boy is a servant who came in the retinue of one of my officers. He attacked a tenant on one of the outlying farms because the man would not give him a loaf baked by his wife. I made an example of him."

Rutgar watched as some of her indignation faded to uncertainty. A flush bloomed on her cheeks. She was a woman whose body revealed every emotion, if a man took the time to read it. "Is that what your indignant summons was about?"

"That was not the priest's tale."

"But that is the truth of it. It seems, little maid, that you foam at the mouth as readily as the good father."

The flush on her face deepened to crimson, even as she glared at him with undaunted challenge in her eyes.

What waste for God to give such iron spirit to one whose face and form were meant for softness.

"Witch of Ardun, what is your name?"

"I am called Gisela."

"Gisela." A sibilant and graceful name that suited her well. "Gisela, you are a very small mote caught up in a wind that is far more brutal than you know. You should renounce your fuming over those you cannot help and spend more time looking to yourself. Of all the Saxons at Ardun, you are the least able to defend yourself. If you would learn a bit of proper humility, your stay on this earth will be easier."

With that, Rutgar turned to leave, satisfied he'd had the last word. Her unexpected plea stopped him with his hand on the latch of the door.

"My lord, wait."

Her tone was softer now, more uncertain. He turned.

"Ercangar's son Lothar? Does he lie wounded in a cell like this one, as Father Gaunt told me?"

A man could melt at the sound that voice. Rutgar was determined that he would not.

"He does."

"You would leave such a noble warrior to rot of wounds gained in defending his own people?"

The pain in her voice congealed to anger, and she

stepped forward, fists clenched, as if she might attack him with her sudden wrath. Absurdly, Rutgar's instinct urged him to retreat.

"Lothar is no more your concern than the others."

"Lothar *is* my concern. We are . . . friends."

Abruptly she turned away, as if to hide her reaction. A momentary slump of her shoulders revealed her distress, however.

"Lothar will recover well enough from his wounds," he told her. "His grandmother Adalinde cares for him."

She turned back to confront him. "Adalinde has not my skill at healing."

"Ah!" he said cynically. "You are an herbwife as well as a witch?"

"I am. Let me tend Lothar, my lord."

He watched the anxiety on her face grow into desperation.

"Please, my lord. How can it harm you to grant me this?"

Rutgar suffered a twinge that felt surprisingly like jealousy. "What is this fellow that he's so dear to you —that your fear for him reduces you to begging for permission to succor him?"

"We are close," she admitted evasively.

They were lovers, Rutgar concluded. No other "close" relationship was conceivable between a young nobleman, whether he be Frank or Saxon, and a comely serf girl. Gisela's spirit and fire, her artless grace and indignant passion—all were fodder for the Saxon's lust. The thought vexed him, and the fact that it vexed him irritated him even further. With the elvish beauty of her face and a wealth of golden hair, Gisela was fair as any woman Rutgar had seen, but he had possessed some of the finest ladies of the king's court without paying one of those noble ladies the tribute of his jealousy. If the ache eating at his guts was indeed that cursed senseless affliction, he didn't like it one bit.

He climbed the steps to the cell's exit, then turned to give her his answer. Her body was drawn tight as a bowstring as she waited. Perhaps she really loved this Lothar, or perhaps she believed she could bring the old lord's son back into power and benefit from his gratitude.

"I suppose if conquest necessarily involves unpleasantness, it must also leave room for healing. You may see to Lothar under the condition that a guard is present," Rutgar conceded.

Only a subtle shift in the tempting curves of her body revealed the girl's relief. A slight smile touched her mouth as her face softened. "Thank you, my lord. The guard will not be necessary. I give my word that Lothar and I will not plot an escape."

"Nay, Gisela. The guard will be there to protect Lothar. Saxon or not, the man doesn't deserve to be left alone to your mercies."

He shut and bolted the door before she could talk him into even more concessions. Let her at him long enough and she'd have him washing her feet and serving her wine. He had to smile at himself as he strode out into the fresh-smelling night. His men would laugh to learn that Rutgar, known throughout the domain as the iron-hard rock women broke themselves against, was in danger of being wrapped around a serf maid's small finger. She cooled his anger even as he sparked hers. She earned his admiration—an emotion he'd never felt for a woman. Worse, she somehow inspired his jealousy.

Gisela of Ardun was a dangerous woman after all. Perhaps he should start believing in witches.

When Gisela first saw Lothar, she had to admit that she'd done Rutgar an injustice in believing he would mistreat a prisoner. Her brother sat on a bench similar to the one in her cell, reading. Beside him was a stack of well-worn leather-bound volumes that he had obtained from the abbey at Verdun: religious philosophies and lives of the saints. Over the years he had read to her from them, for she herself could not read.

"Look at you—living a life of ease! And after I pictured all kinds of horrors being rained upon your head!"

"Gisela!"

Lothar rose stiffly to greet her as she climbed down into a cell identical to hers. Rutgar's watchdog guard followed. When Lothar eyed him uneasily, Gisela smiled assurance.

"Don't fret, my lord. This stalwart fellow is here to protect you from me. Rutgar hesitates to subject even a Saxon enemy to a plague such as myself."

The Frank glared at her and took up his station by the door.

"Gisela!" Lothar took her hands. His injured arm and side were stiff, she noted. But that was to be expected; she couldn't really blame Adalinde's care for that. "How come you here? Aelrhane . . . ?"

"Is still lurking in the forest, no doubt very angry with me right now. The new lord of Ardun was stupid enough to fall into Aelrhane's hands, and I foolishly thought to help him escape. He repaid my kindness by dragging me back here and throwing me into the cell next to yours. I think I displaced the onions and garlic, for it's quite pungent in there."

Lothar's face flushed with anger. "The dog. Did he hurt you, Gisela. If he did . . ."

"The Frank has done nothing but mock me, embarrass me, and treat me as gently as one might handle a sack of grain. But other than to my pride, which you keep warning me is a useless iniquity, no damage was done."

Lothar's anger faded quickly. Gisela pushed him back to arm's length and surveyed him critically. "You, my lord, look very fit for a man I pictured writhing on his deathbed. You always were very quick to mend."

"I am as well as a man can be without seeing the sun for so many days."

"I had it on a holy rat's authority that Rutgar was letting your wounds putrify and entertaining himself with your moans of agony."

Lothar shook his head and smiled. He spread his arms—the left one with some difficulty—to demonstrate his wholeness. "He's been kind enough, for a conqueror."

"Kind? Can a warlord be kind and still be a warlord?" Gisela led Lothar back to the bench and picked up the lamp. "Let me have a look at you so I may send for my medicines if need be."

Once Gisela had helped her brother shed his tunic and shirt and carefully removed the bandage from his wounds, she was more than satisfied that Lothar's arm and side were healing well. The wounds were closed, the skin and scar tissue pink, healthy, and clean. "Adalinde tended you well enough."

" 'Twas your poultice that kept the poison from the wounds."

Gisela laid a hand gently on his arm. "I didn't want to leave you, Lothar."

"I know you didn't. Aelrhane gave you no choice. In truth, Ercangar and Aelrhane have given us all little choice in our fates."

Gisela helped Lothar back into his shirt and sat wearily beside him. "Perhaps none of us have much choice in what roads we follow. Sometimes I suspect that our fates are laid out for us before we are born. How else would I so often be able to see what lies around the next curve of time?"

"You are very melancholy, Gisela." Lothar took her hand. "Do you see something?"

"What I see, I can't interpret." She intertwined her fingers with his. The touch of his solid flesh was a comfort after so many days of feeling isolated, angry, and powerless. "When I look at Rutgar I feel a permanence about him. I think he will be here for a very long time. I also have the feeling of a strange recognition when I look upon him." She hesitated, not knowing quite how to express what she felt when she tried to see the Frankish warlord with the deep, penetrating sight that her Gift sometimes gave her. Something about Rutgar confused her mind, heightening her perceptions and mixing in emotions that kept her from seeing clearly. She couldn't think properly or feel properly when she was close to him.

Yet she couldn't air such nonsense to her brother.

"I believe . . . I believe this Frankish warlord is someone of whom we should be very cautious."

"Indeed! He's already proven that." Lothar gave her a look that was uncomfortably penetrating. "Tell me of this man who is now our master."

"You have fought him," Gisela said uneasily. "You know him better than I."

"When I fight a man, I see his weapon. Little else. I think you know more of Rutgar than his iron."

She shrugged. "I can tell you little. His temper is close to the surface. He is a hard man, I think, though occasionally he laughs, sometimes at himself. He's arrogant, and can be surly when crossed." She smiled suddenly. "Oh yes, and he doesn't believe in witches."

Lothar grinned. "Will you teach him otherwise?"

"I'd rather stay out of his way—if I'm ever released from these cellars, that is."

"With God's help, perhaps I can attain freedom for us both. I have petitioned Rutgar for my freedom and promised an oath of loyalty in return."

Gisela laid a hand on his arm. "A man's oath is a sacred and powerful thing, Lothar. Are you sure you want to bind yourself to this man?"

"I am bound to God above all." He covered her hand with his and smiled gently. "No oath to a man can take precedence over that. But if I must have an earthly master, also, then surely this Rutgar is no worse than my father, and he is almost certain to be better than Aelrhane."

"What you spoke of many years ago to me—of going to one of King Charles's palace schools and becoming a priest—do you still have such an ambition in your heart?"

Lothar shook his head. "I've grown past the age for schools, I fear. But perhaps if King Charles can keep our people from slipping back into pagan darkness, God will someday grant my heart's desire to be a shepherd of his flock."

Gisela had to grin at her brother's gravity. "A shepherd the likes of Father Gaunt, who says I'm the devil's whore and have naught but darkness in my soul?"

Lothar tweaked her chin with brotherly affection. "Father Gaunt wouldn't know an angel if one stuck out her foot and tripped him. The people may call you witch, but your soul shines as brightly as the sun. 'Tis my opinion that your Gift comes from God, not the devil."

"Wherever it comes from, I doubt my small sorceries are going to help us much."

"Don't give up hope, Gisela. Trust God. His plan is the best possible thing for all of us."

Gisela sniffed in disbelief. She trusted God, whether men named him a Christian God or the deities who ruled the Saxon life. She trusted Lothar as well; but she certainly didn't trust Rutgar.

Gisela was with Lothar once again two days later when Rutgar opened the cell door and looked down at them. His body filled the doorway and blocked the light, casting his face in shadow, but Gisela felt annoyance radiate from him like heat from a fire.

"You look well enough," he said to Lothar. Descending the steps, Rutgar motioned the bored guard to leave.

"My wounds are all but healed, my lord. I've only a minor stiffness remaining."

Rutgar sent a half-amused smile in Gisela's direction. "What a shame I didn't manage to kill him with my neglect and abuse."

"I but listened to the words of the priest," Gisela shot back. "Was I to trust your . . . honor . . . over the truthfulness of a holy man? Such are not supposed to lie, you know."

Rutgar seemed amused rather than vexed by her refusal to back down before him. He gave Lothar a wry smile. "As you can tell by her tone, your little witch doesn't put much faith in my honor. She doesn't seem to realize that honor is something between warriors and peers, not between men and women."

Lothar moved to Gisela's side, as if to defend her. "Gisela has never taken a very realistic view of the exigencies of life, Lord Rutgar. She expects the world to be a gentler place than it is."

Rutgar's brows drew into an annoyed pucker at the sight of Lothar's arm around Gisela's waist.

"She is as foolish as most women, I see. But you may rest easy and release her. I've no intentions of beating her here and now, though no doubt that tongue of hers has earned more than a few blows."

Gisela opened her mouth for a sharp retort, but a warning look from Lothar silenced her.

"I've thought about your petition." Rutgar settled himself on the cell's single bench, legs stretched in front of him and arms folded across his broad chest as he regarded Lothar with speculative eyes. "Your father's people tell me that you recognized King Charles as your sovereign, and that you had no part in Ercangar's decision to surrender Ardun to the Saxon rebels."

The Frank looked battle-ready even sitting in such a relaxed posture, Gisela noted. He relaxed in the same way Silver relaxed, with muscles ready to spring should something make the wrong sound or move the wrong way. One couldn't help but admire the animal perfection of him.

"Still," Rutgar continued, "now that your father is dead and Aelrhane and his rebels are at a disadvantage, what assurance do I have that you won't try to regain the lands that were under your father's stewardship?"

"I have no ambitions in that quarter, my lord."

"I asked for your oath once before. You told me it belonged to God and your people."

Lothar sighed and looked down at the dirt floor. "I have realized that I can best serve Ardun by helping you bring peace here, and maintain it."

"Is peace truly what you seek, Lothar? You're a noble Saxon—the old lord's son. 'Twould be natural for your people to make you a focus for dissension and discontent."

"My oath would be sacred, my lord. I would not break a formal bond of loyalty, even under pain of death."

"So you say."

Lothar stiffened. "You question my honor?"

"I know nothing of your honor, boy."

"As Lothar knows nothing of your alleged honor, Rutgar!" Indignation flooded Gisela's face with heat, and she could hold her peace no longer. "Lothar is the truest—"

"Be silent." Rutgar cocked a warning brow in her direction. "This doesn't concern you."

"It—"

"Silence!"

Rutgar's eyes never left Lothar, and though Gisela was not the subject of that intense gaze, she could feel the power behind it. Lothar's eyes dropped and he backed a step before visibly forcing himself to stay where he was.

"I've decided to accept your petition, Lothar. But there is a condition. You will fight me for the rule of Ardun so there may be no doubt in any man's mind who is lord here."

"You want me to fight you?" Lothar sounded as though Rutgar had asked him to jump off a cliff.

"You're well enough healed to wield a sword. And

since my head was nearly cut in twain by our friend Aelrhane but a few days past, we are matched fairly enough."

"You defeated me once already."

"Not before the eyes of those who might see you as a legitimate Saxon savior."

"But I don't want Ardun. Why should I risk my life for something I have no desire for?"

"Because I demand it. Do you want your freedom, boy?"

Lothar made a sound that was halfway between choking and laughing. "Freedom holds little lure when death follows but moments upon its heels."

"You may yield honorably at first blood, if you wish."

Lothar turned toward Gisela, anxiously searching her face. She met his questioning gaze uneasily, remembering her dream—the duel, the fire. Was Rutgar's demand the beginning of the vision's fulfillment? A chill shivered down her spine. She could hold her brother's eyes but a moment before she had to look away.

"What of Gisela?" Lothar asked quietly.

"Her fate is not linked to yours," Rutgar declared firmly.

Lothar hesitated, then pressed onward. "I would like her to go free also."

Rutgar looked from Lothar to Gisela with an air of annoyance.

"I will give my promise to behave," Gisela offered. If Lothar was to fight Rutgar, she had to be there to see it.

"A woman's promise is a useless thing. From what I've seen, maid, you're not capable of comporting yourself in a manner suitable to your position in the world."

Gisela returned his frown with a level look. "If I were as meek as you'd have me, my lord, you might well be rotting in pieces on the forest floor, and Aelrhane's blade would be stained with your blood."

His eyes caught at hers, but she held steady and refused to lower her gaze. Slowly he began to smile.

"Very well, Lothar. Your little witch may go free as well. Some have been asking for her services as healer, and there is always need of another pair of hands at the women's work. But if trouble is your brew, witch, I'll make you wish you were safe once again in this cellar."

"Gisela is not a troublemaker, my lord. She'll behave."

"I doubt it," Rutgar said, taking his leave. " 'Tis fortunate that she's but a woman. How much harm can she do?"

Seven

The practice yard stretched between the manor and the east palisade, and it was usually populated only by men drilling at their military exercises and a few servants carrying water or setting up targets. But on this day almost all of Ardun crowded around the yard's margins, jostling and straining for a view of the unusual contest that was about to begin. At the rear of the crowd, Gisela craned her neck to see over the shoulders and heads in front of her, but there were too many. Every man, woman, and child had deserted the day's labor to watch the duel between the old lord's son and the king's warlord. Peasants and serfs had come in from the villages and farms, taking a holiday from their work. The hearth in the smithy was cold, the looms and spinning wheels in the weaving house were silent, and weeds in the vegetable plots had a day's respite from the women's hoes. Chores were neglected, with Lord Rutgar's blessings. Only the kitchens hummed with their usual activity—more than on an ordinary day, for a great feast was to be laid for all who attended the contest, as befitted a celebration for the beginning of a new era.

"May the best man win today," a lanky peasant in front of Gisela said to his neighbor.

"The best man is always Saxon," grunted the other.

"Aye, well, most here would say you're right. Rutgar's a bold one, though, and just too. He's giving Ercangar's whelp more of a chance than did the old lord himself. The strongest arm will take the day, and that's as it should be."

Murmurs of approval came from several others.

Rutgar knew exactly what he was doing in staging this spectacle, Gisela realized. Men respected strength above all else, and if Lothar yielded under Rutgar's sword with all Ardun watching, there was little chance Ercangar's son could ever be a danger to Rutgar's rule.

"Maid Gisela!" Panting, Guntar appeared beside her. "Look what I found for you." He set a sturdy wooden box by her feet. "Look here. You can stand on it and watch the fight over people's heads."

"Oh Guntar! Bless you."

A strong voice rang out over the practice yard, announcing the contest. The duel was to be with the spatha—the longsword. No rules restricted the combatants other that the code of honor. The victor would take all. God have mercy upon the vanquished.

The roar of the crowd's approval nearly shook Gisela from her little perch. One hand on Drada's thin shoulder, she stood on tiptoe to watch her brother stride confidently onto the practice yard beside Rutgar. Lothar wasn't feeling as confident as he looked, Gisela knew. Her brother was a skilled swordsman, but he himself had told her that Rutgar fought like hell's own champion. He even looked like hell's own champion, Gisela thought. Taller than Lothar by half a hand, Rutgar also appeared to be broader through the shoulders—or perhaps he wore extra padding under his mail byrnie. Lothar also wore mail, and Gisela detected the bulge where he had covered his healing side with thick bandages.

Lothar donned his helmet and saluted his adversary. Rutgar did the same, though his headgear stuck momentarily on the bandage that still wrapped his head. Men! Gisela reflected scornfully. Both of the fools were held together with bandages, and they were eager to lay each other open yet again. Why God set men as rulers over the earth was beyond understanding.

"What passes?" Drada asked anxiously.

"They are but starting now," Gisela told her. "They circle like two tomcats taking each other's measure."

She didn't want to watch, but neither could she tear her eyes away. The crowd held its breath, waiting for blood to flow.

"What passes, girl? Tell me!"

"There is nothing to tell yet. Oh! Here it starts!" Her fingers pressed into Drada's shoulder. "Lothar lunges bravely. He swings well, but Rutgar deflects the blade with his own. Now Lothar cuts low." She gasped.

"Rutgar jumps the blade—how can he do that with all that mail hanging from him?"

Gisela narrated the contest for the blind woman's benefit, and Guntar's too, since the lad was even shorter than Gisela and could see only the heaving bodies of the crowd. She tried to keep her voice calm as the blades rang and onlookers shouted encouragement or hooted derision. But her heart grew heavier as the minutes passed, as Lothar attacked bravely again and again and his blade was easily turned aside by Rutgar's skill. Rutgar was truly a master at the craft of war, Gisela could see. At first it had seemed that the Frank was losing the fight, for Lothar was the one who hacked forward time and time again, his blade forcing Rutgar into what appeared to be retreat. But never did the Saxon blade even come close to laying an edge on Frankish mail. Lothar was well trained and strong, but Rutgar was playing with him as Silver might play with a rabbit before his teeth delivered the fatal crunch.

As Gisela feared, after a time Rutgar, like Silver, showed his teeth to the victim. Lothar was forced back, and back again. The crowd roared and cheered, its fickle approval clearly with the strongest. Gisela's heart rose into her throat and cut off the words of her narrative to Drada. She prayed that Lothar wouldn't get caught up in the heat of battle and delude himself into thinking he could win. She prayed even more fervently that Rutgar would accept Lothar's surrender after first blood. A man driven by bloodlust might not remember a promise made in a calmer moment. Most conquering warlords would not have made the promise at all.

Through all her prayers and fearful gasps, Gisela's eyes could not leave Rutgar. If war could ever be poetic, then he was the poem. Every movement, no matter how fast, was graceful and controlled, every lunge, sidestep, retreat, part of a deadly dance. He wielded the long iron blade as if it had no more weight than air.

Drada tugged impatiently on Gisela's sleeve. "What is happening, girl? What are all these throats roaring about?"

"Is Lothar winning?" Guntar jumped up and down in an effort to see over the crowd.

"No," Gisela moaned. "Lothar isn't winning. May God have mercy on him!"

Rutgar obviously intended to end the duel with no more time wasted. He forced Lothar back. Gisela could feel the intensity of his deadly focus almost as if it were directed at her. For a moment dizziness swept her. She grasped Drada's shoulder to steady herself, then saw the crimson that bloomed at Rutgar's sword tip as it cut the skin of Lothar's throat.

The vision was clear in every detail, as if she were looking through Rutgar's eyes. She saw the stoic acceptance in Lothar's face, the pallor of his skin, the gleam of the blade as it caught the afternoon sun, the scarlet trickle that dripped from the sword into the dirt. Not real. Not yet. On the field, Lothar still desperately deflected Rutgar's strokes. But a moment later Gisela's vision and reality converged when Lothar's sword flew from his hand and Rutgar pressed the tip of his blade to Lothar's throat. Gisela could not see the smear of her brother's blood, but she knew it was there.

"First blood!" Gisela thought she heard Rutgar say, but how could she have heard anything above the shouting of the crowd? She was right, though, for the people of Ardun took it up as a chant. "First blood! First blood!"

Lothar knelt. "He yields!" someone shouted.

"Kill the Saxon scum and good riddance!" a Frankish voice urged.

Gisela held her breath. Leaving a rival alive was not a mistake most ambitious men would make. Few warriors would fault Rutgar for choosing not to accept any victory short of death. He had said Lothar might yield at first blood. He had not promised to accept such a surrender.

Rutgar lowered his blade, though, and he clasped Lothar's hands between his in acceptance of the oath of vassalage. The crowd roared once again, scarcely caring who they cheered.

Gisela breathed once again. Lothar was alive. The Frank had taken the path of mercy rather than the safer road of slaughter. A flood of gratitude warmed her heart, and she vowed to repent every scathing word she'd ever thrown Rutgar's way. She jumped from her perch, feeling as though she might fly. "I must go to Lothar!"

Drada's veined hand caught her arm. "Nay, child. Leave the man his pride."

"But he's hurt!"

"He'll come to you if he needs mending. You and Guntar must help me to the feast. My stomach has been teased all the day long with the smells coming from the kitchen, and I'd not wait until all of the good food is gobbled up by this crowd."

The press of bodies buffeted them toward the manor door, and the blind woman's grasp on her arm was unrelenting. Drada was right, of course. Lothar didn't need her to cosset him. Still, as Gisela looked back toward the practice yard where her brother was now standing with Rutgar and huge Etich, she longed to run back—not so much to tend Lothar as to thank Rutgar. What kind of warlord chose mercy and honor over bloodlust and expedience? As if hearing her thought, Rutgar looked up. Even at a distance Gisela could feel the piercing gray of his eyes. Suddenly and inexplicably shy, she ducked her head and urged Drada toward the manor.

The rest of that day was given over to a grand feast. Everyone stuffed themselves with roast venison and pig, cheese white with cream, broiled and stewed fish, and sugared pastries. Men and women alike overindulged with mead, wine, and ale until the stronghold looked as though it was beset by some plague, so many limp bodies lay about. Women snored on their cots in the women's quarters—those who made it there and hadn't collapsed in the hall or the yard. Frankish warriors lay draped with Saxon men-at-arms who had been released from their confinement to watch the duel. Upon Lothar's surrender, each Saxon warrior had made a similar oath to Rutgar, and then promptly taken full advantage of his new lord's largesse.

Not everyone at Ardun celebrated in a drunken stupor. Men on the palisade kept vigilant watch to protect the revelers, and a small group of swordsmen worked off the lassitude of their meal by hacking at each other in the practice yard where Rutgar had earlier won his victory over Lothar. Ermentrude and Fredelin diligently worked to clean up the celebration's mess and clutter—with the sullen help of Atruda and Gillan, who had been forcibly sobered up when the cook soaked their heads in the stable's watering trough.

Gisela had partaken heartily of the dishes laid on long tables in the manor's hall—she had the lean days spent in the cellar to make up for, after all. The sumptuous meal had little time to settle in her stomach, however, before those who had overdone their celebrating in both food and liquor came to her for relief. The evening saw her in the little infirmary at one end of the women's quarters, doling out infusions of slippery elm and meadowsweet to calm abused stomachs and pounding heads. The hour was late and she was preparing a similar infusion for herself when Rutgar appeared at her door.

"I can see the people of Ardun are grateful to have regained your services. Surely every man, woman, and child that dwells within the palisade has passed through this door in the last few hours."

"And now the master, also, I see." Gisela tried to still the trembling of her hand on the horn cup she had just filled with slippery elm tea. She was tired, that was what made her so unsteady. She was very, very tired.

"Since you are so diligent in serving my people"—he emphasized the possessive *my* with a smile—"I thought you might also see to this head of mine."

"You could have sent for me, my lord. You needn't have come here."

"I was curious to follow the stream of people flowing toward this little closet. I take it this is where the witch of Ardun casts her spells and brews her love potions."

"The business in love potions has been very slow tonight, my lord. Your people have been more interested in their stomachs than their hearts." She motioned him to sit, then set her lamp on the little table beside him and parted the hair that hung in dark, damp strands on his neck. He had just bathed, she guessed, for the sharp scent of lye soap rose with the warmth of his body. Though just washed, the hair on the back of his head was sticky with blood.

"The bandage stank. I took it off."

" 'Tis well you did. Such foulness will oft inflame a wound. You've opened the gash again." She clucked disapprovingly. "I should have stitched it, but I had nothing to stitch it with in Aelrhane's camp. At least it looks healthy enough."

"Then stitch it now. As you said to me once before, we wouldn't want the rocks to fall out of my head, would we?"

"No. I suppose not."

Gisela set to work cutting the hair around the gash, then wiped it clean with yarrow and witch hazel, which would help stop the bleeding. She stitched the ragged edges together as best as possible, though it would have been better done when the wound was fresh.

While she had Rutgar at such disadvantage, Gisela dared to speak from her heart. "My lord, I thank you for sparing Lothar on the field today." She could not keep the emotion from her voice. Right then, she was in such charity with the Frank that she was startled by the sudden distance in his voice.

"Did you expect me to dishonor my vow to your . . . friend?"

"In the heat of blood, many warriors would not have counted such a promise a true vow."

"A promise and a vow are one and the same and must be kept." He smiled slightly. "Besides, there are those who have said that my blood cannot heat."

Those fools did not know the man, Gisela thought. In her experience, his blood heated rather quickly.

"I expected to see Lothar here," she said hesitantly. "Did you not prick him with your blade?"

"Not so deeply that he needs your attention. If the man's wise, you won't see him."

"How so?"

"I told him to stay away from you."

"Why?"

"Because I choose it to be so," he answered gruffly.

"Surely you don't think the two of us would plot together!" She pricked a bit harder with her needle than was strictly necessary, but the iron man didn't flinch. "Lothar is no danger to you after today, and I . . ." A sudden flash of mischief made her bold. "Are you afraid of *me*, my lord?"

"Afraid of a woman?" he scoffed.

"Then why . . . ?"

"Because I will it! Ouch!"

"Sorry."

"Are you trying to sew my scalp to my skull?"

Gisela applied a salve of knitbone and white willow and smirked to herself. The iron man had nerves after all. "That should hold you together."

Gingerly, he touched the back of his head. "You've a gentle hand, when you're not annoyed."

She gave him an innocent smile.

"So 'tis just as well you're done with your stitching as I say this last. I would that you stay within the stronghold walls until the countryside is more at peace."

"I cannot do that, lord. There are people at the villages and farms who need my tending, and medicinals to be gathered, and—"

"You will do as I say, Gisela, or make your home once again in the cellar. I suspect your friend

Aelrhane would like nothing more than to have his pet witch back to incite a Saxon holy war."

"I thought you didn't believe in witches, my lord!"

"I don't. But your Saxons believe in witches. They look for spirits, trolls, gnomes, and sprites in every log, pond, waterfall, and fire. And since it is Saxons I must rule, it bodes me well to pay some heed to their beliefs."

"What of Lothar?" she demanded. "Why can I not see him?"

"Because I don't wish you to."

"But we're friends. There's no harm in—"

He held up his hand to stop her. "I said that I don't wish you to."

Gisela comprehended no reason for the annoyance in his tone or the stubborn set of his jaw.

"Do you understand, Gisela?"

"I understand that you're . . ." *Exasperating* and *unreasonable* both came to mind, but a look from Rutgar made her think better of voicing her opinion. Her charity with him was wearing a bit thin. With all others he seemed just to a fault. He believed in mercy and honor, healing and tolerance. But with her he was an ogre. "I understand well enough, my lord." She didn't understand, though. She didn't understand at all.

In the following days, Gisela found it easy enough to resume her former life. Much of her time was spent treating the ills and complaints of the people of Ardun, who'd been without her services for too long a time. Thomas the smith was suffering from skin ulcers. His son Geoff had burned his arm and left the burn untreated; now the injury oozed pus. Luitgard returned from the village where Gisela had sent her when Rutgar had first attacked. The girl had begun her monthly courses and was in need of a dose of motherwort to relieve the cramping. A host of others had lung congestions and stomach problems, warts, boils, rotting teeth, and earaches. There was plenty to keep Gisela busy, and when there wasn't, she let Ermentrude put her to work in the kitchen or helped Drada in the weaving house. She avoided Adalinde, however, for she had no desire to be drafted for work in the manor—to be serving Rutgar at his table or cleaning the lord's bedchamber. The less she saw of the new master of Ardun, the happier she was. Gisela was not comfortable with things she didn't understand, and she didn't understand Rutgar. He was a confusing merge of intolerance and mercy, savagery and gentleness, irreverence and stilted honor. She didn't know whether to despise him or admire him.

Five days after the great contest, a freeman peasant from one of the outlying farms brought his daughter into Gisela's little infirmary. The girl was pasty white, with pocked skin, lank hair, and lackluster eyes. She stared sullenly at the ground as her father explained that she'd been forced by two Franks and he'd not have her bear their seed. He had enough mouths to feed without adding an unwanted babe. With the portion of his crop that must go to Rutgar at harvest time and the part that was burned a week ago by Aelrhane, he'd be hard put to feed his own through the winter.

"If Rutgar's men abused your daughter, then he should forgive the rent this season," Gisela said indignantly.

"Nay, maid. The lord gave me the villains who did the deed. Reduced them to slaves, he did. 'Tis enough. They've strong backs, and I don't feed them much."

"Rutgar gave them to you as slaves?"

" 'Twas my choice between that and seeing them hanged. The lord said that they'd do me little good rotting at the end of a rope. He's a fair man, that one. And he's got a practical turn of mind. Not like Aelrhane. Now there's a man who thinks only with his blade and cares not who suffers because of it. I be loyal to the old ways, maid, but sometimes I think we're better off cleaving to the Frankish king's man."

Gisela sighed. She prepared a dose of pennyroyal for the dejected girl and assured her that if her attackers had left any of themselves behind, the potion would free her of it.

"Bless you, maid," the father said.

Two days later, Gisela realized her medicinals were running low and, unless she was permitted to collect more, she would soon be out of several essentials. To make matters worse, summer would soon end. It did not last long in this land beside the northern sea. Already there was a hint of sharpness in the morning air. She needed to collect as much as she could to see them through the coming winter. Not to mention that she ached to visit Silver and know just one more hour's peace at the pool.

She dared not leave the stronghold without Rutgar's consent, however. The cellars would welcome her back if she did.

"So get his permission," Drada advised when Gisela complained of her dilemma. "He's not unreasonable, as men go. He told me that we might take some of our fine woolens to the market fair in Verdun next summer."

"Aye? That's nice. But he seems less reasonable with me than with others."

"Tch! I've never known you to be so timid about asking for what you need, girl."

Drada was right, Gisela admitted. Avoiding Rutgar was a habit that had turned into an obsession—pure silliness, to be sure. Where was the grit and bravado that had always gotten her through life?

Therefore, she left Drada to seek out Rutgar in the practice yard, where he often spent a good part of the afternoon. He was not there. Two of the warriors who thrust at each other with blunted lances stopped their mock combat to regard her with hostile, wary stares. She took the opportunity to ask after their lord.

"He's not here, so be off about your business, witch."

A touch on Gisela's shoulder made her turn to see Galt's face looking down at her. He looked more sober than usual. "If 'tis Rutgar ye seek, maid, he's in the manor. I saw him head that way a moment past."

"Thank you, Galt."

"You keep a distance from those Frankish wolves, little maid. Our lady Adalinde tries to frighten them with stories of your magic, and they like you not."

Rutgar wasn't too pleased, either, Gisela guessed. He would probably have her thrown out of his presence, if not worse, rather than grant her request.

Gisela didn't find Rutgar in the hall as she had hoped. Adalinde lifted a brow when she saw her, then smiled slyly. Gisela didn't return the smile.

"My lady," she said boldly, "it has come to my ears that you've been exaggerating my abilities. You do me no good in this."

Adalinde waved her objections aside. "Your good is not what I seek, girl. It serves these Frankish interlopers right to go to sleep at night with a few nightmares in their heads."

"Is that what I am? A nightmare?"

Adalinde's smile was genuine this time. "You are the symbol of the old ways, the old gods, the old powers, Gisela. Our people remember your mother, and they see her in you. The thought of your magic reminds them that they are favored of the gods."

"I am not the power my mother was."

"No. But perhaps you simply have not learned your strengths."

Gisela silently cursed her grandmother's single-mindedness. Ardun would be burned and all its people dead before Adalinde would admit defeat. "I seek an audience with Rutgar. Is he here?"

The sly sparkle in the old lady's eyes should have told Gisela that trouble was coming. "You will find him in his chamber. Since you go there, help Gillan carry the water up the stairs."

Gillan had a much sturdier build than Gisela, but Gisela willingly helped her with the task of carrying two buckets of steaming water that had been heating on the hearth. Their purpose became apparent when they entered the lord's chamber, for Rutgar was in the midst of his bath, soaking in a wooden tub and attended by dithering maids. Sweat-dampened leggings, shirt, and hardened leather breastplate attested to his recent presence on the practice yard.

They stared at each other, he sprawled in the tub and she frozen in the doorway. For a moment Gisela imagined that he was as disconcerted as she, but then a slow smile revived the boldness of his mien. Even sitting naked in a wooden tub he was imposing.

"Come in," he commanded. "The water grows cold."

Gisela tried to retrieve her composure. It wasn't as though she hadn't attended men in their baths. She had often bathed Ercangar, and Aelrhane as well. She did not especially want to attend Rutgar, however.

Gillan emptied her steaming bucket into the tub. Her face as hot as the water she carried, Gisela did the same.

"Is that too warm, my lord?" Gillan asked.

"Nay. Just warm enough."

"Would you like your hair washed, my lord?" another servingmaid almost pleaded.

Gisela was ashamed for them. One would think they had no better work than to crowd around Rutgar's bath, giddy and giggling, behaving like concubines in a wicked sultan's palace.

She drew herself up with what dignity she could. "My lord, I have a need for words with you."

Rutgar smiled lazily. "Then speak."

Gisela was not fooled by his relaxed posture. She felt the intense focus of those piercing eyes and wondered just how displeased he was about Adalinde's tales.

"Leave us," he ordered the maids.

They obeyed reluctantly, mouths drooping with disappointment.

"That wasn't necessary. What I would request of you is certainly not private."

"Ah. You have a request." He tossed her the wet sponge. "Since my attendants have left, you may bathe me while you talk."

Gisela sighed and tried to pretend that the chore was no more disconcerting than bathing Ercangar. "As you wish." She pushed him forward and began to soap his back. Thick slabs of muscle padded his shoulders and tapered over his ribs. She ran the sponge down sinew-knotted arms and over his chest, watching the suds bubble over hard-puckered male nipples. Her stomach fluttered. This wasn't at all like washing Ercangar.

"What weighty request bade you walk into the ogre's lair?"

"Ah!" she said tartly. "You admit it."

"Admit what?"

"That you're an ogre." The riposte made her feel braver.

He grinned. "The buglet still has her sting. I see I haven't swatted you down yet. I'll give that some thought, ogre that I am."

Gisela thought it best to let the subject of swatting drop. A silence stretched between them that was almost comfortable, broken only by the lapping of water in the tub and the quiet sound of their breathing.

"Gisela?" Rutgar leaned back in the tub and looked up at her. "You had something urgent that needed discussion?"

"Oh. Yes." She'd been mesmerized by the motion of her hand stroking across his chest and the silly reflections of her mind. "Uh . . . I need to collect medicinals from the forest. Otherwise I will run out of several remedies."

He lifted one brow. "You can't just cast one of your spells to relieve people of their aches?"

"My lord, I seldom cast spells." She didn't add that the spells she did try almost never worked. "Magic is much more than spells and incantations. 'Tis a oneness with nature, an appreciation of what the Mother Earth offers, both physically and spiritually."

He sat up, sending a small flood of lukewarm water onto the woven rushes that covered the stone floor. "I'm going to have something very physical to offer if you go any lower with that sponge."

"What. Oh! Sorry!" Gisela's cheeks grew warm. Her hand had journeyed on its own accord as they were talking.

"And I'm going to be as shriveled as Odo if I don't get out of this tub." He stood, and his masculine response to her attentions were blatantly displayed. He seemed not the least embarrassed. Gisela didn't know why her own breath caught in her throat and her face caught fire. Modesty and privacy were were rare commodities in a stronghold such as Ardun, and this wasn't first time she'd seen a naked man in full arousal.

She tossed him a towel and turned quickly away, wanting nothing more to escape the room. She thought she heard him chuckle softly, but her ears were almost deafened by the sound of her own pounding pulse, so she wasn't sure.

"Can . . . do I have your permission to collect my plants?"

"When I can spare a couple of men to escort you, then you may go."

"I don't require an escort, my lord."

"I require that you have one."

"But—"

"Do you want to collect your plants?"

"I . . . Yes."

"Then you will go with an escort."

She sighed. No visit to the pool or romp with Silver, as she'd hoped. No seeking of the peace the forest could bring to her soul. But she still needed those plants. She gritted her teeth. "Yes, my lord. Thank you."

"Is there something particularly interesting in that corner where you're staring so intently? One of your devils or spirits, perhaps?"

The only devil in this room was behind her. Gisela was sure she heard the mocking chuckle this time. Resolutely, she turned. Rutgar had pulled on loose linen braes that were unlaced at his narrow waist. His chest was bare. For some reason he looked more intimidating in that scarcity of clothing than in full armor.

"May I go?" Gisela choked out.

" 'Twas all you wanted?"

"Yes." A good deal more than she wanted, Gisela thought.

"Then go."

Face still burning, Gisela fled.

Eight

Gisela heard Adalinde call her as she ran down the stone stairs into the hall and fled toward the freedom of the yard, but she pretended she didn't hear the summons. The crafty old woman had a scheme in her mind, Gisela sensed. No doubt she had hoped for something momentous to come out of sending Gisela into Rutgar's bath. What had she expected her to do? Bewitch the man as some believed Gersvinda had ensnared Ercangar? Suck the strength and wit from him with some kind of injurious sorcery? Ridiculous. She couldn't do such a thing, even if she wanted to. Whenever the two of them met, it was Gisela who ended up befluttered and helpless as a babe, not Rutgar.

Gisela swept out the hall door and headed for her infirmary, skirting the practice yard on her way. She recognized a few Saxon men-at-arms practicing with the Franks. Gisela paused for a moment to watch. Normally Gisela found little entertainment in watching men practice the art of violence, but right now the hacking, stabbing, and grunting served as a vicarious outlet for her own agitation. She wouldn't mind taking a blunted sword to the arrogant master of Ardun and applying it where it would do the most good.

After a few moments, she noticed one Saxon versus Frank duo whose battle was escalating into a private war. One by one, the other pairs in the yard stopped to watch. A small audience of gawkers gathered as well. The smith was there, along with several stablehands, a kennel boy, a peasant leading a horse laden with firewood, and a woman with a fat hen hanging by the neck in each hand.

One of the Saxons in the yard shouted a raucous encouragement to the Saxon half of the battling duo. A Frankish man-at-arms glared at him, then gave a partisan hoot when the Frank landed a blow to the Saxon's helmeted head. Gisela heard Thomas the smith make a wager with the firewood peasant, and Rolf the stableboy spit in his palm to seal a bet with one of the kennel lads.

More of an audience gathered as the entertainment caught the attention of others in the stronghold. As a small crowd gathered, Gisela pushed herself to the front to see better. The Saxon was restoring some of the Saxon pride lost when Rutgar defeated Lothar so soundly. This Frank was no Rutgar, and his Saxon adversary was no reluctant warrior with a priestly disposition. Gisela's heart swelled in satisfaction as the Saxon beat off every attack and got several telling blows through the Frank's defense. She couldn't remember when she had enjoyed a match so much. When the Frank faltered and stumbled, she laughed softly.

The heads of several of Rutgar's men turned in her direction, and the scowls on their faces told Gisela that her disrespect wasn't appreciated. A bit of frustrated rebellion in her made her stare right back. These Franks were too accustomed to victory, she thought indignantly. They should learn a few things about defeat.

Piqued, she turned her attention back to the match. The Frank suddenly toppled backward and landed on the ground with a pained cry. His foot was twisted beneath him at an unnatural angle. The Saxon immediately broke off his attack.

"Witchcraft!" The Frank who shouted pointed an accusing finger toward Gisela. "She put a hex on Gaston. I saw her eyes glow with the devil's light."

A man standing beside Gisela moved away warily. "I heard her mumble a curse just before he fell."

Gaston's comrades were helping him to his feet. He held his injured foot off the ground and glared at Gisela. "Devil's whore!" He spat. "Someone ought to teach you the folly of aiming your heathen mischief at good Christian Franks."

One of the other Franks on the practice field rolled up the sleeves of his shirt and grinned. "I'll teach the slut!"

"Stone her," someone suggested. "Witches ought to be stoned."

"I can think of a more amusing way to take care of her."

Every Frank in the yard seemed to have his own suggestion for proper retribution, and none of them bode well for Gisela. She backed away from the advancing Franks, confused at how a rousing practice match had suddenly turned ugly, with all the ugliness directed toward her.

Suddenly, Guntar was at her side, narrow chest puffed out, fists bunched at his side. "Leave her alone!"

"Out of the way, boy." A Frank swept him aside with a brawny arm. " 'Tisn't child's play here."

"Hold!" the Saxon victor demanded. With his helmet off, Gisela recognized him as Anselm, Galt's son. He elbowed his way through the Franks, blunted sword still gripped in his hand.

"Stay out of this, Saxon!"

"Leave our Gisela alone!" Anselm insisted.

The injured Frank, Gaston, joined in. "She laid a hex upon my feet so I would trip."

"You don't need a hex on your feet to trip, you clumsy ass," a Saxon from the onlookers shouted.

"And I don't need witchcraft to help me confound your weak blade!" Anselm added.

"Witchcraft should be punished with death! Our good king says so."

"Send the devil's daughter back to the devil!"

Shouts from angry Franks were drowned out by Gisela's Saxon defenders. By now she was surrounded by a crowd; no escape was in sight. Someone threw a stone that missed her only by inches. A second stone flew out of the crowd toward her, to be snatched out of the air by a large, swift hand.

The onlookers, Frank and Saxon alike, melted back

as Rutgar held up the stone for all to see. Somehow he had materialized out of the crowd, surprising both Gisela and her attackers. She resisted the urge to hide behind his broad back.

"I will have none of this!" Rutgar proclaimed. "No one at Ardun will be stoned, whipped, hanged, or otherwise attacked without my sanction!" He swept the crowd with cold eyes. "Do you understand? Anyone who breaks the peace by attacking another will suffer the full force of my retribution."

Gaston and his comrades looked sullen. "The slut's a witch," one mumbled. "She hexed our practice and got poor Gaston a broken ankle."

"More likely Gaston hexed himself by letting himself be diverted by a pretty face. Don't use superstitious babble to excuse your own lack."

Gaston looked at the ground, but not before Gisela saw the resentment in his eyes.

"You men get back to your drill," Rutgar commanded.

Rutgar turned on the crowd. "You have tasks more important than watching grown men make fools of themselves over a bit of superstition. Anselm, Antonius, take Gaston to the infirmary."

"I'd have Antonius set the ankle," Gaston muttered. "I'd not go into the witch's den."

Rutgar shook his head in disgust. "As you wish. Get you gone. All of you."

Gisela hastened to obey. She wanted nothing more than to be out of the yard. She didn't get far, however.

"Not you!" Rutgar bellowed before she had gotten two steps.

She turned slowly and gave him a tentative smile.

"Gisela, you are more trouble than three of your

Saxon warriors taken together. What am I to do with you?"

"I did nothing, my lord! I was simply watching!"

"It matters little if you did nothing. My men believe Adalinde's tales about you, and your Saxons seem foolishly eager to risk life, limb, and the peace within these walls to defend their pet witch."

Gisela raised her arms in a helpless gesture. She had no control over Adalinde's silly tales or her people's eagerness to guard her safety. She had encouraged neither.

"From now on you will serve in the manor where you are not so much in everyone's view."

"But . . . the infirmary."

"There are several empty rooms in the manor. You may choose one as your sickroom."

"My lord! This isn't fair! I didn't do anything wrong!"

"I try to bring peace here, and you are distracting my men and setting Frank and Saxon at each other's throats."

"I didn't!"

"You did! Whether or not you intended it, the result was the same."

She simmered in angry silence.

"You will stay in the manor unless I give you permission to leave it. And you will keep away from the men-at-arms."

"You might as well lock me in the cellar again!" she moaned.

"If that is your choice."

Gisela looked into his implacable face and wondered why Fate had chosen her to come continually to the harsh attention of this man—and why her mind turned to mush every time he looked at her, robbing her of the wit to defend herself from him. She sighed in resignation. "That is not my choice."

"Then obey my command."

"Yes, my lord."

Gisela watched Rutgar stride away. Upon the people of Ardun he showered patience and justice. Why did he never have any left in his heart for her?

Rutgar reined Doomsayer to a halt as the last ruddy sliver of the sun disappeared and surrendered the world to night. Torches cast their wavering red light upon the newly cut timber that replaced the damaged part of the barrier. Ardun's men were working late on repairs tonight. The work was almost finished, and everyone would feel more secure when the wall was impassable. They were lucky Aelrhane had so far limited his forays to the villages and farms, though the damage to crops and livestock hurt badly. When Rutgar apprehended the cur, he would take the price of every slaughtered cow, pig, sheep, and goat out of his hide. The rebel was a crafty son of Satan, though. With all the soldiers Rutgar had sent out to apprehend the rebel, so far only two outlaws had been taken prisoner. What was worse, the outlaw ranks were swelling as lads from the farms, tired of getting hammered by the rebels, were joining Aelrhane themselves.

Stars were beginning to pop out in the darkening sky—angels lighting their candles, one by one. Rutgar surprised himself with the fanciful thought. Such whimsies were not like him. The demands of his life left little time to wonder why the stars glittered or the moon waxed and waned. He usually left such useless cogitations to priests, philosophers, and women.

Women—Rutgar grimaced at the thought. Woman was simply another name for trouble. One woman in particular. A witch, of all things! Rutgar snorted in masculine disgust. A witch with the face of a wood sprite, the body of a siren, the smile of an angel, and the sparkling golden eyes of a mischievous elf. Who would have guessed that trouble could come in such a small, winsome package?

Doomsayer suddenly threw up his head. The horse's ears pricked forward, and the muscles in his great frame tensed as a shape materialized suddenly at the edge of the forest not ten paces away—glittering eyes, pointed ears, and a silver-tipped pelt. The beast looked like a trick of moonlight in the shadowy gray dusk. Rutgar drew his sword. Wolves did not commonly attack human beings, and for the beast to attack man and horse together would be madness. But it was madness for the wolf to appear at all.

The creature showed no fear. Neither did it attack. Amber eyes fastened upon him with almost human intensity. In a way those eyes—golden, upslanted orbs that glinted with an almost otherworldly light—called to mind a very similar pair of golden eyes that so often glared at him from an elfin face. Strange that he was thinking of that very troublesome woman when the wolf appeared. Odo had mentioned that a wolf had been seen from the palisades several times as dusk darkened to night. Could this beast be the same wolf who had attacked Edgar and Notker at the pool where they had found Gisela—the same one who had fled when he'd come upon her in the forest?

All sorts of fantastical notions were preying on his mind this night, Rutgar reflected. His little charlatan witch did not transform herself into a wolf and roam the forest by night. Nor was the savage creature some kind of spirit familiar. The very thought was nonsense. The night air was turning his mind to mush. Or perhaps it was Gisela's strange effect on him that had his mind wandering down these strange roads. She made him want to laugh and curse at the same time. A woman who neither cowed before him nor threw herself at him, Gisela was a novelty. She upset the natural balance of his mind, making him swing between outrageous tolerance and contemptible oppression where she was concerned. A novelty, Rutgar assured himself. That was the hold Gisela had on his mind.

The wolf tucked his haunches beneath him and sat. Still staring at Rutgar, he let his jaw drop in a wolfish, tongue-lolling smile. Rutgar felt Doomsayer relax beneath him, and somewhere inside him he knew that the sword in his hand was not going to be needed. He knew it as clearly as if the wolf had spoken—which, of course, it had not. But there was something in the animal's gaze that was almost intelligent.

"You shouldn't be lurking around here, you know," Rutgar told the wolf. "Someone is going to put an arrow through that fine pelt of yours."

If he was going halfway to dementia, he might as well travel the whole road. Talking to the animal didn't seem as ludicrous as it should, however. The wolf cocked its head as if it understood the words, when by rights it should have fled at the first sound or move that Rutgar made.

"And if you're worried about that little enchantress friend of yours, she's a good deal safer behind the earthworks and log walls than she would be roaming about the forest with you."

The moon must have touched him with madness, but the moon had not yet risen—though the wolf's silver coat seemed to ripple with a milky light.

Rutgar sheathed his blade and turned Doomsayer back toward the stronghold. He did not believe in witches, magic was merely a figment of human fears, and wolves did not appear from the forest and invite conversation from the lord of the domain. Perhaps he needed one of Gisela's curative potions himself.

When he looked over his shoulder toward the forest, the wolf was gone. The vision of golden eyes and a winsome smile that haunted him was not.

Gisela's fingers ached from scrubbing and strong lye. It never failed that after the evening meal, the table planks looked as though the fighting men of Ardun had done battle with their food rather than consumed it. The craftsmen and servants who took their meal in the hall were scarcely better. Pigs and dogs possessed neater table habits.

Fredelin swiped her cloth over the last of the soiled boards. "Grudela of North Point Farm came today with with two calves for the lord's byre," she said. "I saw her in the weaving house talking to Drada. Her husband Wort took a cut in the arm from one of Aelrhane's men. They lost a whole field of barley to the raiders."

"Did Wort talk to the lord?" Atruda asked as she wrung out her scrub cloth.

"Aye. And Grudela said Rutgar forgave them their rent and returned the calves as well. Soon we'll have naught to eat but what we grow within the walls."

"Aelrhane is surely not bold enough to raid the lord's own crops within sight of the walls," Atruda said.

"Mayhap not." Fredelin looked toward Gisela. "What think you, Gisela? You are Aelrhane's friend. Will the man see us all starve rather than surrender us to Frankish rule?"

"I doubt Lord Rutgar will let that happen," Gisela answered.

Fredelin threw her a sharp look. "I heard Adalinde tell old Galt that you had put a spell upon Rutgar to weaken his arm and befuddle his mind. And also that he will never bear an heir. Gillan tells me his horn is as limp as a boiled leek."

Gisela lifted a brow. That certainly was not her experience.

"Gillan would say that," Atruda commented with a chortle. "The girl has tried to crawl in Rutgar's bed often enough, and he won't have her." She looked expectantly at Gisela. "Did you really put a spell on him, Gisela?"

"I'd like to put a spell on Adalinde's mouth," Gisela replied.

"Our lady is wise." Fredelin helped Gisela stack the table planks along the wall. "To Rutgar she is all smiles and acquiescence, but when his back is turned, she heartens our people with reminders of Saxon power. She and Aelrhane will give this land back to us."

"More likely she and Aelrhane will get the lot of us hung up by our thumbs," Gisela replied tartly.

"Rutgar is a kinder master than Aelrhane," Atruda ventured. "He doesn't spend all his time drinking ale and galloping to the hunt."

"That's because Rutgar fears to go into the forest," Fredelin said with a smirk, "for the forest is still Saxon domain."

Gisela said sadly. "I think you fool yourself, Fredelin. We will have nothing but war and destruction if we cling to Aelrhane just because he is Saxon."

Fredelin sniffed. "You need not hide your true sentiments, Gisela. Everyone knows you have congress with spirits and are favored of the old gods. Whatever spells you employ to defeat Rutgar will never be betrayed by *me*." She shot a warning look toward Atruda, who quickly avowed her loyalty.

"Me either, Gisela. Really. But you needn't kill Rutgar, do you think? He is very handsome!"

Gisela sighed hopelessly. She felt an urgent need for peace and solitude. She smiled weakly at the other women and dipped a mug of mead from the kettle that still boiled on the hearth. "I think I'll sit outside awhile."

Neither woman dared to follow her out, no doubt believing that she was going to indulge in some magical incantation. Gisela couldn't help but laugh softly to herself as she sat down on the stone steps of the manor. Everyone seemed to take her sorcery more seriously than she did. For less than five days she had worked in the manor, serving meals, cleaning, and organizing the little chamber Rutgar had set aside for her infirmary. In that time she had heard tales that she had bewitched Rutgar's man-parts, made Aelrhane and his men invisible to Frankish eyes, invoked a host of spirits to sicken those whose loyalty to Aelrhane was suspect, and was soon to raise Ercangar from the dead so he could drive the Franks from Ardun with a legion of demons at his back.

The truth was, all she had done in those five days was to scrub her knuckles raw and discover that the manor as a prison was little to be preferred over the cellars. Far from ensorcelling Rutgar, she had concentrated on avoiding the man whenever possible—a difficult task when he was so often about and seemed to follow her every action with his eyes when they were in the same room.

One night serving at table she had dared to greet

Lothar. Rutgar had growled like a bear and separated the two of them, sending her to pour ale at the lowest of the tables, far away from where Lothar sat. Two days ago when she had paused in cleaning the hearth to play with a hound that had ambled into the hall, his eyes had rested so heavily upon her that she sent the hound away, wishing that she could follow his exit. But Adalinde had bade her stay and finish at the hearth, smiling as she looked from Rutgar to her. She had whispered to Rutgar in a tone that could be heard by everyone in the hall that the dog was the leader of the Ardun hunting hounds and could be touched by no one but Gisela.

That wasn't strictly true, Gisela reflected, looking up at the stars that glittered in the dark sky. Old Stagkiller was cranky, and he'd taken pieces from a few kennel boys in his time. But Gisela had worked no special magic on the dog. She simply took the trouble to talk to the hound. Patience, not magic, had won him over.

She took a sip of the hot mead and leaned back against the stone wall behind her. The warmth felt good slipping down her throat. The days were still warm, but the nights had a chill. And she was exhausted. The honeyed drink spread its warmth into the weary fibers of her body, and she closed her eyes.

She lolled in the forest pool, the warm water coaxing the tension from her body. Suddenly a sleek form surfaced in a gentle surge of water, then dove again. Gisela wasn't frightened. She didn't move. Even when the other nudged her legs apart and surfaced between them. A warm, smooth wave of water washed over her, and when it receded, he was still there—a man, dark and huge. He covered her, enveloped her as thoroughly as the welcoming pool. A heat simmered in her blood, and she folded herself around him. Staring down at her were gray eyes, molten and silvery—and a smile, tender at the same time as it was ferocious on a mouth too beautiful to belong to a warrior.

She ached. She burned. Those gray eyes engulfed her as she arched her body in supplication. His breath heated her skin. His flesh burned where it touched her. He moved, and filled her with sweet fire—so full, she must burst with it. The holy pool washed over them as Gisela, the warm water, and her lover melted into one.

Gisela opened her eyes with a start. The night still chilled her skin. The stars were the only things that glittered down at her. Her breathing came in labored gasps, and her blood still raced through her veins.

Gray eyes. Familiar gray eyes. Rutgar's eyes.

It was only a dream, she told herself, but she knew better.

Nine

A few days passed before any of Rutgar's men could take time to escort Gisela on a plant-collecting foray into the forest. Most were fully occupied repairing the west palisade and reinforcing the rest of the wall. Others cleared brush from the deep ditch and earthen ramparts that protected Ardun, and still others rode out daily on patrols visiting the villages and farms and scouring the forest for signs of Aelrhane.

Finally, on a day when clouds hung low to the fields and almost touched the tops of the trees, Gisela was permitted to go into the forest with the escort of Etich, Antonius, and Notker. The forest floor was damp from the night's rain, and the beginning of autumn's debris rustled beneath Gisela's sandals as she searched through thickets, overgrown grasses, and prickly hedges for what she needed. By the time her collecting basket was half full she was soaked through, and the promise of fall in the air set her to shivering.

"Foolish woman." Etich sat atop his horse at the edge of the clearing where Gisela worked and shook his head at her sodden state. "Rutgar will not thank me if the cold settles in your lungs and you die. Then he will have to explain to all of Ardun why he killed their little witch."

" 'Tis but a passing chill, giant. Stay where you are, ere the great platters of your feet crush the very plants I search for. You great oafs have no notion of what you might trample underfoot."

She had long ago learned that Etich—nicknamed the Bear by his comrades—was not the fearsome ogre she'd first assumed, though from what she'd seen, few could best him in the practice yard. She'd seen him trounce Rutgar one afternoon in a wrestling match, a victory that had immediately won him a special place in her heart, for with anyone else in the military drill, Rutgar triumphed with tedious consistency. After the Bear had pulled his bruised commander to his feet, he'd winked at Gisela where she watched with a throng of other spectators.

"He's having an off day," Etich had confided in a whisper the whole world could hear. "Usually it takes me longer to best him."

Even Rutgar had laughed, and his face had glowed with rare good humor. It made her wonder what it would do to a woman's heart—to her heart in particu lar—if Rutgar were ever to turn a look of such warmth her way.

Gisela's hand lit upon the leaf she had sought. "Ah! There you are! You hide well this morning." As if soothing the living greenery from the hurt of being uprooted, she crooned softly as she plucked it from the soft ground.

Etich sighed impatiently. "If you have found what you seek here, then let us ride to Verhonne. Someone there will have a fire to dry you, and it is closer than the stronghold."

"As you wish, but then we must look along the banks of the river for some plants I am still missing."

Etich grunted noncommittally as she tied her basket to the back of his saddle. "You are wetter than a duck's underside." He swung her up before him and wrapped her in his mantle. "'Tis no wonder you shiver. Summer is too short in this godless country."

The village of Verhonne was nearly deserted, for all who dwelled there were in the surrounding fields. As the three horses plodded along the muddy track that led between the huts, only one voice greeted them.

"Welcome! Welcome, maid Gisela!" The voice was as withered as the old woman it belonged to. She stood in the doorway of a mud and wattle hut, white hair straggling around her shoulders, a ragged gown hanging loosely from her spare frame. "You've come at last."

Gisela smiled down at the crone from her perch atop Etich's horse. "Greetings, Hildegard. How is your daughter?"

"You must come in and see for yourself." The old woman gestured imperiously with a thin arm.

"Have you a fire inside, woman?" Etich demanded.

Hildegard gave him and the other men a dismissive

glance, then beckoned once again to Gisela. "Come! Come!"

There was a fire inside the hut, and abundant smoke as well. No windows admitted light or air; a smokehole in the roof was the only concession to ventilation. The walls were dark with the greasy leavings of many fires that had burned on the little hearth. The floor was packed earth, the furnishings four straw pallets, a wooden table with benches, and another rough table that held a few odds and ends of daily living.

Gisela took no note of the squalid conditions. She had been born in a hut similar to this one, twenty paces farther up the muddy track. Before her mother had died they had lived there together, though Gersvinda's house had been somewhat larger and a good deal cleaner. She remembered watching the hut burn after her mother's death, hiding from the priest behind the scanty shelter of Hildegard's skirts. The domicile of the devil's whore, Father Gaunt had called her home. He had smiled while it burned and muttered the words *maleficus* and *magus* over and over.

A stirring on one of the pallets brought Gisela's attention back to the present. There lay a young woman whose lank black hair contrasted starkly with a pale, almost grayish face. She smiled slightly at Gisela.

"My daughter. Her courses run amuck," Hildegard explained. She glared at the three men who crowded inside the hut.

Etich gestured for Antonius and Notker to leave, but he stayed, facing down the old woman's frown with a formidable one of his own. "I am responsible for her." He nodded toward Gisela.

"She will come to no harm here," Hildegard said indignantly. "She is ours."

Etich merely grunted.

"His comrades name him Bear," Gisela explained impishly. " 'Tis why he sounds so much like one."

The old woman cackled in appreciation.

Etich squinted at Gisela through narrowed eyes. "Do not sharpen your claws on me, little witch cat. My patience is short, and we could just as well ride back to Ardun as spend more time picking your little leaves. Now, dry yourself, so we may leave here."

"Will ye look at Grimalda while ye dry, good maid?"

"Of course I will." Gisela removed her wet mantle and headrail, hanging them close to the warm hearth, then knelt beside Grimalda's pallet.

The young woman grabbed at her hand as if touching her alone might bring a cure. "Have ye a cure for me, magess?"

"How long have you been bleeding?" Gisela asked, lifting the girl's chemise to judge the flow of blood.

"Eight days now. 'Tis what happens every month. I bleed and bleed till there's no blood left in me, it seems. And my womb twists into knots so that I can't stand for the pain of it."

Gisela heard Etich shift uneasily behind her.

"When did you last lie with a man, Grimalda?"

"Nine days past." She chuckled, then grimaced. "Alman's taken a great liking to me, and he's not one to keep his horn tucked away. And a mighty one it is, too."

"Do you bleed when he takes you?"

"Nay."

"Is it painful?"

"Only when he's acting the brute. Sometimes he gets so heated up he forgets 'tis a woman he's skewered and not a haunch of meat."

Etich coughed. Gisela could almost picture the color crawling up his face. For all their lustiness, men could seldom abide hearing a woman's point of view on the act of coupling.

She placed her fingers on Grimalda's abdomen and palpated gently.

"Will ye be singing over me, maid?"

Gisela smiled. "No. I don't believe an incantation is needed."

"I be mighty tired of all this blood pouring out. 'Tis an ugly enough feeling to have a man's seed dripping from between your legs, but at least that lasts but a short while. This bloody river lasts for days."

Another masculine cough. "Uh . . . maid Gisela. I'll wait without."

Gisela kept her face turned from Etich and smiled. "As you wish, O Mountainous One."

She would suffer for that later, Gisela knew, but the satisfaction was worth the price. Etich had done nothing but complain about his mission from the time they had left the stronghold. He was a fighting man, he'd groused, not a lady's maid.

"Well now," she said, returning her attention to Grimalda. "I suspect the bleeding and pain may ease with a dose of motherwort and raspberry leaves. I haven't any with me, but I'll send some along with Guntar when I return to Ardun. Boil the leaves in clean water and let the infusion steep for a bit before you drink it."

"No incantations or spirits, magess?"

"Not this time."

"Aye," old Hildegard grumbled. "That priest has been coming around here, you know. He's been saying 'tis a good thing that Rutgar has you locked up in Ardun. He says you work through the devil and spread wicked superstition."

"He's talked that way for years, and about my mother more than me. There's little harm in him."

"Little good as well. Young Beodolf had a rash, and the priest mixed some dust and water into mud and rubbed it on—said the dust came from some saint's tomb. The rash got worse, and the priest says his cure didn't work because poor Beodolf was thinking unholy thoughts when the mud was put on."

"I doubt Father Gaunt would know a truly holy thought if one kicked him in the shin."

The old woman gave a dry cackle. "He won't speak to poor Grimalda. Says women's pains and problems are punishment for the first woman's sin, whatever that was."

"Woman's first sin was allowing her sons to be trained for war." Gisela embraced the old woman. "I will send the motherwort for Grimalda."

"Tell young Guntar to be wary coming through the woods. Aelrhane's still kicking up dust. Two days ago we lost ten sheep from the sheepfold, and North Point Farm lost two horses—the pride of old Wort's life. Right now every able-bodied soul is sweating to get in the crops before Aelrhane comes round to burn them in the fields."

Gisela sighed. "Perhaps we will never know peace."

The old woman looked cautiously toward the door where Etich had disappeared. In a low voice she confided: "Aelrhane spreads the tale that Rutgar holds you against your will. He rages that so abusing a holy woman is a crime akin to King Charles's burning of the sacred tree Irminsul when he first invaded our land. Some of the young men are listening to his words and raging also."

"Holy woman?" Gisela chuckled as she donned her mantle—now merely damp rather than soaked—and secured her headrail about her head and neck. "Aelrhane has never held me in such esteem before."

Hildegard patted Gisela's arm. "You are the old ways made flesh. Not many of us hear the old gods any longer." She looked up hopefully into Gisela's face. "Have you seen aught to make us glad, maid?"

Gisela shook her head. "My visions bring only confusion of late."

"The world is confused," Hildegard said with a nod. "Mayhap the gods also."

The Bear growled through the door. "Are you through dallying, maid?"

"I'm coming." She turned back to the crone. "I will send the herbs for Grimalda."

Hildegard stood on tiptoe to place a feathery dry kiss on her cheek. "Bless you, maid. And if you can convince yon beast, go to Clearwater Farm. Merta is nearing her time to be delivered. She's a strong woman, for a foreigner. But her hips are narrow as a boy's. 'Twill be hard for her."

"I'll try to see her," Gisela promised.

Etich was reluctant to believe that Gisela's plants grew only on the banks of the river as it cut through the ridge at Clearwater Farm, and he muttered the whole hour it took to ride there. Notker and Antonius seemed amused by their captain's complaints. At another time, Etich's grumbling and the men's cautious mirth might have lightened Gisela's heart, but Hildegard's tales about Aelrhane disheartened her. The man was ripping Ardun and its people apart to regain his power; worse, he was using her as a tool to incite the people to war. Even the quiet beauty of the forest could not cheer her from that knowledge. She wished suddenly that she were alone so she could call Silver to her and gain some comfort from pouring out her heart to her best friend.

Clearwater Farm was actually a small village that cultivated the well-drained uplands above the river. Mud-and-wattle huts huddled in a circle around a common area used for small gardens. One larger house dominated the rest, a timber dwelling with an attached wing for sheep, fowl, and cattle. Fields of gold and green surrounded the little circle of dwellings like a colorful swirl of skirts.

When Gisela and her escort rode up, Merta was bent over in her garden pulling weeds. Gisela greeted her warmly. She had known Merta and her husband, Roland, since they'd first come north from their homeland Thuringia.

"Gisela!" Merta straightened laboriously from her task. Built like a chimney, she was narrow and straight up and down from her feet to her shoulders—except for the protruberance of her gravid belly. "You've no doubt come to chide me for being with child again after the last one nearly killed me."

"Nay, Merta. I simply come to see how you fare."

" 'Tis well you come, for I could use a potion. I see master Etich is here as well. No doubt my husband Roland will be pleased to visit with you again, good sir." Merta explained to Gisela: "When my husband traveled to the stronghold to pledge his oath to the new lord, he took it upon himself to outdrink this giant." She grinned. " 'Twas a humbling experience for Roland."

Gisela slanted a look back at Etich. "The Bear is accomplished at humbling people."

"Only those that need it, little cat."

Merta called to Roland, who waved from the nearest field of barley, where he toiled with half a dozen others. He started to shout back a greeting when an arrow took him high in the chest. His words choked into a strangled shriek.

Merta and Gisela stood stunned. An eerie silence fell over the fields, as if time had stretched out, allowing no sound or movement while it awaited what was to come. Suddenly the surrounding woods appeared to come alive as men pounded into the ripe fields, a few on horseback and others, almost as swift, carried by their own legs. More arrows flew. Blades rose and fell. The serfs and slaves milled in confusion, starting and bounding like panicked rabbits. Merta screamed and started to run toward the fray. Etich grabbed her and dragged her back, depositing the hysterical woman in Gisela's arms.

"Inside the house!" he ordered.

All three men vaulted to their saddles and drew their swords.

"To work, my lads!"

Gisela cringed at the glee in Etich's voice.

Merta was a handful for Gisela to drag into the shelter of the house. Small as she was, she was strong. The peasant woman continued to scream her husband's name and struggle until Gisela gave her a stinging slap with her open palm.

"Merta! You do us no good!"

She stared at Gisela, her eyes wide but no longer wild. "They killed my Roland, Gisela! Those Saxon beasts will kill us all!"

"Nay! Etich and his men will drive them off."

"Never. They're outnumbered!"

"The serfs—"

"Are spineless swine who will stand there and be butchered!" She looked frantically around the one large room with its cots and table and cooking hearth, then flung open the door that led to the attached animal shed.

"In here!" she summoned.

Gisela followed and found a pitchfork thrust into her hands.

Merta held up a scythe. "We'll get those sons of Satan!"

"Merta, no!"

Gisela's pleas were useless as Merta flew out of the house and rushed into battle. Smoke rose from the surrounding fields and flames leapt hungrily, a hellish backdrop for plunging horses and struggling men. Gisela rushed after Merta, but her pursuit was foiled when she tripped over an obstacle. She looked down, horrified, at a body whose head was nearly severed in two by a blade that had cleaved helmet and skull alike. It was Notker.

Gisela fell to her knees, retching. A woman's cry rose above the thundering of blood in her ears. She got up and stumbled toward the sound. Smoke stung her eyes and filled her lungs. Her own breath roared through her head so that she could hear little else. The moments before she found Merta seemed an eternity, but some instinct guided her to where the woman lay over her husband, the scythe still in her hand. The blood that coated Roland's tunic and leggings belonged to her, not him. When Gisela turned Merta over, she saw that the Frankish woman's throat had been slashed open. Gisela promptly lost whatever was left in her stomach.

Roland groaned. He was alive, despite the arrow that protruded just below his right collarbone. Gisela gently moved Merta's body off him, but before she could tend him, the thunder of hooves coming from behind made her swing around.

"Gisela!" a harsh voice called. "By Freya's mighty tits, Gisela!"

Aelrhane's horse skidded to a stop in front of her, kicking dust and stones on the two bloody heaps lying at her feet.

"This is good fortune. Come! We must leave quickly. One of the cursed Franks escaped to fetch his devil lord." He reached down a bloody hand to assist her onto his horse.

Gisela stared at the crimson hand, stunned. Finally she found the wits to answer. "Nay!"

"What is this nay? Come!"

"Bloody swine! Murderer!"

"They were foreigners, the lot of them. This is Saxon land!"

"They were my friends!"

"Then you should choose friends more wisely. Come! Now!" He grabbed her arm to drag her into the saddle. Frantically she pulled away. His hand left a crimson smear on her skin.

"I'll have no part of this!" Gisela shrieked.

"We have no time! Do as I say!"

Gisela flinched back as Aelrhane came for her again. Suddenly a broad body interposed itself between them. Etich. Scarlet runnels coursed from beneath his helmet, and his right arm hung uselessly at his side. But the left armed raised a gore-stained blade in Gisela's defense.

He didn't have a chance. Even Gisela knew that Aelrhane held all the advantages. The Saxon laughed as he sent his blade slicing downward. Etich thrust it aside with his own, but his left hand was not his fighting hand. Two more slices and he went down. Aelrhane jumped from his horse to finish the giant.

Gisela screamed and interposed herself between

Aelrhane and Etich. The Saxon sword could not cut its victim without slicing through her first. Aelrhane knocked her aside, but she threw herself over Etich's barely breathing form.

"Damn you! Aelrhane grabbed her arm, cursing. "Stubborn bitch!"

The ground shook with the approach of riders. Rutgar's war cry made Aelrhane jump with alarm. Frantically he glanced around, then turned back to Gisela and scalded her with the wild fire in his eyes. "You're a fool, Gisela! A fool!"

He vaulted to his saddle and called out the retreat. Stones from beneath his mount's hooves pelted Gisela as he fled.

She laid her ear to Etich's chest. His heart still beat. The mountainous bulk of muscle rose slightly as he drew in breath. Face pressed against the bloody iron scales of his armor, Gisela gave herself over to tears.

Ten

Rutgar's rage rose to choke him as he surveyed the destruction. The fields still blazed. Clearwater's defenders were but ragged and bloody heaps in the stubble of the half-harvested crops. The dwellings themselves were aflame, belching a column of black smoke to join the lowering clouds.

Beside Rutgar, Antonius paled. "Etich said he and Notker could hold them, sir."

Etich was known for his exaggerated opinion of his own considerable prowess, but in this case the Bear had been given little choice but to take on more than he could handle.

"You were correct in following his orders to fetch help. One man more or less would not have made a difference." He urged his horse forward into the destruction. "Check each body. There may be some alive."

Rutgar's heart weighed him down like a stone as he searched. At each bloody heap, he feared to see Etich's face. He should be accustomed to losing comrades in battle, but Etich was more than a comrade; he was a friend, almost a brother.

"My lord!" Lothar called. "Here is Etich!"

There was not only Etich, but Gisela as well, blood-spattered and filthy, hunched over Etich's body like a hen protecting a huge egg. Rutgar stared in surprise. He had expected the Saxon witch to be far away, fleeing with Aelrhane.

"Take her," he ordered harshly.

Gisela fought the two men who pulled her away from Etich. Her eyes stared wildly from a blood-smeared face, and her gilded hair flew in tangled disarray about her shoulders. When her eyes lit upon Rutgar, however, she calmed, like a child waking from a nightmare and realizing the horror was only a dream.

"Rutgar?"

"Aye, 'tis Rutgar." He dismounted, but kept hold of the saddle, white-knuckled, to hold himself from doing her harm. "You are a fool to still be here, at the site of your treachery. What game do you play now?"

"Game?" She still looked like a bewildered child, until her gaze came to rest upon Etich. The horror returned to her eyes. "Etich is—"

"He's alive!" Lothar interrupted from where he knelt beside the giant's body. "He breathes. Roland also!"

"No thanks to her!" Rutgar could rein in his anger no longer. He advanced on Gisela, fury making his hands tremble as he reached for her. Her eyes widened in alarm. No innocent pretense of bewilderment remained, only fear. "Treacherous woman! Antonius told how you lured them here with a pretense that your damnable plants grew only in this one spot. How easily men are befuddled by a woman! Why did you not escape with your rebel friends, fool? Did you think I wouldn't suspect?"

"Nay!" Her voice choked on the hoarse denial as Rutgar pulled her from the restraining hands of his men. "I had no part—"

"Liar!"

"Nay!" She cast desperate eyes on Roland, who sat with Antonius's assistance. "Ask Roland. He can tell you . . ." Her voice trailed off as Roland's furious eyes met hers.

"I saw her talking to the scum," came Roland's hoarse testimony. "She took his hand . . . was going to get . . . get on his horse. Etich prevented her." The farmer sank back against Antonius and shut his eyes.

Rutgar's fury solidified in his chest like a block of ice, burning and frigid at the same time. Fool that he was, he had softened toward the bitch, had thought her softhearted, had allowed the golden eyes and disarming sweetness to make him forget that women were treacherous and stonehearted. Notker and Etich had paid for his mistake. Fury out of control, he reached for Gisela's throat and closed his fingers around the fragile white column of her neck.

"Nay, Rutgar!"

Rutgar scarcely heard Lothar's protest, nor felt the

man try to break his lethal hold. Gisela's small hands curled around his wrists, but against his strength she was powerless as a babe. Where were her spells, her treacheries, her impudent words now? Her eyes clung to his, like the eyes of a wild creature caught in a trap, hopeless, bright with the certain knowledge of death. Those eyes. Those wild, helpless, golden eyes.

He couldn't do it, much as she deserved to feel the life choked from her. Rutgar threw her at Antonius.

"Take her. She rides with you."

Lothar made for the gasping Gisela, his face anguished. The poor man was truly a bewitched fool, Rutgar noted. He put out a hand to stay him. "Don't. Leave her be."

"She's hurt."

"She's not hurt. The blood on her clothing belongs to others who died because of her plotting. Go with Gaston to make a litter for Etich and Roland. The rest of you men start burying the dead."

He turned back to Gisela, who stood stiffly in Antonius's grip. She held out a pleading hand. "Rutgar, I did not—"

"Silence! If you provoke me into laying hands on you again, you'll not escape with your life."

Her face grew even paler, a stark contrast to the crimson that smeared her skin—Etich's blood.

"Take her somewhere out of my sight," he ordered Antonius.

The ride back to Ardun was a grim one. Rutgar fumed at Aelrhane and his cutthroats, at the stubborn, superstitious Saxons who accepted the Cross and the rule of their rightful king only under pain of death, at the gullible nature of men who would allow themselves to be led into a trap by the smile of a woman— himself as well as Etich and his men, for Rutgar was the one who had let Gisela out of the stronghold with three of his men on her leash.

Rutgar looked to where Gisela rode with Antonius. She slumped wearily over the mailed arm that held her prisoner on the horse, her eyes never leaving the litter that carried Etich and Roland. Guilt, misery, and concern played across her face like a troubled wind rippling across a pool. A shadow of doubt dulled the hard glitter of Rutgar's certainty. The Saxon witch looked genuinely anxious over Etich and the farmer. And if only Etich's intervention had prevented her from escaping with Aelrhane, why had she not fled after Aelrhane struck Etich down?

Rutgar wrenched his eyes away from her, reluctant to let doubt mar his anger. She was anxious, of course. Like most women, her anxiety would be for her own fate. But why had she stayed? Had she thought she could fool him into believing her innocent?

Rutgar didn't want to listen to that dispassionate part of his mind that questioned Gisela's guilt. He wanted to wallow in his fury. Anger was an old friend. It didn't weaken a man as did the worry, fear, and guilt that waited to pounce upon him the moment fury lost its hold. Worry and fear over Etich; guilt for Roland and his family, vassals that he had failed in his responsibility to protect. Gisela was a convenient target to fuel a defensive wall of rage, and his rage was made more bitter by the realization that, even smeared with gore and covered with her own perfidy, she still sang through his blood, just as she had since he had first seen her sprawled naked and indignant in the forest. She was like a disease in his mind—the tilt of those golden elfin eyes, the sound of her voice, the gentle curve of her smile.

Damn the woman for getting under his skin! And damn himself for growing soft and foolish because of a woman's allure. He would like nothing better than to be exorcised of her bewitchment, which had nothing to do with magic and everything to do with his own undisciplined, undiscriminating lust.

"My lord Rutgar . . ." Lothar urged his horse even with Doomsayer. "If I might have a word with you."

"What is it?"

"The maid Gisela—she would not be part of such a bloodthirsty scheme of Aelrhane's."

Rutgar snorted his contempt. "I would be a fool to regard your opinion of the matter. You're obviously enamored of the woman."

"I am not that, sir."

"Indeed?"

"I swear to you. Gisela is . . . dear to me . . . as a friend. I've known her for most of her life. She would never knowingly cause another creature to come to harm."

Doubts again. Rutgar ground his teeth. Certainty was much more comfortable.

Lothar continued. "Aelrhane would not have staged such a bloodbath if he'd known Gisela might be there. He would not have risked her getting hurt. He simply came to vent his spleen on a family of Franks that held Saxon land."

"Roland and Merta were Thuringians."

"Aelrhane doesn't split hairs. They were Franks as far as he was concerned, I'm sure. I'd venture that was why he laid low the farmers as well as the livestock. When he saw Gisela, he must have tried to convince her to go with him. That was the conversation Roland must have seen."

"Hmm." Rutgar was noncommittal. "The people

hereabouts certainly seem to put great store in Gisela as some sort of symbol of their pride."

"They do. Old ways die hard. Gisela's mother was a powerful sorceress, though it was mostly a gentle magic she wielded. The people invest Gisela with the same potency that was her mother's. She is a talisman of sorts, a small bit of power that can intervene between them and the cruelties of this world," Lothar said. "But I swear to you, my lord. There is no harm in Gisela, symbol or not."

An idea began to blossom in Rutgar's head—one that satisfied a measure of his frustration and pleased the dispassionate tactical side of his mind as well. He smiled. "You Saxons should learn that it is dangerous to put much store in symbols. They can so easily be used against you."

Gisela's little infirmary stank with the odor of blood; the air was heavy with a burden of pain. Right now, the pain was Gisela's. The knowledge that Etich had been cut down defending her sliced into her soul as sharply as any sword. When poor Etich awakened, Gisela knew, the sting of her guilt would be as nothing compared to the agony he would bear from the great slash that cut his midsection. She was grateful he remained senseless while she stitched muscle and flesh together. When she applied a heated iron to sear the flesh closed, he came awake screaming, then dropped back into the comfort of oblivion.

She cleaned her patient, cleaned herself, straightened the infirmary, then found one task after another to keep her there. Not much was left to be done for the giant, but Gisela was reluctant to leave him. Moment by moment she checked his pulse, his breathing, his color, willing him to live, willing his wounds to mend cleanly. When she could think of no more prayers to utter, she simply sat beside him, his mighty paw cradled in her hand.

" 'Twas not my doing, Etich; I vow it was not." Emotion crowded her throat and solidified into words. The unconscious man made a safe confidant, so she didn't hold them in. "Rutgar is convinced that I'm a villain, you know. The man has a brain the size of a gooseberry. If your King Charles sets such store by men such as he, then 'tis a wonder his great kingdom hasn't split into a dozen warring pieces."

She paused to dab a soothing salve onto Etich's abused flesh.

"Stubborn, pigheaded, suspicious-minded, arrogant, brutal, shortsighted son of a snake. He's the most treacherous, irrational man I've ever known."

"You forgot overbearing," came a rasping, laborious answer. "That's Rutgar."

Gisela froze, her fingers poised above Etich's flesh.

"Keep on, little witch cat. 'Tis better you sharpen your claws on Rutgar than on me. Feels as if a bigger cat than you has been digging around in my guts. Or mayhap my bowels spilled onto the floor and got trampled by my horse."

"Nothing quite so terrible." She finished the work as gently and rapidly as possible. Etich didn't flinch as she coated the stitched and seared flesh, but he let out a great sigh as she cleaned away the fresh blood and laid on a fresh poultice of knitbone and white willow.

"Can you bear it, Etich? Or should I give you a sleeping draught?"

"Nay. I'll be sleeping permanently if this little cut festers."

Gisela couldn't meet his eyes.

"Don't give me that look, maid. This is none of your

doing. 'Twas my duty to protect you, and that's what I did."

"I did not summon Aelrhane, Etich. I swear I did not."

"I know. I saw the look on your face when that devil reached for you." He closed his eyes, his face sagging with weariness and pain. When he opened them again a moment later, Gisela could see the apprehension in their depths. "Will I live, or is the devil preparing me accommodations in hell?"

"Most likely the devil will have to wait for your company. Aelrhane's blade hit nothing vital, and I cleaned the wound well with myrrh and willow before I cauterized it, so I have hope it will not fester."

" 'Tis my hope as well," he said with a wry smile. The smile turned into a grimace as he tried to sit.

Gisela pushed him gently down. "You must lie still for a few days, my good giant, or you may accomplish what Aelrhane's blade did not. 'Tis a miracle Aelrhane's sword did not cut clear to the gut. It seems you Franks are not vulnerable to Saxon blades."

"Would that we were not," Etich grunted painfully. Gisela covered her patient with a blanket and moved about the little room, cleaning the dishes she had used to mix the poultice. Etich's eyes followed her.

"Did Aelrhane put those bruises on your neck?" he asked in a soft voice.

Gisela touched her abused throat. "Nay. 'Twas Rutgar gave me those. He believes I lured you and your men to Aelrhane's trap, and all but killed me for it."

"He has a hasty temper where you are concerned, and you've given him fuel enough to keep his temper burning." He lifted his bushy brows. "I'm amazed you haven't been squashed yet. In his heart, Rutgar must like you."

Gisela laughed at the notion. "The man has no heart."

"So he would like the world to believe," Etich replied with a slow smile.

At the evening meal, Rutgar was in a chillingly strange mood, even though Gisela had made it known that Etich would likely recover. She picked at her own meal in between her duties at hearth and table, her appetite dulled by the events of the day and the way Rutgar followed her with the frozen iron of his eyes. His attention unnerved her as it never had before. Unadulterated hatred would be easier to bear, she decided, than the speculative, overwhelmingly male scrutiny that followed her every move.

Trying to keep the most distance she could between herself and her master, Gisela left the duties of the high table to Atruda and busied herself serving the common soldiers and craftsmen—many of them serfs like herself—at the lower tables. It was a feeble defense, and doomed to failure when midway through the meal, Rutgar summoned her with a curt wave of his hand. She had no choice but to obey.

"I would have more ale," he commanded.

Gisela exchanged a brief look with Atruda, who could have easily served the ale without Gisela's coming half the length of the hall. With a barely perceptible shrug, Atruda left Gisela to the mercy of Rutgar and took herself to the lower tables.

"More ale, Gisela. Is the task so difficult?"

Gisela picked up the pitcher of ale and moved to go behind Rutgar's chair to his other side, where his goblet sat. Quite deliberately, he tilted his chair so that its back met the stone wall. She couldn't get around.

He raised a brow as she hesitated.

"More ale, woman. Are you deaf?"

The whole hall watched them. Gisela gritted her teeth, her face heating with embarrassment. She was tempted to upend the pitcher in the swine's lap, but given his current humor, that would no doubt be the end of her. She leaned across him, her breast brushing his arm despite her attempt to not touch him. As she poured the ale, she could feel his eyes roam along the curves that were displayed by the gaping neckline of both kirtle and overtunic. The goblet took an eternity to fill.

When Gisela finally straightened, Rutgar's knowing smile tempted her to hit him.

"You have more magic to you than I suspected," he said in a voice meant for her ears alone. But his appreciative perusal of her figure was apparent to everyone in the hall. "You will go to my chambers after the meal, woman."

Silence fell over the hall. Everyone was listening, Gisela knew, and Rutgar had made no attempt to keep his words for her ears alone. No one was naive enough to think he merely wanted his chambers spruced up before he retired for the night.

"I . . . I . . ."

"What?"

She searched desperately for an excuse. "Etich must be tended, my lord. I cannot leave him."

"If Etich is doing as well as you reported, he can do without you for a few hours."

Her face heated until she was certain her cheeks were red as the coals on the hearth. "I . . . have other duties, my lord."

"I prefer you tend to the duties I would set you."

The insufferable pig, to humiliate her before the eyes of all! She drew her lips into a tight line and fixed him with a stare that would have sent Ardun's true believers running for cover. "I would rather not . . . my lord."

Rutgar's smile was chilling, yet at the same time sparked a peculiar heat in the core of her belly. "Gisela," he said, his head shaking slightly in warning, "your preferences in this do not matter one bit."

Gisela desperately combed her mind for an excuse to forestall him, but at this most crucial of moments, her mind was blank.

"Fetch more ale before you depart, wench."

Stifling the urge to hit him, Gisela went to fetch a fresh pitcher of ale from the kitchen. She gambled that no one would notice the few moments she took to dash from the kitchen to her infirmary. The white powder she fetched from the shelf had not been used since Gersvinda had died, had never been used by Gisela herself. She would use it now, though, and be damned to those who drank and laughed with Rutgar this night.

Ignoring the knowing looks that bombarded her from all sides, Gisela carried the fresh pitcher through the hall and set it on the head table at Rutgar's elbow.

"Enjoy yourself, my lord."

He smiled at her with a purposeful heat that made her face burn. "I intend to enjoy myself, Gisela. I certainly intend to."

An hour later, Gisela's angry pacing had seared a molten path between the wardrobe and the washstand in the lord's chambers. The hot wind of her passage stirred the curtains of the great bed that dominated the room like a crouching beast—a constant reminder of the purpose for which she was there. Rutgar must think himself very clever to combine punishment for her with a night of frolic for himself. How like a man to think only in terms of conquest—if not with the sword of iron then with the sword of flesh he carried between his legs.

In the stronghold, the village, and the farms, other girls surrendered their virginity, willingly or otherwise, even before they grew breasts. Not Gisela. No man had dared to force her, and when she chose a man, he would be one who wanted her for herself, not for the power he imagined her to wield. Aelrhane had wanted her as a symbol of power. Rutgar wanted her as a conquest of the Saxon old ways. She would not allow herself to be used in such a way.

A small tendril of "what if" clouded the certainty of her indignation, however, creeping past the defenses of Gisela's outrage. What if Rutgar craved her for herself? Might she willingly yield? He was a rare man, this conquering Frank, with a heart that showed occasionally behind that iron facade and a courage grounded in mercy, not brutality. There was inside him a need that called to her, a chink in the iron she could sense but not quite see. She wanted to reach out and touch it, touch him—the real man, not the warlord. Foolish, but something in the flash of his eyes and the slow curl of his rare smile lured her further into foolishness. What if he truly wanted her . . .

He did not, Gisela warned herself. Rutgar did not crave the maid Gisela; he craved the witch of Ardun.

And she would not be used in such a way. She would not! She vowed it over and over to herself as she stopped her furious pacing and stared out the window at the rapidly aging night.

"I'm glad to see you are not so foolish as to disobey me."

The sound of Rutgar's voice made Gisela whirl

away from the window. Apprehension sent a rush of renewed energy through her body as he closed the door behind him and dropped the bolt.

"How could anyone presume to disobey the great Rutgar?" she returned sarcastically.

"Indeed! If you had, I would have dragged you out of whatever hiding place you fled to, and no doubt the trouble would have soured my temper."

"You mean it can get more sour than it already is?"

"Considerably," he warned. He unclasped his embroidered mantle and flung it across the chair by the wardrobe. "You would be well advised not to test it."

"As you would be well advised not to test mine."

"Is that so?" He chuckled. "Do your worst, buglet. Call down your devils. Shrivel my ballocks." He spread his arms and waited, smiling a taunt. "Where are your old gods when you need them?"

"Careful, mighty warlord." Gisela returned his taunt, wondering all the while when the powder she had slipped into the ale would do its work. "Your precious ballocks may shrivel yet."

He grinned. "In that case, we will both be disappointed."

"Speak for yourself. I want no part of your goatish rutting."

"Perhaps I can change your mind." He sat and removed his boots, then his tunic. The soft material of his shirt pulled across broad shoulders and hinted at the sculpted power of his chest. The cloth wrappings that bound his leggings climbed over sinewy calves and thighs bulging with muscle. The sight of him inspired an ache in the pit of Gisela's belly, and the faint curl of his smile tugged at her heart with an insistence that was impossible to ignore. Beneath all that muscle dwelt a man who called to her. Perhaps she heard the call because she was a witch, or perhaps simply because she was a woman.

Gisela told herself to ignore it.

"I have no wish to play whore for you, Rutgar."

"I would never mistake you for a whore, Gisela. A whore generally tries to please a man. Besides, I have no intention of paying for your services."

"You may pay more dearly than you think!"

"You are overbold for a serf, but I can understand that, now that I've seen how the people here cosset you."

"I am not cosseted!"

"Are you not?" He stood. The room filled with an overabundance of raw masculine power. "You need to learn something of the realities of this world." Rutgar untied the laces of his shirt and drew it over his head. Molten muscle flowed beneath tautly stretched skin. A white, jagged line that angled over his ribs must have once almost cost him his life, Gisela noted. Other scars attested to years spent enduring the brutalities of war. Suddenly she felt very small and not a little frightened.

Rutgar threw his shirt on the chair beside his mantle and tunic. Like a lion stalking his prey, he came toward her. She backed a step, then two.

"I have done nothing to deserve such treatment from you, my lord."

"You think not? Count yourself a casualty of war, then. You involved yourself in this fight, so you pay the consequences when you lose."

She backed into the bed, then jumped like a startled rabbit to put distance between her and that dread piece of furniture. "I . . . I had nothing to do with today's raid. I swear it!"

"Perhaps not. But your people think you're some

sort of witch who can weave magic to protect them from the consequences of their rebelliousness—a talisman, of sorts, that guarantees the survival of Saxon power."

He seemed in no hurry to catch her. Rather, he appeared to enjoy the chase. Her determination to resist faded with every step she retreated.

"That's not true!" Gisela knew she lied, for Adalinde and Aelrhane had made it true.

Rutgar shook his head. " 'Tis true enough, Gisela. You are the personification of foolish dreams of a Saxon kingdom. When you are conquered, your people will be conquered as well."

"Liar!" She felt the cold stone wall at her back. She could retreat no further. "You use that as an excuse. You're nothing but a rutting he-goat."

Rutgar halted, folded his arms across his naked chest and sent her a smile that ignited an explosion of heat in parts of her she was just now discovering. His eyes surveyed her appreciatively. "A rutting he-goat, am I? Another crime you should answer for, witch maid, for 'tis you who've made me so. Perhaps you're no witch at all, but a siren come in from the sea to drive men mad with lust."

"Nay! Do not lay your randiness at my door! I'm a virgin and know naught of men!"

He laughed. "A virgin? An unlikely defense, little maid."

"I am! I swear!"

"You swear to many things, Gisela. This claim at least I will know the truth of very soon."

"No!" She tried to dodge away as he reached for her, but he was faster than a man his size should have been. He pushed her back against the wall and swooped down upon her mouth. His insistent lips forced her to open to the thrusting invasion of his tongue. His hard body molded itself to her, fitting against every curve as though Mother Earth had made them to be locked together in such a way. Against her belly his weapon rose into a hard, hot, lethal sword.

A traitorous pleasure shivered through every nerve of Gisela's body, and reason became a small voice trying to shout through the clamor of a hurricane. Her heart sped until she could hear her own pulse pounding through her veins—or was it his?

The assault ended, but Rutgar's eyes—every bit as invasive as his tongue—still bored into her soul. His mouth gentled to a sensuous smile. "Little Saxon witch, you needn't be so afraid. This is a battle we may both enjoy."

Eleven

Gisela attempted to regain control of her rubber knees and push away the strange lassitude that infected her body. Anger and indignation were her allies; the honey-sweet urge to surrender was her enemy. She summoned the energy to duck under one of the arms that caged her and dodge away.

"I will not surrender, Rutgar. I am not a stronghold to be taken by conquest!"

He didn't chase after her. Infuriatingly relaxed, he leaned against the heavy carved bedpost, folded his arms across his naked chest, and regarded her with a gaze that started heat simmering in the pit of her belly. A warm, slow smile softened his face. "You are more than a conquest, Gisela."

"I am the witch of Ardun. That is what you want."

"Witch!" he scoffed. "You are not a witch, you're a woman. I'm going to prove it to you. You can call down your curses and pray to your old gods for help, but I am the only help you have."

Something in his eyes made her want to yield—a need that went beyond conquest and a yearning that was more than lust. It was gone as quickly as it came, shuttered by iron hard gray.

"Gisela. You know you can't deny me."

She lifted her chin in futile determination while his eyes made a slow, appreciative journey from her uncovered hair to the crude sandals on her feet.

"Remove your clothes, Gisela. When I first saw you, you were naked as God made you, sleek and golden as Eve tempting Adam. I would see you thus again."

Defiantly, she drew the loose folds of her tunic about her.

Rutgar lifted his brows in mock surprise. "Do you have so many gowns in your wardrobe that you can spare these rags to be ripped from your body?"

She stood undecided, fists clenched tightly in her armor of coarsely woven wool. When Rutgar took a determined step forward, her nerve broke. "Do not!"

Too late. As she tried to dash away, he caught her by the neck of her loose tunic. Frantically Gisela tried to twist away, but the tunic was weaker than Rutgar's grip. It ripped with a great tearing sound.

"Now look what you've done!" she cried.

"Be still, woman! You'd try the patience of a saint."

"A saint would not be doing this!" she shot back.

"Hold still!"

Something in his tone made her obey. Slowly, inevitably, he drew her to him, fitted her tightly against his body, where the hard promise of his arousal pressed against her vulnerable softness. As his mouth came down upon hers once again, she clung to the last shreds of her resistance as a drowning man might cling to a floating log. His strength invited her to melt against him. His need was a cry that the woman inside her yearned to answer. Sensations jolted through her; desire awakened, hungry and demanding as any other newborn.

"You are a stubborn thistle in my mind and soul." Rutgar's voice was a quiet rumble. Implacable eyes looked down into hers, glittering like a polished blade. "Perhaps only fire can free me from you."

Gisela drowned in sensation as he kissed her again, more gently this time. One hand cupped her buttocks and pressed her more firmly against his erection, and the other slipped over her breast, now protected only by the thin material of her kirtle. She fought the instinct to fit herself even more snugly to his invitingly masculine contours. She should not want him, but she did. Desire washed through her in a hot, molten flood, and when Rutgar's hands smoothed over her body and paused to untie the laces of her girdle, she made no move to stop him. His eyes surveyed her with satisfaction as the girdle and torn tunic fell away, leaving only the tightly fitted kirtle.

Squeezed between desire and apprehension, ricocheting from indignation and embarrassment, Gisela stood mute. Rutgar's unwavering gaze made her feel giddy and afraid at the same time as he reached for the kirtle's laces.

Finally, the kirtle fell into soft folds around her ankles and only a threadbare chemise covered her from those seeking eyes. Rutgar's hand reached out to rest where his eyes had feasted, palm smoothing the coarse material over the nub of her erect nipple, fingers curling gently around the smooth curves of her breast. Gisela's breath stilled; her heartbeat thundered in her ears, and a traitorous excitement coiled between her thighs.

"You should have finer garments, Gisela. Such treasure should be clad in silk."

His hands jerked with sudden violence, and the chemise tore as if it were tissue. Gisela jumped, her nerves on edge. Rutgar's eyes darkened almost to black as they rested upon her bare flesh. Her hands fluttered upward in an attempt to cover herself, but he caught them in his own and spread her arms wide.

"You are the most beautiful woman I've seen in a very long time," he said quietly.

Gisela closed her eyes, pulsing with the heat of her mortification and at the same time tingling with the strange excitement of his admiration. Why was the powder and the spell she had said over it not working? Of all the magic her mother taught her, all the spells she had bungled, why did this most vital sorcery have to fail?

Rutgar lifted her in his arms and laid her on the bed, settling close beside her. She lay helpless while his mouth explored the contours of her body, starting at her lips, gliding down the column of her throat, pausing for a slow, sensuous journey around her breasts. She heard a quiet moan of desire, and realized with surprise it came from her own throat. He murmured a sound of comfort, his mouth moving once again to her lips while one hand dipped between her thighs and gently caressed the moist flesh that blossomed at his touch.

His tongue played within her mouth, then over her lips. "Open your legs," he whispered.

She made a small sound of protest as he wedged his leg between her knees, forcing them to part for him.

"Don't be afraid." His voice was a rough caress. "I'm not going to hurt you."

His finger slipped inside her, and she gasped at such an intimate invasion.

"Be still, little one. You are like silk here, made to drive a man wild."

He opened her slowly, first one finger, then two, deeper and still deeper, until she forgot about the potion she'd fed him and the spell cast to save herself. Her senses overwhelmed her mind, and those senses screamed for him to finish his sweet conquest. Willingly she yielded and spread her legs wider. Eagerly she arched against his hand, flowing molten against him, seeking relief from the need pulsing through her.

His touch withdrew, leaving her aching and cold. He rose to his knees and worked hastily at the ties that held his braes. Gisela had only a moment to be anxious at the sight of his impressive erection before he wedged his naked hips between her thighs and moistened the head of his shaft with the warm wetness of her femininity.

She sighed as his touch sent a jolt of renewed desire through her. His breathing came faster, then hesitated. A frown drew his brows into a pucker that was definitely not passion.

"Rutgar?" Gisela whispered, feeling hopeful and bereft at the same time.

"What the . . . ?" His imprecation trailed off into a moan. His eyes widened, then narrowed, suspicion gleaming in their depths. "Stay here!" he commanded, his voice no longer gentle with passion. "Christ's holy bones!"

His lunge for the slop jar landed him there just in time, Gisela judged from the miserable sounds that rose from behind the privacy screen. Frazzled, dazed, still dizzy with desire and light-headed with relief, Gisela wanted to laugh and weep at the same time. Her spell had worked only too well. Her mother had assured her that the powder and incantations would cool any man's ardor; she didn't say it would have him embracing the slop jar. Gisela only hoped it didn't kill him.

Gisela slipped cautiously off the bed and quickly donned the tattered remnants of her clothing. The sounds coming from behind the curtain made stealth unnecessary, but just the same, she crossed to the door on tip-toe and opened it slowly to avoid creaks. There was no sense in disturbing Rutgar with her leaving, and she certainly didn't want to be in this room when he came out from behind the privacy screen. She suspected he was not going to be in a mild humor.

By the time Gisela reached her cot in the women's quarters, the excitement of her escape had faded. She shook with exhaustion and a strange disappointment. As she pulled off her clothing, she recalled the mixed agony and excitement of having Rutgar gaze at her nakedness, of his hands traveling over her flesh. Gooseflesh rose at the memory. Honesty compelled her to admit that when she was lying beneath Rutgar, she had forgotten all fear and pride and wanted him with every fiber of her body. Now, safe in a darkness filled with snoring women, she felt a yawning emptiness in the pit of her belly. One of the few times her magic had actually worked, and she wasn't sure she was all that happy about it.

Gisela pulled the blankets of her cot tightly to her chin, chiding herself for such weakness. Rutgar was a dangerous player in a brutal game, and letting herself weaken toward him could destroy her. Despite her small victory this night, her magic was no match for his power, just as her resistance was no match for his magnetism.

She drew herself into a tight little ball, feeling ill from the turmoil of her emotions.

Curled upon her cot, she vainly sought the comfort of sleep.

Next morning, the view from the window of Rutgar's chamber revealed the unfolding of a peaceful late summer day. The sun crested the ridge to the east and set the trees glowing in fiery splendor. The gates of the palisade were open, flung wide as if to gather in the warmth of the newly risen sun. Cows filed through the open gate to the pastures that skirted the stronghold. In the garden against the north wall, women bent over the damp soil plucking weeds from among the turnips and beets. One shooed away a pair of geese that strayed from the gaggle being herded across the yard by a diminutive goose-girl. Ringing up toward the bright blue sky, the clanging from the forge attested that the smith was hard at work.

The morning's peaceful warmth stopped at Rutgar's window, however. His chamber was sour with the reek of sickness, and Rutgar felt worse than the room smelled. He sat slumped in the stone window embrasure, holding his head against the cheerful clanging of the forge. The braes he'd worn the night before, wrinkled and sagging about his knees and calves, were his only apparel. His skin was clammy. His bones felt as though they ground one upon the other. His hair was damp with sweat and hung in lank strands about his face, and his eyes were hot pokers burning in his skull.

"Looks like a case of bad ale to me," Gisela said as Odo pushed her into the room.

" 'Twas not that the ale was bad so much as the woman who served it," Rutgar managed to grate out.

Gisela lifted her brows in offended surprise.

"Do not play the innocent with me, woman. You think I do not recall your words about enjoying that pitcher of ale? I am not so dull-witted as these Saxons you hold in the palm of your hand."

"I would not presume to call you dull-witted, my lord."

"No, witch? You presume enough to almost kill me!"

Gisela bridled at his tone. "I did not almost kill you. And if I had, it would have been no more than you deserved!"

"Aye! That's the truth. I deserved such for my stupidity in not locking you permanently in the cellar as a rebel, an outlaw, and a heathen troublemaker. I'm growing softhearted and softheaded both." His eyes narrowed. "What did you put in the ale, Gisela? All those who drank from your cursed pitcher are ill."

Gisela raised her chin. The amber eyes were calm and undaunted. "It won't kill you, my lord. You'll recover in a few hours, I think."

"You think?" he asked ominously.

" 'Twas a potion strengthened by a spell to cool your lust. Perhaps I mixed it a bit strong."

He came toward her slowly in a stride that lacked

its usual flowing strength. "Cool my lust? It curdled my lust, and a good deal more."

At his tone, Gisela backed away, only to bump against Odo, whose hands curled around her arms like manacles.

"What do you think should be the punishment for a serf who tries to poison her lord?" Rutgar inquired with seeming politeness.

Gisela beamed him a smile that wavered only slightly. "Perhaps she should be rewarded for protecting her virtue?"

If he hadn't hurt so much, Rutgar might have laughed. He had thought to conquer her with raw strength and lust, and she'd reduced him to the weakness of a puling babe. Indeed, as she had promised, she'd shriveled his ballocks and more besides. And now she stood before him with taunting smile and dancing eyes. A man had to admire a woman like that —right before he throttled her, if he'd a mind for his own sanity, or at least banish her to a place where the only creatures she could bedevil were rats and worms.

Yet something within him had a yen to continue the duel—if he managed to survive the first blow she had dealt. He'd never yet backed down from a challenge, and if that wasn't challenge lighting Gisela's eyes, then he was the king of Naples. Woman she was, there was no question about that, yet she'd proved herself a worthy opponent.

He managed a grim smile, though the muscles of his face ached with the effort. "You think such a one should be rewarded, do you. 'Tis only fair. She will be rewarded, to be sure!" The sudden wariness in her eyes was a balm to his pride. "Odo. Fetch Gisela a pail of water and a scrub brush. Since I've taken the whole night making a mess at her behest, she can clean up my leavings."

Rutgar painfully pulled on a shirt and tunic before turning to look at her once again. She had gotten her nerve back, from the look of her, for she glared at him unrepentantly. "Odo will bring you what you need to accomplish your task. You are not to leave this room. Tonight when I feel strong enough, I will give you what you deserve."

"But . . . 'twill not take me all day to clean the mess."

"Then you can spend the rest of the day waiting for me, thinking about the second round of our duel. If you are not here, I will find you. And when I find you, Gisela, you will wish you had stayed."

He left the room without a backward glance, his back burning from the twin flaming arrows launched from furious amber eyes. Dramatic exit safely accomplished, he leaned weakly against the stone wall outside the chamber, strangely bemused. For a moment he allowed himself to imagine having all that spirit and beauty smiling at him, instead of glaring. The thought weakened his limbs past their already pitiful state. How fortunate Gisela did not know she had such a powerful weapon in her arsenal. She was dangerous enough as it was.

Rutgar didn't feel up to braving the hall. The very thought of the food that would be set on the tables there made his stomach flip. Instead he wandered toward Gisela's infirmary. Every time he had come by the day before, Etich had been oblivious. Rutgar had been able to assure himself that his friend did indeed still have both feet firmly planted in the land of the living, and that was all. This morning when Rutgar walked into the infirmary, Etich's eyes opened.

The Bear looked as bad as Rutgar felt. Rutgar took perverse comfort from it; no one liked to suffer alone. Etich, however, had been laid low in honorable combat, while Rutgar had been bested—albeit temporarily—by a woman. The Iron Warrior, as King Charles's court flunkies had once dubbed him, had been outmaneuvered, outflanked, ambushed, and taken down—not by the sword but by a female who scarcely came up to his chin.

" 'Twasn't her fault," Etich croaked from his cot.

Rutgar sighed, guessing the Bear was talking about Gisela. She was prisoner in his chambers, and still he couldn't escape her.

"Whose fault?" he asked, hoping he was wrong.

Etich grunted painfully. "Gisela's."

Of course. Gisela. "What wasn't her fault, Etich?"

"Attack."

"I didn't say it was."

"Thought it. No?"

"The possibility crossed my mind," Rutgar admitted.

A smile twitched Etich's mouth. "Always . . . you believe . . . women faithless."

"I have reason," Rutgar reminded him.

"Aye." The Bear panted for a moment, closed his eyes, then opened them again. "Shielded me," he said with some difficulty. "Her own body."

"Gisela?"

"Aye."

A pang of guilt added to the already uncomfortable roil in Rutgar's stomach. The Saxon witch had thrown herself in the path of Aelrhane's sword for Etich's sake, had she? He suffered a recollection of his rage, of taking that smooth, fragile throat in his hands and wanting to choke the life from it. He cursed under his breath.

"What?" the Bear croaked.

"Nothing."

Etich's dry lips cracked a grin. "Doubt . . . or two, Stoneheart?"

"If you didn't strain your flapping mouth so freely," Rutgar observed sourly, "you might enjoy a faster recovery."

"Flapping mouth . . . all I can move."

"Then talk about something else, if you please. I came to comfort a wounded comrade, not to receive a sermon on the virtues of a troublesome woman. What is your obsession with the girl?" Rutgar asked irritably.

"Nay . . . not *my* obsession."

Rutgar lowered himself to a stool beside the cot. His sigh was an admission of Etich's implied accusation. "Etich, my friend. She's more than a woman. She's a symbol of Saxon power—of their cursed pagan ways and a power that is in the past, not the present."

Etich made a rude noise.

Rutgar smiled, almost against his will. "You think 'tis an excuse?"

The Bear had been a father to him since Rutgar had been sent to fight with King Charles's army at the tender age of twelve. The giant knew him entirely too well, Rutgar acknowledged ruefully. Having him around was worse than having a conscience.

"What of . . . the other?" Etich asked. "Bertrice."

"Bertrice of Stringau has nothing to do with Gisela."

Etich managed a pained chuckle. "You know naught . . . of women. And . . . you lie . . . to yourself. Take you out to the yard . . . straighten out your brain."

More comfortable with manly banter than the awkward discussion of Gisela, Rutgar grinned. "Brave words, Bear. We'll see if you can deliver on that promise once you're on your feet."

"Done it before," Etich reminded him.

"Aye. And no doubt you'll do it again, you great hulking brute. To that end, I'll leave you to get some rest." Rutgar's legs wobbled beneath him as he rose—an uncomfortable reminder of the woman who lured him and infuriated him at the same time. He would have to thank her for her courage in saving Etich's life—right before he demonstrated that his will was law at Ardun. For whatever reason he wanted her, he did want her. And she would damned well enjoy herself and be sorry she'd ever thought to resist.

"Rutgar," Etich said as Rutgar shuffled out the door. "If you ever open your heart to a woman . . ." He paused for breath and strength.

"Small chance of that, my friend."

" 'Twill not bleed out your lifeblood."

Rutgar smiled. "Save your hits for the practice field, Bear. There at least you know what you're doing."

Twelve

Gisela had the entire day to wallow in the mire of her too fertile imagination. The door to the chamber was barred from without, and her pounding on it brought only Odo, whose disapproving glare halted her appeal for freedom before it even began. Meekly she asked for vinegar and lye to help clean the room. Odo nodded curtly and shut the heavy door in her face. She heard the bar drop again with an implacable thunk.

She was truly in trouble this time, Gisela admitted to herself. Men had killed women for lesser offenses. She would have been far wiser simply to lie down and submit to her fate, and probably would have done so if she'd known the potion and spell would nearly kill her victim in the process of cooling his lust. She tried to remember who had been at the head table with Rutgar. Who else might have drunk from the pitcher and how did they fare? A flood of guilt washed over her. She had thought merely that those who drank would discover the joys of celibacy for a night or two, not suffer a plague of her making. But then, when had she ever produced a bit of magic that didn't somehow whip around and bite her in the backside? Never.

Gisela pushed aside her dire imaginings and bent to her task. The waste jar had been inadequate to Rutgar's needs, but she was accustomed to such messes, and after an hour's work, the chamber smelled of lye soap and vinegar instead of the sour leavings of illness. Without a word, Odo collected the bucket and soiled rags and left her alone again behind the barred door. When she asked who else was sick, he didn't answer. When she pleaded, he merely smirked. She longed for the days when Ardun was populated by men who were wary of her wrath.

As the day dragged on, Gisela tried to sleep, but the bed seemed to burn her when she lay upon it. The comfort of the feather-stuffed mattress reminded her of how it had felt when Rutgar had laid her upon it the night before, how it had sunk beneath his weight when he had stretched out beside her, his hands stroking and playing, coaxing an all too eager passion from her flesh.

How potent was a man's power over a woman. How easily that potency could be wielded for pain or joy. The thought of it drove Gisela off the bed and into the chair, which was far too hard and sharp-cornered to allow sleep. The stone window embrasure was no better. She gave up and surrendered to restless anxiety, pacing the floor and listening to the sound of her worn sandals against the woven rush mats.

As the sun sank below the sharpened tops of the western palisade, Fredelin brought Gisela a meal of bread, cheese, and mead—and the welcome news that those who were ill, whose number included Father Gaunt, Lothar, and several others, were rapidly mending.

She set the platter beside the chair. "Ye'd best eat," Fredelin warned.

Gisela huffed in frustration. "Little strength is needed to sit all day in a room and count the minutes as they go by."

"For what's to come." Fredelin picked a piece of cheese off the platter and popped it into her mouth. "The whole stronghold knows ye're penned here in the lord's chamber, and Rutgar's been growling at one and all the whole day. This afternoon in battle practice he whacked one of the men so hard that the poor fellow had to be carried off the yard."

Gisela was horrified. "Was he dead?"

"Nay. 'Twas only the flat of Rutgar's sword that caught him, but a hard blow it was. His poor head must have rung his helmet like the clapper of a bell." Fredelin sniffed. "I'm glad I'm not the one who got Rutgar into such a fine fit. His men are taking bets on whether you'll bloody the sand around the whipping post or have your neck stretched hanging from the watchtower. I heard one say that the lord will just take you apart with his bare hands."

"That's ridiculous!"

Fredelin shrugged. "That's what I heard. You'd better eat that so I can take the platter back to the kitchen."

Gisela's appetite had waned since Fredelin started spinning her tales, and she pushed the food away.

"Are ye not hungry, Gisela? Ermentrude'll have one of her snits if ye send back her food. I'd best eat it for ye, then."

Gisela picked at the cheese and sipped at the mead while Fredelin polished off the rest of the platter. When she was finished, the cook's girl let loose a satisfied belch and smiled craftily. "Can I have the new kirtle Drada's making you when you're gone? 'Twould be a shame to waste the gown on Gillan or one of the others when you and I are just the same size."

"I'm not going anywhere!" Gisela declared. "Rutgar may be angry, but he's not going to whip me, or hang me. He's not such a brute as that, and he knows he deserved most of what he got!"

"Ye needn't get so huffy!"

With an indignant sniff, Fredelin took the platter and left, and Gisela once again had only her own thoughts for company. Dusk darkened into night. The yard outside the chamber window grew quiet as the people of Ardun found their cots in the hall or barracks or women's quarters. One of the hounds in the kennels bayed at the full moon, his howl sounding lonely until a chorus of yips and howls joined in harmony. From her window Gisela could see the dim glow of a lamp in the stables, and finally, as the night grew old, that glow extinguished.

A tightening in Gisela's chest told her Rutgar was coming before she heard the sound of his footsteps. The bar grated; leather hinges groaned as the the door swung inward. Gisela turned from the window. Rutgar seemed to fill the room. His face had lost its waxy pallor and he no longer swayed on his feet. The stride that carried him into the chamber was steady and lithe, and he stood straight and strong once again—strong, solid, and hard as stone.

He set his lamp upon the table and regarded her with a satisfied half smile. "I see you didn't change yourself into a crow and escape through the window."

"If I were to change myself into a bird, it wouldn't be a crow," she declared.

"True, a songbird would be more suitable, caged to wait upon my pleasure." He circled her, like the predator he was. Gisela stiffened her spine and clenched her jaw, refusing to retreat. "You should know by now that I wait on no man's pleasure."

"I should have you whipped," he said, still stalking. "If you were a man, I would not hesitate to do it."

"If I were a man, I would not have been forced to defend myself in such a fashion!"

"Under both God's law and man's, I am your master. You can't defend yourself from me, Gisela. Part of you doesn't even want to."

" 'Tis not true!"

He laughed. "Was it fear and loathing that made you so warm and willing before your evil potion did its work? Were you defending yourself when you opened to me like the petals of a flower parting before the sun's rays?"

"I did not!"

"You have convenient holes in your memory."

Gisela couldn't keep the flush from heating her face. She was too transparent, and he read her too well.

He held out a hand to her. "Come to me, Gisela."

She conjured up enough resistance to slap the hand aside.

His smile took on an edge. " 'Tis fitting I first saw

you naked and running through the forest, for you are that wild. You need to be tamed, woman."

"Not I!"

"Aye, you! Don't make me come after you."

"Come ahead, Frank!" She expected him to meet the challenge with anger, but instead he laughed—and in the blink of an eye, lunged.

Gisela danced out of the way. "Clumsy oaf! Is that the best you can do?" Giddiness bubbled within her, and she saw an answering gleam in the flash of Rutgar's eyes. She dodged again, beneath an outstretched arm, leaping out of range of his hands. Did she only imagine that somehow their grim confrontation had become a game?

"You slip through my fingers like water, Gisela, but even water can be captured."

"Pah! You are slow as an ox. 'Tis no wonder the Bear downs you with so little trouble."

"The Bear is not so enticing a prey," Rutgar said with a smile.

He tried to trap her against the bed. She allowed herself to fall back, pulled up her knees, rolled, and landed neatly on the other side.

"Clever," Rutgar admitted.

Gisela laughed.

"But not clever enough."

He was around the bed in a flash. She dove for the mattress, thinking to use the same trick, but before she could roll he was on top of her. Laughter died in her throat; this was a game no longer.

"Fairly captured, maid," he said, his face very close to hers, the hard, muscular length of him immobilizing her futile struggles. His mouth lowered to take the prize. She was momentarily lost in the heat of him as he feasted upon her lips and thrust boldly into her mouth. When he released her, she had to sharply remind herself that she was not supposed to be enjoying herself.

"Let me up," she demanded halfheartedly.

"Nay. I like you where you are."

"You will not rape me," she declared with some confidence. "I've heard your judgments in the mallus, and you are not such a one to hold your men to a line that you yourself freely cross."

"I will not need to rape you." He rolled off her and watched with a disconcerting smile as she struggled to climb out of the depression they'd created in the mattress. Just as she had gained the edge of the bed, he pushed her gently back down. The weight of his hand on her shoulder kept her there. " 'Tis what bothers you the most, is it not—that your people see one favored of your old gods fall willingly to Frankish charm."

"I see no evidence of charm!" she scoffed.

He laughed softly, and the richness of the sound sent of queer quiver from breasts to the juncture of her legs. "Then we are well suited, are we not? For you are not exactly a polished jewel." Suddenly he was dauntingly intense. "You want me, Gisela, as much as I want you. I feel it every time I touch you. What nature has decreed for a man and woman is impossible to set aside."

The iron gray of his eyes had deepened to pitch, and they burned with a dark fire that sharpened the ache between her legs. He leaned over her, slowly descending, until their lips were only a finger's breath apart. She wanted him to close that small distance so badly she could taste his lips on hers. Instinctively, she lifted her face toward his. He slid one hand behind her head, tangling his fingers in her hair, holding her still as he sealed his mouth to hers. His other hand cupped her breast, kneading, playing, rolling the nipple between gentle fingers through the rough wool of her clothing.

"Am I going to have to rip your clothing off again?" he whispered against her lips.

"No. Please." Unhesitatingly, she helped him drag the tunic over her head.

"This is a pitiful garment, Gisela. I would not have you wear it again."

"You ripped my only other," she reminded him.

"I'll find you better." The unwavering intensity of his gaze made her forget even token resistance when his fingers deftly unfastened the laces of her kirtle.

"Dressed in silk and fur, you could outshine every nobleman's wife in King Charles's court."

He peeled the kirtle from her body and tossed it to lie with the tunic. Her meager shift followed shortly after. Gisela resisted the urge to shield herself from the heated appreciation in his eyes.

"Dressed in nothing at all," he whispered reverently, "you outshine any woman I've ever known. How does such comeliness survive in such a brutal place?"

On his knees above her, he pulled off his tunic, then his shirt. The rise and fall of his chest made the lamplight ripple across hard slabs of muscle. Impatiently he sat back to unlace his fine leather boots and rid himself of the encumbrance of leg wrappings and braes. His sex sprang free, and to Gisela, mesmerized in confused fascination, the potent male weapon seemed to leap for her. He was huge and magnificent, the beast's wild, lithe beauty in human form. Gisela was frozen, unable to move. She thought she might break into a thousand pieces when he touched her.

He reached for her, and her very bones seemed to

melt as their naked flesh came together. The heat of his desire flowed into her, possessing her body like a demon spirit. The warmth of his breath on her ear made her melt and flow against him like hot wax.

"You feel it, do you not, Gisela? Desire can be sharp as a blade, and just as compelling." He thrust with his hips, letting her feel his erection against the taut muscle of her belly. In the hot, moist region between Gisela's legs, a yawning emptiness pulsed and contracted into a tight sphere of need. She arched against him, realizing suddenly that he was right. She had fallen under his spell. Anger, pride, and indignation had fled; what filled her was passion and a heart-melting yearning for surrender.

He pressed her down into the mattress. Tentatively she touched him—ran her hands along the broad shoulders, slid down the muscled slope of his back. The light in his eyes challenged her to continue. She found the flat male nipples on his chest. His breath caught. Coarse chest hair tickled her fingers as she explored further. She ran her fingers along the scars that marred his perfection. Over his ribs, along his collarbone, down a lean hip. He caught her hand and kissed her fingers, then her mouth. The kiss stole her breath; his slow smile stole her soul. Her whole body hummed with the rhapsody of being so close against him. "By all the saints' bones," he whispered against her ear. "If ever in this world there was a woman truly a witch, 'tis you."

He parted her thighs with one iron-muscled leg and slipped his fingers deep inside her. Unconsciously, blissfully, she arched against him. Rutgar's face loomed above hers, dark, sensual, and predatory. His breath hissed in and out between clenched teeth, and for a moment, he looked down at her with hooded eyes. Then he kissed her less gently than before. His tongue thrust in time to the caress of his fingers, which stroked and retreated in a demanding rhythm that wound the fibers of her body impossibly tight. Helplessly Gisela moved to his rhythm, no longer in possession of her own body.

She groaned when he took his hand from her and left her at the peak of desire. His mouth pressed a hot, moist kiss into her belly. Even the stubble on his face rasping against her skin seemed an erotic caress.

"Witch maid. Sorceress. You could draw the anger from the devil himself." He spread her legs far apart and ran his hot tongue down the inside of each thigh, ending the caress with a reverent kiss on the damp triangle of curls that guarded her sex. "You take to loving well," he said with a throaty chuckle. "Mayhap I'll sentence you to warm my bed for many nights to come."

His body pinned her firmly as he positioned himself at the moist entrance to her inner folds. Eyes half closed and dark with desire, he rubbed along her wet cleft. His mouth drew into a tight grimace of mixed pain and ecstasy as the hard tip of his penis became slick with her readiness. Gisela instinctively raised her hips to capture him, unmindful of anything but the need to have him inside her.

He thrust, swift and hard. Pain took Gisela by surprise, and she cried out. Her hands clutched at the muscular arms that caged her, as if Rutgar's hard strength could relieve the sudden agony.

Rutgar groaned. "Be still!" He held himself motionless inside her, grimacing as though he were the one in pain. His head dropped until his brow rested lightly on hers. "Gisela, you're too old to be a virgin." Gently he tasted her lips, licking away the saltiness of her tears.

She gasped. "Please stop. It hurts."

"No more pain," he promised in a tight voice. His jaw clenched, Rutgar drew back, then thrust again, slowly and deeply. And again. And still again. Gisela buried her face in the warm hollow of his throat as the pain faded and desire once again began to grow into a tight, sharp coil. She matched his rhythm, meeting his thrusts in an instinctive counterpoint. His ragged breathing warmed her hair; his heart thundered against her cheek. More than their bodies fused and twisted together, and for a moment she felt as though she could touch his soul and gaze into the hidden chambers of his being.

Rutgar's cry of release left her suspended high on the spiral of her own desire. She felt the hot stream of his climax, the pulse of his orgasm a second heartbeat within her. Something inside her swelled with satisfaction, while another part grieved like an angel ejected suddenly from paradise.

She moved beneath him restlessly as his still warm offering began to wet her thighs. Rutgar wedged his hands beneath her buttocks and sealed her to him. "Lie still, my love" he whispered against her brow. "I want to stay inside you yet a while.

He could stay inside her forever as far as Gisela was concerned. Now she understood why her mother had bade her not yield her virginity without caution. A woman lost herself in loving a man. All else in the world faded before the desire to be one with him. Gisela closed her eyes and wallowed in Rutgar's closeness.

* * *

Rutgar experienced an unpleasant pang of guilt at Gisela's pliant stillness. He pushed himself off her and rolled away from the enticing body that had just catapulted him closer to paradise than he had ever come. Damn her to hell! No female of her ripe age had a right to be an untried virgin.

She lay relaxed and limp beside him, looking like a wanton siren with her tangled hair spread wildly over the pillow, her full breasts ruddy and wet from his suckling, her legs still spread as if for loving, moist with his seed and her virgin blood.

Cursing himself for his softness, he reached out and pulled her against him, snugging her into the curve of his body, where she fit as if Satan had made her especially to be Rutgar's own private temptress. She was all spirit and impudence, honey and vinegar stirred together and heated to a boil. The lamplight turned the tangled skeins of her hair into purest gold. Her skin was like warm silk beneath his hands. Her breath warmed his chest, while her hands splayed against him, as if undecided to push him away or embrace him.

An unfamiliar surge of protectiveness swelled within Rutgar, catching him unawares. He should have believed her when she declared her virginity, unlikely though the story was. He should have gone slower, made their joining easier for her, but his desire for her had been like a plunging, runaway stallion that trampled all control beneath galloping hooves. Never in his life had he needed a woman so desperately—to the point where his passion instead of his usual iron control dictated the pace of their mating.

And she had been untouched, just as she'd declared. He'd never before opened a virgin, preferring to use more experienced women to slake his appetites.

Women of casual virtue were much easier to understand than females who prattled of their purity and hid hearts of stone beneath soft, tempting breasts.

And saints above—Gisela was soft and tempting. Sweet rounded breasts teased his chest. A slender thigh wedged unwittingly between his own. The tender curve of her belly pressed against his groin. He wanted her again. Once had not been enough. No fine lady from the king's court had ever tempted him so much.

"Gisela." Her name came out of his mouth a husky whisper. Just thinking about taking her again had him fully aroused.

She moaned into his mouth as he kissed her—a little sound of passion that he devoured with a thrust of his tongue. He coaxed her to meet his thrusts with her own, to play with him, to welcome him into her warm, wet, sweet-tasting mouth.

"No pain this time, my love. I promise."

His hands started a slow exploration of her body. Already he was desperate to bury himself inside her, but he wanted to give her pleasure, bind her to him with passion. She was the only tenderness in his world, and he would not let her escape.

He felt her relax under his caressing hands. Her legs parted as he fondled her, his finger gently circling the tender nub that was the center of a woman's desire.

"You are mine," he crooned against her ear. "Your fire, your soft heart, even that sharp tongue you wield like a stinger. From this night forward you don't belong to the Saxons, Gisela. You belong to me."

His mouth roamed over her beautiful, soft breasts, and the ache within his groin grew almost unbearable. He thought he would burst from his own urgent desire. Her breasts swelled and tightened beneath the ministrations of his mouth. Her hips arched against him. Mercilessly he drove her onward with mouth and hands, until finally he kissed the silky curls that guarded her sex.

She jerked in surprise as his mouth closed over the soft, moist folds of her flesh. Her whispered exclamation of shock was belied by fingers twisting in his hair begging him to continue. He breathed in the warm, womanly scent of her. The honey-sweet taste of her filled his mouth. He wanted her so badly that he was dizzy with the wanting, his world narrowed to the urgent pressure at his groin and the moist cleft that was so sweet and warm against his tongue.

He stroked, and stroked again. Slowly, deeply, feeding on her shudders of pleasure. He drove her on, until she cried out and convulsed in the grip of ecstasy. Then and only then did he allow himself relief. While her body still quivered with its own release, he sank into her, and she enveloped him like flowing honey. So willingly did she give to him—yielding, open, trusting where he'd given little reason for trust. He drank in her spirit and courage, fed on her sweetness, devoured the sweet sorcery of her soul.

She moved with him, taking as well as giving. Her passion demanded a tenderness he didn't know he possessed. Her surrender crumbled a wall within him that he hadn't known existed. Time became endless as they flowed together, one into the other, until her tight inner muscles convulsed around him in a frenzy of completion. With breath-stopping, heart-pounding violence he came with her, buried so deeply within her that he was lost, pulsing so hot and furiously that he feared his soul itself might explode.

Black spots swam before Rutgar's eyes as he waited for his body to slide down the other side of that erotic wave. Beneath him, Gisela lay limp as a rag doll, her lips gently curved into a smile, her lashes like crescents of gold on her cheeks. She slept, sated and peaceful. Rutgar couldn't help but smile at the innocent sensuousness of her beauty.

Careful not to wake her, he rose and wet a towel in the pitcher of tepid water that sat on the washstand. He cleaned her first, then himself. Both of them were smeared with the stickiness of his seed and Gisela's virgin blood. Then he lay down again beside her, gathering her to his body and covering them both with the goosedown bedclothes.

That's showing the wench, he chided himself with a wry chuckle. *You made her truly sorry, you did!*

As he slipped into sleep, Rutgar wondered just which one of them had been conquered.

Thirteen

The morning sun streamed through the half-open shutters and fell in a bright band across Gisela's face. She stirred, groaned, and burrowed more deeply into the warm bed. Something was not right. For a groggy moment she couldn't pinpoint the wrongness, then realized that her hand encountered nothing but emptiness on the other side of the bed. Where Rutgar had lain the bed linen was wrinkled and cold.

Rutgar. Memory came flooding back in vivid detail. Gisela covered her eyes with her arm and moaned. A flush of chagrin heated her cheeks. Far from behaving like a proper martyr, she had been a wanton. The Frank hadn't had to force her; she'd almost begged him to possess her. In fact, if memory served, she *had* begged him at the last. Instead of fighting for her virtue, she had yielded much more than her body.

She waited for the flood of shame to drown her, her arm still covering her eyes as if she could shield herself from remorse as well as the sun. The old gods should be thundering their anger and raining fire down upon her conscience. She tensed to await the sting of censure. When it didn't come, she cautiously moved her arm and opened her eyes. She ought to be rigid with the guilt of her behavior, but surprisingly her conscience felt quite free. She was warm and peaceful, with a fuzzy contentment at the back of her mind that made the world soft and bright. Rutgar was not the enemy, a newly awakened womanly instinct told her, and in the end, he had yielded as much as she.

In sudden eagerness to greet the new day, Gisela flung back the warm bedclothes and admitted the cold outside air into her warm cocoon. The water in the pitcher on the chest was cold, but it could not chill even the edges of the warmth that still enveloped her.

Beside the pile of her torn clothing lay a linen kirtle and finely embroidered tunic, along with a shift, cross-cut stockings, and a finely wrought girdle with tiny chips of some jewelstone set in a swirling design in the leather. Gisela touched the garments with reverence. Never had she worn such fine things, but they must be for her.

The first pang of shame pricked her heart. If this was payment for her virtue, then she was a whore indeed. She pushed the thought away. If she didn't wear the garments, then she must go downstairs naked, for her own poor clothes were nowhere to be found.

The floor-length blue kirtle fit Gisela surprisingly well and felt wonderfully soft against her skin—so different from the coarse wool she'd worn all of her life. The tunic was a lighter blue, its neckline, sleeves, and hem embroidered with silken thread. The chips of jewelstone in the girdle caught the colors of the cloth and seemed to grow to twice their size—to be real jewels instead of merely chips.

As Gisela smoothed the tunic around her hips, she thought that now she knew how it felt to be a nobleborn lady, clothed in such luxury, with jewels winking at every step. She felt much too grand to be a mere serf.

When Gisela walked into the kitchen, Ermentrude froze and stared. She dropped her spoon into the batter that she'd been so vigorously beating, then briskly retrieved it and came back to life. "You're very late," she commented, but her words lacked their customary bite. "Breakfast has been long cleared away, and the dinner's well in the making."

Gisela suddenly felt awkward. Fredelin and Gillan both stared at her as if she were a stranger. Of course everyone knew what Rutgar and she had done in his chamber the night before. Any of the other women of Ardun could have gone to the lord's bed with scarcely a comment heard, but Gisela knew her own fate would not be afforded that blessed indifference.

The silence in the kitchen was unnatural. Gisela felt heat rise into her face. Suddenly the door banged open to admit Guntar laden with two pails of water from the well.

"Where do ye want . . ." He spied Gisela and all but

dropped the buckets. As it was, his sudden discomfiture caused water to slop onto Ermentrude's freshly scrubbed floor.

"Mind what ye're about, lackwit!" Ermentrude thundered.

The boy put the buckets safely down. "Gisela!" He sounded as though he hadn't expected her to be alive. "Are ye . . . are ye all right?"

"Aye."

"Ye look . . . different."

" 'Tis the borrowed clothes. Mine were . . ."

"I can imagine what condition your own are in," Ermentrude said pragmatically. "But your mother's clothes fit ye well."

"My mother's?"

"Aye. The lord asked this morning for something to dress you in. I gave him the one of the gowns that Gersvinda left behind when old Ercangar sent her to the village to live. Her clothing looks as though ye were made to fill them, and 'tis right that they do."

Gillan leaned toward Fredelin and spoke low into the girl's ear. Fredelin sniggered.

"Back to work!" Ermentrude scolded. "Lazy slatterns. Those turnips will be shriveled with old age before ye have them peeled and cut. And you, young Guntar! There's wood to carry for the fire and more water to haul before that big kettle is full. And you—" She turned upon Gisela. "There's bread and cheese and cold sausage to break your fast." Her eyes swept over her in an evaluation that made Gisela blush. "I'd imagine you need some strength after your night, my girl. Eat your fill, then take yourself upstairs to tend the giant. He's been growling like a bear all morning long."

" 'Tis why they name him the Bear," Gisela said as

she cut a hunk of cheese from the round on the table and sat herself on the bench.

Ermentrude lowered her hefty bulk to the bench on the opposite side of the table. "If he wants to act like a bear as well as look like one, then he should live in a cave, not in a civilized house such as this one." She waved a hand imperiously at Gillan. "Bring Gisela a loaf with some butter."

Gillan obeyed, raking Gisela with resentful eyes when she set a platter of coarse bread and a crock of butter on the table.

"Get about your work," Ermentrude warned the girl, "and quit looking like curdled milk."

Gillan huffed and walked away. Gisela sighed.

"Don't pay them any mind," Ermentrude advised. "You'll be getting looks and words, too, from more than these girls, and if ye let such get under your skin, ye'll be in a sorry state."

The strange elation Gisela had awakened with was fast draining out of her. She stared at the table in front of her, unable to meet the old cook's eyes.

"Don't look so, girl. 'Tis not your fault, nor theirs either. Ye know the people hereabouts hold you to be the one who can bring magic to the side of Saxons. Now it seems you've given all your magic to Rutgar. There's many here who regard the Frank as a good man, but he's still not a Saxon, is he?"

"There's no magic about what happened between Rutgar and me," Gisela said in a low voice, knowing even as she spoke that it was a lie. Magic came in many guises, not just spells, incantations, potions, reading the turn of fate in cast bones, and seeing the future in dreams. What had changed Rutgar from a conqueror to a lover in the dark hours of the night was surely magic. What had made her surrender so blissfully—that also had to be magic, but not the kind of magic Rutgar could use to conquer her unruly people.

Ermentrude reached out and squeezed Gisela's hand, looking a bit awkward in the unaccustomed gesture. " 'Tis not fitting for you to look so puny-faced while wearing your mother's gown, for Gersvinda was a well of power, was that woman. You raise that chin of yours, girl, and be your mother's daughter. 'Twasn't as if you had a choice in going to Rutgar, and all of them that cast you looks now will understand that once they've gotten over their startlement. And pay no mind to Gillan, for the slut's merely jealous. After all, your Rutgar's a fine-looking man."

"Not *my* Rutgar."

"Maybe not your Rutgar, but my old woman's eyes tell me that ye're going to be *his* Gisela for some time to come, so ye'd best learn to live with it. Now, stop crumbling that bread into pieces and eat it, then get up to that grumbling giant and pour something down his throat to make him silent."

Etich had been moved from Gisela's little sickroom to a chamber on the other side of the manor. As Gisela made her way there, she noted that old Ermentrude was right. The girls cleaning the hall followed her with curious eyes as she passed through. Guntar and the smith's son Geoff shoveled ashes from the hearth. They glanced at her quickly, shamefaced, then glued their eyes to their work. Even Guntar—dear friend that he was—apparently didn't know what to think of her anymore.

Worst of all, though, was the pair of Rutgar's men whom she passed on the landing in front of Etich's chamber. Their leers made Gisela's skin crawl, as though the hunger in their eyes had reached out to actually touch her. Obviously everyone—every single maid, scrubwoman, kennel boy, and soldier—knew of her downfall and regarded her with disillusionment, disappointment, and lurid speculation. She would be surprised if the villagers and outlying farmers didn't know as well.

The Bear greeted her with a growl that was worthy of his name. "There ye are, maid! Ye've no call to leave me to the mercy of the old biddies in this moldering place. They give me nothing but broth—same color as horse piss. Same taste, too."

Gisela tried to give Etich a stern scowl, but couldn't suppress a smile. "I see you've regained enough strength to grumble. Do you make it a habit to taste horse piss, giant? Perhaps that's what makes you so large."

"If I had, it would taste the same as the brew that old black scarecrow has been pouring down my throat."

"You shouldn't call Adalinde an old black scarecrow. She's a very nobly born lady. Her clothing is dark because the fate of her people is dark."

Gisela unwrapped the bandages from around Etich's barrel chest and sniffed them for sour pustulence. They were damp with sweat and leakage from the wound, for apparently Adalinde had not deigned to change the dressing while Gisela had been shut away in Rutgar's chamber. The odor was healthy, however—a very good sign. A little blood stained the wraps, but it was clean and vigorously red.

"You're recovering remarkably well, my fine mountain of a man. It seems that Frankish flesh defies the power of a Saxon sword."

"Aye, maid. It takes more than a gold-haired witch and a wild fool rebel to bring down the Bear."

Gisela's smile dimmed, and Etich was immediately contrite.

"Nay, Gisela. I but jest with you. I know you had no part in planning that fray. I've said it to you, and I've said it to Rutgar."

Gisela shook her head. "Who knows what your lord Rutgar thinks." Last night she'd known, or so it had seemed. She'd felt what he felt, believed what he believed, so much a part of him, their souls were inseparable. In the harsh light of day, however, the night's magic faded like a dream.

As Gisela washed the raw flesh of Etich's wound with an infusion of yarrow and myrrh, she felt his eyes roam her face.

"Was the stubborn fool harsh with ye last night, maid?"

Gisela grimaced. "Maid no longer, as you and everyone else in the stronghold well knows. Why do all hereabouts take such an unnatural interest in my downfall?"

"I did warn you, little cat. Sharpen your claws against Rutgar's tough hide and you're like to get swatted down."

The huge Frank was a strange one to loose her feelings upon, but Gisela couldn't stop the raw emotions from suddenly rising to the surface, more powerful for her having stoppered them inside all morning long. Tears filled her eyes and rolled down her cheeks. "The woman who woke in my body this morn is not the same maid who Rutgar ordered to his chamber. I don't know how to feel or what to think, other than I want to be left alone! Is that too much to ask?"

"Aye, it is."

Gisela desperately tried to stop her tears, but to her shame, they continued to flow.

"Was he so rough with you, maid? I see no broken bones or bruises."

"No," she said between sobs. "He wasn't rough. But he . . . he made me forget who he is . . . for a while."

A knowing smile curved the Bear's wide mouth. "And do ye hate him now?"

"No," she sighed. "I never hated him. But I think I'm afraid of him now. I wasn't afraid of him before."

" 'Tis wise to be afraid of Rutgar." He scrutinized her tear-streaked face for a moment, then chuckled. " 'Twas bound to happen, Fate being the wily jester that she is. You'll be good to the poor man, won't you, little maid?"

Gisela looked up in surprise and wiped the wetness from her cheeks. "Me be good to him?"

"Rutgar's not known many women in his lifetime, other than whores and bitches. I doubt he'll know what to do with you."

Gisela thought privately that Rutgar had known very well what to do with her the night before. She didn't have a notion of what Etich meant. "The goatish lummox knows better how to deal with me than I know how to deal with him! Perhaps he'll leave me be now that he's shown everyone how easily I'm brought to my knees."

Etich chuckled, then grimaced as his tortured flesh objected to the movement. "I don't think so, maid. But I doubt Rutgar wants you on your knees; more likely he'll have you on your back again soon, or he's not the man I think he is."

Gisela flushed, intensely sorry that she'd exposed her raw feelings. "What is it about men that makes you ignore the brains God gave you and think with either your swords or that puny weapon you carry between your legs?"

"Was it puny, little maid?"

Heat crawled up her face. "I should have known better! Next time you can change your own bandage, and you can drink horse piss the rest of the week for all I care." She huffed out, followed by Etich's hoarse chuckles. Puny indeed! No, she admitted. Nothing about Rutgar was puny in the least, including the sensual power he had trapped her with last night. That was the very problem.

Rutgar was not in the hall when she descended the stairs, and Gisela was grateful. Sooner or later she would be required to face him. Could she still look in his eyes and see the man she had discovered the night before, the one who had, in the end, poured his strength into her along with his passion, who had seemed to protect her at the same time he possessed her, who had stolen her soul and given his in return?

Or had it all been a fantasy? Gisela almost did not want to find out. Soon she must face him, but not now. With no one to stop her, she fled to the weaving house.

Seated at her loom, her eyes fixed sightlessly on the cloth she was weaving, Drada called Gisela's name as she walked in. Gisela smiled, wondering as she always did how the old blind woman knew everything and everyone who moved about her.

"Yes, old mother," she called above the clacking of the looms. " 'Tis I. Gisela."

Drada cackled and the other women looked up from their wheels and looms. "Have you escaped your duties in the lord's house then?"

"For a time." Until Rutgar came looking for her. Or mayhap longer. Might it be that once the chase was finished and the prey brought down, the hunter would lose interest?

"Good." Drada nodded. "There's wool that needs carding if your hands are idle."

The other women followed Gisela with their eyes as she made her way to the stack of fleece at one end of the room. Before last night she would have been greeted with chatter and gossip. Now they said nothing. But their eyes spoke plainly of sorrow laced with pity and contempt. Sighing, she took up the carders and resigned herself to spending the afternoon as a stranger in the midst of women she had known all her life.

When Drada sent her to fetch a bucket of water from the well, Gisela was relieved to go. The atmosphere among the women had begun to oppress her. She would almost rather endure Etich's teasing or Ermentrude's well-meant lectures. She waved at Thomas as she passed the forge. The smith stared at her for a moment, then smiled and waved back. He turned to say something to his son Geoff, who then bounded toward her and took the wooden bucket from her hand.

"My father says to tell you that the burn on my arm is much better, maid Gisela."

She stopped and peered down at his arm, which was indeed healing well. "I'm very glad to see it, Geoff."

"We had to butcher our old cow, and my mother is making you a fine pair of shoes from part of the hide."

"That's very generous of her, Geoff. She needn't do it, though."

"For treating my arm. She says an arm is worth ten pairs of shoes. If you'll come to be fitted, she'll make them to size."

She was suddenly rich in fine garments, Gisela reflected—clothing earned for services rendered. But the services performed for little Geoff rested much more easily upon her conscience than those rendered to Rutgar.

"I'll stop by and talk to your mother on the way back from the well."

"I'll carry the water for you," Geoff offered.

"Aren't your supposed to be pumping the bellows for your father's fire?"

"My father won't mind. He says folks hereabouts should be treating you more like a lady than a poor bastard slattern."

Gisela smiled, quite certain that Thomas would be horrified to hear his words repeated, but the sentiment gave her mood a lift. "Then your assistance is very welcome, sir. And most grateful I am for it."

They did not make it to the well, however. Lounging against the stone corral next to the stable were the same two Franks Gisela had encountered on her way to tend Etich. One looked up. His eyes brightened when he saw her. Nudging his companion, he pointed her way. Gisela's hand tightened on her bucket as the men grinned and pushed themselves off the wall.

Rutgar ran the curry comb through Doomsayer's glossy coat. The familiar animal scent of the stable was a balm he drew into his lungs; the horse's muscular bulk was as comforting as a mother's breast. He almost gave in to the urge to lay his cheek against the smooth back and draw on the solace of the bond he felt with the big beast.

It was hard for a man to admit he was a shrinking coward, but today that was exactly what he was. Rutgar had fought more battles than he could count. His sword had drunk the blood of more men than he wanted to think of. Yet this morn he ran from facing one small maid who couldn't defend herself against a fly, despite her brave words and huffy threats.

The Bear had been right, Rutgar conceded. He hadn't known what he was getting into. He'd bedded his share of women—ladies of the court, slave women, serfs. They'd all been willing partners. Enthusiastic, even. None had inspired a need in him as Gisela did. Taking her had been more than possessing an alluring body. Much more even than conquering a maid who had become a symbol of her people's stubbornness. Taking Gisela had been losing a part of himself and gaining confusion, distraction, and vulnerability to fill its place.

Women were dangerous creatures; Rutgar had known that from a very tender age. He should have remembered it the first time he'd felt an amused twinge of interest in Gisela. The interest had become an obsession he didn't understand, and Rutgar was no longer amused.

Sounds from outside the stable slowly eroded his self-absorption. A ruckus on the other side of the stable wall was making Doomsayer fidget and the other horses in their cubicle stalls stamp and whicker. Rutgar cursed. The world was out of joint when a man couldn't find peace hiding in a stable. He stormed out, glad for the opportunity to vent at least part of his frustration on whoever had the temerity to break the morning's peace.

"What passes here?" he demanded from the stable door.

A scuffling knot of men and boys jerked as if he'd laid a lash to their backs. Rutgar's sharp gaze rested momentarily on Thomas the smith, whose nose dripped blood, the smith's son Geoff, and a scuffed and somewhat bruised band of adolescent allies. Four uneasy Frankish men-at-arms backed away from his gaze, which finally came to rest, as if drawn by an invisible thread, on Gisela, who sat in a dazed-looking heap next to the corral. An instant surge of alarm quieted as she pushed herself to her feet and glared at the men-at-arms, all her bones and her spirit apparently intact.

"You," he sighed. If the Saxon old gods were alive, they were certainly determined to rob him of any moment of peace. "I should have known you would be at the center of any storm brewing."

"This is not my fault!" Gisela declared. "Your goatish men are the cause. Young Geoff and I merely passed by on our way to the well when these two"—she stabbed a finger toward two of the men-at-arms—"assaulted us. Then, when they could not handle the job of subduing a mere woman and child, they called in these other two."

Rutgar stifled a sudden flash of jealous ire. He turned to the men-at-arms, who shifted uneasily under the burden of his gaze. "We were but having a bit a sport with the slut," one said. "The smith figured he'd stop our fun, and the whelps, too." A tentative grin twisted the Frank's lips. "Toublemakers, all of them. I figured it was our duty to whip the trouble right out of them."

"My lord!" Thomas the smith grew redder in the face than he already was. "The bullying scum was shaking my Geoff like a hound shakes a hare, and the boy was just trying to defend our Gisela!"

Rutgar's gaze swung once again to Gisela, who stood stiffly indignant under his scrutiny. He wanted to reach out and touch her, to assure himself she was not hurt past her bruised dignity, but to show such weakness in front of his men would be a mistake. "You say these men attacked you?"

"They did!" Her eyes swept contemptuously over the Franks. "And when poor Geoff defended me, they near to choked the poor lad!"

Rutgar nodded toward the smith. "You have my thanks, Thomas. Your son as well."

"My lord!" one of the Franks objected. "They lie. The bitch came along swinging her hips and jiggling her tits with an invitation no man could resist."

Rutgar pinned him with a furious look. "In any domain under my rule, no woman shall be taken against her will. The penalty for rape is death or slavery, as it has been in Frankish law down through the ages. Bear that in mind next time you lust after an unwilling maid."

The Franks studied the ground.

"This woman is mine," Rutgar declared to every man within hearing. "Remember that, for I do not share." He advanced upon Gisela, and wide-eyed, she retreated until the rough planks of the stable wall pressed into her back. Rutgar put a possessive grip on the back of her neck and pulled her to stand beside him. "Is that clear?"

One of the men-at-arms, a mercenary from Thuringia, had the misguided bravado to snort in amusement. His mirth ceased abruptly as Rutgar released Gisela and grabbed him, slamming the grizzled mercenary against the stable wall by his neck.

"I will have obedience to my commands!" Rutgar declared in a cold voice. "The woman Gisela is fodder neither for your lust nor for your insults. Next time you disobey me you will find my sword at your throat instead of my hand."

"Ah . . . aye, my lord!"

Rutgar released him and swept the others with hard eyes. The men-at-arms faded back, their attention fixed nervously on the ground. Gisela's troop of young champions grinned broadly, and their triumph echoed as smiles on many of the Saxon faces in the crowd.

"There's work to be done," Rutgar reminded them crossly. Out of the corner of his eye, he saw Gisela begin to fade back. He reached out and took her arm.

"Gisela."

"My lord," she replied stiffly.

"I have some words for you, also."

She rolled her eyes and sighed. "I thought you might."

Fourteen

"Well, little witch? Is it true?" Rutgar demanded as he closed his chamber door behind them. Gisela couldn't decide if the silver glint in his eyes came from humor or anger.

"Did you find our sport so entertaining that you're now casting out lures for others to satisfy you?"

"Did I what?" Now she knew he had to be joking. Rutgar couldn't possibly believe she would do such a thing, the arrogant toad! "I would sooner plunge my hand into the hearth fire than invite some strutting man into my bed. This is all *your* fault. You've made me fair game; your men are simply emulating their lord."

"You are not fair game. I don't intend to share you."

Gisela uttered a Saxon curse under her breath. The morning's incident had left her feeling soiled where the night's encounter had not. Right at this moment, she didn't want anything more to do with men. They were arrogant as strutting cocks and had the hearts of asses.

Rutgar's eyes probed her face for a moment. One corner of his mouth twitched up in the beginnings of a smile. "Plunge your hand into the fire, will you? Was it so bad, then?"

"It was!"

"You seemed to like it well enough last night." He put a hand on her shoulder. His thumb idly caressed the side of her neck, inspiring an involuntary tremor in response. "Those shudders that shook the bed were not from revulsion, I think."

Gisela's face heated. "You're a beast."

"Aye. Sometimes. You've commented on the fact before."

She tried to shrug out of his grip, but he held her fast and captured her other shoulder as well. He continued to look at her, and his scrutiny made her want to squirm.

"You liked it," he reminded her.

"I did not like it," she lied, to save what little dignity she had left, parrying his sharp gaze with a determined glower. Embarrassment crystallized to anger. "And I do not like you."

"You liked it," he asserted confidently. "And me."

"When the sea boils, and the sun freezes."

He released her and laughed. "My little witch, from my experience of you last night, I think that you have enough passion in you to make the sea boil. And mayhap I could scowl at the sun and freeze it to solid ice. From what women have told me about the coldness of my heart, it might be possible."

"If you're through jesting, my lord, I have work to do." Gisela headed for the door, but he pulled her back by the arm.

"I did not give you permission to leave. Neither did I this morning. I expect your obedience, Gisela. Defy me, and you will regret it."

Gisela glared at him. "Why do you do this? You've demonstrated your power over me and what I stand for. Must you torture me endlessly?"

"Torture, is it?" he asked with a wry smile. "Poor little witch, beset so sorely. What a shame your magic cannot save you from me."

He pulled her toward him, fitting her curves to the hard planes of his body as he claimed her mouth. Her lips opened to receive him, defying her will. His tongue played with her, gently, then fiercely. Her body responded with a warm melting between her legs, a traitorous tingling in her breasts, and an empty ache in the vicinity of her heart. But as desire heated, so did anger—anger at him for using her so. Anger at herself for being so vulnerable to her need for him.

She clung to the anger, fed it, nursed it—and bit him. Rutgar jerked away, cursing, but didn't let her go. "You little fiend from hell!"

"Let me go!"

"Stinger still intact, is it, buglet?"

Gisela struggled to get free, then stopped suddenly when she felt what she was rousing in him. He grinned down at her, infuriatingly sure of himself.

"What are you doing? Why—"

"It should be obvious what I'm doing."

" 'Tis broad daylight, you randy goat! I have work to do. Duties . . ."

"Your duties lie here with me, beneath me. Or on top, if you prefer. I wouldn't want to be an overbearing ogre about it."

Her face flamed with embarrassment, and he grinned.

"Innocent little buglet, did you think I wanted you for just one night?"

Her breath caught in her throat as the heat in his eyes caught her full force. "Yes. I thought . . ."

He kissed her again, and this time she was past resisting. The feel of his mouth on hers was inescapably right, as if it were something she'd been awaiting all her life.

"Ah, Gisela," he whispered against her lips. "You are vinegar and honey in one vessel, fire and frost. If you thought I would be satisfied after just one night with you, then whatever bones you divine from or lots you cast deceived you."

She protested halfheartedly when he laid her on the bed. Her body cried out for him. Her spirit, enslaved by her senses, could complain but feebly, and as Rutgar undressed her, baring her flesh inch by inch and paying sensual homage to each inch with his mouth, even that small complaint was drowned in a flood of desire.

By the time he covered her with his own body, she was ready to beg for him to complete their union. She helped him peel his braes from his hips, and he murmured her name in a way that could have made the wildest beast in the forest sit tamely at his feet. The low, husky sound of his voice reverberated in the chest that pressed warmly against her cheek. It surrounded her, invaded her very soul as he invaded her body. Slowly he filled her. Gently, deeply, until she felt his flesh had touched her very heart. She gasped as he withdrew, bereft at the emptiness he left.

"Am I hurting you, little witch?"

"No." She moaned quietly as he pushed forward again, ever so slowly, so that she could feel every inch of him slide into her welcoming body. "No," she whispered. "You're not hurting me."

"Then wrap your legs around my waist."

She obeyed, then gasped as he settled himself even deeper inside her. Instinctively her hands reached around him to grasp his tight, muscular buttocks, urging him still deeper.

"Easy," he crooned in her ear. "The fire built slowly burns hotter, and longer."

She burned. If she were any hotter, she would have exploded into incandescent ash. Still he drove her onward, stroking slowly, sensuously, holding her from the crest that she struggled toward. Their eyes locked and battled, as if they were warring, not mating. Rutgar's face was rigid with the strain of holding himself back. Gisela spoke his name, hearing her voice, husky and sensuous, as if it were spoken by another person —a woman steeped in passion and rich in love. Rutgar's eyes widened, as if she had just pulled the plug on his self-control. He thrust fiercely, desperately plunging into her as if he would bury his very soul in her center. Unafraid, Gisela moved with him, part of him—one flesh, one need. As he erupted, hot and pulsing, her world contracted to a hot, white pinpoint of ecstasy, then expanded in a warm explosion. Every muscle in her body, every nerve, every fiber, seemed to ripple in a wave of satisfaction.

For several moments they lay perfectly still, locked together, frozen in a world that was somewhere between paradise and earth. Gisela counted the dark lashes that lay against Rutgar's cheek. She noted the way thick brows rose over his closed eyes in so clean an arch. Admired the high molded prominence of his cheekbones, the clean curve of his jaw. Then he opened his eyes and looked at her. For the first time she noticed that his eyes had a few tiny flecks of gold buried in the clear gray. Her mother would have said they were the reflection of his soul.

"Gisela." The usual mockery was absent from his voice, and the slight smile he gave her was almost reverent. The afternoon light slanted through the window and painted his splendid body in a mosaic of light and shadow. She could see muscles flex in his arms and shoulders as he braced himself above her. His hair swept down his cheeks in dark waves. Every hair in the curly mat on his chest was afire with the light that played over his body.

He was beautiful, Gisela decided, still dizzy with erotic exhilaration. He was beautiful, and seemed to have very little connection to the man who had taken her people and her home, or the man who had almost choked the life from her in a field at Clearwater Farm.

"Gisela," he repeated in a whisper. One finger traced a line from her brow, down the straight slope of her nose, and over her cheek. "If I could believe in magic, I would believe in you. I think maybe you are a talisman. You are this place, its soul and its spirit. As long as I have you, I have Ardun."

Gisela's life calmed into an uncertain peace for the next stretch of days, but it was far from the life she'd known. The people of Ardun treated her with a new deference, and a new suspicion. Gradually, the smiles and friendly greetings returned, if a bit more hesitant than before. The Saxons settled under the yoke of a Frankish master, and found the yoke easier to bear than defiance and war. Most were too occupied with the business of survival to care whether it was a Saxon or a Frank who called himself lord of Ardun. There were fields to harvest, fruit to gather and preserve for the winter, game to be brought in and butchered, meat to be salted or smoked to see the people through the lean, cold months to come.

Aelrhane continued his raiding, but with the crops in, many of the peasants took refuge in the stronghold with their families and livestock. Little was left for the Saxon rebels to slaughter or burn, and in answer to Aelrhane's pillaging, a trickle of Saxon men came to Rutgar to pledge service and receive military training. Several of the Franks who had ridden with Rutgar in conquest left, their service to the king fulfilled. Several sent for their families and pledged themselves to the lord of Ardun as his vassals.

As the days passed, Gisela fought with a contentment that threatened to overcome her. The whole of Ardun accepted that she was Rutgar's woman. Nightly she lay in the lord's bed. He taught her the joy of passion, and she admitted to herself that she no longer wanted to hold herself from him. He had become a fire in her blood. When she lay beside him, curled securely in the curve of his strong body, she felt safe. When he came inside her, loving her, he touched the core of her soul.

Gisela didn't know when it had happened, how she had let herself be so foolish. But it was there, foolish or not. She loved Rutgar of Belthane, now Rutgar of Ardun. She wasn't foolish enough to believe he loved her, of course. He was a nobleborn warlord and she merely a serf. He used her for his own pleasure and the imagined hold she had over the people he had made his. Gisela told herself that she was fortunate Rutgar treated her well and protected her from insult. Even Adalinde dared not scold or take a switch to her for fear of Rutgar's retribution, and since the incident at the stable, the men-at-arms treated her as though she were lady of the manor rather than their lord's leman.

Still, fool that she was, Gisela longed for more than Rutgar's passion. She wanted his heart, unobtainable though it seemed.

As the season wore on and the coughs, congestions, bellyaches, fevers, and boils of Ardun's people took their toll of Gisela's medicinals, Rutgar himself escorted her into the forest to renew her stores. After what had happened the last time she went into the forest to collect, he didn't quite trust her with anyone else, Gisela concluded. Whatever the reason he went with her, however, she enjoyed having his company. With him at her side, she felt secure from the worry that Aelrhane might appear to snatch her back into his service. Foolish as it was to believe that Rutgar could defeat a whole party of raiders on his own, Gisela believed it nevertheless. With her own eyes she had seen his lethal skill with weapons, and knew Aelrhane would be wise not to challenge him, no matter how many of his ragtag outlaws he could call to his aid.

"How did you learn the uses for all these little plants?" Rutgar asked during a stop in one glade. "To me they look all alike."

"My mother taught me. She was renowned as an herbwife and healer."

"And a witch as well?"

"Aye. The sick and lame flocked to her. She would

give them a potion or sing a spell, and always they would feel better, even if they weren't completely cured. Sometimes they needed a balm for their spirit more than for their ills, and she gave them that."

"As do you." Rutgar smiled. He settled on the ground beside her while she worked. " 'Tis the healer and the killer who see most clearly the link between spirit, mind, and body. Be grateful you have come by such experience through healing."

For a moment the iron armor of his soul slipped to reveal the man behind the warlord. Both a healer's and woman's instinct urged Gisela to reach out and touch him, but before she could, the armor was back in place. He looked sharply away.

"Your mother is the one who taught you witchcraft, then?"

"She tried," Gisela said with a sigh. "As you've discovered, I'm not as adept as she was. If I try to use the things she taught me, more often than not they don't work—or they backfire."

"I discovered that right enough," he said with a snort. He watched her for a while in silence, his eyes reflective. "I've heard it said that you see the future. So Adalinde says, and the common people as well."

She was silent, but his level gaze compelled her. He wanted an answer, and in Gisela's experience, Rutgar seldom was satisfied until he got what he wanted.

"I have visions, sometimes," she admitted. "And dreams. They aren't something I conjure up deliberately. In fact, 'tis a gift I could well do without. My mother had them as well, but not as strongly as I."

A slight smile slanted Rutgar's mouth. "And do these visions come to be?"

"Yes." She thought of her eerie foretaste of Rutgar's making love to her. At the time, she had tried to convince herself that it was merely a dream, but even then, she knew that it wasn't. Someday they would make love at the fairy pond, just as she had envisioned. "Yes," she repeated quietly. "They almost always do."

His smile turned skeptical. "What do your visions tell you about the future of Ardun?"

She looked at her hands digging in the soil, but instead of damp black dirt and tangled vegetation, she saw the blood and flames of her recurrent dream. "My visions tell me that the fighting has not yet ended."

"In this world the fighting seldom ends. Have you not yet learned that?"

" 'Tis not something I want to learn."

He shook his head, then stiffened, his eyes fastened at a point behind her. Alarmed, she turned—to see a gray head emerge from the underbrush. Amber eyes seemed to glow in greeting.

"Silver!" She held out her hand, inviting the wolf into the clearing, before she realized that Rutgar had an arrow notched to the bow that had been slung across his back. Careless of the danger to herself, she lunged to place herself in his line of fire. "Do not! Please! He means no harm."

For a moment eyes hard as gray flint focused down the line of the arrow, looking straight at her. Gisela wondered suddenly how many men had seen a similar sight as their last view of this mortal world. Slowly Rutgar lowered the bow. Blithely ignoring the arrow meant for his fine pelt, Silver trotted into the clearing and pushed his broad head under Gisela's hand.

"A pet?" Rutgar asked incredulously.

"Not exactly." She ruffled the plush fur between the wolf's ears and smiled down into the yellow eyes. "A friend. I'm amazed he's here. He's very shy of everyone but me."

Rutgar regarded the wolf cautiously. Silver sat, licked his jaws, and regarded him right back. Gisela drew her breath in wonder, stunned that her special friend should show Rutgar such favor. As if reading her thoughts, Silver gave her hand a quick swipe of his tongue, just to let her know she was still his chosen.

"You keep very strange company, little witch."

"At times." She smiled impishly, and Rutgar smiled in return as he perceived the reflection on himself.

"I've seen your friend before, at dusk, lurking at the margin of the wood around the stronghold. He behaved most strangely for a wild animal, and I thought then that he looked a bit bewitched. I hope you don't make a habit of trying to tame predators." He fixed her with a pointed look.

"Most predators don't wish to be tamed, my lord."

He snorted contemptuously. "For most predators, taming would mean the death of them. You'd better keep your fine pelt away from the vicinity of Ardun, my fine-looking beast, or the men on the walls will stick it through with arrows."

Silver gave him a wolfish smile that brought a chuckle of amusement from deep in Rutgar's chest. The interplay between them brought a strange warmth to Gisela's heart.

"Lady witch, have you gathered enough leaves, roots, and whatever else you're grubbing for?"

"Yes," she said, her voice catching.

"Good hunting," Rutgar bade Silver as they got to their feet and the wolf disappeared into the brush.

"Silver has never been so tame with anyone but me," Gisela told him.

Rutgar grinned. "You shouldn't be surprised. You've called me beast often enough."

"Aye. Likely he recognizes a brother predator."

"Likely he does."

Rutgar bent down to kiss her, and Gisela wished suddenly they could stay in the forest forever, simply a man and a maid, instead of warlord and slave.

Silver's strange acceptance of Rutgar marked the completion of Gisela's surrender, and as the last days of summer passed, she was surprised to find that she was quite happy. Rutgar had something special in him. She had sensed it from the first time she'd seen him, though she'd fought admitting the truth of it, for circumstances and their own stubborn pride had them ever at odds. When Silver confirmed the man's uniqueness, her heart used the excuse to plunge even deeper into thralldom. For the first time in her life, Gisela began to understand why her mother had been content with Ercangar, even though the old lord of Ardun had never even pretended to love her.

The first snows fell. Rutgar promoted Lothar to be captain of the guard, a post he fulfilled meticulously if not enthusiastically. Etich healed and left his bed. As soon as the giant recovered his strength, he left Ardun with a contingent of men. Escort duty, he told Gisela with a grimace. But he was reticent as to the details of his mission.

One damp, cold morning, Gisela received an unexpected visit from Father Gaunt's wife, Hilde, who worked as diligently as her husband in badgering the formerly heathen people of Ardun to pay proper respect to the Church.

"My husband would flay the skin off my backside if he knew I'd come to you for a potion," Hilde told Gisela miserably. "He thinks ye deal with the devil."

Hilde had voiced that opinion herself more than once, and had made Gisela's life miserable when she was a child. Often she had lectured her on the torture Gersvinda was surely enduring in hell, and on one occasion, shortly after Gisela had come to live at the stronghold, Hilde had used pig's blood to paint a cross on her cot. The smell of the blood had lingered for days.

In recent years Hilde had been more restrained, but her contempt had been no less. Gisela resisted the temptation to comment on Hilde's willingness to accept help from the devil's handmaiden now that she was the one in discomfort.

"Gaunt says the trials of childbirth are a woman's legacy from Eve," Hilde told her. "The more difficult it is, the better for her soul."

Gisela filled a cup with a steaming infusion of motherwort and handed it to the priest's wife. " 'Tis easy for a man to say such when they're not the ones who must labor to produce the babe."

"Aye," Hilde agreed with a dramatic sigh. "They don't know what agony we bear. Not that you know, either, Gisela. But I expect you will soon, seeing that the lord Rutgar is laboring so between your legs. And him supposedly sworn to wield his sword in protection of the Faith! I'm sure my husband has given him a penance for it, but he doesn't seem disposed to repent and cast you aside."

Gisela sighed. "Drink the brew, Hilde. It should ease you a bit, and 'twill not grow you horns. Come back in three days for another dose. And when the pains begin, send for me, or if Father Gaunt won't have me, get old Mother Gottweld. She's seen more babes into this world than anyone at Ardun."

Hilde regarded the motherwort tea with a suspicious eye, tasted it gingerly, then downed the cup with a look of martyred resignation. She left without a word of thanks, but her comments lingered behind in Gisela's mind, starting her to dream about Rutgar and babies . . . and other hopeless fantasies.

She was indulging in such a daydream the next day when Gillan snapped her roughly back to reality. "What're ye woolgatherin' about?" the girl chided as they labored together under Ermentrude's watchful eye.

Gisela glanced up from the pile of garlic and onions in front of her. Her place as Rutgar's mistress did not exempt her from duties in the kitchen when she had time, though she would rather lance a boil than peel an onion.

"I've chopped a pile twice the size of yours in half the time," Gillan complained. "With all the work to be done around here because of Rutgar wanting his food just so, it seems you could lend a hand without woolgathering your way into uselessness."

"I'm working at it," Gisela retorted. In truth, she had been thinking about Rutgar, loving nights, babies, and impossible dreams, tending to her task with hands only—halfhearted hands at that. Gillan's sullen tone set her back up, however, and she wasn't about to apologize to the jealous little slattern.

Gillan sniffed and regarded Gisela as if the huge pile of vegetables before them was her fault. "I've never known a man to be so particular about his food. You'd think the damned Frank was a king instead of a king's lackey. You didn't see our good Saxon Aelrhane putting on such airs and mincing so about the meat being tough or the bread stale."

"Aelrhane wouldn't know if what he was eating was

raw, overcooked, or putrified," Gisela replied sharply. "The kitchen grew sloppy while he ruled here."

"Well aren't you grand?" Gillan sniped. "You aren't the mistress here, even if you are entertaining that Frankish devil between your legs every night, so don't go acting as if you rule us all. You're a serf just as low as the rest of us. Lower even. At least I can point to Gudalf and claim him for my father."

Ermentrude shot them a stern look from over the chicken she was dressing. "If you two would do more chopping and less bickering, ye might get some work done."

"I've been working till my hands are raw," Gillan complained.

"Ye do more whining than working, ye lazy strumpet. The lord doesn't require anything of us that isn't reasonable. And you stop your dreaming, Gisela, unless you're seeing something that's going to tell us whether the boys are going to bring in enough grouse for tomorrow's stew. The both of ye get to your work."

That night, lying in the circle of Rutgar's arms, Gisela wondered if Gillan was right. She had come to love the invader; she sometimes speculated, perhaps half hopefully, about bearing his child. Did she harbor somewhere deep inside her the hope of becoming mistress here—a lady where she'd once been a slave? Feckless fantasy—silly as a toad dreaming of becoming a prince. All the same, to have Rutgar as her own, to be raised above her humble life by his strong hand, to be called wife, to have his heart as well as his passion . . .

She relaxed in the heat of his body and allowed herself to dream. After all, dreaming had never hurt anyone.

Or so she thought. Gisela learned the folly of dreaming the next afternoon as she watched a string of riders and baggage carts file through the palisade gates, Etich at its head. Escort duty, he'd told her days ago when he'd left. Who had Rutgar sent him to escort?

"Who is that?" she asked Adalinde, who stood surveying the heavily cloaked figure who rode beside Etich.

Adalinde's gaze never left the cloaked woman. Her face was drawn and sharp, her eyes narrowed and assessing. "That is one our own," she said bitterly. "A weak and traitorous little fool. Bertrice of Stringau. Ercangar's niece. My granddaughter. And Rutgar's bride."

Fifteen

The hall that took up the greatest part of the manor's space was used for many things. The lord's mallus was held there to judge offenses and arbitrate disputes. The main meal of the day was eaten there, with serfs, craftsmen, and soldiers rubbing elbows with nobles and stewards. Servants and a handful of men-at-arms slept on the benches that lined the walls, or when the weather was cold, on pallets laid beside the hearth.

On this night the hall was glorious with festivity. Trestle tables ran down both sides of the central hearth, the planks groaning with such an immense weight of food that Ermentrude complained the whole lot would crash to the floor if they brought out so much as one more dish. The benches also groaned, crowded with serfs and peasants, craftsmen, and warriors—Frank and Saxon side by side—who jostled and crowded, elbow to elbow and sometimes jowl to jowl, paying homage to the fine feast.

Above them all, the head table presided from the dais. There sat Rutgar, dressed in a fine black tunic embroidered in silver. On his left was Adalinde, dressed also in black, as was her custom, and down the line Lothar and Etich. On Rutgar's right sat the woman who drew the eyes of everyone in the hall—Bertrice of Stringau. Skin like creamy milk, hair the color of autumn chestnuts, and eyes limpid as pools of . . . of . . .

Pools of pig shit, Gisela decided, setting a platter of roast venison on the head table as she surreptitiously surveyed Rutgar's bride. She had begged Ermentrude to be relieved of the duty of serving at this welcoming banquet, but Ermentrude had insisted. There were few enough hands to help, the cook complained. No one could shirk the duty, and why should Gisela seek to be excused? Did she fancy herself too good to turn her hand to honest labor now that she slept in the lord's bed? The awkwardness of the situation seemed never to have entered the cook's mind.

Gisela set the platter down and turned away, studiously avoiding a direct look at Rutgar. She didn't want to see him admire Bertrice. Though what there was to admire about his pasty-faced betrothed she couldn't imagine. The girl possessed as much liveliness as a slug, as much expression as a cockroach. Her nose was too big; it looked as though it had been pasted sloppily onto her face from some other face entirely. And her eyes were as small as a pig's as well as the color of a pig's leavings. Most unattractive.

While she went up and down the lower tables refilling tankards of ale and fetching wine, Gisela savored these obvious lacks in Bertrice's appearance. Cautious glances toward the head table revealed other flaws as well. The woman was so spare of flesh that her hands looked like the claws of a crow and her eyes were sunken and shadowed like the empty sockets of a skull. A fine passion she would bring to Rutgar's bed— like to that of a dried-up corpse. A wonderful mother she would make for his children—maternal as a dead stick.

"Damn ye! Watch yourself, ye clumsy, addlebrained lackwit! Your jostling made me slop sauce on my shirt."

"Sorry," Gisela said absently.

Not satisfied with her halfhearted apology, the man —a servant who had come with Rutgar's military retinue—grabbed her wrist and drew back his hand for a blow, but before he could wreak his punishment, Gisela landed a kick in the instep of his sandaled foot. He yelped and promptly released her, but the look that followed her retreat was a black promise. Few around them had noticed the exchange of unpleasantries, immersed as they were in doing justice to the feast spread before them.

"You should be more careful," Gillan warned Gisela as she brushed by the table with a platter of sweetbreads. "Rutgar has a wife to warm his bed now. You're going to have to learn how to be a mere serf again."

Gisela was fortunate that her pitcher was empty. If

it had been full, the temptation to empty it over the girl's head would have been irresistible.

"Bertrice is very beautiful, don't you think?" Gillan asked, eyes glinting.

"What I think is that I have work to do. I don't have time to be jabbering."

At the head table, Adalinde summoned her peremptorily. From the grate straight into the fire, Gisela thought ruefully. Would this evening ever end?

Rutgar did not look at Gisela as she filled the goblets at the table. His attention was all for Bertrice, of course. Bertrice of the knobby wrists and too-large ears. Bertrice of the insipid smile and crooked teeth. A stone settled on Gisela's heart as she admitted the truth. The wretched woman was, indeed, very beautiful, just as Gillan had declared. All Gisela's harping on imaginary flaws would not change that. Bertrice had a sweet face and a fragile, ethereal look about her that would move a man to protective tenderness—damn her!

"Are you going to stand there all evening, Gisela, or may I have some ale?"

Rutgar's voice startled Gisela out of her trance of misery. She swung quickly around—too quickly by far, for her elbow hit the back of the master's chair and the entire contents of the pitcher cascaded over Rutgar's shoulder, down his tunic, onto the table, and into his lap. The hall fell suddenly silent. Gisela's horrified gasp seem to ring from the rafters and echo from the stone walls. Then an explosion of laughter burst from one and all—except those sitting at the head table. Rutgar in particular did not seem amused.

Without uttering a word, Gisela fled to the kitchen. She had provided enough entertainment and been the victim of enough gossip and snide remarks for one night. Atruda looked at her curiously as Gisela stormed through the kitchen and out the door. Frigid night air brought instant gooseflesh to her skin, but she ran on, running from Rutgar, Bertrice, herself, and the cold. Without conscious thought she sought refuge in the little chapel that backed up to the west palisade. The timber and mud walls provided some shelter from the cold, but the rest of her problems followed her there, or so it seemed, for they chased her mind like a pack of hounds after a stag.

Fool! Gisela chided herself as she sat down on one of the hard benches. What had she expected, after all? Rutgar was lord of a vast domain. He must marry and produce heirs. Did she expect him to marry her—a serf, a witch, a Saxon?

Bertrice was Saxon, but Bertrice was nobleborn. She was born to be mistress of a great domain, lover to its lord, mother of his children, while Gisela was little more than a slave, worthy only to be used as the lord saw fit, in the kitchen, the poultry yard, or attending him in his bed.

Gisela's heart twisted at the knowledge that she had lost Rutgar's loving, his companionship, his touches and rare tenderness. Strange to think how she'd once fought his possession. Now its absence would leave a gaping, miserable hole in her life. She lowered her head into the cradle of her hands.

Slowly, the peace of the little chapel soothed her. She raised her eyes to the crude altar, where a carved crucifix seemed eerily alive in the flickering light of three small candles. She understood why Lothar was so attracted to the place. It had a magic that was not unlike the benign sorcery found in shadowed forest glades, calm blue lakes, or the swirling mist of the fairy pond.

"There you are!" came a quiet exclamation from the darkness behind her. Lothar dropped onto the bench beside her. "Has this holy place calmed you, Sister?"

Lothar called Gisela sister only when he thought the circumstances very dire. She must have made even more of a dolt of herself than she'd realized.

"What is it that has you so upset, Gisela?"

"What do you think?" she snapped.

"I cannot guess. I've never before observed you to be so ill-mannered. You openly showed contempt to one to whom you owe obedience."

Gisela expelled her breath in a whuff of disgust. "I wasn't contemptuous; I was clumsy. I didn't spill the ale deliberately."

"Indeed? I've never known you to be so careless."

"I was . . . distracted."

"Every time I've seen you today, you've been wearing a scowl fit to curdle milk."

She shot up from the bench, angry once again. "What do you expect? If I had emptied that pitcher over Rutgar's head, it would have been less than he deserved from me. He gave me no warning, no hint that . . . that he planned to import some little strumpet who is willing to sell her loyalty for a secure match of marriage."

Lothar nodded. "Ah," he said in a way that made Gisela want to shove the word back down his throat.

"What do you mean, 'Ah'?"

"I thought you would be grateful to be rid of Rutgar."

Wasn't that just like a man, to reduce such a mix of emotions to its most simplistic state?

"Of course I am!"

"Gisela, I'm sorry I could not protect you from Rutgar. But as his sworn vassal . . . well, his tactics with you, painful though they might have been, were probably in the best interests of peace here. And I didn't think he would really harm you."

"He didn't," she declared. Rutgar had never asked her to love him. Her own foolish heart had been the culprit.

"Bertrice is a lovely girl, don't you think? I've not seen her since our uncle died and she was sent away to be cared for by the nuns. I wouldn't have recognized her as that skinny little maid who wailed every time I teased her. Now she's so . . . so . . ."

Gisela could think of a few choice descriptions to finish Lothar's worshipful ruminating, but didn't. She did their cousin an injustice, but she couldn't quite purge the hurt bitterness from her heart.

"I'm going to Verhonne," she told Lothar. "I can't stay here."

"Are you daft?"

"I can live with the widow Hildegarde. The villagers will be glad to trade a share of the harvest and hunt in exchange for my skill at healing. 'Twas how we kept ourselves when my mother lived."

"Gersvinda was a free woman, Sister. She could live where she liked, but when she died, you sold yourself into serfdom in return for your keep. You are part of Ardun, just like the stables and the fields and livestock, and Rutgar is your master. Do you think he would give you leave to dwell in the village?"

"He should have no more use for me," Gisela said with a sniff. Self-pity stalked her again, but she refused to give in to it. "I will do very well. Rutgar won't care if I go."

Lothar ran his fingers through his hair in a swipe of frustration. "You can't leave now, in the dark of night," he reasoned. "Go to the kitchen and eat something. You'll feel better then."

Gisela took Lothar's advice, but the fish stew and venison that Ermentrude dished out for her didn't make her feel better, for Ermentrude served up a steady stream of rebukes and comments with the meal. How could Gisela be so flighty, so clumsy, so rude, so ill-mannered and ill-behaved? 'Twas a wonder the lord hadn't fetched her back for a beating, which she richly deserved. And wasn't their new mistress a gentle soul? Though the girl didn't look sturdy enough for childbearing. But whether or not the new mistress could survive birthing children, King Charles had done the right thing in arranging for the old Saxon bloodlines to continue in the rule of Ardun—for hadn't Bertrice been heir to Stringau, which had been held by their own lord Ercangar's brother? The marriage would soothe a few ruffled Saxon feathers, the cook predicted, then shot a canny look in Gisela's direction.

"Ye didn't go and become attached to the man, did you, Gisela?"

"Of course not! I'm no such fool."

"Aye? Well, even if ye did, I doubt you'll lose him to her for long. There's no fire in the girl, and she'll not satisfy a man like Rutgar, mark my words. But then, ye can't fault her for the lack, for she's a nobleborn woman, and such are made for finer things than lust."

Gisela snorted into her stew.

"When you're through eating, take the water heating on the hearth and carry it to the lord's chamber. Rutgar will be wanting a bath after the dousing you gave him, and the other girls put in a full night's work while you took yourself off."

Gisela passed the task off to the lad who tended the

kitchen fires. Rutgar could bathe himself if he wanted to smell sweet for his bride-to-be. He wouldn't find Gisela waiting for him in his chamber from now on. Tonight she would take refuge in the women's quarters, and at first light she would leave for Verhonne.

Gisela did not make it to the village; she did not make it until the dawn; in fact, she scarcely made it to her cot in the women's quarters before Rutgar came for her. He stomped around the crowded little room with its rows of snoring women and paused at each cot until he had located her. Gasps and startled shrieks met his methodical search, but he seemed not to care. When he finally found Gisela, he pulled her off the cot and to her feet.

"You are not where you are supposed to be," he said in a dark, quiet voice.

Gisela stiffened her spine. "And where is that?"

"I wouldn't think that you'd need to ask by now."

"Your bed is going to be rather crowded with three of us in it, don't you think?"

A titter issued from the darkness of the room and reminded them they had an avidly interested, if somewhat groggy, audience.

"Come with me," he commanded.

Gisela twisted out of his grasp and hissed a refusal. His hands landed heavily on her shoulders and his face lowered to within mere inches of hers. Even in the pitch-blackness Gisela could see the iron glint in his eyes.

"Do not refuse me, Gisela, or I shall carry you over my shoulder like some booty of war, and you may kick and scream all you like. Don't fool yourself that any will come to your rescue."

Gisela hesitated, rebellion and anger warring with good sense.

"Do you doubt I will do it?"

She breathed a small sigh of surrender. "I will come."

With what dignity she could muster, Gisela preceded Rutgar toward the door. That dignity was somewhat marred by stumbling into a cot and hearing the occupant's amused snicker.

Once in Rutgar's chamber, Gisela let loose her temper. "Where is Bertrice?" she demanded, gesturing to the empty bed.

"Bertrice is not yet my wife. And she has nothing to do with what is between you and me."

"There is nothing between you and me, not from the moment your bride rode through the gates of Ardun."

"You are mistaken, Gisela. Nothing has changed between us. I still require you to obey me, and I thought in the past few weeks that your obedience was not so onerous a chore." He stripped off his shirt and bent to unlace his boots. "Now be done with this woman's tantrum of yours before the water cools in my bath. You soaked me to the skin with ale. I have never known a woman so clumsy."

"Ooooh!" Gisela grabbed the ball of soap and flung it into the bath, producing a splat that sent a small cascade of water to the floor. "Call your bride to bathe you. She will need the practice in her duties. And if you want a woman to warm your bed, you may introduce her to that task as well!"

"Are you jealous?" Rutgar laughed, and his expression thawed. "What silly womanish notion is this? My marriage has nothing to do with you."

"I will not dishonor your bride," Gisela declared.

Rutgar unwrapped the cross bandages that bound

his calves and untied his braes, still chuckling. Gisela grew madder at each insensitive, ignorant, arrogant male chuckle.

"I thought you an honorable man, Rutgar, in spite of your being a Frank. But you have no notion of honor. You have no heart as well."

He looked up at her with eyes suddenly devoid of amusement. "Say what you want about my heart, Gisela, but do not slander my honor. Women have little understanding of the concept. Nor do they have such soft hearts as they so often plead."

The chill in his gaze warned her that she trod on dangerous ground.

"I have no intention of sacrificing the pleasure of your company simply because I am taking a wife. My marriage to Bertrice is a matter of politics and economy, and I will treat my wife with all due honor, giving her my name, my protection, my children, and sharing with her all my worldly goods."

"And what of fidelity?" Gisela demanded.

"Fidelity? A man does not owe his wife fidelity. Where did you get such a nonsensical idea?"

"The union of male and female is the highest bond in the universe. All nature pays homage to it. It is a bond that should not be broken—by either party. To do so threatens the order of nature."

Rutgar gave a great bark of laughter. "Is this some sorcerous paean taught you by the gnomes and elves, or perhaps the fairies in the woods?"

"By my mother," Gisela growled.

"Then she was as daft as the fairies!"

"You obviously know nothing of loyalty!"

"I know everything of loyalty! And I begin to doubt there is a scrap of it in you!"

"You only—"

"Silence!" He cut off her retort with a peremptory sweep of his hand. "I do not wish to discuss this any further." With swift, angry motions he peeled off his braes and stalked to the tub. "You are going to perform your duty and tend my bath—and any other service I require. Is that clear?"

Gisela noted ruefully that the force of his arrogance was not a bit diminished by the fact that he stood in the middle of the room without a stitch on. If anything, his naked physique was more intimidating than full battle armor. He lowered himself into the tub and threw her the cloth, watching her from under sardonically raised brows.

"I will bathe you," she conceded.

"Indeed. How generous of you."

Rutgar did not make the task easy, insisting that she soap every square inch of his skin. He closed his eyes and let his head drop back as her hands did their work, and she noticed the deeply etched lines between his brows and at the corners of his mouth. He looked very tired, and unhappy with more than their battle of words. For a moment she almost felt sorry for him, but only for a moment. When his hand took hers and directed it to the heretofore neglected region at his groin, indignation fired once again to life.

She pulled her hand away, splashing his face with soap in the process. "You can wash that area yourself, my lord."

He smiled enticingly. " 'Tis much more pleasant when you do it."

"My duty here is to clean you, not pleasure you."

"Efficient servants know that tasks can be combined."

"I have only one task here," she said with a rebellious sniff.

"You believe that truly?" He lounged back against the edge of the tub and regarded her with a lazy amusement that almost disarmed her anger—almost, but not quite. But she was sufficiently mesmerized by the sensuality in his gaze that she didn't move fast enough to evade his sudden grasp for her. "I think you'll have little will for rebellion if I set my mind on seducing you to less tedious tasks."

"Curse you, Rutgar, I'll—"

"Poison me? Put a spell on me? I don't know why I put up with such a bothersome stinging little beastie."

Growing more furious with every taunt, she yanked hard in an attempt to escape, sending water everywhere—until suddenly he yanked back, and she was dragged over the rim of the wooden tub and into the lukewarm water with him. A wave worthy of the open sea rose between them, overflowed onto the floor, then subsided. Gisela sputtered. Soapsuds stung her eyes and water burned in every cavity in her head.

"That's more like it, buglet. I'm glad to see you striving so to please me. And you do please me." His last words dropped to a serious tone. Straddled upon him as she was with her kirtle riding up her hips, she could indeed feel how much she pleased him, the randy Frankish pig.

"I don't mean to please you," she proclaimed. "Never again. You know very well you can have me, Rutgar, anytime you like, morning or afternoon or in the dead of night—unless I could somehow run far enough that it wasn't worth your time to search me out. But you will not have me willing, I promise you that. If you enjoy rape, then take your pleasure. I don't have the strength to deny you. But I will not dishonor your bride by going willingly into your embrace. I will not."

He scowled at her like a boy-child robbed of a toy, and she scowled back at him. For all the determination of her spirit, she could feel herself weakening. Her thighs ached to grip him in a lover's embrace. She longed to see the intimate smile he gave her only when no one else could see; she hungered for the secure, comfortable warmth of snuggling next to his hard body in the small hours of the night. The emptiness that began inside her at Bertrice's first appearance grew and swelled and cried out to be filled. How long could she deny him?

Unwilling to test her strength further, she rose and stepped out of the tub, eyeing him warily.

"Get me a towel," he commanded coldly.

Still dripping herself, Gisela obeyed. He erupted from the water, dried himself, and dressed, all without glancing her way.

"Clean clothes," he barked.

She laid them on the bed and hastily backed out of his reach, but he didn't come at her as she halfway expected him to. He buckled on his sword, threw a heavy cloak over his shoulder, and turned to regard her with forbidding eyes.

"Leave the stronghold, and I will find you. Keep in mind that my patience is limited."

He stalked out without looking back. The slam of the heavy door rattled every loose object in the room.

Sixteen

Rutgar slammed his fist into the logs of the palisade, breaking skin as well as bark. Why, why, *why* did he let the damned woman get away with such behavior? No man would dare to so defy him, to challenge him at every turn, to question his honor, of all things. What did a woman know of honor? Nothing! The very concept was foreign to the female mind.

The frigid night air was not having the hoped-for cooling effect on his temper. If Rutgar had stayed with that devil's imp a moment longer, he would have done something truly worthy of the beast she named him. She was a fever in his blood, and a pain in his ass, that rivaled the sting of a viper's bite.

What he should have done was bend her over the bed, saucy little behind topmost, and beat her until she begged for mercy. He couldn't though, God help him! At least a dozen times the little witch had richly deserved a whipping, a beating, a stoning even, but when Rutgar looked into those big golden eyes, what he should do to her melted into what he would like to do to her. That body, with its sweet curves and lush womanly secrets, was made for better things than a beating, and crushing that lively spirit, troublesome though it often was, would be a cruelty he couldn't stomach.

Rutgar had always believed that mercy should be tempered with firmness, that a man who allowed himself to be swayed by sentiment or desire was a fool—and now look at him, his tail in a knot, his cock on the rampage, and his mind turned to mush because of a damned female. And why? Women were much the same; tall, short, plump, thin, nobleborn, peasant, or serf—they all could take a man inside their bodies and relieve his need. What was special about Gisela, that he needed her, wanted to be with her, even when the desire for sex was not upon him?

A tide of frustration rose through his chest and flooded into his head as though it would burst his skull. He slammed his fist into the logs yet again. The pain that lanced up his arm was easier to bear than the confusion that ate at his gut. He wanted to choke Gisela and make love to her at the same time. Damned if he wasn't serving a bit of his Purgatory time here on earth. God, omniscient and omnipotent as He was, could have found a better solution to the problem of procreation than to make Woman.

Rutgar looked out into the night-shrouded forest, letting the quiet and the darkness seep into his soul. Women. God rot them. They were either treacherous, using their wiles to gain what they wanted for themselves, or they were cold, like his own not so tender mother, who had abandoned him to the mercies of his stepfather when he was scarcely as tall as his dead father's sword. That gentle dame had wed Belthane's conqueror—his father's murderer—then watched her new husband send her young son off to battle for the king as part of Belthane's war levy. Not a tear had she shed for his going.

The bitterness of memory was a contrast to the night's peace. The moon was a mere crescent sliver riding the tops of the forest. It lent little light to the sky, even less to the woods. Rutgar wondered if Gisela's wolf was out there, waiting for her to come for a visit. He sympathized with the poor bewitched creature; he was feeling a bit ensorcelled himself at the moment.

No lonely howl rose toward the moon, however. What did reach Rutgar's ears, now that the din of his own temper had quieted, was the soft sound of a woman weeping. Rutgar put a cautious hand on his sheathed knife and went in search of the sound's source. He found it where the new west palisade met the north. Rutgar stood for a moment to observe. Of all the people who resided within these walls, Bertrice of Stringau was the one he would least expect to find on the palisade, and yet here she was, splayed against the logs in an agony of weeping, her face buried in the rough bark as though it were the bosom of her mother.

He spoke her name quietly; she jolted to attention, her face pale in the dim light of stars and moon.

"Lady, what do you out here at this time of night?"

"My lord Rutgar? Is that you?"

"It is."

"I . . . I'm sorry." She dabbed at her wet face and attempted to set herself straight. "I thought I was alone."

"What makes you weep so, lady?"

" 'Tis . . . 'tis nothing, my lord. I miss the convent and the sisters. I . . . I apologize. Usually I am not this undisciplined."

"You have lived with the sisters at Gandersheim much of your life, have you not?"

Bertrice sniffed quietly. "The king sent me to the convent there when I was but twelve—when my parents died and my uncle Ercangar assumed responsibility for Stringau."

"So the king informed me. 'Tis only natural that you miss the sisters, but your home is now Ardun."

She smiled bitterly. "So the king informed *me*." As if daunted by her own brief show of spirit, she lapsed into awkward silence.

"Lady, you should not be wandering alone at night," Rutgar warned. "I waited until the people here had quieted to send for you, but there are those here who still cherish a spark of rebellion."

"These are *my* people," she said quietly. "They would not harm me."

"Perhaps not. But there may be some who are loath to see an alliance of the old bloodlines with the new, simply because they do not wish me to succeed in winning Saxon trust and loyalty."

"Oh." She gave a melancholy sigh. "Yes. Of course. I should not have come out."

She was a gentle-faced girl, winsome and attractive, though the headrail that covered her hair and draped beneath her chin left little enough for the eye to behold. Rutgar wondered why he did not stir at the sight of her. She was young, pretty. What's more, she was meek, submissive, respectful, and quiet—everything a woman should be.

And beside Gisela, she was dull as watered milk.

The thought of Gisela pushed his frustration another notch to the fore. She was just a woman, he told himself, a woman no different from any other except that she was a good deal more trouble. Bertrice could just as easily light the fire in his blood.

Rutgar stepped closer. Bertrice flinched away, wide-eyed.

"Be still, Bertrice. We are to be husband and wife, after all."

She stood and endured as he kissed her. Her mouth was stiff and cold beneath his, her body rigid. When he released her, Rutgar could see that her eyes were squeezed shut. She looked as though she'd just been forced to kiss a frog.

No matter, he told himself. She would learn, and when she softened, his body would respond as it ought. Surely it would. Gisela did not have a stranglehold on his passion. He would not allow it.

Determined to feel something—anything—he kissed Bertrice again. The effect was not what he'd hoped for on either of them. She struggled so fiercely that he was forced to either let her go or hurt her.

Wild-eyed and panting, Bertrice cringed back from him.

"Bertrice," he chided, stifling his impatience, "you have no need to fear me. We are betrothed by the king's word and the Church's sanction—all but wed."

Her breathing calmed somewhat, though she chewed anxiously on her lower lip. "Please forgive me, my lord." She bit both lips and stared down at her feet. "I beg for a few days to adjust to my new circumstances. From the time I was sent to the convent, I never thought to leave its sheltering walls. The idea of marriage is very new to me."

"Is the thought of being a wife so fearful to you?" He put a comforting hand on her shoulder, and she shied away. Apparently the thought was so fearful.

With visible effort, Bertrice touched his hand in apology. "I'm sorry. I beg your forbearance, my lord. If we could postpone the wedding for a short while . . ."

Rutgar sighed. "If that is your wish, lady. I want you to be content with your lot. You have no reason to fear me. I am no soft-handed scholar nor a polished courtier, but neither do I eat maidens alive."

"You are very understanding, my lord. I am grateful."

"You will allow me to escort you back to your rooms."

"Of course." She did not look up into his face as he took her arm and led her back to the manor, but stared straight ahead, her expression martyred—a pure maiden sacrificed on the altar of expedient matrimony.

Rutgar's mood was not improved by finding Gisela gone from his chamber when he returned. He had expected it, but still it stung. No doubt the damned woman would bury herself in the infirmary mixing her potions or in the weaving house where he would not see her for days. So sure was she that Rutgar would not force her! She thought she knew him, did she, that little daughter of the devil? She thought she could pull his strings like a puppeteer and make him dance to her will?

The hell she would, Rutgar fumed. He jerked off his clothing and dashed cold water onto his face. The hell she would! Gisela had been so anxious that he give due honor to Bertrice, she should be grateful for the opportunity to see that the lady was well served. Bertrice needed a woman to attend her, and Gisela was the perfect choice. Rutgar would have the little troublemaker under his eye every day, and he would discover if her so-called woman's honor could resist the intimacy they'd forged between them. She wanted to come to him; he knew she did.

He climbed into his empty bed and stared moodily into the dark. All the Moors, Huns, and Bavarians together on one battlefield would be more easily dealt with than one coddled, stubborn woman who was determined to have her own way. And now it appeared he had not one but two of the creatures on his hands.

The morning sunlight streamed through the weaving house windows and glistened on the fibers of fine white wool that slipped through Gisela's hands. The wool caressed her fingers as it twisted into a slender strand and wound itself onto the spindle. The spinning wheel hummed in time to the click of Gisela's foot on the pedal. The wheel sang, Gisela's fingers flew, and the fluffy pile of carded wool beside her stool diminished bit by bit. On either side of her, a chorus of wheels sang their own tunes, and the looms clacked in harmony. All labored together to produce a fabric fine enough to adorn a pure and noble bride.

The project was Drada's idea—that the women of Ardun should present their new mistress with her wedding raiment. There was no silk to be had in

Ardun, so the undershift and headrail would be cut from soft linen, the kirtle and overtunic from Ardun's finest wool—the kirtle dyed the blue of the northern sea in summer, and the tunic the gold of a warm day's sun. A heavy wool mantle was in the making also—a deep blue to match the kirtle, its inner folds lined in bright gold.

Gisela didn't mind that she had been pounced upon and put to work the moment she had shown herself in the weaving house the night before. She was unpracticed enough at spinning that she must focus all her concentration on keeping her thread fine and even, and that concentration kept her mind from wandering to other matters—painful matters. She did not want to think about Rutgar wedding her noble cousin; Rutgar taking his bride to bed, whispering to her in the same gentle tones he had used with Gisela during the dark hours so many nights; Rutgar and his smiles, his scowls, his laugh—coming warm and unexpected in those precious moments when they had shut out the world and relaxed in their cocoon of passion. She did not want to think about Bertrice, with her shy smile, milk-white skin, long silky lashes, rich brown eyes, and maidenly diffidence.

Gisela had never expected to become a used woman as her mother had been, nor to make the same blunders of the heart that had made her mother suffer. But she didn't want to think about that. She had thought about it so much the last day that her mind staggered in misery. She wanted to think only of the wool slipping through her fingers, the steady humming of the wheel and click of the pedal—and she was succeeding in her concentration, until Rutgar opened the door to the weaving house and stood within the doorway. His tall figure was haloed by the blinding brightness of the morning sun, and his long shadow reached across the room to fall across her wheel. Gisela's heart skipped a beat. Her foot slipped off the pedal, and the whirr of her wheel whimpered slowly to a stop.

"Welcome, my lord," blind Drada said. Her loom didn't miss a clack in its rapid rhythm.

"Good Drada," Rutgar greeted her. "I've come to rob you of Gisela. I have duties for her elsewhere."

Old Drada's head turned toward Gisela as if she could see her, then moved on to a woman who sat at one of the looms. "Luitgard, take Gisela's wheel. When Karis comes in from fetching the wood for the hearth she can finish at your loom."

Gisela was forced to give up her place to Luitgard and follow Rutgar from the weaving house.

"Just what are these duties you have for me?" she demanded, running a few steps to bring herself even with him. "Is it not a bit unusual for the lord of the domain to run about fetching servants and marshaling their tasks? Adalinde delegates which women shall work where, and there are lads about with nothing better to do than carry messages and fetch people."

"Is it not equally unusual for a serf to question her master's actions?"

When Gisela stopped, he took her arm and pulled her up the steps to the manor entrance.

"Slow down! Ouch! Not everyone has legs as long as yours!"

"Or a tongue as impertinent as yours. I have no time for leisured strolling."

When they reached the private receiving chamber off the hall, Rutgar spun her around to face him. His regard made her distinctly uncomfortable. A glint of triumph in his eyes told her that the victory of the night before hadn't been as decisive as she'd thought.

"As you say, the lord of Ardun has more pressing tasks than overseeing the duties of servants, but this is a personal task I have for you, Gisela."

Was it excitement or dismay that made her pulse suddenly pound? Had Rutgar not believed her declaration that he couldn't have her short of rape? Had her confidence that he wouldn't stoop to such a thing been a fool's naiveté? She backed a step away.

He smiled wolfishly as he spoke. "My bride Bertrice needs a woman to serve her. I've decided you are the one best fit for the task."

"What?" The rapid drumbeat of her heart slowed abruptly to a dull thud. "Best fit . . . for . . . ?" Indignation and hurt made her chest ache so that the pain robbed her of words.

Rutgar strolled to an upholstered bench, dropped himself onto it, leaned back against the wall, and stretched his legs comfortably out in front of him. "The noble lady Bertrice is having some difficulty adjusting to her new situation in life," he said airily, as if the very mention of Bertrice didn't cause Gisela to flinch. "She needs a woman companion near her own age, a sympathetic ear, someone to help her with . . . whatever it is that women need help with when they are about to marry."

"No." Gisela said the word firmly and definitely, so the heartless dog would have no doubt about her refusal. "No, no, and no again."

Rutgar's lips curved into a deceptively amiable smile.

"You insist on believing that I *ask* you to attend your duties, Gisela. I don't ask. I *tell*."

Gisela curled her hands into fists so tight that her

nails dug into her flesh. "You are cruel, Rutgar. You enjoy watching people squirm beneath the thumb of your power."

"I do enjoy watching you, Gisela, squirming or no, and I would have you close by in the manor."

"And what of your bride?"

"Bertrice will be happy in your company. You can teach her the ways of Ardun, and she can teach you the virtue of womanly obedience. 'Tis a quality you noticeably lack."

"As compassion is a quality you noticeably lack!"

"Compassion?" He shook his head and smiled in a mockery of forbearance. "I am the most compassionate of men, buglet, to ignore your stings and try to save you from your own foolishness."

"Am I foolish to expect the lord of Ardun to possess some shred of honor? I will not do it. There are any number of women at Ardun more suitable to companion your wife. Choose one of them!"

"Enough! I lose patience."

"Since when did you count patience among your virtues?"

"Cease speaking of things you little understand. You will serve Bertrice." One moment he was at ease on the bench, and the next he had her by the shoulders, his face a mere inch from hers. "You will serve Bertrice, Gisela, or . . ."

He kissed her, deeply, thoroughly, a potent reminder of what had been between them and still could be. Gisela could no more struggle against his possession than she could fight the rising of the sun or the flood of a tide. From the beginning, his touch had seemed so natural and inevitable that resistance had been futile.

"You'll serve Bertrice," he whispered against her

lips. Her senses swam as he kissed her again, briefly and hard. "You'll serve Bertrice, or you'll serve me. Make your choice."

"This is lovely, is it not?" Bertrice swirled the peach-colored silk about her, laughing like a delighted child. Her unbound chestnut hair swirled with her, gleaming with golden highlights that rivaled the glory of the afternoon sun. "Oh my!" She tottered dizzily. "Such behavior! Mother Angelique would call me a silly goose and say well brought up young women should not indulge in such flightiness. But Mother Angelique has never seen a silk of such stunning color, I suspect. To think the king himself has dowered me and provided all these wonderful gowns. 'Tis all . . . quite overwhelming." Her smile faded, and a shadow darkened her eyes, driving away the brightness like a cloud banishing sunlight.

" 'Tis lovely," Gisela admitted. "Finer than anything I've ever seen."

Bertrice fingered the silk and smiled gently. " 'Tis easy to love such beauty, but a king's gifts are cold. They are merely an offering he makes for his use of me. Now this"—she held up the length of fine linen that Drada had sent that afternoon. "This is a labor of love. A true gift from my own people. This has a beauty that warms the heart." She lovingly caressed the linen, smoothing tiny wrinkles from the material with the tips of her fingers. "If the entire wedding garment is as fine as this piece, it will be special indeed. I am so touched that the women of Ardun would labor so to make such a gift to me."

"Of course they would labor to honor you," Gisela said. "You are to be their mistress."

Bertrice's smile was faintly uncertain. "Will they love me for that, I wonder?"

"Of course they will."

Who wouldn't love Bertrice? Gisela reflected with a touch of bitterness. Gisela herself had tried all afternoon to despise the woman. She had failed miserably —she who had more reason than anyone to loathe her. Who at Ardun, therefore, could not love the child?

And Bertrice did seem a child in many ways, though she was Gisela's elder by a year. Her innocence, honesty, and needfulness were unflagging, just as in a child. Gisela wished her rival were cynical, vain, pompous, or cruel. Then she might hate her. But she wasn't any of those things.

"The evening meal will not be such a fuss as it was last night, will it?" Bertrice asked. They were examining the kirtles, tunics, and jeweled girdles that King Charles had commissioned made for her while she was still at the convent awaiting Rutgar's summons. "I should not like to appear too grand." Her hand shook slightly as she ran it along one beautiful gold kirtle. "So many people," she sighed.

" 'Twill not be such a fuss," Gisela assured her. "Last night was a feast in your honor. Usually the hall is not nearly so crowded nor chaotic."

Bertrice laughed softly. "Chaotic indeed! I did enjoy the dunking you gave Rutgar last night, Gisela. He was not overly harsh with you about it, was he?"

"Rutgar has ways of avenging himself," Gisela said, her mouth pulling up into an wry smile.

Bertrice's eyes at once grew round and worried. "Is Lord Rutgar a cruel man?"

"No." In spite of the accusations she had flung in Rutgar's face that very morning, Gisela told Bertrice the truth. "He's a strong man who does right by those who serve him—at least he does the best to his way of thinking, which is a man's way of thinking and not always understandable to a woman. But Rutgar is a good master, as masters go."

"You like him, then?"

Gisela looked down at the floor in silence, not knowing what to say. She loved Rutgar. The conqueror of Ardun should be her enemy, but he was the light of her day, the passion in her nights. But did she like him, the irritating, arrogant, insensitive, manipulative, underhanded Frankish pig?

"Yes, I see," Bertrice said softly, though Gisela was sure the girl didn't see at all. "You can be honest with me, Gisela. I can understand how hard it is for a woman not to cringe from him—I, who have lived my whole life among women. Even the man Etich, big as he is, has not the same effect upon one's spirit as Rutgar."

"Rutgar is much more bluster than bite," Gisela assured her.

"He has been the soul of consideration and kindness since I arrived," Bertrice said with a small sigh. "And yet . . . Well, we will muddle through together, won't we, Gisela? I'm so grateful to have you with me, so I may have someone to talk to. Mother Angelique always said my primary flaw was my chattering mouth. And she was right. Just look! The sun has set while I stand here and talk your ears off. Now I must rush to dress for the meal. Will you braid my hair or should I leave it loose? Nay, braid it. Hanging loose it looks so wanton, and I would not want Rutgar to think that I invite his attention."

Bertrice chattered on as Gisela sat her on a stool and attacked the task of taming the thick waves of chestnut hair. She talked of the sisters at the convent, whom she had hoped to join in holy vows. She talked of the other young women who had come to the abbey for their education. She talked of the loveliness of the convent gardens, and the sweetness of days filled with prayer, study, and the homey tasks at which the sisters spent their day.

"Your hair is finished, lady. Let me help you into a fresh gown and you may go down to the hall."

Bertrice grasped her hand as a drowning man might grab on to a branch that might keep him afloat in a flood. "You will come up with me after the meal?"

"I must help in the kitchen, lady."

"Nay! I will tell Rutgar that he must excuse you from all other duties. I must have you with me, Gisela. I need you beside me. Please."

"My lady, you needn't beg. You are mistress here, and I am but a serf. I am yours to command."

"Nay, I do not need a slave," Bertrice continued in the same pleading tone. " 'Tis a friend I need. Say you will be my friend, Gisela."

Gisela squeezed Bertrice's hand reassuringly, but couldn't meet her eyes. This woman would marry Rutgar, sleep with him, make love with him, have his children, and someday learn to love him. And Gisela would be her friend, listening to her wifely stories about her husband, watching the two of them weave a life together.

How had the skein of her life ever become so tangled?

Seventeen

"This is very beautiful indeed." Bertrice handed the sample of cloth back to Drada and smiled politely. The women of the weaving house smiled tentatively back at her. "The cloth that comes off the looms at the abbey at Gandersheim is not nearly so fine. I am most grateful for your gift of wedding clothes."

Drada nodded her head. " 'Tis our joy to be able to honor you, lady. May your union with our lord bring peace to this land."

Bertrice examined the looms, wheels, spindles, and fleeces with polite attention but no real interest. Gisela had spent the morning showing her the ins and outs of the stronghold where she would be a virtual queen, and had yet to spark anything beyond courteous regard. The vegetable cellars—which once again housed turnips, beets, beans, and onions instead of prisoners—had held no interest for her, nor had the smokehouse, the smithy, the armory, the kennels, the poultry yard, nor the byres that sheltered the cattle and sheep. The horses in the stable frightened her; she had clung to Gisela at every snort or stomp of a hoof.

"I've always much preferred to ride in a wagon than atop a horse," she'd confided to Gisela as they left. "Of course, at the convent there was little opportunity to do even that, for we seldom went beyond our own walls."

As they left the weaving house amid amiable but reserved good-byes, Gisela admitted the day was not proceeding well. Bertrice knew nothing of spinning, weaving, food preservation, cooking, meal planning, candle- or soap-making, nor any of the thousand bits of knowledge that any mistress of a domain such as Ardun needed at her fingertips. She greeted the women servants with amiable courtesy, but close proximity of a man, whether warrior, serf, or free peasant, inspired her to fold into herself like a turtle hiding in its shell. Her hands withdrew into the long sleeves of her tunic and her arms folded tightly around her middle. If she could have draped her headrail completely over her face, she would have, Gisela suspected.

To give Bertrice credit, however, she did try to treat all who greeted her with a kindly regard. She showed no distaste when the grubby children of the stronghold crowded around her, reaching out to pat her with dirty hands and vying with each other to be the loudest in demand for her attention. In the chapel where she paused to pray, she looked like a saint, Gisela thought—or at least how Gisela thought a saint should look. Composed, peaceful, so totally focused in prayer that she seemed removed from the everyday world and its petty concerns. Even Father Gaunt hesitated to disturb Bertrice when he came in wearing his finest priestly vestments. Gisela suspected that he wished to impress the new mistress of Ardun with the grandeur of his position. When Bertrice rose from her prayers to acknowledge him, he turned his greeting into an impromptu sermon about the heresies and paganism still rife in the Saxon people and cautioning her—with disapproving glances toward Gisela—against trusting too readily or keeping company with those who might endanger her soul.

"What a pompous blowhard," Bertrice whispered to Gisela as they left the chapel.

Gisela laughed and surrendered to a sudden urge to like this girl as well as pity her.

Their last stop was the herb garden Gisela had been diligently preparing for next spring in a sunny corner where the north and east palisades met.

"I helped Sister Bernarde with the herbs at the abbey," Bertrice told Gisela, her eyes sparkling with interest for the first time that day. "I've a fascination for the medicinal properties of plants. 'Tis wonderful that God gives us plants that will cleanse and heal us—if we but bother to learn of them. Rutgar mentioned to me that you are a healer. I haven't the stomach for doctoring, but I would be honored if you would share your knowledge of the plants with me."

They spent a happy hour discussing what might thrive in the garden come spring and where they could obtain herbs and plants that did not normally grow in the region. They might have carried on so all day had a spurt of activity on the practice yard not drawn Bertrice's uneasy attention.

"Perhaps we should return to the manor," Bertrice suggested.

They skirted the practice yard, where several youngsters were hacking away at the dummy post that was the inanimate opponent for the boys just starting to use the spatha. Two mounted warriors practiced with shield and lance. Several bowmen had set up targets against the palisade, and a pair of duelists fought with the sword.

The dueling pair caught Gisela's eye as they passed. No one but Etich was so big, and the only man who dared oppose Etich with the bared sword was Rutgar.

"Is that . . . ?" Bertrice's voice trailed off into a quaver.

"Yes. 'Tis he."

In spite of the day being cold and blustery, both Rutgar and Etich were stripped to their braes. The Bear boasted a fur pelt that rivaled that of his namesake; curling reddish hair covered him from his beard to his navel.

Rutgar, on the other hand, displayed more flesh than hair. The sight of him made Gisela's face grow warm. With every powerful lift and stroke of his sword, muscles rolled smoothly beneath sweat-moistened, glistening skin. She knew every scar that marked his torso, had run her fingers through the short, dense hair that arrowed from breast to groin, had cupped those tight, straining buttocks in her hands, had kissed the calluses that made his palms as hard as horn, and felt the rough skin of his hands slide gently over every inch of her soft flesh. As he moved flawlessly to the rhythm of the duel, he was power in motion, grace cast into the mold of a man.

A surge of guilt cut off the line of her thoughts. She was longing for another woman's betrothed, and that was wicked. Not only was it wicked, it was foolish. Only unhappiness could come from such lack of discipline.

A small sound of distress brought Gisela's attention back to Bertrice. All blood seemed to have drained from the girl's face, so pale was she. Her hand reached out and grasped Gisela's in a crushing grip.

"Look at that!" she moaned. "They could kill each other!"

"They but play at war," Gisela assured her. "Rutgar is the only man who dares to practice with the Bear at swords or wrestling."

"So brutal! Like beasts tearing at each other."

"We live in a brutal world. Be grateful you have such a man to protect you and yours."

"The most brutal thing I have seen at Ardun is Rutgar!" Bertrice snapped. "Who will protect me from him?" Immediately her eyes dropped in contrition. "I am sorry, Gisela. I mean no insult to Ardun or its lord. 'Tis simply that I am accustomed to the gentle, feminine surroundings of the convent."

Gisela guided Bertrice away from the practice yard, looking one last time over her shoulder at Ardun's lord. "You have no need to fear Rutgar, Bertrice."

"So he has assured me," Bertrice replied in a flat voice. "I'm sure Lord Rutgar is a fine and honorable man. I'm told King Charles values him greatly and calls him friend. Mother Angelique believes this is a very advantageous marriage for the orphaned daughter of a minor Saxon noble." She sighed and darted a fearful glance back toward the practice yard. "He is so big, though. So savage. When I am near him I feel that one glance from his eyes will break me into pieces. A man such as Rutgar has no gentleness in him."

Gisela knew how wrong Bertrice was. She remembered how Rutgar's hands and lips could coax and caress. She recalled his eyes in the glow of the lamp beside his bed, how they would soften from iron gray to quiet mist as he looked at her lying beside him. A shaft of pure, hot jealousy shot through her at the thought that all his gentleness as well as his power and passion would belong to Bertrice, a woman who didn't want them. For a moment Gisela choked on her pain, unable to speak.

"Now I've offended you," Bertrice lamented as they paused on the steps into the manor. "You are right, Gisela. I should be grateful for such a strong man. I should learn to love him. But from the time I left Stringau and was welcomed into the convent, all my love was for God and the beautiful life the sisters led as the brides of Christ. Now the king declares I shall be the bride of a warlord."

Gisela laid a comforting hand on the girl's arm, jealousy and pity warring within her. "Rutgar will make you happy, Bertrice. He is a better man than you think."

Bertrice sighed and lowered her head. "I will do my best to be a good wife, with God's help. Happiness is not necessary."

"Maid Gisela!" Guntar pelted up the steps toward them, his breath puffing raggedly into the cold air like clouds of smoke from a mythical dragon. "Gisela, come quickly! Geoff got slashed by that old boar that's penned over by the cow byre!"

"Oh mercy!"

"He was showing off for Luitgard—walking on the rail of the pen, and he fell. That nasty old pig would've killed him, but Luitgard pulled him out before the boar got him too bad!"

"Tell them not to move him while I fetch my medicines."

"Yes'm." He bobbed a little bow to Bertrice before running off with his message.

"I will help you," Bertrice volunteered in a small voice.

"Lady, I think 'tis best that you not." What to do with Bertrice, who was probably fragile-spirited enough to swoon at the sight of a messy wound? The answer walked out of the chapel just then—Lothar. "You wanted to know more about the relics in the chapel, my lady. Here is the man who can tell you."

Lothar was happy to offer Bertrice escort while Gisela attended to Geoff. Gisela watched for a moment as the two of them walked together toward the chapel. Lothar looked down at his cousin and said something, and Bertrice's beatific smile glowed from her face. The fearful little convent flower seemed comfortable enough with Lothar, who was a warrior by trade and almost as big as Rutgar. But then, Lothar was her cousin, and family of a sort, and he had a truly gentle heart. While fighting came naturally to Rutgar, it came to Lothar only with great effort. Perhaps Bertrice sensed the difference.

With a sigh, Gisela hurried off to the infirmary.

Two days later, Rutgar, Bertrice, Gisela, Lothar, Odo, and ten armed men set out for Stringau. Bertrice desired to visit the home of her childhood before her wedding, or so went the story that all Ardun believed. Gisela knew the truth of it: that the journey to inspect the other half of Rutgar's domain was simply another excuse to postpone the wedding preparations.

The day was a miserable one, and from what Gisela could see, Rutgar's mood matched the glowering clouds and cold drizzle. His ill humor wasn't a result of the weather, for he had been quite similarly bad-tempered the day before, and the day before that, when the sun had been brilliant in a bright blue sky. Nearly everyone felt the sharp edge of his tongue, and even Adalinde had stayed out of his way these past days. Gisela didn't need to fear crossing his path, for she was with Bertrice when duty did not call her to the infirmary, and Bertrice scampered away like a little mouse whenever Rutgar was near.

The rain grew harder as the morning hours passed, but Rutgar and his men seemed impervious to the cold water pelting down upon them and the half-frozen mud that splashed up from beneath the horses hooves. Gisela also paid little attention to the misery of the day, for her mind was occupied in its own troubles. Contradictory emotions fought a war within her that rivaled any battle old men remembered over their tankards of ale.

Since Gisela had started serving Rutgar's bride-to-be, Ardun's lord hadn't made a single move to return her to his bed. In one way Gisela was relieved that he had recognized the finality of her decision; in another, she was hurt that he had given up the fight so easily. Emotions were contrary things, Gisela decided morosely. Life would be a good deal easier without them. Less interesting, but easier.

All in all, Gisela had enough on her mind to make her forget about the rain and cold. Bertrice was not similarly blessed, however. Though she said little, dejection was plain to read on her face. She sat uneasily upon her mount and was entirely unsuccessful in convincing the beast it should move at anything faster than a plodding walk, therefore slowing the entire party.

The night caught them well short of Stringau, the weather and the women both stretching what was normally a one-day trip into two. They camped in a grove of birch and pine. The men-at-arms quickly erected three tents: one for the women, one for Rutgar, Lothar, and Odo, and another for themselves.

Gisela wanted nothing more than to crawl into her blankets and sleep. Her body was cold to the very core, her backside was sore from riding, and her spirit was tattered from the incessant raging of emotions across the battlefield of her heart. Bertrice was not ready for sleep, however. As soon as they had retired to the privacy of their tent, the dejection that had sat upon her face all the long day took voice, sobbing out in tears and hiccups of misery. "Did you see the expression on his face?" she sobbed.

"Whose face?"

"Rutgar's! All day long he's looked like he could chew up iron spikes. He's scarcely spoken to me in two days."

Gisela sighed. She didn't bother to mention that Rutgar had scarcely been talking to anyone.

"Oh, Gisela! Obedience to the king is my duty. I must accept it. But it is very hard. All day I've been watching Rutgar and telling myself I should be grateful he's such a fearful man. I'm safe with him to protect me. But I cannot help how I feel."

She continued her sobbing. Gisela began to feel more pity for Rutgar than for the sad little would-be nun. She lay back on her blankets, weary of trying to convince Bertrice of what a fine husband Rutgar would make. She doused the little oil lamp that lit the tent. "You should try to sleep, lady. Tomorrow will be another long day."

Bertrice's crying gradually smoothed into the shallow, even breathing of slumber. Gisela wished she could fall asleep as easily. She stared into the darkness and wondered if she could manage the night without a last trip outside to relieve herself, and decided she could not.

The sentry nodded to her as she headed toward the thicket that she and Bertrice had found earlier. "Don't go far, maid. There might be beasts prowling about."

The clouds had scattered, leaving only wind-tattered remnants to play hide-and-seek with the moon. The birch grove had a ghostly cast in the darkness, tree trunks glowing faintly white in the moonlight, bare branches stretching toward the sky in dark and skeletal supplication.

It was no wonder that the sentry was uneasy, for the darkness was alive with subtle sound. Small creatures rustled in the damp vegetation, dead leaves rattled in the night breeze, and water dripped and spattered like the quiet conversation of fairies. The night sounds held no fear for Gisela, however. The forest was a welcoming haven, even damp and cold as it was. The Earth Mother's bosom, Gersvinda had called it—a place where all creatures could find shelter and comfort.

By the time Gisela found her thicket, the camp had been swallowed by the darkness behind her. Gisela tended to her business, then lingered, reluctant to return. Back at the camp her troubles awaited her, coiled like snakes in her blankets, where she had left them behind to go into the clean, comforting night. They could not follow her here, where the forest soothed her heart and guarded her as a mother might guard a hurt child.

In the far distance a wolf howled. Gisela smiled, thinking of Silver. The howl was not his, but belonged perhaps to a cousin or sister or aunt. She wished Silver might step out of the night, so she could bury her face in his warm, plush fur and forget that she had to go back to her tent, to her blankets, to the snakes of turmoil waiting there.

As if she had conjured up her wish, the thicket rustled as a figure emerged stealthily from the brush—not a wolf, but a man. Faint moonlight gleamed off a flash of white teeth as Rutgar grinned.

Gisela sprang into instant flight, but she wasn't quick enough. Rutgar grabbed her and pulled her back into the thicket.

"Quiet, little maid. 'Tis only me. Would you bring the whole camp down upon us?"

Gisela mumbled in protest, and he released her. "What are you doing here?" she whispered.

"I might ask the same of you."

"I was attending to the call of nature."

He grinned. "When I saw you, I was hoping you were attending to the call you heard from me."

"Were you calling?"

"Not aloud, witch maid. I'd though perhaps your magic had allowed you to hear the call of my need."

She sniffed indignantly. "What you need is to visit your wooing upon your bride-to-be, my lord, not me."

"She would rather do without my attentions."

"I didn't notice you stopping when I expressed a desire to do without your attentions."

He sighed. "Ah, Gisela. I'm not a warrior of words. Still your sharp tongue and sit beside me a while. The day has been a long one, and I came out here for a dose of peace, not an argument."

Gisela had come for peace, as well. She saw no real reason why she couldn't share it with Rutgar. A half rotted log offerred a seat off the damp ground, and for a moment they shared it in relative peace. The tension that ran high in both of them made their peace a short one, however.

"I have missed you," Rutgar ventured into the strained silence.

"I have been close at hand, just as you ordered."

"Close at hand, but not where I want you. You are fortunate I'm such a patient man, Gisela. But I wonder how long it will take for you to realize that I'm right about your place in my life."

"You mean in your bed?"

"There too."

Gisela sniffed. "I've not changed my mind, my lord. My place in your life is serving your wife, as you ordered. Serving her, not betraying her."

"No wife expects her husband to cleave only to her. Most are grateful to be shed of a man's attentions. Where do you get the notions that are in your head?"

His frustration was like a palpable presence between them. His voice became quiet, frighteningly so. "Gisela, I am being patient with you, but my patience will not last forever. I am still your master, and when I choose, you will forget these womanish notions and come back to me."

He reached for her, and her body rebelled when she ordered it to retreat. She stayed beside him, close enough to see the determined glitter of his eyes, to sense the heat and hardness of his body. His hand cupped her chin and forced her eyes to meet his. She read his hunger, frustration, and, buried deep in the gray depths, a wealth of loneliness.

Longing flooded Gisela with such force that she almost cried out. His mouth descended toward hers, temptation coming closer and closer. A tingling ache spread outward from her heart. Gisela had never wanted anything as much as she wanted his mouth upon hers, the scent of him in her nostrils, the heat of him on her skin. Her heart was weak; it could not obey the demands of her spirit.

As Rutgar's lips touched hers, Gisela felt all her noble vows shatter. He deepened the kiss, and she wanted to fold herself into him and give everything he would take. Desperately, she did the only thing she could think of to keep herself from slipping into the maw of complete surrender.

She hit him.

Eighteen

An instant after her fist crashed against Rutgar's face Gisela realized what she'd done. A serf who struck her master could die in a number of inventive punishments, none of them pleasant. She gasped at her own foolish audacity.

Rutgar's eyes burned into hers. "Witch!" He spat out the name as if this time he believed it.

Still stunned by her own action, Gisela didn't resist when he jerked her toward him and savaged her mouth in a bruising kiss. Roughly he forced her mouth open; his tongue thrust inside, taking possession of her very breath. A fire fueled by both anger and passion leapt inside her. Gisela's nails dug into Rutgar's thick woolen cloak. Had his back been bare, she might have shredded it. Her tongue fought with his. Her teeth bit at his lips, and he nipped and bit in return.

When he released her, Gisela gasped for breath. All she could see in the darkness were his eyes looking down at her, the cold light of the moon glowing in their depths. The fire inside her calmed to a warm, liquid longing. The lines of his face seemed to soften to reflect her own mellowing, and when his mouth came down upon hers again his kiss carried more passion than anger.

Rutgar whispered her name against her lips. Gisela lapped up the sound of his voice, savored the feel of his hard body against hers, melted against the thick ridge of his arousal that pressed into her belly. She had missed him, starved for him, and now was overwhelmed by the feast of sensation his embrace brought to her. He moved against her, thrusting with his hips. His hands captured her buttocks and rubbed her against him. She melted, floating in a warm sea of desire, forgetting Aelrhane, the forest, the night, the cold. Knowing only the man who held her.

"Come with me," he moaned into her mouth. "My tent. We'll oust the others to find another bed."

A cold trickle of reality chilled the edges of Gisela's passion. She remembered Bertrice, sleeping innocently in her blankets, trusting Gisela to be her friend.

She pushed Rutgar away. "I can't."

He drew her close again, his warm hands slipping from her shoulders, down her arms, and up to slowly caress the sides of her breasts. She closed her eyes. "I can't."

"You can. You will."

"No. Nothing has changed."

She pushed at him, but he held her. "God rot it, Gisela! I want you! I need you, goddamnit!"

"Let me go!"

She twisted out of his grasp and fled toward the camp before she could change her mind and succumb to the demands of her yearning. Every fiber of her being seemed to hum with the need to go back to him, but she didn't. She ran heedlessly, stumbling over roots and stones, picking herself up from the wet ground and running again. And as she ran she cursed the king for his schemes, Rutgar for his determined passion, and herself for her weakness.

Bertrice stood in the center of Stringau's hall and surveyed the cold harshness of the bare stone walls. She scarcely remembered the place, even though it had been her home until she was twelve years old. She did remember that hangings had softened the walls when her mother had been alive. One had shown a scene on a Saxon ship where prisoners were being sacrificed to the god of war—a reminder of the ancient days when Saxon ships had raided freely up and down the coast of Europe. Others had pictured tales of the Frost Giants, the Great Earth Serpent, and Loki, the immortal mischief-maker. Her favorite had shown the Fenris Wolf in all his fearful evil. It had made her shiver whenever she looked at it, and many a childish nightmare had formed around the evil-looking beast with his long fangs, but it had fascinated her all the same.

They were gone now, though. All the hangings, the woven wool rugs that had once covered the floor, the cushions that her mother had lovingly embroidered to pad her father's chair. Now the hall was bare and cold as a tomb. The walls of the hall were damp and cold; the floors uncovered by anything but the day's accumulation of dirt; the chambers above the hall were bare and unwelcoming as stone caves. Stringau seemed an appropriate place to be ruled by a man who was also without softness or refinement.

"This place is such a mess!" Gisela tripped down the stairs. Her face was smudged and cobwebs were woven into into her hair like a delicate net. "But the steward showed me where the furnishings are stored—your family had some wonderful things, my lady. Oh, good. The fires on the hearth have been lit. Soon it will be warmer in here. The kitchen and pantry are quite clean—cleaner than the rest of the manor, at least. They're the only places that have seen much activity over the past years, I think." Gisela ran a finger through the sooty deposit that coated a stone wall. "Eccch! A good bit of vinegar and lye are needed here."

Bertrice attempted to look interested as Gisela rattled on with plans of making Stringau into a livable home once again. For one who had looked quite pale and despondent when they had arrived here this morn, Gisela certainly showed a lot of energy now—an almost desperate energy. Bertrice herself found little interest in such a project, and she didn't know why she allowed Gisela to talk her into going along with such nonsense. She wished intensely that she herself were but a simple serf girl with an uncomplicated life that left room for enthusiasm over such simple things.

By the time the evening meal was served, the hall was warm and clean, thanks to Gisela. Bertrice toyed with her food while Rutgar and Lothar conversed with the steward about defenses, stored grain, and the estate's records—subjects of absolutely no interest to her. She made an excuse to retire early—a headache, which Mother Angelique had once told her was a feminine reason for getting out of almost anything. The thought of the dear abbess made Bertrice suddenly and painfully homesick. The wise old nun had often assured her that God would never ask anything of her that she couldn't bear. Bertrice was beginning to suspect in that one thing, at least, the good abbess had been mistaken.

When Gisela came up to their chamber, Bertrice didn't want to talk. She didn't want to be cheered, or to talk about how fine Stringau was, or listen to her maid's dutiful encouragements. She sent the girl to her pallet, and when she was certain that Gisela was asleep, she donned her mantle, stole through the sleeping manor house, and slipped into the night. The moon was high, and she quite easily found her way onto the platform that ran the length of the log palisade. There she stood looking into the night, shedding the troubles of the past few weeks and letting her mind go blank. She had discovered as a child in the convent that the quiet of a dark night could often soothe away the troubles of the day. The night air was a balm, the moon and stars reminders that human concerns and troubles were insignificant in the glory of God's universe.

"Gisela? Is that you?"

Bertrice turned with a gasp to see a tall figure coming toward her. Instinctively she poised to flee. Once before Rutgar had found her in just such an isolated place, and she didn't care to repeat the experience.

"Bertrice! What are you doing here? Wait!" The intruder brushed the hood of his cloak from his head. " 'Tis only I. Lothar."

Bertrice expelled a sigh of relief. "Lothar! I thought

perhaps it was . . . well, I didn't know who it was. 'Tis very late."

"Aye. That it is. What are you doing up here? Is something amiss?"

"No. Of course not. I often wander out late at night to speak to the moon and stars." She smiled whimsically. "Sounds silly, doesn't it?"

"Not at all. I've been known to do that a time or two myself. This is a very peaceful time of day. The most peaceful, perhaps."

"A warrior who values peace? How strange."

Lothar smiled. "Very few of us in this world have a choice of what our lives will be. Wielding sword and lance would not have been my choice, but for a nobleborn man there are few other paths to follow."

"Yes. I suppose. You are not like the others, though." Bertrice raised shy eyes to Lothar's face, and realized her words were true. Most Saxon warriors boasted long hair and a face full of beard, flamboyantly forked. Lothar was clean-shaven. His hair was cropped in neat waves just below his collar. His was the face of a poet, or a scholar. His eyes, also, did not belong to a fighter. They were gentle, with laughter twinkling in their depths.

With this man Bertrice felt very safe. Not because Lothar seemed devoid of a man's desires, but because she sensed a pervasive gentleness in him. Warrior or not, he would never hurt anything if he could help it. Of that she was strangely certain.

"Like what others, Cousin?"

Bertrice instantly lowered her eyes, mortified by the unseemly focus of her attention. "The other warriors," she explained quietly. "Rutgar, Etich, the men who ride with them."

"Rutgar is a fine and honorable man."

"Yes, I know he is."

Bertrice stood for a while looking out into the night, silent but very aware of the man beside her.

"I scarcely recognized you when I first saw you," Lothar told her. "You were but a child when you left. Now you are a beautiful woman."

"Am I beautiful?"

"Aye. You are."

Bertrice smiled. "I remember you from the years before, when my father and mother were still alive and each year at Midsummer Day we would visit Ardun for feasting and games. You were but a gangly boy. You . . . you never seemed very happy."

"I wasn't, but I've learned to accept what I cannot have."

"And what is that?"

He shook his head and smiled gently.

Bertrice looked down at her feet. "I have almost no family left besides you, Lothar, and yet I do not feel as though you are family. We have not been together in so long."

Lothar hesitated for a moment, then spoke. "You have Gisela also."

"Gisela?"

"I suppose she did not come to Ardun until after you had gone to the convent. She is your cousin, just as I am. Ercangar was her father, though he never acknowledged her. All at Ardun know she is his."

"But why . . . ?"

"Her mother was Ercangar's mistress, but he put her aside shortly before Gisela was born. I think perhaps he feared the power she had over the people."

Bertrice huffed in contempt. "Men still cling to the *friedelehe*—even though the Church does not recognize the old way of marrying. And the Church should not. 'Tis the women who suffer in such unsanctified casual arrangements that can be set aside so easily. Now poor Gisela suffers because her mother was *friedelehe*."

Lothar shook his head. "Gisela suffers more because her mother was Gersvinda. She was a very powerful witch. Some say Ercangar was ensorcelled by her power—perhaps even Ercangar believed that."

"Poor Gisela."

"Gisela has powers of her own. She will find her way in the world."

Lothar looked at Bertrice in a manner that suddenly made her feel awkward, but she didn't want him to leave. With him she was more content than she had been since she had first ridden through the gates of Ardun as Rutgar's betrothed. She couldn't resist the urge to reach out and touch his face. "You are a good man, Lothar. If the world were different, if I were not promised, if we were not so closely blood-tied . . ."

His long, supple fingers closed around her hand, but he did not take it from his face. "You are beautiful, Bertrice."

For an eternal moment they stood looking at each other, until Lothar finally cleared his throat and backed up a step. "I . . . I envy you your time at the abbey," he said quietly. "To my father's great distress, 'twas always my chief ambition to give myself to the Church. I petitioned him to gain me admittance to one of the king's schools, for they take all bright and willing students who wish to learn, not just the sons of the great families. I wanted to attain enough learning to become a priest."

Bertrice's heart swelled with admiration. "You would make a fine priest. But . . . you do not need to be learned to take your vows. I have heard of ignorant serfs being ordained simply so there may be someone able to perform the holy offices at their lord's command. Sometimes they have not even enough learning to read the Scriptures."

"So have I heard, also, though Father Gaunt reads and writes well enough. But I think those chosen to speak for the Church and for God should be the most knowledgeable and wisest among us."

"I too!" declared Bertrice, feeling a swell of longing. "I wish you could know the joy of the religious life, Lothar. It lifts one high—so high. To be able to spend the day in prayer and contemplation, to escape the cares and distractions of this mortal world . . ."

She sighed, and looked up to find Lothar's face very close to hers. Without thinking about it she offered her mouth for his kiss, and he took it. Gently, reverently, and then with a passion that inspired an ecstasy within her that was anything but holy.

Suddenly frightened, she cringed back and pushed him away. "What are we doing?"

"Cousin . . . !" Lothar reached out to her. Shaken, confused, she let him draw her to him for comfort. "Bertrice, sweet cousin, you were not meant to be any mortal man's wife. And my devotion also will always belong first to God. But in the sad vale of this earth, let my affection for you shine like a pure and holy light. I admit my love for you, Cousin, but 'tis not a sinful love. 'Tis only right to worship one of God's most lovely creations."

Bertrice inhaled sharply. "God may not have meant me to be wife to a mortal man, but the king has declared that I will be wife indeed, and to a man very much of this world, a man reeking of worldly power and violence."

"Bertrice. Rutgar is a good man. Twice he has

spared my life when it would have been more convenient to kill me. The people of Ardun are learning to trust and respect him, and you will also, my dearest one."

Bertrice bowed her head in acquiescence. "I will do what is required of me by God and king." She raised her eyes to Lothar's. "I would never importune upon your honor, Cousin. But I would have you know that if I must marry in this world, I would that it were you instead of Rutgar. If ever I could learn to be content with a man, 'twould be you."

Lothar placed a chaste kiss upon her brow, and together they let the night bring peace to their souls.

Adalinde swept through Ardun's hall like like a stiff, dark broom, seeking dust, soot, and litter. "Atruda, do you call this hearth clean? 'Tis not clean, you lazy girl. Clean it! And then find someone to help you replace these filthy rushes."

"They were replaced but yesterday, mistress."

"They stink today. Replace them!"

"Yes, mistress."

"Gillan! Get those hounds out of here and back to the kennel. Do you want the wedding guests to believe we live with those noisy, quarreling, smelly animals underfoot all the time?"

"But we do."

"Not while guests are here. Get them out!"

Earlier Adalinde had inspected the bedchambers and kitchen, giving Ermentrude and every one of the housewomen pounding headaches. Wedding guests would be arriving that afternoon—some had already arrived. By tomorrow evening they would all be here —some making the journey from as far east as Hamburg and others coming from as far south as Bremen and Verdun. It appeared that the arrogant Rutgar was one of the king's favorites, for all the king's counts and vassals within two days' ride wanted to show their support—or curry Rutgar's favor—by being present at the auspicious occasion of his wedding. The king himself was far too busy with court intrigue and his wars to attend, of course, but he had designated a highborn bishop from Aquitaine and a favored count from Thuringia to be his *missi dominici*—deputies to represent the royal presence and also to ascertain the condition of the properties Rutgar held in the name of the king.

Adalinde would have liked to send the *missi* back to their cursed king with instructions on what he could do with one of the sharp points of his royal crown.

"Guntar!"

"Yes, mistress?"

"Tell your grandmother I want more women in the manor. The looms can be still for one day. And hurry about it. There's work to be done."

"Yes, mistress."

As Guntar ran off to do her bidding, Adalinde caught a glimpse of Bertrice on the landing at the top of the stairs. When their eyes met, the cowardly mouse of a girl bit her silly lip and fled toward her bedchamber. Adalinde snorted. Her blood ran in Bertrice's veins, yet the girl had less backbone than a worm. Bertrice had to know that her marriage would cement Rutgar's position in what had once been the one of the proudest Saxon domains. She should have refused the marriage and told the Frankish king to burn in his Christian hell. Adalinde had entertained hopes that she might do so, particularly when Rutgar had continued his lustful pursuit of Gisela after Bertrice had arrived. But the emptyheaded fool couldn't see past her nose to the insult her betrothed had dealt her. And Gisela—another fool—had fended off her lover when she should have flaunted his indiscretion in front of Bertrice's very eyes. Surely Gisela realized that unless Bertrice was driven back to her convent, the Saxon cause at Ardun was lost.

The door to the hall banged open and Rutgar strode in, looking like a thundercloud. The servants glanced at him uneasily, then hurried back to their work. Indeed, he'd been more curt and impatient than usual since his return from Stringau. He and Bertrice had little to say to each other, it seemed, and Gisela fled whenever Rutgar was near. She seemed to sense his coming even before he appeared, and scampered to wherever he was not.

"Adalinde," Rutgar greeted her.

"My lord."

"Has the bishop arrived yet?"

"He sent a messenger ahead to say his party would arrive tomorrow, my lord."

Rutgar grunted. For a man who was about to acquire a beautiful wife and cement a political position as well, he seemed little pleased.

"Have you seen Gisela?"

Adalinde raised a thin, black brow. "I believe she went to the forest, to the pond known as the fairy pool."

"She left the stronghold without escort?"

Adalinde's mouth twitched in a smile. "I believe so."

"And you did not prevent her?"

"There is no need to raise your voice, my lord." The truth was that Adalinde herself had encouraged Gisela to go to the pool, knowing that Rutgar would ask her whereabouts—as he did every day—and hoping she could send him after her. It suited her purpose to have their passion reignite. "I beg your pardon, Lord Rutgar, but it was my understanding that Gisela had the freedom to do what she pleased."

"Not to go into the forest without protection, the dim-witted little idiot! Christ's holy bones, if God had to put women on this earth, why didn't he at least give them brains?"

Adalinde watched impassively as the invader marched furiously out of the hall, but her heart gave a leap of hope. Such high passion the man had when he was angry! How could Gisela resist? Indeed, she still had hopes that one of her granddaughters would still save the Saxon cause.

Nineteen

The sun was high, but within the forest the world was damp and shadowed, redolent with the pungency of wet wood and rotting vegetation. The farther Rutgar rode the thicker the forest became, until the denuded branches and prickly thickets tangled together in an almost impenetrable barrier. Finally he dismounted and tethered Doomsayer to a tree—just as he'd done months ago when he had first ridden this way in search of Edgar and Notker. And he'd found Gisela —disrespectful, disobedient, troublemaking, irresistible Gisela.

Rutgar pushed through the bare shrubbery, his temper growing more frayed with every step. His addlewitted little witch suffered a foolishness that knew no bounds. She might have the forest animals at her feet, but Aelrhane was another sort of creature entirely. Rutgar did not want to contemplate what the rebels might do to Gisela for what they must think of as her betrayal. She might naively think they wouldn't harm her, but she was little acquainted with man's baser nature. Gisela thought Rutgar a beast, but she might learn he was a lamb—in some ways at least—compared to Aelrhane.

The forest dampness condensed into a thick white fog as he walked, and the air seemed to grow warmer. Then the little pool was before him. With a warrior's instinctive caution, he drew back into the tangle of thickets without a sound. The little pond looked like a scene plucked out of time, for the warmth of the water and the air around it made the banks softly green and mossy even while the surrounding forest was bare. Steam rose from the water's glassy surface and curled through the fog in eerie tendrils.

Nothing else in the scene seemed alive. All else was frozen—even Gisela, who was little more than a shadow in the mist. She knelt in the shallows, so still that for one moment Rutgar fancied that some magical spell held her entranced.

Then she stirred. Her head tilted back, and her arms rose from her sides, making the steam swirl around her in veils of filmy white. Her fingertips trailed streamers of mist. Her hair shone golden even in the ghostly dim light. She was naked, clothed only in beauty.

Rutgar's heart and loins tightened in a mighty spasm. His anger fell away, leaving only longing and tenderness. He realized then that he would never be free of this woman. She was bound to him with more than the ties of serfdom, and he was tangled so completely in her coils that no hope of escape remained. No matter how she might resist him or how he might tell himself that he merely used her, theirs was a union that went beyond Church or politics or even their own preferences. She might despise him for what he was and what he did, but he would never let her go. Since the day he had first been sent from his home to fight in the king's armies, Rutgar had prided himself on needing only himself. Now honesty compelled him to admit that he needed someone else; he needed Gisela with such intensity that he might die of it.

Careless of noise, Rutgar stood. The snapping of twigs broke the eerie peace. Like a startled woodsprite, Gisela spun to face him. The mist whirled with her, spiraling around her naked torso in a sensuous path that Rutgar itched to follow with his hands.

"You!" Her voice was hushed and vibrated with tones of suprise and—was it welcome? Was it possible that despite her stubborn refusals, she needed him as much as he needed her?

"You should not be here," Rutgar said mildly.

Her chin tilted up. She stood proudly, unashamed of her glorious nakedness. "None would dare assault me in this place."

Except Rutgar. His eyes never left her as he pulled off his boots and removed his cloak. "The water looks warm."

A slight smile tilted her mouth. " 'Tis said that this pool will swallow whole any trespasser who dares venture within."

"You are still here."

"I am a witch."

Grinning, Rutgar unwrapped his leggings, discarded his tunic and his braes. "If your pool likes witches, it should like me as well."

"Why?"

He stepped into the water. "Because I am a witch's lover."

The pool was indeed warm, and so was the steam that curled about his legs like a living thing, swirling upward over his hips and chest as if it would taste him. Gisela's eyes widened in surprise. She backed away, then stopped. A soft tendril of mist uncurled from her fingers and stretched toward him.

He touched her. She quivered, ready to spring away yet somehow frozen in wait of his caress. "Don't fight me, Gisela. Don't refuse me."

Rutgar's restraint was at an end. Like a man starving he devoured Gisela's tempting mouth. Her lips opened beneath his; her tongue met his thrusts with a hesitant welcome. The mist wet her skin, making it slick and warm. His hands slid down the curve of her back and found her buttocks—lovely, firm mounds made to fit perfectly into the cup of his fingers. He pressed her against his own nakedness and felt her melt against him.

"Gisela," he whispered against her lips. "Gisela, I've been cruel to you. Forgive me."

Her eyes were soft with passion and bright with the beginning of tears. She touched his cheek. "What is this? The mighty warlord begs forgiveness?"

A smile twitched at his mouth. The muscles felt unused, he had not smiled in so long a time—not since she'd torn herself from him. "A rare occurrence," he assured her. "I should not have made you serve Bertrice." With infinite tenderness he brushed the wet gold of her hair back from her elfin face. "But you made me very angry. 'Tis a weakness when a man needs a woman so, he becomes ruled by his emotions, whether they be anger or desire. I wanted to hurt you, and to punish you, so I forced you to bow down to Bertrice."

Some of the warmth left Gisela's eyes as she drew back. "Bertrice is a most gentle and considerate lady. She deserves well of you."

He could almost see Gisela fold in upon herself, like a blossom that seeks to protect its heart from the cold night. Rutgar refused to let her go. His hands tightened around her waist.

"Bertrice will receive well of me. But I don't wish to speak of Bertrice. She is the woman the king gives me. As he orders the troops of his armies, so he orders the lives of men and women with conquests and political maneuverings in mind. You are the woman who sets my body aflame and has the power to trouble my heart. You have cast a spell over me, Gisela. Not a witch's spell, but a woman's."

She shook her head in silent denial, but he held her fast. The mist swirled between them, and even though he touched her only at her waist, his skin tingled as if her soft flesh were everywhere against his, inciting him to a need that was hot and urgent. Seeming to experience the same phenomenon, Gisela's eyes grew languid and her head fell back in irresistible invitation. He lowered his mouth to the hollow of her throat and sucked away the warm water that gathered there. Then he bent her back and suckled gently at her full, taut breast, filled with both a child's longing and a man's. For a moment she grew soft in his grasp. A small sigh escaped her lips. When he lowered her into the warm, shallow water and pillowed her head on the moss that grew at the pool's edge, she struggled against his domination only feebly.

"Nay, Rutgar. Please."

"I cannot let you go," he said softly. "I've used you cruelly, and—God help me—I'll do so again if need be to keep peace in this land; but mostly I've wanted you for myself. Touching you brings me the joy that water brings to a man who has thirsted all his life."

As Rutgar moved against her, warm currents eddied around them as if the pool had a life of its own. He lifted her to his seeking mouth and she grew soft and pliable in his hands. Her breasts were a feast that only sharpened his hunger, her belly a delicacy that tantalized his desire. He tasted lower, opening her with his tongue teasing until she cried out for him to take her completely.

He returned to her mouth, allowing his torso to slide enticingly over her belly and breasts. She moved beneath him, fitting them more closely together, and he felt a surge of power greater than any he'd ever experienced in battle.

"Water?" Golden eyes twinkled up at him, their brightness no longer clouded by doubt. "I'm like water to a thirsty man? Not even wine?"

He kissed the teasing slant of her smile.

"You need practice with your seduction speeches, my lord."

"Do I?" He lifted himself from her, depriving her body of his, and was gratified to see her smile falter. "You're overbold for a mere wench."

"So you've told me." Her fingers circled his nipples and drifted over his chest, teasing, coaxing. Rutgar thought he might burst with need. Their play had become a contest of self-control—and the witch was winning. He shook his head and flung himself backward into the pool, surfacing to see Gisela sputtering and wiping water from her face. Her eyes locked with his as she laughed and leaned back onto the bank, her impudent breasts thrust upward and her legs parted in shameless invitation. Rutgar groaned aloud, shaken with the fury of his own desire. The witch had won their little game, and surrender was going to be sweet. She was there, waiting for him, and his only thought was to take her. He dove beneath the surface. The water stroked him as he swam, its touch driving him to frenzy. He surfaced between her legs, which closed around his hips in welcome. The wave of his momentum drove him forward, and he buried himself in her sweet, slick warmth. She rose to meet his thrust, clinging to him, crying. He thrust, and thrust again, far beyond the point where he could be gentle, but Gisela needed no coaxing to respond. Her legs wrapped around him and urged him on. She met his passionate savagery with her own fire, taking him deep within her, rocking with him, opening to him, clasping him with her body until he lost the knowledge of where he stopped and she began. The first wave of her climax triggered his. He threw his head back and cried in triumph as their bodies locked together, rigid in ecstasy.

Long after he was drained and limp, Rutgar clasped Gisela to him, loath to release her. They slipped farther into the warmly welcoming water, her face buried in the hollow of his throat, her legs still wrapped around him in intimate embrace. Content to lie there, Rutgar felt Gisela's breathing slow and the muscles of her body relax, one by one. The need still filled him. It didn't quiet even when his body was satiated and limp with satisfaction. This need was a thing foreign to his life. He wasn't sure he liked it; it turned the gray plain of his existence into bright highs and black lows. But like it or not, there was no escaping it.

Just as there was no way for Gisela to escape him.

Exhausted by a confusing combination of guilt, elation, and melancholy, Gisela slumped in Rutgar's firm grip as Doomsayer plodded quietly along the forest trail. A cold night gathered around them. The leaves under Doomsayer's hooves crackled with frost, and her breath combined with Rutgar's in an icy cloud. Above the featureless blackness of the forest, the cold sky was lit with a million pinpricks of light. The combination of drear darkness and jeweled splendor fit her mood exactly.

"We have sinned," she told Rutgar with a sigh.

He kissed the side of her neck. A chill shivered down her spine in reply.

"We haven't sinned," Rutgar said against her ear. "There is too little pleasure in this life for us to discard this one as sin. Besides, I wouldn't expect a woman reputed to be a witch to be overly concerned with such a notion."

"I am a Christian, baptized as your wretched king commanded."

"*Our* wretched king."

She was silent.

"Be as it may, you are a Christian witch. Do you believe that God is marking every offense you commit in some great ledger so He may damn your soul to perdition?" He chuckled. "If so, I assure you that God will have very little company in heaven and the Church will have a very great congregation in hell."

"You make a jest of it."

He kissed the back of her neck.

"But what we did was wrong!" She tried to ignore

the tremors of warmth where his lips caressed her skin. With a great effort of will, she wrenched herself away and twisted to look back at him. "In two days you will take holy vows with Bertrice."

He scowled. "I told you that I didn't want to talk of Bertrice."

"Do you think not talking of her will make her disappear?"

"I don't want Bertrice to disappear, Gisela. She will be my wife. There is no connection between my marriage and what I feel for you."

Gisela uttered a soft curse and faced forward again. Rutgar's arms tightened about her. His breath was warm in her hair.

"Will you continue to fight me, Gisela?"

She was silent.

"You'll never win, buglet. You can't hold yourself from me any more I can keep from taking you. Bertrice will be content. I will give her security and children, but you I will give my passion."

Gisela turned her head so that her cheek rested against the warm wool of his tunic. He draped his cloak so that it enfolded them both, and in the warmth of their cocoon, she could hear his steady heartbeat pound in his chest. She had won some portion of that heart, for all that he insisted he didn't have one. Rutgar told the truth; she could not hold herself from him, no matter how wrong her surrender might be. He was too strong, and she was not strong enough.

All the next day Gisela suffered pangs of guilt as she helped Bertrice prepare for the wedding. Rutgar had offered to release her from his bride's service. Now that he had her snared once again on the horns of his passion, there was little need for him to keep her constantly under his eye. Gisela refused. She was not comfortable bearing constant company with the woman she had wronged, but Bertrice needed her. Only Gisela knew how miserably unhappy the bride was as the nuptial day approached, for the girl put on a brave face, smiled at their guests, and was flawlessly courteous when she received the king's *missi*—the bishop who would perform the wedding ceremony and the noble count from Thuringia who would give her in marriage in the king's place. Only when she was alone with Gisela did Bertrice let her guard slip and her face fall.

Gisela feared she was not much help to her mistress's spirits, however, for she could not help going about her duties in a shamefaced depression. She was not accustomed to guilt and deception, and they did not sit comfortably on her soul. She despised herself for yesterday's surrender, and she despised herself for the surrenders she knew would come every time Rutgar summoned her. Her will was too weak to free her from the trap her heart had landed her in.

In the late afternoon of the day before the wedding, as they sat in Bertrice's bedchamber and made the final adjustments to the bride's wedding clothes, Bertrice took Gisela's hand and led her to a pair of upholstered stools that sat at the foot of the bed. There Bertrice sat facing Gisela and regarded her with a kind eye.

"My dear friend, there is no need for this long face you are wearing. I know of your tryst with Rutgar."

Gisela's heart sank.

"Nay, Gisela. Do not look so. You have not offended me. Indeed, if my lord Rutgar eased himself upon you to the point where he never touched me, I would be very content—though I would not wish his lust upon you. I suspect you had little choice in receiving his attentions."

"Did Rutgar tell you?" Gisela asked softly, scarcely believing that Rutgar would be so cruel.

"Nay. Our grandmother took great delight in informing me that the two of you were trysting in the forest yesterday."

"Our grandmother?"

"Lothar told me we were kin, dear Cousin. Others may pretend that you are merely another serf, but I cannot. I am too happy to have a woman of my own blood nearby to love."

Gisela could not keep back the tears that flooded her eyes.

"Don't cry." Bertrice wiped away the tears with the embroidered edge of her own headrail. You have not wronged me. Adalinde made much of Rutgar's lusting after you and thought I should care greatly, but truly I am relieved. I am not a person of such pride that it is so easily wounded.

They embraced, and Gisela still sniffled.

"Do you love Rutgar?" Bertrice asked, almost shyly.

Gisela nodded.

" 'Tis a wonder to me that he doesn't frighten you."

Through a shaky smile, Gisela confessed: "I am difficult to frighten. Though he has tried, and a time or two he's succeeded."

"Yet you love him." Bertrice looked at her hands for a moment, then bit her lips and regarded Gisela with misty eyes. "I believe I could feel a similar affection for . . . for Lothar. When I am with him, I am happy. We met by accident once at Stringau, on the wall—and he kissed me, or I kissed him. I don't know which it was. The feeling was . . . quite nice."

"Oh, Bertrice!" Gisela exclaimed sadly.

" 'Tis quite all right. I do not deceive myself with silly dreams. We're cousins, he and I, and even were I not pledged to Rutgar, I could never marry Lothar. The Church would have no reason to grant us dispensation. And there is Lothar's ambition to become a priest, and the most devoted priests don't have wives, you know. I believe someday the Church will forbid it altogether."

Through Bertrice's chatter Gisela could hear her hopeless pain.

" 'Tis what makes me admire Lothar the most, I think—his dedication to the Church." She sniffed. "You shouldn't feel bad for me, sweet Cousin. I have become quite resigned to this marriage. Truly."

Gisela squeezed her hand. "What a tangle our lives have become."

"Yes," Bertrice sighed, but she managed a brave smile. "The devil's own tangle."

"Try to keep from spilling a pitcher on anyone important," Ermentrude cautioned Gisela during the banquet the night before the wedding. "We cannot have the haughty bishop with ale running down his holy robes, now, can we? Though that Count Lucius looks as if a dousing might do him good. Don't get any notions in your head, though, girl."

As if Fate was punishing her for her transgressions, Gisela found herself with the task of serving the head table, though she had no desire to be close to Rutgar and Bertrice, or to the others who sat with them—as gloomy a group as she had ever seen. Adalinde sat straight-backed and rigid in her chair. She looked down at the celebrants with a face devoid of expression. Beside her, Bertrice toyed with her food and looked utterly miserable. Whenever Rutgar spoke to her, she tried to smile, but the resulting expression was merely a stiff stretching of her lips. Rutgar himself looked forbidding enough to frighten off someone with considerably more spirit than poor Bertrice. On Rutgar's left, the most holy Bishop Galvan ate and drank with a relish that demonstrated that his earthly appetites were undiminished by his holy office; and Count Lucius of Thuringia made sport of trying to grab each serving girl who was unfortunate enough to be within his reach. Sitting next to the count, Lothar studiously kept his gaze from Bertrice. His food was little touched, but his intake of wine and mead kept his stomach full and his eyes glazed.

How glad Gisela was when the feast was ended and the last guests had found beds—the manor, the barracks, the women's quarters, the hayloft in the stable, and even the chapel overflowed with them. The trestle tables had been wiped down and stacked neatly, and the hall vibrated with the snores of those who made their beds on the benches along the wall or laid pallets near the hearth. In the kitchen, Gisela sat at the worktable and stretched her feet toward the smoldering fire. Since being assigned to Bertrice's service, she had slept on a pallet in her mistress's chamber, but on this night Bertrice had requested the privacy to pray in solitude. Gisela felt the need of solitude herself, though the combination of the hot mead she sipped and the erratic flickers of the flames almost had her asleep. Ermentrude and her helpers already snored on pallets by the wall.

Gisela roused from a light doze when Guntar tapped her on the shoulder and whispered her name. "Is all well with you, maid?" he asked.

"Of course. Why should it not be?"

He wrinkled his nose. The uncertain light from the

hearth made his freckles seem to dance across his face. "Drada said everyone should treat you with special tenderness for a while. Are you sick?"

"No. I'm not sick. Drada is . . ." A meddling old woman, Gisela told herself silently. But Drada loved her, and the knowledge that the old woman knew how she felt somehow made the burden easier. "Drada is just thinking I'm tired," she said to Guntar.

"Oh."

"Why aren't you asleep, Guntar? Can't you find a place?"

"Ermentrude said I could sleep here. And Rutgar sent me for you. He says you should bring some wine to his chamber."

Gisela's heart dropped. Not tonight, of all nights.

"Will you take up the wine for me, Guntar?"

"Aye. If you want me to. You really are tired, aren't you, Gisela?"

"Yes, Guntar. I really am tired."

She would sleep in the infirmary, Gisela decided. There at least she would have privacy if she gave in to the tears that were building inside her. The little stone closet of a room had an empty cot that likely no one had found.

She had scarcely undressed and pulled the blankets up around her before the door slammed back and Rutgar filled the doorway. Backlit by the dim light of the torch in the hallway, he was a black shadow haloed in red—an appearance appropriate to the state of his temper.

"Guntar is a poor substitute for the one I summoned!" he snapped.

Gisela truly was tired, in spirit and body. Unwilling to fight with him, she buried her face in the thin, straw-ticked mattress.

"Gisela! Are you ill?"

Suddenly his hands were on her bare arms, turning her to face him. He rubbed up and down until her gooseflesh was replaced with the warmth of his touch.

"Are you ill? Answer me!"

A note of fear in his voice caught at her heart. "I'm not ill."

He held her a moment more, and she could feel his eyes survey her in the near darkness. Her flesh tingled wherever his gaze rested, and she loathed her own weak will.

He kicked the door shut. "Have you not so much as a candle in here?" he asked, rummaging among the things on her worktable. "Ah, here is one." Momentarily a dull orange light flickered through the darkness.

When he turned toward her, Gisela could see that his face looked as tired as she felt.

"Why did you not come?" he asked.

" 'Tis the eve of your wedding."

His smile was a dispirited one. "All the more reason why I need you tonight."

She covered her face with her hands, unable to resist the lure of his eyes. "I will not insult Bertrice so openly on this night. A woman's wedding is special. I will not lie with you in the bed that she will occupy tomorrow night."

She was surprised when Rutgar's temper didn't flare. His touch, when it came, was gentle. "This cot is very small for both of us."

He took Gisela's hands from her face and pushed her back on the cot. Holding her wrists on either side of her head, he kissed her brow, her nose, and finally her lips. He tasted of wine and smelled of pitch-smoke, sweat, and need.

"Don't refuse me tonight, Gisela. I need you."

"You know I can't refuse you. Foolish lackwit that I am, I love you."

He pulled her from the narrow cot along with the blankets and laid them all on the floor.

"We are going to be very cold here," she said as he pulled her into his arms.

"I'll make you warm. I promise."

The pounding on the infirmary door woke them.

"Gisela! Are you there?"

Lothar's voice demanded a response. Gisela shook the grogginess from her head as Rutgar cursed.

" 'Tis Bertrice!" Lothar said. "She's taken ill. Come quickly and bring your medicines."

Twenty

Bertrice was dying, and Gisela could do nothing to save her. Pale, sweating, and weak, her skin as cold as if the Dark Angel had already claimed her, Bertrice lay with her knees drawn up to her chest, clutching Gisela's hand with the desperation of pain. She would permit no one else in the chamber except little Luitgard, who, wide-eyed and quiet, regularly removed soiled linen and used basins and replaced them with clean ones. At regular intervals Bertrice tried to vomit, but there was nothing left in her stomach to come up. She expelled blood instead—from every orifice possible—and convulsed in spasms that left her panting and spent.

Gisela had given Bertrice infusions of slippery elm and meadowsweet to ease her stomach, and white willow for the pain, but her affliction was much too brutal for such gentle remedies. Finally Gisela resorted to henbane, which could not cure, only sedate and ease the pain. When Bertrice begged for more, Gisela shook her head reluctantly.

"Too much of this and you will not wake."

" 'Twould be a mercy," Bertrice rasped. "I am dying anyway. How much longer must I endure before God takes me from this horror?"

Gisela squeezed her hand. She didn't want to see Bertrice give up the fight, but neither could she lie.

"A little more," Bertrice pleaded. "Just a little more to ease me. Then I must see the priest. I would not exit this world without making my confession."

"Just a bit." Gisela held the cup to Bertrice's lips, then nodded for Luitgard to fetch the priest. Bertrice clutched at her hand as Father Gaunt walked into the chamber. "You will come back?"

"Of course."

"Vow not to leave me to die among these strangers."

"You have my most sacred vow."

The priest eyed Gisela warily as she left the bedside, holding his cross before him as if it might fend her off.

In the hall, where it seemed the whole of Ardun waited and worried, Rutgar handed Gisela a tankard of mead and pulled her to the hearth. Instantly she was surrounded by questioning faces, but they retreated before Rutgar's scowl. Lothar remained, however. Hollow-eyed and pale, he looked almost as bad as Bertrice.

"What ails her?" Rutgar demanded of Gisela.

"I don't know."

Rutgar sighed with the impatience of a man accustomed to defeating enemies by the skill of his sword and strength of his arm. He did not take well to sitting helplessly by while a battle was lost.

"Is there any hope?" Lothar asked quietly.

Gisela took a deep draught of the mead. The bittersweet liquid warmed her somewhat and loosened the knot that tied her stomach, but still a stone seemed to weigh down her heart. "She is dying," she admitted dejectedly. "I have never seen an illness strike so swiftly."

Rutgar's swift, sharp gaze shot her way. "Think you this is not an illness?"

She couldn't voice the possibility that seemed too horrible to contemplate. There was no shortage of poisons that might send a person to such an agonizing death, but who would wish innocent little Bertrice such harm? Aelrhane might curse her for wedding the enemy, but even Aelrhane was not heartless enough to do this, Gisela thought. Even if her estimation of him was too generous, the Saxon rebel's arm was not long enough to reach into the stronghold from the forest.

Rutgar wiped his hand over his face as though he tried to remove some obstacle from his sight. The expression that emerged was grim and full of menace. "If someone poisoned that gentle little maid, I will find him. And when I do, he will wish he had drunk his poison himself."

Father Gaunt descended the stone stairway, a frown marring his priestly mien. When Rutgar rose with the obvious intention of going up to Bertrice's chamber, the priest laid a hand on his arm to detain him. One look at Rutgar's face persuaded the good father to withdraw his hand, and he cleared his throat uneasily.

"The lady asks only that Gisela be sent to her, my lord."

All eyes fastened upon Gisela. Rutgar's expression revealed a vulnerability she would not have guessed he possessed; the priest radiated disapproval from every righteous pore.

Father Gaunt raised his cross defensively. "Take care, witch, that you do not pollute that poor maid's soul, for she has been cleansed to meet her Maker. God will punish you tenfold if you corrupt an innocent with your sorcery."

"Be silent, priest." Rutgar's voice was cold as iron.

"I but defend your lady, my lord."

"We need to hear no more of the sorcery and demons that you have moaned about all night. Be silent or leave."

The priest pursed his lips in holy aggravation while Rutgar motioned Gisela to return to her duties.

Bertrice welcomed Gisela back with a weak smile, then promptly convulsed in a spasm more severe than any that night. Even the henbane was not strong enough to fight the convulsion. When she finally lay limp in Gisela's arms, Bertrice managed to smile. Gisela wondered at the courage of this girl she had thought so weak and fragile.

"Not long now," Bertrice breathed softly. "I see the Dark Angel in the distance." Her mouth twitched upward faintly. "I would have thought he looked like Rutgar, but he doesn't. He is beautiful. Beyond beautiful."

"Bertrice. Don't give up."

"I'm not sorry to die, Gisela. What is there for me in life but unhappiness? God is calling me to heaven as a mercy. Don't grieve. Don't let Lothar grieve."

"Rutgar would speak with you."

"Nay. I mean no insult, but I don't wish to see him now."

"At least let Lothar come to you, then."

"Lothar should not remember me like this." She croaked out a weak laugh. "How strange that I should still suffer the sin of vanity when I am so close to meeting the One whom beauty cannot deceive."

She doubled up, her upper body coming off the mattress as her muscles contracted in pain. Gisela held her as she retched and heaved, then cleaned the blood and bile from from her ashen face.

"You must comfort Lothar," Bertrice whispered as Gisela sponged her. "Promise me."

"You know I will."

"And you must cling to Rutgar, if you truly love him as you said."

Gisela could think of nothing to say.

"God has spared me the fate of becoming Rutgar's wife, so mayhap he will settle the task on someone more suited," Bertrice said with a faint smile.

"God will doubtless have His way." Gisela didn't bother to remind her cousin that noblemen did not wed serfs. They used them. On rare occasions they might even love them, but they did not wed with them.

Bertrice was silent so long that Gisela had to check her breathing to make sure she still lived. As she brought her head close to the girl's mouth, a whispered request came from the bloodless lips.

"Stay with me until I go."

Gisela lovingly stroked her cousin's face. "You know that I will."

In the private receiving room off the hall, Rutgar, Lothar, and Adalinde waited in silent vigil while Gisela waited above. Adalinde sat by the brazier, for once looking limp rather than arrow-stiff and straight. Rutgar stood by the chamber's one window, brooding into the darkness beyond. Lothar paced the length of the room. Two empty flagons of wine stood on the table, the contents of which Lothar had downed with uncharacteristic thirst, causing his steps to falter and his balance to waver. He glanced often at the door, his face dark, his lips moving with words never quite pronounced.

"You don't mourn her," he said suddenly, his gaze sweeping the other two occupants of the chamber. "You don't." He sat down hard on the padded bench beside Adalinde. "You I understand," he said to the old woman. "You never mourn anyone. But you . . ." The last word was an accusation flung at Rutgar, who turned slowly from the window and gave Lothar a cold stare.

"You're drunk, Lothar. Go to your bed. Bertrice won't see you. She won't see anyone but Gisela. Making yourself sick on drink will not help her."

"You have a stone for a heart, Rutgar. Your bride is dying, and you mourn her passing only for the loss of the alliance she brought you."

Rutgar kept an iron grip on his temper. Few men would dare to address him thus, and for good reason. He did not stand still for insult. Yet some allowance must be made for a man whose kin was dying and whose judgment was tottering from an overload of drink.

"Sit down, you fool," Adalinde ordered Lothar. She glared at both men. "Your recriminations cannot help my granddaughter, nor all your mourning, whether it be for lost love or lost power. My lord Rutgar, you realize that this is no chance illness. Someone did not like the idea of a Saxon noblewoman sharing her heritage with a Frankish warlord."

"I am not blind, lady, nor callow. I know well what manner of death has come to Bertrice of Stringau. And when I find the one responsible, your granddaughter will be properly avenged."

Adalinde nodded grimly. She gave Lothar a withering look. "There speaks a true man. A single act of vengeance is worth a year's mourning."

Lothar turned away.

"I will take my leave," Adalinde said, rising stiffly from the bench. "Since my granddaughter refuses any comfort I have to offer, I will go to my bed. I am too old to wait the night for Death to come. Too soon he will be coming for me."

For the first time since he had first met Adalinde, Rutgar thought she did truly look old. Lothar stiffened as she passed, but the two did not look at each other.

"Your grandmother would have made a fierce warrior," Rutgar commented to Lothar.

"Aye. She is more a man than I, and she never lets me forget it." His shoulders slumped. " 'Tis unfair of me to resent her for it. Ardun is her life. 'Twas a bitter draught for her to swallow when my father turned the domain over to King Charles." Lothar shook his head blearily. "All the women of my family seem doomed to hardship. My mother died birthing me. Bertrice's mother died beside her husband when a greedy neighbor attacked Stringau. Now Bertrice. Poor gentle Bertrice. Cursed. They are all cursed." He sent a furtive glance toward Rutgar. "My sister also."

Rutgar's eyes narrowed. "You have a sister?"

"I have a sister." Lothar laughed bitterly, exhaling alcoholic fumes. "A sweet sister with Adalinde's strength but none of her rancor. You know her well.

Too well, a more vigilant brother might say. But then, she has never been acknowledged as kin, so I've not acted the part of brother to her except when it was convenient." He shot a resentful glance toward the door where Adalinde had made her exit.

Realization burst upon Rutgar's mind like the blow of a fist. "Gisela?"

"Aye. Gisela."

Rutgar nearly roared. "What kind of man would permit his own blood to live as a serf?"

Lothar stared at the floor, his face flushed. "Ercangar never called her daughter. When her mother died, Gisela traded her freedom for a place at his hearth. She never made a daughter's claim upon him, but all of Ardun knows she carries his blood. The deference they give her is not only because they think her a witch."

Rutgar sat down. Thoughts were rearranging themselves in his head so rapidly that the process almost made him dizzy. "Why did you not tell me of this sooner?"

Lothar shrugged. "No one dared to speak of it while my father lived. I think Adalinde is secretly proud that Gisela carries our blood, but a silence held so long becomes cast in stone and hard to break. If you had known, would it have saved her from your attentions?"

Rutgar recalled his losing battle to keep Gisela from his heart. Her connection to Ercangar would simply have been another excuse for him to seek her out. "Nay. 'Twould not have saved her. There's not much in this world that would keep me from Gisela. Even my marriage would not have kept me from her."

Lothar grunted unhappily.

"Does all Ardun truly believe Gisela is Ercangar's

daughter?" Rutgar asked. A mad scheme was forming in his mind.

"All who were here when Gersvinda belonged to Ercangar know it, for the witch was besotted with my father and never lay with another." Lothar belched out spiritous fumes, then grimaced. "She was with child when he put her aside. That was Adalinde's doing. I think she feared that Gersvinda's power over Ercangar would become greater than her own."

"Is there any way that Gisela's blood heritage can be proven?"

"What does it signify?"

"Is there?"

Lothar lift his shirt and displayed a tiny reddish splotch under his arm, just to the side of his left breast. It was shaped vaguely like a heart. "Most who carry our blood also carry this mark."

Rutgar felt his stomach tighten as certainty solidified. Gisela was indeed Ercangar's bastard daughter. "If Charles wanted me to wed into the bloodline that ruled these lands before me, he should have given me Gisela."

Comprehension slowly dawned through the fog that clouded Lothar's expression. "You . . . you can't mean to wed her!"

"Why not?"

"She's a serf, and a bastard."

"Freedom is easily granted. I own her; I can free her. And the king himself is a bastard."

Lothar eyed him with unveiled disgust. "God have mercy but you are a cold devil. What of poor Bertrice?"

"Bertrice is beyond insult or hurt, or soon will be, unless a miracle saves her. She would not begrudge

Gisela her place as mistress here. Bertrice loves Gisela well."

"The bishop will never consent to it."

"The bishop will carry out the king's will. Charles wishes me to wed a Saxon woman who will cement the peace in this region, and so will I do his bidding."

Once Charles learned of Rutgar's presumption, he might demand his head on a platter, but Rutgar didn't think so. Charles the Great was nothing if not a practical man.

A knock sounded on the door. It opened to admit a buzz of voices from the hall, and Gisela. Her face was stony, her cheeks streaked with tears.

"My lords, Bertrice is gone."

Lothar buried his face in his hands. Rutgar felt a tightening in his own chest. Bertrice had not deserved such a fate. Neither the fate of being forced to a marriage she abhorred, nor the fate of being murdered for her role in a drama she little understood. He hoped her gentle soul was now at peace.

Father Gaunt pushed into the room behind Gisela. "My lord Rutgar. The body must be moved to the chapel."

"I will help prepare her," Gisela said, her voice quavering.

"Nay!" The priest fingered his cross. "You will not touch her, foul woman! 'Twas bad enough you attended her bedside!"

Gisela turned a shade paler, and Rutgar's temper rose. He took Gisela's arm. "I told you once to be silent, priest! Do not try my patience on this of all nights."

Father Gaunt flinched back from his anger.

"Get you gone! I will see that the body is prepared

and moved. You will conduct a service for the lady Bertrice at sunrise."

The priest backed out the door with such haste that he hit the door frame. Jowls quivering with indignation, he gave Gisela one last glare before disappearing.

Gisela quivered also. Rutgar could feel it where he held her. He suppressed an urge to gather her into his arms and hold her until the quivering stopped. This was no time to grow soft because of a woman.

"Gisela," he said gently. "Go to the infirmary and sleep. There are other women who can tend to Bertrice's body."

"No. It should be me."

He took her chin and turned her tear-stained face toward him. "Bertrice is beyond caring. You can do no more for her. She would want you to take care of yourself now." Their eyes locked for a moment before hers dropped in surrender.

"Lothar. Take Gisela to the infirmary. Give her one of her own sleeping draughts. She must rest."

Lothar looked a question at Rutgar, and Rutgar shook his head. Telling Gisela of his decision would only rob her of much needed sleep.

Gisela left with no further protest, leaning on her brother for support. Lothar murmured a quiet word of comfort, and she briefly touched his shoulder with her head. Rutgar smiled to think how jealous he had once been in thinking Gisela enamored of Lothar.

"Sleep," Rutgar advised Gisela in a voice too quiet to reach her. "Tomorrow will be a new day."

And tomorrow, despite anyone's protest, Rutgar would gain for himself a Saxon wife.

※ ※ ※

"Come, girl, you must get up."

Gisela woke to the harsh sound of Adalinde's command. In the best of circumstances, her grandmother's voice was not a sweet sound, and on this morning it seemed even more austere than usual. The old woman's visage was appropriate to her voice—gray, drawn, and even more deeply lined than usual. In the grogginess of waking, Gisela thought for a nightmarish moment that a skull floated above her. Then she remembered the night before and realized why Adalinde had aged so.

"I'm awake," Gisela groaned.

"Then get you up. 'Tis time."

"Are they having the service so early? Am I late?"

" 'Tis high morning, Gisela. Bertrice was sent to her rest hours ago."

Gisela's eyes widened with dismay. "High morning? How could I have slept so long? Why didn't anyone wake me?"

"You needed your sleep."

Hastily grabbing at her clothes, Gisela scarcely paused to wonder at her grandmother's unusual concern for her welfare. She must go to Bertrice's pyre and bid her friend's spirit good-bye.

Adalinde snatched the kirtle from her hands. "You will not wear that."

The gown had been her mother's—one of the several that Rutgar had resurrected for her. The garments were the best clothing she'd ever had, and now Adalinde was taking them from her.

"I have nothing else to wear." She reached for the kirtle, but Adalinde flung it away.

"I will bring something for you to wear. Wrap this robe around you. We are going to my chamber."

Mystified, Gisela had no choice but to obey. In

Adalinde's chamber, a steaming tub of water awaited her beside the glowing brazier. When her grandmother motioned for her to get in it, Gisela hesitated.

"Go on, child. All will be made clear in time. Right now there is much to do."

She was still asleep and dreaming, Gisela decided as she submitted to her grandmother's ministrations. In all Gisela's days at Ardun, Adalinde had taken note of her only to assign her tasks or to punish her for some infraction. Gisela had never in her life sat in a tub of warm water and lathered herself with soap that smelled of the distilled essence of lilacs. She had never entered Adalinde's rooms except to clean them. Now she bathed in luxury, and Adalinde herself wrapped her in a linen towel when she rose from the tub, then took a brush to her hair until it dried and fell in soft, sweetly scented waves to her waist.

Once Gisela was clean, brushed, and buffed, her grandmother dressed her in Bertrice's wedding raiment of blue and gold, the fine, soft linen and wool the women of the weaving house had labored so diligently to produce. A jeweled headband secured the sheer veil, and slippers of soft white leather adorned her feet.

"Come. Make your mark upon this." Adalinde presented her with a scroll of thin parchment. "Rutgar has given you your freedom."

"Is that what this is about?" Gisela asked. "Freedom?" Her heart warmed that Rutgar would make such a gesture, though in itself, freedom meant little, for she could not leave Ardun, serf or freewoman. Even if she could, Rutgar knew that she would never leave him.

"You will do," Adalinde said, regarding her critically. "You show your blood, and you have more mettle than most. You will do what you must."

Gisela asked warily: "What must I do?"

"You must marry Rutgar, Sister." Lothar's voice startled Gisela. He stood at the chamber door, the sickly green tinge of his skin clashing with the bright colors of his best clothing. Drawing a pensive breath, he smiled faintly. "I am to escort you to your wedding."

Gisela didn't answer. Now she was certain that she dreamed.

"Gisela?" Adalinde demanded. "Have you nothing to say?"

Gisela opened her mouth, but nothing came out.

" 'Tis for the best, Sister. Rutgar is a good man, and he will treat you as well as any man treats a wife."

A crowd awaited them in the yard between the manor and the chapel. Gisela spotted Thomas the smith and little Geoff, Drada, Guntar, Ermentrude, and Luitgard. They smiled encouragingly as she walked past on Lothar's arm. The men-at-arms were dressed in their finest. Etich smirked as though he had planned this whole event. Gillan looked positively green. The abbess from Gandershiem was properly solemn—she had come to see Bertrice wed but had sent a message the day before that her party had been delayed and would not arrive until the day of the wedding. How sad, Gisela thought distractedly, that she had not been here to bid Bertrice farewell.

On the steps of the chapel, Rutgar was a splendid figure dressed in black and gold, his eyes possessive and almost tender as he watched her approach on Lothar's arm. Bishop Galvan was resplendent, as befitted a favorite of the king. Beside him, looking as though someone held a knife to his back, stood Father

Gaunt. Count Lucius watched from the front ranks of the crowd and gave Gisela a cold smile as Lothar handed her into Rutgar's care. Rutgar's large hand folded about hers and squeezed in gentle encouragement. Nothing seemed real—except that Rutgar's hand felt so hard and warm, and her own felt so cold.

The ceremony was a blur. The chapel was very warm from the bodies crowded within. Gisela felt giddy, as if she were floating above the floor, her body made of air. Rutgar steadied her as she swayed against him. She shook her head, and suddenly everything became real—the drone of the bishop's voice above the restless noise of the crowd, the odor of so many bodies packed into a small space, the empty ache in her stomach, the steadying grip of Rutgar's hand upon her arm.

This was not a dream—madness, but not a dream.

The bishop declared Gisela to be Rutgar's wife. Her new husband pressed a gentle kiss upon her brow. Gisela's eyes rolled up into her head and, for the first time in her life, she fainted.

Twenty-one

Gisela felt enthroned as she sat in Rutgar's chamber—like queen of epic legend with a feast set before her. Rutgar lounged in a nearby chair, legs stretched out languidly before him, joined hands pillowing the back of his head. He watched her with the satisfaction of a predator who had just brought down a particularly toothsome doe, smiling tolerantly as she downed her second venison pasty.

Downstairs in the hall, the wedding guests feasted while Gisela had her own private repast in Rutgar's chamber. There was little wrong with her that could not be cured by food in her stomach, but Rutgar still acted as though she might break at any moment. He spared her the stress of the wedding feast, and attended her himself while Alalinde and Lothar stood in for them as hosts.

"I'm sorry I fainted," Gisela said around a bite of cheese.

"Adalinde should have fed you. Are you sure you're not ill?" His eyes surveyed her with dark concern.

"I'm fine. In fact I'm stuffed." The day behind her was a blur, no more lucid than if it had been the dream she had thought. Her head was clear now, but the world still seemed a bit uncertain. She no longer knew her place or even who she was.

"Are we truly wed?" she asked hesitantly.

A slow smile softened Rutgar's face. "As truly as if the Holy Father himself had joined us."

"This is very odd, my lord. You would wed a serf? A lowborn female with no father, no position other than slave?"

He shook his head, fond amusement lighting his eyes. "Serf no longer. You are mistress of all the land from here to the northern sea."

Gisela closed her eyes, thinking that when they opened, her world would have returned to its former dreary state. It didn't. She still sat in Rutgar's chamber—now her chamber as well—with Rutgar's eyes burning over her with a hunger that had nothing to do with the food set before them.

"Bertrice . . ."

"Would not begrudge us this."

Gisela believed it. But the haze of unreality remained. "Nobleborn warlords do not marry common serving women."

"Gisela, you are anything but common. Did I not

once tell you that you could outshine any noble lady in King Charles's court?"

A flush heated her cheeks, and a softer warmth stole over her heart. She had dreamed of becoming Rutgar's wife, but never, ever believed the dream could come true. Yet here she was. She would live her life with him, bear his children, be his lover, his wife. Such a future seemed too bright to gaze upon.

He lifted the small table that held their supper and set it aside. Gisela recognized the look in his eyes and felt an answering tension in her own body. She smiled impishly. "Do you think we should go downstairs?"

"No." He took her hands and pulled her to her feet.

"Your guests might be insulted."

"Our guests, wife."

"Our guests," she conceded with a smile. Rutgar did not look as though the state of their guests' sensibilities was foremost in his mind. Never before had his eyes savored her as they did now, regarding her with a slow relish that made every nerve in her body quiver.

"Our guests are tending very well to their revelry," Rutgar said, drawing her close. "They will not miss us if we have our own private celebration." He touched her cheek, then lifted the jeweled headband that held her veil. "After all, you are overwrought. All of Ardun knows you collapsed at my feet." His fingers gently pushed the headrail aside and combed reverently through the heavy fall of her hair.

Rutgar's touch made Gisela forget about the strangeness of the day. She breathed out a sigh of pure contentment as he ran his hands down her arms, up over the sides of her breasts, lingering while his thumbs circled her nipples. He tortured them with the many layers of clothing that separated them, yet it was sweet torture, with a promise of sweeter to come.

He unlaced her girdle and let it fall to the floor. Her tunic followed shortly after. "I have endured this whole day by thinking of this moment," he said softly. His eyes caught hers in an iron gaze of molten possession. "You are truly mine, now, in the eyes of Holy Church and all of Christendom. Tell me that you come willingly, that your heart is mine as well as your body."

"There is no part of me that is not yours," she whispered. "You know that I love you, my lord."

He sat her on the bed and removed her shoes, then her stockings. Slowly he rolled the cloth down her legs, then went exploring over the flesh he had bared. He stroked, tickled, stroked again until she no longer needed the brazier to warm her. She longed to lie back on the bed and feel his touch on all of her.

"Rutgar," she whispered fervently, her head thrown back as the pleasure of his caress made her muscles go limp. "Please."

He smiled, took her hands, and pulled her to her feet. "Turn around, love, so I may attack these laces."

The kirtle slipped to the floor. She would have stepped away and turned around, but he held her against him, her back pressed to his chest. He kissed her hair, her neck, her shoulders while she moved restlessly against him. "Patience," he soothed, but his hands coaxed her to higher passion. He cupped her full breasts. They swelled and grew taut, the nipples thrusting against his palms in heady challenge. The thin material of her shift still stood between them—an exquisite torture. Gisela wanted to rip it off, to feel the familiar hard calluses of his hands scour her heated skin. That he was as tortured as she was plain from the rasping of his breath, the tension of the muscles that strained against her.

"This is a wedding in truth." His voice was a mere growl as one heavy, broad hand traveled over her belly and dipped between her legs. He pulled her back against the hard column of his arousal. "This is the mating that binds us together so none can part us. You are mine for all eternity, to bear my lust, and my seed, and hold my heart in your hands." Against her cheek, Gisela felt the curve of his sudden smile as he took one of her hands and wedged it between them to where his erection strained to be free of his braes. "And perhaps hold this in your hand as well."

She turned and gladly complied, torturing him as he had her until he gripped the bedpost for support. Impatient now, she untied his braes and worshiped his velvet hardness with her hand, until he set her back from him with a groan.

"You will have this game over before 'tis well begun." His eyes devoured her. "Take off the shift. I would see this wife I have taken."

Without hesitation she stripped it off and stood proudly before him. He stared at her breasts as if he'd never before touched them, teased them, feasted upon them, and his mouth slowly curved into the smile of a conqueror. His tunic and shirt came off in one shrug of his broad shoulders. Naked, eager, and fully aroused, he held out his hand to her.

"Witch," he said softly. "Come capture me with your spell."

Rutgar's playful slap on her rump brought Gisela fully awake. "Lazy wench. Do you still sleep?"

She eyed him reproachfully as he stood beside their bed, then yawned, for she'd not been granted much rest during the night. Though the wedding night had begun with the sun still resting on the horizon, Rutgar had not permitted Gisela to rest until the predawn, when she had fallen asleep—comfortable and satisfied as she was weary—with his satiated flesh still inside her.

She reached down to massage the slight sting of his swat, but his hand quickly replaced hers to rub the sore spot.

"Did I hurt you?"

"No." A lassitude crept over her as his quick massage turned into a caress. His fingers slipped from her backside to brush enticingly against the delicate flesh between her legs. Her breath caught. Sore as she was from the night's exertions, she wanted more.

"Witch." He dropped a light kiss on her belly. "You weave such magic that I could stay a lifetime in this bed with you." He looked almost serious. A muscle in his jaw jumped as he dragged his hand away from her. "No more of this, though. We have guests who must feel neglected. A man is not supposed to be so enamored of his bride."

She started to rise, but he pinned her back to the pillows with a quick, fervent kiss. "Sleep if you are still weary. I loved you too well last night."

"Nay," she mumbled. "I would not have your . . . our guests believe you have me tied to the bed for your pleasure."

His mouth slanted into a suggestive smile. "Not a bad idea, now that you suggest it."

Her face heated. She didn't know she had any blushes left within her. "That wasn't a suggestion."

He tilted a brow and opened the door. "I'll send someone to you," he promised as he left.

Now, what did he mean by that? Gisela wondered.

Her question was answered when a timid knock upon the door announced Luitgard's arrival. "The master has said I will be your maidservant," the girl told her.

"My maidservant?" Gisela laughed. What need had she of a maidservant?

Luitgard continued to regard her with unaccustomed deference. "Would you like me to bring you something to eat?"

"No. Of course not. I'll go down to eat."

"Everyone else ate long ago."

"Then I'll find something in the kitchen."

Luitgard puckered her mouth disapprovingly. "If I were mistress, I would have honeybreads and sweet cream brought to me each morning. And perhaps blood pudding and wine."

Suddenly Gisela realized that her changed status meant much more than simply lying unashamedly in Rutgar's arms each night. It meant she was the lord's wife—mistress of all those she had yesterday called friends, mentors, adversaries. An impish smile lit her face as she contemplated how Father Gaunt's wife, Hilde, must squirm to know that the child whose cot she had once filled with dead toads was now mistress of the domain—and Gillan, with her prickly insults and snide words. Gillan must be livid with jealousy and worry.

The possibilities were entertaining, but, of course, she couldn't use her new position to avenge herself. That would be petty. Gentle Bertrice would never even have thought of such a thing.

A sudden jab of reality followed on the heels of Bertrice's image. Surely this marriage to her was a very precipitous thing for Rutgar to have done. No wonder so many of the guests had looked stunned and disapproving at the wedding, including the resplendent bishop who had presided. Rutgar had married on the very day of his betrothed's death service—certainly not a very respectful thing to do. And whom had he married? A serf. A bastard. A woman not even known to his king, much less given to him by his king, as Bertrice was.

Gisela's stomach knotted at the enormity of what Rutgar had done. He must love her very much indeed to defy propriety and risk the wrath of the great Charles.

"You could wear this. 'Tis the color of your eyes." Luitgard tossed a kirtle onto the bed, then dove back into a trunk.

"What is that?" Gisela belatedly noticed the ornate wooden trunk that Luitgard rummaged in.

"Adalinde had it sent up here yesterday." Luitgard surfaced and threw a fine blue headrail on the bed. "She said it was your mother's. Some of the things are really beautiful."

Gisela peered into the trunk, and soon she was rummaging with Luitgard. The clothes were indeed beautiful—more beautiful even than the few things of Gersvinda's that she had already seen. There were definitely going to be some advantages to being a grand lady.

When the new mistress of the house went to the kitchen to break her fast, Ermentrude made a great dither, insisting that she should be served in the hall.

" 'Tis too much trouble," Gisela insisted. "I'll just grab some cheese and—ummm! Is this roasted chicken?" With an puckish grin she pulled a leg from the chicken. Atruda and Fredelin smiled hesitantly at her. Gillan frowned sullenly into the batter she mixed.

"Get your fingers off that bird. You will eat in the hall," Ermentrude commanded. "No mistress of

Ardun will break her fast like a naughty serf child snatching tidbits. Out!"

Gisela retreated, but not fast enough to forestall further indignation.

"Out!" The cook's shout followed her into the hall, followed by the cook herself bearing a platter of cheese, the choice portions of a roasted hen, several slices of honeybread, and a bowl of boiled oats.

"I can't eat all of that!" Gisela exclaimed.

"Eat it!" Ermentrude ordered. "Now that you are a wife you will need your strength. I know. I have buried three good husbands."

Probably because she fed them to death, Gisela reflected. To think that this was the same woman who used to whack Gisela's hand with a mixing spoon for sampling a pudding or snitching a shred of meat before they were served to the company in the hall.

Gisela ate undisturbed. Most of the guests had gone with Rutgar to ride to the hunt, and those who had not still lingered in their beds, nursing aching heads and uneasy stomachs from an overconsumption of spirits. Not until she was almost finished with Ermentrude's generous portions did Gisela have company. Lothar joined her at the table on the dais and sent a servant scurrying to fetch him mead.

From her brother's rather gray face, Gisela surmised that mead was the last thing he needed. He dropped into the chair beside her with heavy, graceless lethargy.

"Are you well, Lothar?"

"Well enough."

She didn't know quite how to comfort him. Bertrice had confided her affection for Lothar, but Gisela hadn't realized that Lothar was similarly afflicted. She'd never seen Lothar so much as glance at a woman, so firmly wedded was he to his ambition for the priesthood.

"Bertrice . . ."

"Is much happier where she is," Lothar finished. "I miss her, 'tis all."

"I miss her too."

A sad smile touched Lothar's lips. "Yes, you must. You have always been one to take hurt creatures under your wing."

Atruda brought him a tankard of mead, and he downed a mighty gulp. Looking at Gisela's frown, he said, "Do not reproach me, Sister. I'm not going to drink myself into a stupor, much as it would suit my humor. 'Twould shame the memory of our cousin."

A sudden pang of guilt made Gisela wince. Sensitive as ever to her moods, Lothar reached out for her hand.

"Do not think that you have done her insult," he said. "She would be happy to see you take her place as Rutgar's wife. When I told her of the injustice that has been done to you in the matter of your birth, she cried for your misfortune."

"What did you tell her?"

"That we are brother and sister. Why should we not acknowledge what everyone knows? Our father will not rise from his grave to shout my words down. Our grandmother does not deny the truth. And your husband will want all to know that he took Ercangar's daughter to wife."

"Rutgar?" Suddenly Gisela's breakfast congealed to a stone in her stomach. "You told Rutgar?"

"Why did you think he wed you? At first I was amazed that he would do so, but 'tis a good solution for you both. He needs a Saxon wife of the old blood to cement the peace. And you gain freedom, position, security . . . everything you've always been denied. I am glad for you, Sister mine."

"That's why he wed me." Gisela felt incredibly stupid.

" 'Twas a feat to convince him of your birth," Lothar admitted. "He found it hard to believe at first, so I told him about the mark." A grin relieved the haggard cast of his face. "I wasn't sure that you bore it. Sometimes the women of our line don't, you know. But you must, because after learning about that mark he was determined that the bishop, the king, all hell itself wouldn't stand in the way of his having you."

She should have known. Nobleborn men did not marry for love. She remembered how he had smiled as his fingers brushed the tiny mark under her breast. Rutgar had never denied using her as a tool to subdue her people. She should not be angry for it. He had not deceived her; she had foolishly deceived herself. The knowledge cast a pall over a day that had started bright with wonder.

Lothar regarded her uncertainly. "Should I have held my tongue, Gisela?"

"You did what you thought was right."

"Do you not want to be Rutgar's wife?"

"That is what I wanted." She had wanted more than that. Impossibly more. She had wanted to be a woman, not a talisman, craved for herself rather than for what she might represent.

Lothar's eyes were keen even though bloodshot. They penetrated to the heart of her. "Gisela," he said gently. "Love is a rare thing. 'Tis best when reserved for God. You have Rutgar's passion and his regard. He will care for you well."

She returned the squeeze of his hand. "I know he will, Lothar."

She carried vexation with her throughout the day. In the morning hours, the scales were evenly balanced, vexation with herself on one side, vexation with Rutgar on the other. As the hours passed, letting all the ire slip over to Rutgar's side of the scales seemed the natural thing to do. Therefore, when the hunt returned, Gisela was only too happy to attend her husband in his bath.

"Was your hunt successful?" she asked as she helped him remove his tunic.

"Aye."

Of course it was, Gisela reflected with irritation. When Rutgar hunted, his prey always fell, whether that prey be stag, stronghold, man, or woman.

"We brought in two stags. They gave us a good chase, though."

Probably a nobler chase than she had led him, Gisela reflected peevishly.

Rutgar sank into the tub with a grateful sigh. "Count Lucius is a fair man with a bow. He brought down one of the beasts."

Gisela soaped her husband's chest and listened to his purr of contentment—the purr not of a kitten but of a tiger. She had his passion, Lothar said. That was something.

His shoulders and back received her next attention. She enjoyed feeling the sculpture of muscle and sinew. Her finger traced the ridge of an old scar that ran along his ribs. Rutgar was a fighting man. He lived for conquest, and accomplished it any way possible. She was a weapon just as his sword was a weapon—something to be wielded to gain and hold power, and to be cherished for its use to him.

Four long scratches marred his back where she'd unthinkingly raked him with her nails the night before. She had his passion, and he had hers. Why wasn't that enough?

He grunted as she traced the scratches with the same nails that had inflicted them. Darting her a wary look, he asked, "Does something ail you?"

She smiled innocently. "Let me wash your hair."

He endured her vigorous scrubbing like the stoic warrior he was.

"You're in a strange humor, wife. Should I be wary about taking wine from your hand this night?"

"Close your eyes," she warned.

The rinse water was fresh from the well, as cold as it had come from the ground. He roared impressively when she poured it over his head. Revenge was sweet.

Rutgar erupted from the tub and furiously dashed the water from his eyes. "Christ's holy bones, woman! Are you trying to kill me?"

Gisela hastily backed to a safe distance and grinned impishly.

"What is the meaning of this foul trick?" He grabbed a towel and glowered.

"Was the water not properly heated, my lord husband?"

"Women!" He stepped out of the tub and threw the towel aside. "I'd rather face a battalion of Huns. At least they are straightforward about their intentions."

Gisela danced out of his way as Rutgar stalked her, stark naked and every bit as intimidating as those Huns he had wished upon himself. "What has brought your stinger out this time, buglet?"

"Why did you not say you wed me because I am Ercangar's get? Why did you let me believe . . . believe . . ." She couldn't put words to her own foolishness.

"Believe what?"

"Answer my question first!"

"I scarcely had wed you before you passed out as limp as a wilted weed. And then after"—he grinned lasciviously—"I had much better things to do with my mouth than talk. Why does that make you angry, silly maid?"

His arousal was becoming only too obvious, not only from the blunt weapon that rose from between his legs but from the heat in his eyes as well.

"Don't try to distract me," Gisela warned.

"Distract you? With this?" He glanced downward and smiled knowingly. "Is this distracting you?"

"No." She jumped aside as he grabbed for her, but found herself in a corner, his muscular arms caging her against the cold stone.

"Tell me why you're angry, then."

He should understand without her telling him, the coldhearted weasel. She stiffened her spine and regarded him with haughty unconcern.

"Tell me." He bent his arms to bring him closer. "I would resolve this before you give me some brew that would have me making love to the slop jar all the night long. Tell me."

She could feel the heat of his bare flesh. He came forward with a sly smile, and his arousal prodded her —an effective distraction that made her grope desperately for the scattering wisps of her anger.

"You let me believe that . . . that you wed me because of . . ."

Comprehension lit his eyes as he looked down at her. "You thought I wed you out of high passion?"

He had the presence of mind not to laugh, but she saw the amusement in his eyes. In a fury she shoved him backward and brushed by him. Only quick and agile movement saved his splendid distraction from being bruised.

"Gisela! Come back here!"

She felt like a fool. She was behaving like a fool. Unable to face him, she marched toward the door, only to be grabbed from behind and dragged up against her husband, whose patience appeared to be wearing thin.

"What do you want from me, Gisela?"

"Nothing!"

"Yes you do! You want me to kneel at your feet and spout useless poems like some fool courtier at Charles's court?"

She tried not to smile picturing Rutgar in such a pose. Some of her vexation drained away.

"You want me to lie to you about love and devotion and how I would slay ten thousand dragons at your merest whim?"

"No. I don't want you to lie to me."

He tilted her head up and kissed her, a thorough, possessive, thrusting kiss that reminded her of the strength of what was between them. "You have all my passion, Gisela. Could you ever doubt it?"

She didn't resist when he carried her to the bed, where he efficiently rid her of the encumbrance of her clothing. There would be no denying him. She didn't want to deny him. He knew he could seduce her into his power, and he was right.

"Marriage is but a contract," he said, then lowered his mouth to one puckered nipple. "A legal ritual," he murmured against her wet skin. He blew, making the rosy nub stand to attention. "It has nothing to do with what is between us."

He shifted his focus to her other breast. "I wed you for this." His tongue flicked to one side of the soft lower curve, where the small heart-shaped birthmark marked her heritage. "But that is not what I long to make love to. Without you, my life is pale—meat without salt, bread without honey. A marriage is a thing of politics, Gisela. What binds us is sweeter than that."

A glowing sheen of sweat covered his skin, despite his chilly bath. His breath came in ragged gasps as his hand slid over her body and settled between her thighs. His name soft on her lips, she opened her legs to receive him. Tongues of fire shot from his fingers, and she arched toward him with a desire equal to his own.

His mouth brushed her lips, then her brow. "Still angry, buglet?"

She had to smile. At least he was straightforward in his bribery. "Limp as a weed?" she inquired archly.

"What?"

"You said I looked limp as a weed at the wedding. You could have thought of something a bit more poetic, considering it was our wedding."

"I'm not a poet; I'm a warrior." He rubbed the hard length of his erection against her desire-swollen flesh and smiled down at her. "I know something that's not limp as a weed."

"Do you?"

He demonstrated. She wrapped her legs around him as he impaled her. Anger melted in the scalding heat of their joining.

"I need you. God help me but I need you."

His words were but a growl as he reached his release, but Gisela took them with her as she soared up the heights of rapture. He might not truly love her, but he needed her. That would have to be enough.

For a long while they lay entwined as their sweat dried and their breathing slowed to a normal pace.

The room was dark. Night had stolen upon them while they were otherwise occupied. Rutgar still clutched her closely, his thigh wedged firmly between hers, keeping her open to him as if his only ambition at the moment was to have her body at his command.

"I scratched you again," she said. Her fingers gently traced the paths of new injuries.

He chuckled. "Still trying to kill me, are you? Better to rip my back than slip more of your witch's brew into my wine."

She stirred reluctantly, but his body pressed her down again.

"We shouldn't desert our guests for still another night."

"They are all drunk by now," Rutgar said against her ear. She felt him come to life between her legs. They would get no supper tonight.

A banging on the door ruined the mood entirely. "What?" Rutgar demanded.

"Fighting, my lord." The voice was Odo's, and it was strained. "The rebels have penetrated the ramparts and ditch and are attacking the walls. We are under siege!"

Twenty-two

Gisela made her way through the press of guests and servants in the hall and exited into the yard, where night was just beginning to fade into the gray of a new day. Ardun was full of frantic activity. Every ablebodied man hurried to the walls, clambering up the ladders to the platform that ran the length of the palisade. Women hauled buckets of water from the well to be heated for doctoring. Wedding guests, awakened from their sleep, shouted demands to be told what all the ruckus was about. A few hardy souls who had not yet retired from the wedding revelry looked up blearily from their tankards to discover that their host's celebration had come to a rude and abrupt end.

Luitgard ran up to Gisela, hair flying and cheeks rosy with the chill of the air. "My lady!" she panted. "Drada wishes to know if the women should stay in the women's quarters or come to the manor."

My lady, Luitgard called her. The greeting pressed home the fact that Gisela, not Adalinde, was now responsible for seeing that the women and children of the stronghold were protected, that the stores of food and water were safeguarded, that the wounded were cared for.

"Wait a bit," she said. "I don't think we are in much danger."

"As you wish, lady." The girl bounded away, looking more excited than frightened.

Gisela could hear shouting from the walls. This ridiculous attack should be over before the sun made its appearance. What could Aelrhane be thinking, to stage a straightforward attack on the stronghold? His ragged, hungry, ill-disciplined men couldn't hope to penetrate the walls. Normally Aelrhane was not such a fool.

She started for the spot in the palisade where she knew she could peek through the logs to see their attackers, the same place from where she had watched with the other servants as Rutgar had ridden out of the rising sun that summer morning so long ago. Halfway there, Adalinde caught up with her and reached out a thin arm to detain her.

"Gisela! You must tell Drada to bring the women in!"

"Surely there is not that much danger."

Adalinde's rapt gaze surveyed the walls, where Rutgar's forces seemed to be throwing as many insults as arrows at the encircling rebels. Her eyes seemed to glow. "The fools agree with you, child. They think they're safe within their walls. Safe behind their iron armor and their iron commander."

Adalinde's tone sent a chill down Gisela's spine. She glanced up to where Rutgar stood on the platform. The iron scales of his armor caught the light of the just risen sun and seemed to catch fire, just as they had that morning when he'd first ridden into her life. Then he had seemed larger than life, unstoppable. Now he seemed even more so.

"The rebels can't hope to win," Gisela said. "The breach where Rutgar gained entrance has been repaired, and Rutgar has more men to defend the stronghold than ever Aelrhane had."

"Aye, he does. And half of them are drunk from the celebration of your wedding, Granddaughter. Do not ever underestimate Aelrhane's cunning, nor the fighting spirit of your own people. Those who fight for their freedom have twice the strength of those who fight to enslave. You are mistress here, for now. Take care of those who need you."

Gisela watched her grandmother march toward the manor like a reigning queen. Something surely was amiss. Aelrhane was not a fool to waste his men on a futile attack, and neither was Adalinde a fool to glow with the expectation of victory when defeat was inevitable. A terrible suspicion blossomed in Gisela's mind. She turned and ran back toward the manor.

Gisela's fears were well grounded, for when she reached the dim passageway outside the lord's chamber she met a familiar face, a face she hadn't seen since her days in the forest with Aelrhane.

"Gareth!"

Her horrified whisper was cut off as the rebel Saxon pulled her back into the shadows with his hand clamped over her mouth. "Quiet now, maid. 'Tis slow going through that tunnel, and we've got to get enough men through so we won't be slaughtered ere we've done our job."

Gisela struggled briefly, but she was no match for Gareth's strength. Stealthy sounds within the lord's chamber told her that others were coming through the bolt-hole tunnel that led to the forest. Someone in the manor had moved the heavy carpet that covered the trapdoor and unbolted it so Aelrhane's men could gain access.

"Be still," Gareth advised. "Ye should be happy to see us, maid. We heard what that devil Rutgar's done to you, and we're here to set you free and see Saxon land ruled by Saxon blood again."

"Or watered by Saxon blood again," Rutgar said from behind them. "Beginning with yours if you don't release my wife."

Gareth whirled and tossed Gisela toward Rutgar, who stood with bared sword and narrowed eyes. Rutgar's arm deflected Gisela away from his blade, and he pushed her toward Etich, who caught her and held fast.

"Rutgar," Gisela cried. "The bolt-hole!"

"So I gather."

Gareth had raised his sword and was backing toward the door to the chamber that held his comrades, whose number doubtless grew by the moment.

"Tell Lothar to bring a detail of men," Rutgar told Gisela. "We'll stuff these snakes back into their hole."

The door burst open, spilling Saxons into the hallway.

"Go!" Rutgar commanded her.

A grand sweep of Rutgar's blade kept the enemy at bay while he made sure Gisela was safely away. Gareth leapt forward, his sword arcing downward in a blow strong enough to cut through helmet and skull with one mighty slice. The blade caught on Etich's upraised weapon, and Rutgar plunged ahead into the mass of eager Saxons. He had to cut his way through to the bolt-hole before it belched up even more of the enemy.

"To Rutgar!" Lothar's cry sailed up the stairway, followed momentarily by Lothar himself and five Saxons who had once defended this very manor from the Frank's invasion. Rutgar suffered a moment's uncertainty when he saw only Saxon faces in Lothar's troop, but they plowed through Aelrhane's men with a ferocity that sent the invaders stumbling back in a snarling, bloody mass.

The battle was short. Blood spattered the walls and soaked the carpet that had been pushed back to free the bolt-hole. Of the six rebels that had made their way through the tunnel before Rutgar managed to bar the trapdoor, three lay in lifeless bloody heaps on the floor. Three others surrendered their weapons to save their lives.

"Someone had to open this from within," Etich pointed out.

"Aye. Someone did."

Any number of rebel sympathizers, from the lowliest serf to Adalinde herself, could have plotted with Aelrhane. Even Gisela knew of the bolt-hole. She had used it to escape with the rebels when Rutgar had first come to Ardun. For a painful moment an alarm clanged in Rutgar's brain. He'd mistrusted women from the time his lady mother had abandoned him to the less than tender mercies of his stepfather. Using that ungentle dame as a model, Rutgar had read treachery in every pair of soft eyes and self-interest in every feminine deed. But Gisela was different.

He would stake his life that she wouldn't betray him.

"It matters not who opened the bolt-hole, for today is going to see the end of Aelrhane and his rebels." Rutgar wiped his bloody sword on the cloak of a fallen Saxon and regarded the prisoners with pitiless gray eyes. "Bind those who are still standing and take them to the main watchtower. The dead also. Lothar, take your men and clear the tunnel of any of these rodents who might think to hide there. I want men in the forest to block Aelrhane's retreat."

Lothar hesitated for only a moment before Rutgar turned on him with deliberating eyes. "These are your people, attackers and defenders alike. You have to make a choice."

"I'm your sworn man," Lothar finally said.

"Then go."

Aelrhane and his men had never entertained any hope of scaling Ardun's walls and overcoming Rutgar's troops. They were merely a distraction to draw attention away from the infiltration from within; nevertheless they put heart into their task as they hurled insults, arrows, and stones against the walls. The first Saxon body that was thrown into their midst from the watchtower effectively silenced them, however. The second and third inspired growls of dismay.

"Aelrhane!" Rutgar called from the watchtower. "There are three of your men. Here are three more." He shoved the bound and bloodied survivors to the forefront, so their comrades could recognize their faces. "Your others are still scrambling to flee the tunnel before Lothar cuts them to pieces."

A few rebels shook weapons in futile fury. Rutgar had pulled the teeth from their attack, and now the best they could hope for was to gain the protection of the forest still in possession of their lives.

"The fight is over," Rutgar shouted. "Not only this insane attack, but all of it. Two days ago I wed a maid who carries Ercangar's blood. The old lord's line will continue to hold sway over Ardun. In honor of my bride, I will grant amnesty to any rebel who will lay down his weapons this day and swear loyalty to me."

"Take your amnesty and stuff it up your ass along with your ballocks, you Frankish pig!" Aelrhane thrust his sword high into the air and roared, but his defiance was the lone challenge from a silent field. The rebels looked uneasily at each other, at the ground, at Rutgar where he stood in the watchtower—anywhere but at their leader.

"Get a ram to the gates!" Aelrhane commanded. "We are not defeated! There's no Frank alive who can hold off stout Saxon warriors fighting for their homeland!"

A rumbling sounded in the Saxon ranks. A few fingered the hilts of their swords.

"Will you fight until you lose everything?" Rutgar shouted. "Aelrhane will never rule here."

Several of Aelrhane's men turned to retreat through the ditch and earthen ramparts. They stopped, cursing, as Lothar and his troops appeared at the edge of the forest. Aelrhane turned to see the trap sprung and whirled to face Rutgar. He swung his sword in a fit of rage, cutting the air in front of him in silent fury.

"The war is finished!" Rutgar warned. "Surrender and give me your honor in a sacred vow, or spill your lifeblood on the field."

"Frankish thief!" Aelrhane raged. " 'Tis my right to

rule Ardun! You fought Lothar for the domain, but *I* am the one Ercangar named successor. Fight me!"

Rutgar's hand tightened on the hilt of his sword. His heart leapt. More gladly would he fight with blades than with words.

"I will fight you, rebel. We will settle this for all time."

Aelrhane laughed with glee. "You will see your death today, Frank."

Rutgar merely smiled. "If that be the case, you will vow to give safe passage to any who wish to leave after your . . . victory."

"Aye. I can be generous."

"And your men will hold the peace when you go down in defeat."

"My men know what is required. I will win this day, Frank!"

"We shall see who will win." He motioned to the gatekeeper. "Open the gates."

It took only a few minutes for the crowd to migrate to the practice yard. Striding through the gates as cockily as if he had already won the day, Aelrhane led the way. His men followed, clumped together in a knot of glaring uneasiness. Rutgar's men-at-arms scrambled down from the wall, and as news of the duel traveled, the heavy oak doors of the manor swung open and discharged a gaggle of women, old men, and children. Rutgar saw Gisela among them. She pushed her way through the throng to the edge of the circle that formed the human arena. Her face was pale, her sweet mouth a tight line of despair. Fleetingly he gave in to doubt and wondered who it was she feared for—Aelrhane or him. But he knew in his heart that her fear was for him.

Gisela did not need to fear, Rutgar told himself. He

would defeat Aelrhane and win his bride the peace she craved. He would present peace to her as a wedding gift. And if Aelrhane's head came with it, then so be it.

Aelrhane made the first lunge. His sword slashed downward in a vicious arc. Rutgar met it with his own, somewhat surprised at the other man's strength. Aelrhane recovered quickly and carved the air within a hairsbreadth of the gleaming iron scales that protected Rutgar's chest. Rutgar sidestepped and gave Aelrhane a small salute to his skill. The rebel returned the salute with a bloodthirsty grin, which promptly turned into a grimace as Rutgar took the offensive.

Attack and retreat, lunge, slash, and duck. Cut and parry. The rhythm of combat sang in Rutgar's blood. Frustration and fury expunged themselves in savage blows and furious retreats. Soon the coppery scent of blood mingled with the odor of sweat. Rutgar felt a warm slickness along his ribs where Aelrhane's sword had found its way through the side joining of his cuirass. Scarlet runnels coursed down his left arm and dripped off his fingers from a slash that had carved his upper arm, probably to the bone.

Aelrhane was worse off, however. The Saxon had lost his helmet, and a cut along his scalp spilled a curtain of blood down the side of his face. His movements had become awkward as he favored his right leg, whose thigh flashed the white of bone through a gash that ran from groin to knee. A myriad of other nicks and slices smeared him with crimson.

Still they fought on. This was not a fight that Rutgar was willing to lose short of death, and Aelrhane's eyes glowed with determination as well as pain. The Saxon's strength of body was not equal to his strength of purpose, however. Aelrhane slowed, while Rutgar milked his own pain as a source of brutal strength.

Finally a vicious sweep of Rutgar's blade sent Aelrhane's sword flying from his hand. Rutgar mercilessly pressed his advantage, slashing forward as the Saxon dove to retrieve his weapon. Just as Aelrhane's hand closed over the hilt of his sword, Rutgar's blade came to rest at the rebel's throat.

"You've lost," Rutgar growled. "Yield, or forfeit your life."

Blood began to darken the dirt where the Saxon lay. Rutgar had to admire a man who could glare with such bold defiance even as his enemy's blade pricked his throat.

Aelrhane's eyes shot unerringly to Gisela, who clamped Etich's huge hand in a fearful grasp at the forefront of the crowd. He muttered a curse in the Saxon tongue that Rutgar didn't quite catch, then turned bitter eyes back to the victor. "Yield!" he said, his surrender as defiant as any war cry.

An anguished howl followed Aelrhane's surrender. One of the rebels raised a mutinous sword. "Nay! Never!"

A flurry of confused movement rippled through Aelrhane's men, then died as the people and men-at-arms of Ardun surrounded them and pushed them out onto the bloodied dirt to taste defeat with their leader. Ragged and ill-kempt, their bodies reflected the lean times of winter. The forked Saxon beards were matted, the crude leather armor worn and stiff with blood and dirt. But their hands were firm upon their weapons.

"Will you swear to me?" Rutgar asked. "Or share a cell with Aelrhane?"

The rebels shifted uncertainly. The group drew tighter as if to draw strength from each other. Rutgar motioned Etich to bring Gisela into the circle.

Rutgar saw surprise and reluctance on his wife's face, but drew on the last of his determination to see the scene through to its end. He had never deceived her; she knew her purpose well enough. She, like his sword, was a weapon for peace; and like his sword, he would use her.

Rutgar grasped Gisela's hand and drew her to stand beside him. "Behold my wife," he said, both to the rebels and the crowd. "Gisela. Daughter of the last rightful Saxon lord of Ardun, niece to the last Saxon lord of Stringau, and favored of the old Saxon gods. At one time you thought her magic would bring you victory, and it has. She has surrendered herself to me in the bonds of Christian marriage, and the children of her womb, descendants of the old Saxon line, will rule here after I die. Be wise and follow her lead in surrendering your loyalty."

Rutgar's implacable gaze fastened onto Aelrhane's men. "Swear to me and King Charles, then help me build Ardun into a strong domain where you can live with wives and children in peace."

Silence thickened the air, broken only by the restless wail of a child. Rutgar squeezed Gisela's cold hand, but she didn't respond. A glance at her face confirmed her displeasure at being thrust before her people as a symbol of surrender.

One by one, the rebels threw their swords to the ground. One by one they knelt, placed their hands between Rutgar's, and swore their faith. Gisela was coiled to flee the moment he loosed her hand, but he held her beside him with a glance of warning. He could feel the heat of her ire warm the air between them, but her expression masked all feeling.

Gisela's anger could be turned to a more constructive passion, Rutgar knew, and she would have her much-longed-for peace. The war was over.

Gisela was surprised at how quickly the stronghold returned to normal at the end of such conflict. The crowd dispersed, the wedding guests to resume their merrymaking, the men-at-arms to congratulate themselves on a bloodless victory—bloodless at least for them—and the women to the pile of work engendered by having so many strangers within the walls.

Gisela made her way through the crowd and tried to ignore the stares that followed her. She waffled between relief that the conflict was over and wrath that she'd been paraded before her people in such a way.

It didn't take long for anger to win out. As the hours of the day passed, it built like a storm inside her. The force of it cleaned away the clammy residue of fear that had been building since she woke to the news of Aelrhane's attack. She embraced her anger, burned with it. In fact, she must have glowed with it, for Rutgar did not come to her to have his wounds dressed. He bound the cut on his arm with a rag and busied himself about the work of setting the stronghold back in order and soothing their guests' agitation. Perhaps the yelps coming from Aelrhane after Gisela descended into the cellar with her medicines discouraged her husband from seeking her aid. She was not particularly gentle with Aelrhane. After the trouble he had caused both her and Ardun, he didn't deserve her gentleness. But neither had she deliberately hurt him. His yelps were more anticipation than pain. Gisela had never yet met a warrior who didn't dread the stitching of a wound more than the earning of it. They bore the cauterizing iron more stoically than the needle. Still, Aelrhane was indignantly loud, and Rutgar likely thought Gisela had more of the same torture in mind for him.

After the evening meal, at which the lord's high seat was conspicuously vacant, Gisela gladly retired to her infirmary to treat a serf who had been kicked in the eye by a mule. Fortunately, the eye was not permanently damaged, only scratched and greatly irritated. She washed it with a warm infusion of eyebright and applied a dressing.

"Thank you, lady," the peasant Gautier said with a grateful nod. "Feels better already."

"Keep that patch over your eye at least until tomorrow at this time," Gisela warned. "Otherwise the poultice will have little effect."

"Anything you say, my lady."

Gisela smiled. "Gautier. I'm the same little maid you used to chase from your wife's garden every spring—hardly a lady."

The old farmer took her hand into his worn and gnarled one. "Ye're a lady, right enough. 'Tis glad we are—my Clothilde and me—to see ye take ye're rightful place. Your lord Rutgar's a good man. Aelrhane's a good man, too, but he's no match for Rutgar."

"Aye," Gisela agreed quietly. "Rutgar's a good man. He'll do whatever he must to hold the peace."

Gautier nodded. "At the mallus he made Seldane return the sheep he'd stolen from my brother. Made the vermin give my brother a week's labor to pay for taking them. Aye. Your Rutgar's hard as stone, but he's fair. We could have worse." He squinted his one uncovered eye at her. "Do ye see peace for us, lady?"

"I haven't seen much of anything for these past few weeks. Perhaps the Gift has left me."

"Nay, lady. The gods would never desert one such as you."

It would be a blessing if they did, Gisela mused when the old man had left. Foreknowing was more a curse than a gift. She hadn't seen her wedding, or the fight between Rutgar and Aelrhane. At first she had thought their duel was the one foretold in the vision that had plagued her since Ercangar's death, but it was not. Though she'd been almost beside herself with fear for Rutgar, the fear hadn't been the same as the taste of dread she always suffered in the vision. The world was cursed with many kinds of fear, each with its own flavor, and the fear she had experienced that afternoon, nor the embarrassment that had flooded her when Rutgar had pulled her before the crowd, was not the tragedy of her vision.

"Ah, Gisela! I thought you might be here." Adalinde sailed through the doorway of the little infirmary. "Whenever your heart is troubled you turn to your healing skills, do you not? 'Tis fortunate for Ardun that you are of such a humor. When your mother was troubled, she used to make objects sail through the air to crash against the wall. Your solution is much more constructive."

"I am not troubled, mistress."

"Do not call me mistress, Granddaughter. I am no longer mistress in this manor. And do not tell me that you are not troubled. Of course you are."

Gisela suspected that Adalinde was the one who was troubled. She had seen her grandmother's expression that morning when the Saxon rebels had thrown down their weapons and pledged themselves to serve Rutgar. Her face, always rather cadaverous, had assumed the haunted look of an empty-eyed skull.

Adalinde inspected the shelves that held crocks of dried roots and herbs, the tinctures brewing on the worktable, the neatly folded scraps of cloth that served as bandages and slings. Then she turned and gave Gisela a sour smile. "Of course you are troubled, Granddaughter. How could you not be? I know you. You may have been birthed in a mud hut and raised in its dirt, but you are a true daughter of Ardun, and it cannot rest well on your mind that the Frankish pig has used you to subjugate a proud and noble people— your people."

Gisela turned away. She loved Rutgar. He was a good master to Ardun. Aye, he had used her mercilessly, and he would again if the need arose. But had Aelrhane not tried to do the same, with even less regard for her own feelings and need?

"I am growing quite accustomed to being used," she said softly.

Adalinde's eyes seemed to glow in the dim light of the infirmary's one sputtering lamp. "You can stop it."

"How?"

"You are Rutgar's wife. You sit beside him in the hall while he eats. You milk him of his lust in the darkness of night. He trusts you—I have seen it. He loves you with a man's foolish passion."

"He does not love me," Gisela denied suspiciously. "And if he did, what has that to do with anything?"

"Kill him."

Adalinde's stark words hung in the air between them. She could have hit Gisela with a piece of firewood and shocked her less.

"Kill him," the old woman repeated, her voice low and vibrant. "There are a thousand ways you could do it. You possess the means, and you will gather the will."

"You can't mean it!"

"I mean it! It must be done, and you are the one who will do it! You are my granddaughter. You have liquid iron running through your veins as blood, as do I. The women of our family have always had the strength to do what must be done, even though the men of our line have the backbone of a worm."

Stunned, Gisela could only stare at her grandmother with unbelieving eyes as the old woman turned regally and walked to the door.

"Think on it well," Adalinde advised before she left. "You can be Ardun's downfall or its liberator. Good night, Granddaughter."

Gisela stood perfectly still for a long while, then sank down on a stool and covered her face with trembling hands. All she had ever wanted from life was peace for herself and those around her; all she had gotten since Ercangar's death had been strife. She had thought this day had seen the end of it, but there was more.

It came again, then, burning through the darkness of her closed eyes. Blood, fire, iron blades singing a song of death. The sour taste of a desperate, despairing fear.

Fate marched to its own drumbeat, inexorably, no matter what she did or Adalinde did or even Rutgar did. Her other visions had come true. This one would also.

Twenty-three

When Rutgar did finally present himself at the infirmary to have his wounds cleaned and stitched—late that evening—Gisela was far too distracted by Adalinde's proposal to remember her vexation with her husband. She debated whether or not to tell him. If Rutgar knew Adalinde plotted his death, the old woman would be sharing the cellar with Aelrhane. Gisela couldn't bear to see her regal grandmother subjected to such treatment. She would watch Adalinde closely, Gisela vowed, and let harm come to neither her husband nor her grandmother.

"You are very distracted this evening," Rutgar commented. "Watch that you do not stitch my arm to my ribs while your wits are out dancing around your fairy pond."

"I wouldn't be so careless," she returned. "Who then would lift his sword in defense of our fair home?"

"Your voice has an edge as sharp as my dagger. I suppose you're still angry."

Gisela sniffed.

"I regret you were embarrassed this morning, Gisela."

"But you would do the same again."

"If I had to."

Gisela sighed. "I suppose you do what you must."

She pulled her mind back to her task. Rutgar didn't squirm and yell as Aelrhane had, but then perhaps she took more care with her husband's arm than with the rebel's leg.

"Your vexation fades very quickly," Rutgar said suspiciously. "This afternoon the daggers of your gaze were sharp enough to slice me to ribbons. 'Twould have taken more thread than you have here to sew me back together."

Gisela smiled. "Perhaps I think you have enough holes in you." She tied the last stitch and rinsed the new seam in his arm with a tincture of myrrh. "I'm glad you didn't kill Aelrhane. What will you do with him?"

"Let him think on his sins in a cell for a good long while. Then I'll see if I can't find a use for him."

"He's not a bad man."

Rutgar seemed unwilling to discuss Aelrhane further. He pulled Gisela down upon his lap. "Are you done with your torture, wife?"

She gave a delicate snort. "If I had wanted to torture

you, husband, you would have been begging for mercy."

"Not I." He chuckled. "My nerves are like iron, as a warrior's should be. Should I show you what else is like iron?"

She squirmed in his lap. "As a warrior's should be?"

"Bold wench! I'll have you begging for mercy!"

"Will you beat me?" she teased.

"Nay." He worked her kirtle up above her hips and turned her so she straddled him on the stool. "I've no need to beat you."

"Starve me, then?"

"Nay."

She deftly untied his braes and took him in hand. He was hard and huge, straining toward her with the hunger of desire. He grasped her hips and brought her over him.

"Are you begging for mercy yet?"

The jolt of his unyielding hardness meeting her soft woman's flesh shot through her like a white-hot spear. She sighed and moved against him, sliding her moist, welcoming cleft along the length of his erection. "You're the first man I've ever known to get a cockstand from having a wound stitched."

He pulled her down so that her ear was next to his mouth. " 'Tis not the stitching, but the stitcher."

She squirmed against him playfully, enjoying the feel of him swelling even larger. "You should rest, husband. 'Tis not wise to tax your strength after a loss of blood."

"I will rest in good time. After I've taught my wife the consequences of her boldness." He moved so that just his seeking spearhead parted her. "Begging for mercy yet?"

She gasped as he tortured her with the promise of paradise.

"Cry mercy?"

"Aye," she sighed in surrender. "Mercy, fair lord."

He gave her what she wanted, every last bit of it. Together they rocked until the stool threatened to collapse. Gisela held on for dear life and laughed as hard as she loved. They both laughed, until the pressure of their desire sent them both over the summit of rapture.

Still gasping with his own fulfillment, Rutgar set Gisela back on her feet before they both ended up on the floor. "Now I'll rest," he consented with a satisfied smile. "Come with me, wife. A soft bed awaits."

They went to their chamber together, and there rested, for a short while. . . .

The next week saw Ardun return to a semblance of normalcy. The wedding guests began to take their leave. The king's *missi*, Bishop Galvan and Count Lucius, stayed to hear the concerns of the people. The war was finally over. Aelrhane languished in the cellar awaiting Rutgar's pleasure, and his men, twenty-three in all, accepted Rutgar's amnesty and fit themselves into the stronghold's routine as if they had never left it. Most of them joined Rutgar's fighting forces. One returned to ironsmithing, the trade he'd followed before following Aelrhane, and joined Thomas as his assistant. Several others declared their intention to take up the plow come spring, and busied themselves at whatever tasks they could find to earn their keep until the planting season.

Several of the rebels accompanied Rutgar's men to bring in the women of the rebel camp and the two men who had been left to guard them. Matrude,

Frieda, and Gruda were happy to return to the stronghold, and the two Saxon warriors readily joined their comrades in pledging loyalty to Rutgar.

Gisela could almost convince herself that the tentative peace might last. Her people seemed happy. Rutgar was strong enough to win their confidence and just enough to earn their respect He could be ruthless when necessary—Gisela had learned that through painful experience—but was fair to all, Saxon and Frank. When Lothar asked Rutgar's permission to travel to Verdun to speak with the bishop about entering the priesthood, Rutgar readily consented. Rutgar rewarded Etich for his loyal service by giving him Stringau to hold as vassal. The jest among the men-at-arms, Frank and Saxon alike, purported that Ardun couldn't support the Bear's prodigious appetite, so he was being sent to Stringau to strip their larders. The Bear merely growled when the jest reached his ears.

Gisela had been Rutgar's wife for two weeks when tragedy shattered the peace of a snowy evening. Father Gaunt's wife, Hilde, who had twisted in the throes of a difficult labor for nearly two days, delivered a babe that was hideously deformed. Missing its entire lower jaw and suffering a malformed spine, the child died within minutes of its birth. A day later, when Gisela left Hilde's bedside to fetch the desolated mother a bit of soup from the kitchen, Hilde took her husband's eating knife to her own throat.

The priest wasted no time laying the calamity at Gisela's feet. While his poor wife's body was still warm, the priest raged that the witch had always hated Hilde. She had lured his silly wife into drinking some devil's potion while she carried the babe; Hilde had confessed her sin to him. And he'd heard Gisela crooning evil chants while she attended Hilde during the delivery. He ranted until Rutgar put a stop to his accusations and pulled Gisela away from the grisly scene.

That night, drifting between waking and sleep, Gisela lived her vision once again. She smelled the blood, heard the shouts and screaming, felt the heat of the fire, tasted fear laced with despair and betrayal. Rutgar's voice was a far-off beckoning that slid off her trance like oil off water. The sting of his slap finally brought her back to the real world. His face swam above hers, scowling his concern.

"Hold me!" she pleaded.

Even the reassuring strength of Rutgar's arms couldn't completely banish the aftertaste of horror. Somehow, sometime, the world she saw in her vision was going to become the real world.

The next morning Hilde's body was burned on a small pyre outside the walls. Her husband refused to say a service over his wife, since suicide, according to him, robbed her of any chance of God's mercy. The poor babe was not placed on the pyre with its mother, as the child's body had disappeared during the night. Demons, the priest ranted for all to hear. The deformed thing had been snatched back to hell by the demons that had spawned it. Would that they had taken their wretched earthly accomplice with them.

Gisela tried her best to ignore Father Gaunt's ravings. As she stood in the snow watching Hilde's pyre send flames streaking toward the sky, she urged herself to make allowances for the priest's shock and grief. In his own way, he had loved Hilde. Of the children she had borne him, only one had survived childhood, and now the priest had been most cruelly deprived of any hope for another. Still, Gisela longed to lash out at him for daring to imply she had had a part in this tragedy. The potion of motherwort she had given Hilde was nothing more than a tonic to ease female sufferings of all kinds. Neither was there harm in the soothing chant she had sung to Hilde during the extremity of her pain.

When Gisela dealt in sorcery—or tried to deal in sorcery—it was not of the evil kind. She would not taint her soul with black magic. Yet thanks to Father Gaunt's accusations, others who stood with her saying farewell to Hilde's spirit—people she had known all her life—now looked at her with a fearful doubt in their eyes. When she turned to go back within the palisade, a low murmur of comment followed her.

The worst was yet to come, however. Waiting for her in the infirmary was the stiff little body of Hilde's child, still caked with the blood of its birth. Gisela was accustomed to death and the horror of its various guises. She was used to the effluents of sickness, the ugliness of malformed and twisted limbs. But about this little deformed body was an aura of malice she'd seldom met. When she saw the grisly corpse lying on the cot, she did something she had never before done: she screamed.

Rutgar and Lothar both were there within moments. The two men crowded into the doorway, nearly getting stuck in their haste. When they saw what lay on the cot, both turned a shade paler.

Rutgar was the first to recover. "Get it out of here," he told Lothar.

Rutgar bent over Gisela and blocked her view while Lothar took away the body. She suppressed the urge to babble and to cry, contenting herself with merely throwing her arms around him and letting his strength steady her racing heart. "I'm sorry," she murmured against his chest. "I just . . . I . . ."

"Hush." He picked her up in his arms. "Always you are comforting and tending others. Let yourself be tended for a change. I want you to rest in our chamber and drink one of your own vile-tasting restoratives."

Gisela allowed herself to sink into the comfort of Rutgar's embrace, but a sick foreboding coiled in her mind. She could feel the priest's hatred as a lingering miasma in the little infirmary. She had no doubt it was he who had crept in to leave the pitiful thing that had been his child. The future pressed in upon her with certain knowledge that her peace was soon to end.

Only a day passed before events proved the truth of Gisela's fears. Rutgar was in the stable examining a mare that had been bred to Doomsayer when Bishop Galvan strode down the straw-littered aisle in full holy regalia.

"You are a hard man to find, my lord," the Bishop proclaimed.

"Am I?"

"Indeed. I expected to find you in the hall, but you weren't there."

"Obviously."

"Fortunately, the lady Adalinde was able to direct me here to the stable."

"How fortunate," Rutgar said with a sigh.

"I have a matter of great import to take up with you, my lord."

"Which is?"

"I think we should perhaps discuss it elsewhere."

"The horses won't spread any stories, Your Excellency. Nor will the hens. What is it you wish to say?"

The bishop pursed his lips and folded his hands

beneath his sable-lined cloak. Rutgar began to suspect he wasn't going to like what the bishop had to say.

"How well acquainted are you with your wife, my lord?"

Rutgar elevated a brow in surprise. "Gisela?" His slow grin brought a slight flush to the churchman's face. "I know her every bit as well as a man is supposed to know his wife. Why do you ask?"

"Your marriage was most irregular."

"The circumstances were irregular," Rutgar said cautiously. "I tried to follow the spirit of the king's wishes that I marry a Saxon woman with close ties to these people."

The bishop harrumphed. "I appreciate that, but some alarming things have come to light about this woman you married." He lowered his voice, as if the horses and hens might care what he said. "She is reputed to be a witch!"

Rutgar merely laughed. "These Saxons believe that demons dance in every flame and watersprites cavort in every pool. They may have accepted the Christian faith, Your Excellency, but they're still pagans at heart."

"All the more reason why we must be diligent to root out any source of heathen power."

"Gisela is not a source of heathen power. I wouldn't be concerned."

"But I am concerned," the bishop said, pursing his lips. "The tales that I heard the people tell of her made me uneasy, but I was ready to overlook that as harmless. The people are ignorant heathens at heart, after all. Now, however, good Father Gaunt has come to me with a complaint that I cannot ignore. He accuses your wife of dealing in the black arts to accomplish several crimes, not least of which is the birth of his child in the form of a demon."

An uneasiness in Rutgar's gut bloomed suddenly into alarm. "'Tis ridiculous, Galvan! And well you know it! There is no such thing as sorcery."

"You're mistaken, my son. Satan has his minions in this world, just as God has his saints."

"Well, Gisela is not one of them!"

"You are scarcely in a position to know that. The woman has undoubtedly stymied your better judgment with a hex of some sort. Father Gaunt suspects as much, and he is concerned for your soul."

"Your Excellency, I have not been duped by a woman since I was twelve. Father Gaunt is an ignorant, narrow-minded little ball of fat who wouldn't know a saint from a shitpile."

The bishop drew himself up and pressed his already thin lips into an even tighter line. "My lord, I would expect a loyal king's man such as yourself to show more respect for a representative of Holy Church."

"Gaunt represents little besides himself."

Galvan huffed indignantly. "Father Gaunt is a duly anointed priest of God, he has brought alarming charges against your lady Gisela. Besides the demonic birth, there is the matter of several poisonings—one of which affected yourself, I believe."

"A harmless mistake," Rutgar declared.

"Several sorceries involving deformed animal births and magical healings of conditions that God had obviously laid upon the sufferer as punishment."

Rutgar was positive by now that God had laid both the bishop and Father Gaunt upon Ardun as punishment.

"And the most serious matter—the good father has

accused your wife of poisoning your intended true bride, Bertrice of Stringau."

Rutgar felt his face turn to stone. His expression must have reflected the fragile hold he had on his temper, for the bishop backed away two full steps.

"I'm afraid I cannot ignore a charge of murder, my lord. I have sent a messenger to the king, so he can bring the charges personally. He feels very strongly about witchcraft, and he . . ." The voice trailed off as Rutgar took a step forward.

"This is madness," Rutgar grated out. He wanted to take the silly bishop by the throat and shake some common sense into him. "I will let it go no further."

The bishop scuttled back. "I fear 'tis out of my hands. The king has been notified. He will send instructions for both of us, I'm sure, within the week."

"The king will instruct you to mind your own business!" Rutgar snapped.

"I think not, my lord. Now, if you could fetch your lady for me. She should be confined until—"

"She will not be confined! And neither will she be questioned by you or Father Gaunt. Stay away from my wife, Galvan."

"When the king's messenger arrives—"

"Then we will discover the will of the king. Until then, 'tis *my* will that rules. Do you understand?"

Galvan expelled an indignant breath. "I expected more cooperation from you, my lord."

"And I expected more intelligence from you."

Seething, Rutgar watched the bishop huff his way out of the stable. A stone sat where his stomach should be. He slammed his fist against the partition of an empty stall, and every horse in the stable erupted in alarmed whinnies. Several landed kicks against the stall walls.

"I'll tell you where you can aim those kicks," Rutgar offered as he stormed down the center aisle.

Gisela was not in the hall. Nor was she in their chamber. No one in the weaving house had seen her, but Ermentrude reported that the mistress appeared a bit sickly when she had passed the kitchen earlier in the day.

She knew, Rutgar decided. Somehow she knew. And she had fled.

Rutgar found her at the holy pool, where he knew she would be. Back to him, Gisela sat upon the green, mossy bank and dabbled a bare foot in the steaming water. Silver was with her, leaning against her and enjoying the circle of her arm. The glade was indeed a place of magic: a place of summer in a world frozen in winter, a place of peace in a land ravaged by war. The green grass and warm water, the girl and her wild, faithful friend, and framing it all a glittering halo of clear ice that coated brush and trees.

Rutgar had a crazy urge to fade back the way he'd come and leave Gisela here where she seemed so much at peace. But before he could, she smiled at him over her shoulder. "Did you think I had run away, my lord?"

"No. I've never known you to run away from anything."

He had no choice but to join her on the grassy sward. He unbuckled his sword, laid it carefully on the ground, and sat down beside her. Silver sent him a cautious glance, then relaxed once again against Gisela.

"The water's very warm," she said. "It feels very good on the feet."

"I think you cautioned me once that this pool would chew me up and spit me out."

She laughed softly. "It didn't, did it? The spirits that dwell here know that you're a part of me."

Rutgar pulled off his boots and took her up on the invitation. Cold as his feet were, the water was hot almost to the point of pain, but gradually his flesh thawed. The water's warmth seemed to spread throughout his whole body.

"You know," he said. No question. Just a statement.

"Yes."

"How?"

Her delectable mouth tilted in a smile. "No magic about it. Guntar overheard Father Gaunt talking to Bishop Galvan and came to me with the tale."

She paused, and there was a moment of silent peace between them.

"I came here to say good-bye." Her arm tightened about Silver's furry, muscular body.

"Gisela," Rutgar said gently. "There is no need for a good-bye. Nothing will come of this."

She met his gaze with clear, honest eyes. "My husband, I know what is important to you. You are the truest man I've ever known. I've seen you sit in judgment at the mallus. I've seen you deal with my people. Never have you let personal preference enter into the fairness of your decisions. And always you have kept the promises you made. These are some of the reasons I love you."

He started to speak, but she held a slender finger to his lips to silence him. "You have taken an oath to your king. And you have made a promise to Ardun, to hold it in peace."

"King Charles will not condone this madness. He is a practical man."

Gisela sighed and leaned against him. This was too

much closeness for Silver, who got up, shook himself, then sat down again several paces away.

"Why does your king hate witches?" Gisela asked with a sigh.

Rutgar dredged up his memories of Charles the Great, sometimes called Charlemagne—the man he'd fought for, and often beside, since he was a scarcely grown boy. Almost as much as Etich the king had been a father figure to him. He was everything a king should be, everything a father should be—taller even that Rutgar, superbly fit, recklessly courageous. Charles was a man of soaring ambition and limitless energy, a man of power and presence. He was the man who had given Rutgar a life and a home, and what he demanded in return was loyalty.

"The king is a man who takes loyalty very seriously. He has pledged himself to the defense of the Church and its tenets, to the spread of the Christian faith, to the welfare of the Holy Bishop of Rome."

"Aye? And what has that to do with witches?"

"The Church holds that witches receive their power from Satan."

Gisela surprised him by laughing. "Does your Church believe the earth we live upon is Satan? Do they think the wind is the devil's breath, and the crash of the sea is his roar? They think that God can invest power in the bones of the dead and splinters of cloth and wood, yet they deny that the same power can flow through the natural things of the earth—through people themselves?"

Rutgar sighed wearily. The blade of a sword was more straightforward than such ideas, and certainly more easily dealt with. "It matters not, Gisela. You are not a witch. And you are certainly not a murderess."

Her eyes slanted up toward him with a look he couldn't read. "Are you sure?"

"I don't believe in witches."

"But your king does. And you must obey your king."

Rutgar shook his head, wanting to deny the gnawing doubt within him. "Nothing will come of it. Galvan dares not act without the king's direction, and I have sent my own messenger to the king. Nothing will come of it."

She smiled one of those smiles a woman uses when she is indulging a man. "I love you, husband."

He traced the line of her sweet mouth with one finger. "You are the joy of my life."

He lowered his mouth to follow the line his finger had drawn. She opened eagerly to him, nestling within the circle of his arms and clinging to him for a moment that seemed almost desperate. The glade seemed to be just a bit warmer when they finally parted.

"Night comes," he said. "We must go."

Gisela cast a longing look around her. Her gaze came to rest on Silver, who sat watching them in silent appraisal. She motioned the wolf to her side and gave him a hug. His tongue kissed her face with a quick swipe, then he danced away. His eyes rolled toward her in wolfish playfulness.

"Not tonight," she said in a tight voice.

He sat, gave her a look of disgust, then padded to the edge of the glade.

"Good hunting, my dear friend," Gisela whispered.

His jaw dropped in a semblance of a smile, and then he was gone.

Twenty-four

Eight uneasy days had passed when the messenger from the palace at Aix-la-Chapelle rode through the palisade gate. He bore messages for both Rutgar and Galvan. The missives stated approximately the same thing: witchcraft would not be tolerated in the Christian kingdom of a Christian king. Anyone even suspected of such foul practices would be tried, no matter the person's station or connections. As the king's representative at Ardun, Rutgar was to ensure that justice was expedited.

Rutgar's missive included an expression of

sympathy for his personal dilemma and the king's confidence in the honor and loyalty that had made Rutgar one of Charles's most trusted comrades-in-arms. Galvan and Gaunt had their victory, for a time, at least. Rutgar was required to forget he was a husband and remember he was the king's man, and Gisela must be tried for witchcraft and murder.

Rutgar felt as though his life had become a nightmare.

Three days later the trial commenced. Rutgar sat beside Lothar at one end of the dais and watched as Gisela was led into the hall by Etich, who had returned from Stringau to attend the trial. The judges of the mallus waited with solemn faces. One or two looked uneasy at the decision before them, and Rutgar guessed that those who had the impassivity to hide it were nervous as well. They were all respected elders from Ardun, purportedly full of wisdom and impartiality. Rutgar hoped that they had enough wisdom to see through Galvan's posturing and Gaunt's superstitious prattle. He could not advise them, however, for he had removed himself from the judging panel because of prejudice.

Etich led the accused to a seat where she would face her judges and accusers, then sat beside her. Gisela's face was calm; her eyes bright. To Rutgar's eyes she looked achingly lovely, even after three days spent confined in the cellar while the mallus was being assembled. Some in the stronghold had speculated that she would magically disappear from her prison and laugh at those who would judge her. Rutgar almost wished that she had. He longed to hear her laugh again, see her smile without constraint, see the amber eyes sparkle with elvish mischief.

Bishop Galvan presented the king's charges and

acted as questioner. He called forth Father Gaunt, who waddled up to the bench set before the dais and stared at Gisela with a look of loathing. Under Galvan's careful questioning, the priest detailed every sorcerous deed he could lay at Gisela's feet—a two-headed lamb that had been born two years past, the blight that had struck the crops of a man who had insulted her, the people she had cured of afflictions where his holy relics had failed. With voice rising and face growing red, he told of how Gisela had lured Hilde to drink her devil's potion, how she had brought forth a demon's child from Hilde's body. He went on to lay the death of Bertrice at Gisela's feet. All had seen with their own eyes that Gisela had served Rutgar's betrothed at the wedding banquet and that the witch had used such means to wreak havoc once before with less deadly results. Worse, the priest declared, poor innocent Bertrice had confessed on her deathbed that Gisela had held her spellbound and forced her to perform satanic rituals that blighted not only her body but her soul.

At that accusation, Gisela fixed Gaunt with such a stare that half those present looked as if they expected the priest to burst into instant flames. "That is a lie," Gisela said.

"Does that mean all else is the truth?" Galvan asked slyly.

"None of your twisted accusations are true."

"Silence," one of the judges chided. "You will have your chance to speak, my lady."

When the priest was finished, others took their turn. A Frankish man-at-arms recalled the day Gisela had watched their practice and had cast a spell that caused him to be injured. Odo, with some reluctance, told of how sick his master and several others had become the night Rutgar had ordered Gisela to his chamber. Gillan recounted her version of Gisela's anger at Bertrice's arrival at Ardun, and how the witch had revealed her ambition to become the lord's wife during conversations in the kitchen. To finish the damning evidence, Father Gaunt questioned a few frightened Saxon serfs about amulets and potions they had purchased from the devil's handmaiden, about the huge beast that had been seen with her on more than one occasion in the forest.

Rutgar's hope diminished as he listened. The common people were always delighted to find a scapegoat for fate's ugly turns. Everything was twisted to point to Gisela's guilt. Everyone knew how Hilde had tormented the girl her husband had so despised; even Rutgar had heard the stories of how the priest's wife had echoed her husband's hatred of the local "sorceress." It would be easy to believe that Gisela had taken her opportunity for revenge. Further, the manner in which Gisela had benefited from Bertrice's death was obvious. No one could deny it. Nor could anyone deny that Gisela had cured ills that had defeated Father Gaunt and his more holy methods, that she had given people amulets and tokens when they'd asked. The truth was twisted and damning. The whole thing was madness—a nightmare of madness with the king's seal of approval.

Gisela endured the proceedings as calmly as she could, determined not to disgrace herself or the memory of her mother. The Saxon culture honored magic and respected the men and women whom the gods had chosen to wield it. She was unaccustomed to thinking of magic as wicked and herself as the servant of some evil demon. In all her life, only Gaunt and

Hilde had chided her for it, and since they had seen sin everywhere and in everyone, Gisela had thought little of their animosity.

As Galvan's witnesses to her wickedness spilled their words into the hall, Gisela tried not to look at Rutgar. A sense that had nothing to do with sight or hearing made her aware of him, though, sitting on the far end of the dais looking like a thundercloud about to spit lightning. She could feel his frustration and anger, his fear. What an irony that a warrior who strode so boldly into battle could fear for her. While he had changed her life to suit his purposes, she had torn a rip in his, Gisela realize. She had awakened his heart, and now that heart warred with the two things most precious to him, loyalty and honor. She would have spared him this if she could. She would have spared herself as well. But Fate had mercy for no one.

"I call Gisela, daughter of the witch Gersvinda, wife of the lord Rutgar, for questioning," Galvan droned.

Etich gave her hand a squeeze as she rose to stand before the dais.

Galvan attacked immediately, drilling her with hate-filled eyes. "Did you poison the lady Bertrice?"

"No." Gisela met the bishop's gaze with a cool stare.

"Did you incite her to perform the devil's rituals at the risk of her immortal soul?"

"No."

Galvan smirked his disbelief. "Did you cause a demon to be born from the body of Father Gaunt's wife Hilde?"

"No. I have no such power."

"Yet Hilde confessed to her husband that she had drunk a potion you brewed for her."

" 'Twas a remedy for the discomfort of pregnancy."

"A sin in itself!" Galvan declared. "For God has decreed that the daughters of Eve shall bear their children in pain as punishment for Eve's sin. Therefore you admit holding God's laws in contempt."

Gisela wasn't too clear on just what Eve's sin had been. Perhaps she had been thought a witch as well. And what the pain and punishment of childbirth had to do with poor Hilde's deformed child she didn't know, but on his bench, Father Gaunt nodded wisely and sadly.

"Do you deny that you hold sway over the vicious beasts of the forest?" Galvan demanded.

Gisela sighed wearily. "I do deny it."

"Do not lie to me, foul creature!" the bishop warned. "Must I waste the judges' time by calling to question all the numerous people who have seen your predatory servants circling the stronghold and who have seen you cavorting and talking to bloodthirsty predators while in the woods? You heard the wench Gruda tell of the wolf who waited upon you when you were with Aelrhane's rebels."

This man could make even the most beautiful things seem ugly, Gisela thought sadly. "Two years ago I rescued a motherless wolf cub and brought him food until he could fend for himself. We are friends, this wolf and I. There is no sorcery about it, unless you count love and companionship as magic."

"And the accounts of your changing yourself into a wolf and running through the forest?"

"If I could change myself into a wolf," she said with a slight smile, "I would be running the forest now instead of trying to answer your questions."

Indeed, Gisela began to wish she could transform to a wolf or a bird to escape Galvan's endless badgering, which seemed less designed to find the truth than to impress the mallus judges. Everything in his mind was sin or evil. Healing was tainted with sorcery, amulets were tools of the devil, the creatures of the forest were manifestations of demons and wicked spirits. Finally, with a dramatic flourish, he summed his accusations into one damning question.

"Are you a witch, Gisela of Ardun? Will you confess it in the hopes of redeeming your soul from hell?"

Gisela hesitated. She dared a glance at Rutgar, whose eyes were fastened upon her with unnerving intensity. If she lied, if she denied her heritage, would these self-righteous churchmen allow her to stay with her husband, bear his children, love him, carry on with the life that they might build together? Yet even if she could convince the judges she wasn't a witch, would Rutgar still want her after all of this ugliness?

The silence stretched. Galvan gloated. Gaunt smiled knowingly. Rutgar lifted one brow ever so slightly. He seemed to be willing her to say something, do something. He did not believe in witches. He'd told her so a dozen times. Did he believe in her?

"Well, my lady?" Galvan insisted. "Do you confess?"

"Do I confess to being a witch?" She met his smirk with calm eyes. "Just what is a witch, Your Excellency?"

"Impertinence! Answer the question I put to you, woman!"

"I will if you will tell me what a witch is."

Galvan huffed in impatience. "Satan's handmaiden. A woman who receives magical powers by having congress with the devil. That is what a witch is, and that is what you are. Confess it!"

"No," Gisela said confidently. "I am none of those things. I did not poison Bertrice. I did nothing to Hilde and her unborn. I have not willingly harmed a single living thing in my entire life. I am not this creature you call a witch."

She saw Rutgar smile, and her heart warmed.

"I say that you are a liar!" Galvan shouted. "A liar! You will find that God has ways of discovering the truth."

When Gisela was finally allowed to go back to her seat, Etich took her hand in a hairy paw and squeezed gently. "Be not afraid, little cat," he whispered. "Rutgar will not let these jackals have you. He holds what is his, and woe to anyone who tries to take it from him."

She returned the squeeze, but couldn't share Etich's optimism.

A few brave souls offered testimony in Gisela's defense, but they were effectively torn apart by Galvan's questioning. All they could do was stutter out that she'd cured their cough or stomach ailment, which was more damnation than defense, or that she presented too sweet a nature to be evil—a common deception of the devil, Galvan concluded. At the end, the bishop looked confidently at the judges. "Good sirs, I expect you to please God and your king by bringing this foul creature to justice."

The judges shot anxious glances at Rutgar, at Adalinde, and at Gisela as they conferred. They were simple, honest men. Most of them had known Gisela for most of her life. She had treated their ills, delivered their children, and given two of them amulets to guard them from some of the many ills that beset this land. Gisela knew the judges suffered for her, but glances they sent the bishop were full of fear. Silence fell upon the crowd as they awaited the decision. A cough, a sneeze, the wail of a child—the small noises only emphasized the tense stillness.

The chief of the court cleared his throat. Cronar was an old man—a woodcutter who had lived all his life at Ardun. Normally full of confidence, now he looked nervous. "Uh . . . my lord Rutgar, we have reached a decision."

Gisela's stomach did a slow, painful flip.

"Yes?" Rutgar replied steadily. "What is it?"

"We . . . we have decided that the king's charges have some merit."

A muscle in Rutgar's jaw twitched. Gisela willed herself to have courage, to keep her dignity, to not disgrace herself in front of her husband and her entire world.

Cronar hastened to continue. "We find that the King's case has merit, but we are unable to agree about the absolute truth of the matter. That must be decided by judicial combat. We will leave the final judgment to God."

A hundred excited voices seemed to babble at once. Cronar shouted above them. "Bishop Galvan, Your Excellency, will you choose a champion to fight for the king's cause?"

"There is no choice to be made," Galvan declared. "Rutgar is the king's champion at Ardun. He will fight for the king's cause."

Beside Gisela, Etich groaned quietly. Rutgar's face froze as all eyes turned toward him. Gisela's heart turned to stone. She had known it would come to this, known with the unerring knowledge that had cursed her entire life.

"Choose another!" Rutgar growled. "Or better still, Galvan, since you are so thoroughly convinced my wife is a witch, enter the field of combat yourself and let God guide your righteous arm."

"I am not king's champion, merely his messenger.

Do you deny the king specifically instructed you to see justice done in this case?"

Rutgar was silent. Gisela felt his pain as if it were her own.

"Well, my lord?" Galvan demanded. "What say you? Do you deny the king's command and break your oath to your sovereign?"

Rutgar fastened Galvan with a look that made even Gisela want to back away. Etich's hand tightened on her arm.

"Perhaps you would invite the king himself to fight to prove his charges," the bishop suggested in an oily tone. "Do you doubt he would? He slaughtered five thousand Saxon hostages after the uprising at Verdun. Do you think he has any tolerance left for Saxons who cling to their pagan ways—or arrogant lords who fancy themselves a power apart from their king?"

Rutgar's gaze shifted from Galvan to Gisela. To all others his expression might have looked carved in granite, but Gisela knew him too intimately to be fooled. She saw the ache and the anger, and cursed the king who would put him to such a test. She summoned all her strength to raise her chin and give him a smile that said she understood.

"I will fight." His voice was a snarl, alien and cold, but the eyes that met Gisela's gaze were dark with a wealth of sadness and regret.

"Lady Gisela," Cronar said. "Who will champion your innocence?"

"I will defend her!" Aelrhane, who had been released from the cellars even as Gisela was imprisoned, stepped forward. "My lord, I made my oath to you but four days ago. Do not doubt my vow, but I am still ready to swing a sword in defense of a Saxon against these invaders." He spat in the direction of Galvan and Gaunt.

"You are not fit to do battle," Rutgar growled. " 'Twould not be a fair fight. Aelrhane still suffers from a wound in his thigh."

Aelrhane grinned. "And you from one in your arm."

" 'Tis not so serious a cut."

Gisela felt Etich tense, ready to spring to his feet. She placed a hand on his arm to prevent him. "Do not."

"I am your only hope," Etich muttered.

"Nay. Rutgar was my only hope."

Before Etich could argue, Lothar rose to his feet from where he sat beside Rutgar. "I will defend Gisela." He smiled at her, ignoring a furious glance from Adalinde.

"No!" Gisela denied. "No, Lothar. I will not accept."

He seemed not to hear her. " 'Tis my right!" he said to Cronar. "Gisela is my sister, and I am proud to claim her as such. 'Tis my right to defend her."

"Done!" Cronar hastened to bang his hand on the table before more argument could ensue. "Tomorrow at sunrise, and may God favor the right!"

The day was still well shy of dawn as Rutgar readied himself for combat. Etich helped him examine the thick leather cuirass with its overlapping iron scales and inspect his sword for any flaw or weakness that could mean death for him who wielded it. Rutgar tested the sword's edge; razor sharp, and hard as iron could be forged, it left a small line of blood on the pad of his thumb. The sword had been his father's, the one thing Rutgar had left of the man who had sired him. It was a noble weapon. The grip was inlaid with gold, partly worn away from years of use. The hilt bore the motto "Courage First and Last" inscribed between twin blood-red rubies. An ironsmith in Milan had spent over two hundred hours forging the double-edged blade, and his father had spent a fortune to purchase it. From the day it came off the forge the blade had been kept in a scabbard lined with oiled fur.

Rutgar valued his sword above all else. It was his life and his livelihood; it was his family. When he looked upon it on this early morning, however, his stomach roiled at the sight of it.

The scales of Rutgar's cuirass rattled as Etich laid it upon the bed. The Bear had spoken little this morning. He had performed the necessary tasks almost as if Rutgar were not in the room. Rutgar had been surprised when Etich had come to his chamber to help him prepare for the duel, but old habits die hard. They had been comrades for many years. He wondered if their friendship could survive the insanity that had taken over his life.

"You should get dressed," Etich suggested. His voice was flat. The usual banter that men use to bolster themselves for bloodletting was not there. "Not that you'll need all this iron about you. You should have no trouble laying that pup Lothar low in one or two strokes if you're serious about it. He's no match for you."

"Old friend," Rutgar said quietly, "you know I must fight."

Etich snorted with ursine vehemence. "That innocent maid is no more a murderess than I'm king of the Moors, and if she's a witch, I'll take her sorcery over Gaunt and Galvan's Christianity any day."

"Then God will prove her innocent. That is the point of the combat."

"Horseshit. You know better than that, Rutgar. God

might enjoy it if we could make our own decisions once in a while instead of always putting the burden in His hands."

Rutgar held up his arms so Etich could slip the heavy cuirass over his head, then pulled the armored tunic down to cover his groin and thighs. He'd spent a sleepless night exhorting God, the saints, the devil himself—anyone or anything that could help him resolve duty to the king with the dictates of his heart. The answer was always the same, bitter, sharp, and clear. He was bound to the king by oath and honor. He must fight and pray God would somehow have mercy on all of them involved in this madness.

Etich yanked at a strap that fastened the sides of the armor. "You should tell old Galvan to stick his sanctimonious nose up his own arsehole and keep it out of your business."

"Galvan's is merely the mouth," Rutgar said. "The will is the king's. He's made himself a champion of the Cross and vowed to snuff out paganism and sorcery."

"And he's not above taking advantage of the situation to test your loyalty now that you've got power and a holding of your own. Wily devil that he is, 'tis just like him to do such a thing," Etich grumbled.

"I've been Charles's sworn man since I was twelve," Rutgar said in a flat voice. "When my stepfather sent me to the king with his war levy, he expected me to be killed. Charles taught me how to fight and survive. I've fought at his side and guarded his back for too many years. I can't betray him."

Etich grunted a curse. "But you would betray Gisela! Do you remember that the penalty for practicing witchcraft is death?"

Rutgar hadn't forgotten. Nor had he forgotten the feel of Gisela against him. Gisela of the soft eyes and slow smiles, who could charm a wolf out of the forest and a lonely warrior out of the prison he'd built for himself, who could smile tenderly at the man who had just agreed to fight against her—the very man, he thought bitterly, who by rights should be fighting for her. Rutgar's whole body seemed to contract with pain centering on his heart.

"It will not come to that," he said with quiet determination.

"What makes you think it?"

"Because God is not that cruel."

Etich shook his head. "You put much faith in a God who appoints priests like Gaunt and Galvan." The Bear's eyes narrowed as he regarded Rutgar closely. Then he smiled. "Or are you planning to give God a little push?"

Rutgar saw the gleam in Etich's eyes. Apparently the Bear was confident he had divined how Rutgar would resolve the situation. Rutgar wished the same understanding had come to him.

The morning was gray and cold, but Gisela shivered from more than the chill in the air. Dressed in stark white, she walked between Antonius and Gaston onto the field of combat. Neither escort laid a hand upon her, but their vigilant attention revealed their suspicion that she might bolt at any moment. Or perhaps they thought she might change her shape to a bird and fly away. Gisela had no thoughts of escape, however. Running would do her no good. The events of her life were out of control and rolling toward a horrific conclusion.

She had spent the last hours praying—to the old gods, to the Christian God, to Mother Earth and the spirit of her own mother. The avenues of the spirit world were littered with her entreaties. She prayed for Ardun, for Lothar, and for herself, but mostly she prayed for Rutgar. Once again Gisela was being used, this time by a man she had never seen, a king far removed in his palace beyond the land of the Saxons. King Charles was using her like the point of a lance to make Rutgar twist and writhe in pain. She couldn't imagine a leader so cruel, but then she had never understood the warmakers or the things they demanded of themselves and others.

The walk down the length of the field seemed endless. Gisela wished her heart were as frozen as the ground on which she walked. She would like to be numb on this morning. Ahead of her was the platform where she would sit to watch her fate be decided. Behind that was a higher platform where the mallus judges waited. Adalinde sat with them, a bit to one side—a position of honor for the matriarch of Ardun. Her grandmother gave her an encouraging smile, but Gisela turned her face away. The old woman had a use for her as well, as Gisela had only realized the night before, when Adalinde had come to her cell.

For once the old woman had regarded her with something akin to affection. She had observed Gisela's dry eyes and calm mien approvingly. "I knew that one of my granddaughters would be of use to me in this fight," she'd said.

Gisela had not questioned her meaning. She was weary from a surfeit of emotion. The dry eyes and calm mien were not so much the result of courage as of having no more tears to cry.

But Adalinde had answered the unspoken question. "You had your chance to use your position to rid Ardun of the invader, Gisela. You have chosen your own path. I have come to give you courage. A woman with my blood running in her veins must know that the only face to show to the world is a valiant one."

"I don't know what you mean," Gisela had sighed.

Adalinde had taken her hand in an almost affectionate grasp. "You have a role to play, Granddaughter, and you will be magnificent. The men of Ardun are sheep, but the women are strong. The women are the ones who have the courage to sacrifice. Now more than ever you are the heroine of your people. Do not let them down."

On those enigmatic words the old woman had marched from the cell, straight-backed and regal as ever. And now she smiled down at Gisela from the high platform, and her smile sapped Gisela's courage rather than bolstered it.

Gisela tried desperately to maintain her dignity as she reached her seat below the judges. A glance at Rutgar almost broke her studied calm. He stood with Lothar, facing the mallus judges and looking every inch the grim and fearsome warrior—hell's own champion, as Lothar had once said of him. Gisela wanted to reach out and somehow ease his torture, for she could feel it as though it tore at her own gut, even though no hint of it showed in the iron set of his features. She feared for him. She feared for Lothar, and she feared for herself. Nothing her mother had taught her, no spells, no incantations, nor conjurings, could help any of them on this day.

Cronar spoke at some length. His words blurred into a senseless gibberish in Gisela's mind. She heard only his declaration that the combat should begin. As Rutgar and Lothar moved to the center of the field, the sun crested the horizon. The first ray of morning light struck crimson fire off the champions' poised blades, and Gisela knew, suddenly, that her nightmare vision had finally sprung to horrible life. The clash of metal on metal rang in her ears, and blood would shortly spatter the icy practice field. This she knew. Finally the anonymous contenders in her vision had faces.

Twenty-five

If God was on Gisela's side, He certainly was taking his time about showing it, Rutgar thought as he drove Lothar back still yet again. The boy fought well. He fought better than he had on the day he had defended his birthright, but he didn't fight well enough. His heart was in every sword stroke. Rutgar could see it in his eyes. Sweat streamed down Lothar's face, converging with blood in a pink smear. One of Rutgar's first blows had knocked his helmet from his head and crowned him with a nasty gash. Wearing blood, sweat, and fiery determination—

Lothar should have looked like a warrior, but he still looked like a priest. He should have left for Verdun a week ago as he had planned.

Rutgar sidestepped a swipe of Lothar's blade and stepped in to hammer him yet again. In a moment's trick of vision, Rutgar saw every familial similarity Lothar bore to his sister: the straight, short nose, the high curve of a cheekbone, the firm line of chin, the raw courage in eyes that refused to flinch away in fear or lower in defeat. Suddenly the face before him was Gisela's, not Lothar's.

Shaken by the perverse trick of his imagination, Rutgar momentarily lost his focus. Lothar landed a bruising cut that bounced painfully off the iron scales of his armor. Rutgar pulled himself together as he lunged forward, raining blows on Lothar's shield until the boy stumbled back in retreat. The contest could have ended there. The watching crowd knew it; they waited with a group intake of breath for the fatal blow to fall.

Rutgar stayed his hand. He could no more kill Lothar than he could kill Gisela; a fatal blow would mean the same thing for both. Rutgar fought as instinct told him to fight, as he had been trained to fight —with victory uppermost in his mind. But this was a battle he could not win. What was God in heaven thinking to let him come so close to winning?

In his mind's eye, Rutgar could see Gisela as she had looked when he had walked onto the field of combat. Dressed in stark white, looking like a sacrificial lamb, she sat on a platform at one end of the field, just in front of the higher platform from which the judges of the mallus watched. Antonius sat on one side of her, Gaston on the other, both looking stern and solemn. Her face was ashen, her eyes red, as though she'd been weeping. But she held herself straight and proudly, not hesitating to meet Rutgar's eyes as Cronar prayed God to decide her fate. She had not condemned him with those beautiful golden eyes, nor entreated him. But he had seen there a great depth of sorrow that tarnished the bright gold. The laughter in her was gone.

The snow-covered practice yard had turned to churned mud beneath the contenders' feet. Rivers of sweat coursed down Rutgar's ribs beneath his shirt and the heavy armor that covered it, and his own heartbeat hammered in his head. He could hear the bellows of Lothar's breath as he allowed the boy to beat back yet another attack that he hadn't the heart to finish. Out of the corner of his eye Rutgar spied Gisela. As Lothar made a spectacular lunge that Rutgar just managed to deflect, she half rose from her chair before her escort pulled her back down. Gisela was afraid; Rutgar could feel her fear in his own gut. Fear not for herself, but for both of the men who fought on the field before her. She was afraid even for the man who fought to condemn her—afraid for him, not of him. Rutgar didn't think about how he knew this with such certainty, but he knew all the same.

How like her to be concerned for him and for Lothar, without regard for her own fate. How like her! Suddenly Rutgar felt a great weight lift from his heart. To hell with the king. To hell with Ardun, his sworn duty, and a warrior's honor. Lothar might be Gisela's champion, but only Rutgar could save her. God didn't seem much concerned with justice this day, so, as Etich had suggested, Rutgar was going to give the Almighty a little nudge on that throne of His.

He fell back before Lothar's next attack. Lothar pressed on, his face dripping sweat, his hair drenched.

Against all instinct and training, Rutgar continued to falter and retreat. The boy had skill and determination, and Rutgar worked to make Lothar appear even better than he was, to make the victory look real. Rutgar stumbled and went down. The noise of the crowd battered the field—surprise or enthusiasm, he couldn't tell. He raised his shield as Lothar pounded on him from above. His mouth did not want to speak the word "yield." Never in his life had Rutgar surrendered. But he would now.

Then God pushed back, or so it seemed. Rutgar had not had time to speak when the blade of Lothar's sword parted from the hilt, spun through the air, and buried itself in the ground point first. Lothar cursed as he raised his useless weapon.

A roar overwhelmed Rutgar's senses—the voices of the crowd combined with the hot rush of blood through his ears. Stunned by how suddenly and capriciously the decision had been snatched from his hands, he threw his shield aside, leaned back on his elbows, and shouted every curse he could think of toward the heavens. As the pounding roar of the crowd became more insistent, he got to his feet and buried the point of his sword in the ground beside Lothar's. He would not take his opponent's life, but the contest had been decided. Victory was Rutgar's—and the king's.

Cronar rose from his seat. As the crowd hushed to silence, he called out in a shaky, quavering voice. "God has judged the maid Gisela guilty of practicing malicious witchcraft. By the laws of King Charles, the witch must die."

Gisela sank down upon the bench of her little cell, glad that Lothar had gone at last to seek his bed. Not that her brother's visit hadn't brought some comfort. It had. Yet in a strange reversal of roles, she had been the comforter, not the comforted. Lothar had been abject at failing her. She'd had to force a promise from him that he would carry on with his plans of going to Verdun to speak with the bishop there. She thanked all the gods she knew, both Christian and Saxon, that neither Lothar nor Rutgar had been seriously injured during their combat. Watching them, fearing for them both, was the most excruciating experience she had ever endured. Her nightmarish vision had come to life before her eyes, and the taste of such fear had been bitter indeed.

Now it was over. Tomorrow at sunrise her fate would be fulfilled. She had not been surprised when Bishop Galvan declared that fire must be the method of her execution. Stoning and hanging were both too merciful, the holy man insisted. The fire would give her a taste of what she would find with her master in hell.

Gisela's vision had always shown the duel culminating in fire—fire so hot, so real that she could feel it scorch her skin. Tomorrow the fire would be real. She would feel its searing kiss, and there would be no waking to the comfort of the fairy pond or her own secure bed. There would be no waking at all. She hoped that she could die with some dignity, without shrieking and babbling her terror. She wasn't sure she had the courage, however. Even the thought of what was to come sent her heart racing in fear.

The bar to her cell door grated open, and Rutgar descended the three steps to her prison. Gisela's heart jumped into her throat. There stood the man whose battle prowess has condemned her, and all she could think was how glad she was that he had come to her.

If she had hated him for putting duty to king above affection for her, it had lasted only a moment or two. He had never wooed her with falsehoods or led her to believe anything but the truth: Ardun and his duty to the king was everything to him.

She turned away quickly before he could see tears fill her eyes. Cursed weakness. When had she become such a puny, weeping maid? His hands lit upon her shoulders, warm, solid, and strong.

"Gisela." The warm male voice was husky, recalling nights of loving, of lying within the warmth of his embrace, of teasing until she provoked his rare laughter. At the sound of it Gisela gave up any pretense at control. She covered her face with one hand and wept openly.

"I'm sorry," she gasped. "I'm sorry." Desperately she tried to get her rioting emotions under control.

"Gisela. Look at me."

She couldn't. The thought of him believing that she had committed the hideous crimes that his sword arm had convicted her of—that was worse even than the anticipation of tomorrow's torture. "Rutgar. Do you really believe me so foul a creature that I could have killed Bertrice?"

"No, Gisela. I believe that you're the gentlest maid I've ever known."

Her heart warmed in relief, but still she couldn't meet his eyes for fear all she would see was pity. "Grant me a boon, husband—for the sake of what we had together."

"What would you ask?"

"I . . . I don't want to die in the flames." She took a deep breath. "I haven't the courage of a martyr or a hero. I would not be so afraid if . . ." Swallowing hard, she turned toward him and glanced at his sword.

To Gisela's great surprise, Rutgar smiled. "Gisela—my love, my wife. I have not come to tell you goodbye. I've come to help you escape."

"You what?" She looked up sharply.

"I've come to take you out of here." His hands slid down her arms and gripped her as though she might try to escape him. "I've never before asked a woman's forgiveness," Rutgar said quietly. "But I ask for yours. I should never have let you be brought to trial. The whims of the king are not worth the turning of one golden hair on your head, or the fall of a single tear from your eyes. I was a fool to think they were."

"But the decision of combat—?"

"Is a pile of horse crap. You are too gentle to harm a flea, much less another human being. God did not decide that contest, a faulty sword did."

Gisela drew a deep breath of relief and laid her head against Rutgar's chest, wondering if there was any way the tangle of their lives could be straightened. His fingers combed through her hair, soothing, comforting.

"Buglet, I'm ready to slay those ten thousand dragons at your merest whim, and when I declare my love and devotion, 'tis not a lie."

She made a small sound of surprise and looked up into his face. His chagrined smile made him look like a boy.

"Don't look at me thusly, Gisela, or I'll not have the courage to confess." He gathered her firmly into his embrace and pressed her head back down against his chest. " 'Tis harder to spill your heart to a woman than to fight all the Huns in the East. All my life I've prided myself on being hard as iron, on not needing anyone but myself. But love can melt even iron. It takes a man unawares, while he's distracted by lust and doesn't see it coming."

Gisela burrowed her face into his chest. His words cleared the last cobwebs of nightmare from her soul. For the moment she was content simply to be in his arms, feeling the solid hardness of his chest beneath her cheek and the warm strength of his arms surrounding her.

"You really love me?" she asked, propping her chin upon his chest and smiling up at him.

He grinned like a boy. "I do. Though it took a hammer blow from God to convince me it was true."

"You know I've loved you all along."

His grin grew even wider. "Of course you have."

"Arrogant rooster! Caught in your own trap. Is it so bad?"

" 'Tis heaven and hell joined. I don't know if you are truly a witch. I don't think I want to know. But if this is magic, we need more of it in the world. Kiss me, wife."

He didn't wait for her consent, but took her mouth in a kiss that had more of love than passion.

"I thought you would never kiss me again," Gisela whispered against his lips.

"You'll have kisses and more for many years to come, God willing." He set her back from him, grimacing as if the effort cost him sorely. "Morning will soon be here. We must leave. I'm going to take you to the village, where Odo waits to guard you. Lothar doesn't know it yet, but he will take you to Verdun with him—to the abbey there. You'll be safe with the nuns until I can get to the bottom of what has happened here and prove your innocence."

"But if your king says all witches must die . . . ?"

"If you are proved innocent of these crimes, who can say that you have practiced witchcraft? None at Ardun will speak against you. I will see to that. The king will relent. He needs me to ward this land."

Gisela sank down onto the bench, suddenly realizing the risk Rutgar took in tempting the king's displeasure. She slowly shook her head.

"You could lose everything—your land, your power, your position in the king's regard. I cannot ask it of you."

"I know you would not ask it of me." He cupped her chin in his big hand. "Gisela, all my life I've hungered for land and power. I've ruled my life with honor and a warrior's code. Now I find it means nothing without you. If I lose it all—well, I've lived by my sword before. There are other kings, other lands, and other estates to be won. But there are no other witches with golden eyes and golden hair and an impudent mouth too bold for her own good." He pressed his lips to hers in a soft kiss. "Now, before you distract me even more with that mouth, we must go."

The door, which Rutgar had closed, creaked as it swung cautiously open. Rutgar sprang to his feet. His sword was out of its scabbard by the time Aelrhane stepped into the cell. Both men froze.

"What are you doing here?" Aelrhane demanded.

"I have every right to be here, Saxon. Not only am I lord here, but Gisela is my wife."

"Aye! Not that being your wife has helped her any." Aelrhane drew the long dagger, the scramasax, that hung from his belt. "I'm your sworn man, Rutgar, but I mean to take Gisela out of here, whether you will have it or not. I'll not permit a Saxon holy woman to burn because of that fat pig of a Frankish priest."

Rutgar lowered his blade. "Then we are here for the same purpose, Saxon."

Aelrhane's eyes narrowed. "You fought as the king's champion."

Rutgar shrugged. "I tried to lose. Someone should teach young Lothar to check his equipment before he fights. Either that or make sure he gets his wish to become a priest."

For a moment more Aelrhane scowled, then he laughed. "You're a good man, my lord. But what of your king? Perhaps this time 'twill be you taking to the woods as an outlaw."

Rutgar grinned wolfishly. "If that comes to pass, you can be sure I'd make a better job of it than you did."

"We shall see."

"For now I must see Gisela to a safe place."

"I'm with you, my lord. The night is quiet, but one never knows when another sword might help." He grinned. "Never let it be said that Aelrhane passed up an opportunity to make trouble."

Adalinde sat in her dark chamber staring at the wall. The wick of the lamp had long ago guttered in the fat that was its fuel. Even the brazier burned low, but the old woman did not bother to add more coal. Darkness was a friend. Adalinde wished it could be dark forever, for the morning's light would bring with it something she might not be able to face. She was a strong woman; she prided herself upon her strength. But she didn't know if that strength would sustain her through watching her granddaughter burn to death.

The old woman had watched Gisela from the time she first came to the stronghold seeking shelter. A grudging admiration for Ercangar's daughter had replaced contempt, and the admiration had over the years grown into a reluctant affection. The girl carried herself well, as should a woman from Adalinde's line. She did not allow her pitiful circumstances to bow her down; she did not allow people to bully her, not even Adalinde. When Rutgar came, Gisela had seen her opportunity and quickly maneuvered her way into a position of power, just as Adalinde would have done in like circumstances.

The thought of Gisela's grim fate was painful, and yet that fate must be fulfilled. The girl could have lived to be her people's savior, had she but heeded Adalinde's advice. She had been weak, though. Now she would save her people through her death. The Saxons would not stand still for this atrocity—the murder of one of their holy women, the insult to Saxon ways and Saxon gods. They would rise up and throw off the Frankish yoke. Gisela's suffering would not be in vain.

Adalinde sighed and rose stiffly from her chair. Her body was tired, yet her mind would not let her rest. She crossed to the brazier and spread her hand above the coals, leaving it there until pain made her draw it away. That agony would be multiplied a thousandfold for Gisela. Curse that wretched bishop for demanding such a cruel method of execution. She had told Father Gaunt a public hanging would be best, but Galvan, the bloated bishop, was out of her control. Gaunt she could have manipulated, just as she had when she'd prodded him to take his complaints to the bishop. Galvan was something else entirely. The worm didn't have an inkling that Gisela's death could be the strategic tap that would dislodge an avalanche of Saxon fury to crash down upon his precious Church and king.

The small, strategic tap. The small spark to set Ardun ablaze. Gisela must die. She would die, and Adalinde could bear that, but she couldn't bear watching her granddaughter burn. Destiny could ask only so much of an old woman, and here Adalinde would draw the line.

She relit the lamp and made her way through the torchlit passageway to Gisela's small infirmary. Without Gisela's presence the room was cold and lifeless. The pungent scent of drying herbs masked the damp mustiness that seeped in from the stone walls. The lamp flickered on rows of neatly arranged crocks and clay bowls. Adalinde searched among them until she found what she sought, then prepared her decoction with practiced, sure movements.

The old woman muttered softly, as if Gisela was listening through the powders and simples that had known the touch of her hands and the care of her labor. " 'Twill be easier this way, Granddaughter. You would not have been happy bringing your people into the Frankish fold."

Done at last, she poured her decoction into a wineskin that held a portion of Ardun's best wine. Only the best for Gisela. Then she looped the wineskin over her shoulder and concealed it beneath her cloak.

The yard was dark. The only torches were set along the palisade and immediately outside the manor door. Once into the yard itself, Adalinde could scarcely see to find her way to the cellar where Gisela was kept. Therefore she didn't spy the trio that came toward her in time to keep from stumbling into them.

Adalinde's exclamation mixed with several masculine curses before they all recognized each other. She stared, her eyes narrowing as she realized what Rutgar and Aelrhane were about.

"Where are you taking my granddaughter?"

"Move aside, old woman. This is not your affair." It was Rutgar the invader who dared to command her. One of his hands curled possessively around Gisela's arm; the other slid his sword back into its scabbard. With a sinking heart Adalinde realized her fatal miscalculation. She had not thought the Frankish devil was so besotted with Gisela that he would defy his king for her.

"What kind of lord defies the pronouncement of his own appointed judges, the laws of his own king?" Adalinde demanded.

Aelrhane stepped to the front. "Old woman, block our path at your peril."

"Aelrhane! What is this, you traitor?" Even Aelrhane had betrayed her. The most loyal of Saxons, the strongest and the best. He had also defected to the enemy. "You have given up, Aelrhane, even as we triumph?"

"There is no triumph here, Adalinde."

How like a man, to give in when sacrifice is required, to wilt when the battle became painful.

"You are like all the others of your sex, Aelrhane. You were a weak leader, good for raising trouble but not knowing how to wield power. And you!" She spat in Rutgar's direction. "You think yourself fit to rule here? A man who puts lust for a woman above loyalty to his king? Pah! Men! Their brains are between their legs and deflate as easily as their cocks do. There is not one of you fit to rule at Ardun. Not one of you."

Even now the fools thought her only a futile, useless old woman—one who had outgrown a female's only function in this world. Or perhaps not. She felt the chill of Rutgar's narrow-eyed stare, saw the sudden suspicion in Aelrhane's face.

" 'Twas you," Aelrhane ventured, half disbelieving.

"You wretched old woman. 'Twas you, wasn't it? Your own blood kin. Your granddaughter. And now Gisela as well."

Pride warred with guilt in Adalinde's breast. Finally Aelrhane understood, and understanding dawned in the Frank's eyes as well. She was the strong one. They had thought her a weak woman, but she was stronger than them all.

"Of course it was me, you useless, spineless oaf. I did what must be done. I have more right to rule here than any man who has set foot in Ardun since my husband died." She raised her arms and turned in a circle, gesturing wide to the few people were drifting into the yard along with morning's first gray light. Thomas the smith came out of the smithy to fetch coal to stoke the forge. A maid yawned her way to the poultry yard to free the chickens from their coop, and three men-at-arms carried wood toward the pyre that was being readied for Gisela's execution. One by one they stopped and squinted into the near darkness at Adalinde's beckoning. "Listen to me, all of you. Do you want to bow down to these puny, weak-willed geldings? Or do you want someone with strength and determination to sit in the master's chair?" Adalinde demanded. She wanted them to hear. She was their true leader, the last Saxon champion. They would rally behind her. They must; they were Saxon.

"I am strong!" she told them. "I had the strength and will to sacrifice two beloved granddaughters so that Saxons will continue to rule Saxon land. That strong am I! Who among you mighty men has the strength to make such sacrifices? Who?"

She pointed a finger at Rutgar, and fancied that her hand appeared as the hand of Fate. "You!" She let all her anger echo in that one word. "You fought Lothar and Aelrhane for Ardun, but I am the true Saxon ruler here. Fight me! I have more claim than they. I have more claim than anyone, as I am the only one here fit to rule!"

Rutgar was not the one who stepped forth to stop her, but the traitor Aelrhane. He held out his hand as though she were an old woman needing a man to lean upon. She looked around her, waiting for her people to vindicate her, waiting for them to hail her as she should be hailed. Blank stares, pity, contempt, loathing, and fear were all she saw. They didn't understand. The stupid swine. They didn't understand.

"Adalinde," Aelrhane said quietly. "Come with me."

No one leapt to support her. Adalinde surrendered to the flood of bitterness that swept through her soul. The dolts would not best her! She was the strong one. If Gisela would not sacrifice herself to rouse her people, then Adalinde would. She flung aside her cloak and lifted the wineskin to her lips.

Gisela broke loose of Rutgar's grasp and flew to her grandmother. She knocked the wineskin from the old woman's mouth, knowing instinctively that Adalinde was carrying no ordinary wine hidden beneath her cloak in the predawn darkness.

"Too late," Adalinde said. The fire had dimmed in her eyes, and she seemed almost normal again. " 'Twas a gift I meant for you, Granddaughter, a kinder death than they would have given you. I never planned such an ugly fate for one of my own blood. Believe that."

"I believe it." Gisela's heart squeezed painfully. She had watched reason flee from the old woman, watched as spittle flew from her mouth and the fevered brightness of mania flared in her eyes. The rigid control Adalinde had maintained upon herself all these years had broken, and what flowed through the broken barrier was madness. "What was in the wine, Grandmother?"

"Nothing you can counteract with your potions, child. I know herbs and poisons as well as you." Her eyelids drooped, she swayed, but still focused on Gisela by what seemed sheer strength of will. "You are no witch, Gisela. The old ways are dead, and our gods have lost their power."

Gisela reached for her, but Adalinde fended her off with a curse. The old woman turned proudly and walked back toward the manor. For a few steps she seemed to have regained her former dignity, but then she stumbled and collapsed. Gisela knelt beside her, waving off Rutgar and Aelrhane. The small flock of early risers looked on, warily keeping a respectful distance.

Adalinde's eyes fluttered open briefly, then closed in great weariness. "Your vision was wrong, Granddaughter. There will be no fire . . . now."

There was a fire. As the evening sun dropped below the horizon, Rutgar and Gisela stood side by side watching as flames consumed Adalinde's earthly remains. Rutgar's arm slipped around Gisela's waist and squeezed lightly. She leaned against him, melancholy with a mixture of emotions—relief, regret, sorrow, hope. Across from them, visible through the orange shimmer of the flames, stood Aelrhane, his face showing the same range of feelings that Gisela felt. Lothar also looked on. All of Ardun had watched, silent and stunned, while the pyre was lit, even Bishop Galvan and a grim-faced Father Gaunt, who had steadfastly refused to say any Christian words over Adalinde's body. The bishop, if not Gaunt, had readily laid

Gisela's supposed sorceries at the feet of the woman who had confessed her dire sins for one and all to hear—especially since the witch was already dead and could make no defense.

Now only the four of them were left. The flames were tamer, settling down to a steady, long burn. After a while, Lothar left. Aelrhane followed shortly. For a time Gisela was content simply to stand in the curve of Rutgar's arm, thinking about the changes that had come to Ardun and the changes that were yet to come.

"Is the war finally over?" she asked Rutgar.

Rutgar smiled down at her. "Our war is over, little witch."

"I'm not a witch," she reminded him. "Remember what Adalinde said."

"Adalinde was too bitter to see magic in anything."

Gisela chuckled. "You don't believe in magic, or in witches."

He leaned down and kissed her, slowly, softly. "Now I do. Who else but a witch, with magic at her fingertips and sorcery in her soul, could have turned a man of iron into flesh and blood?" He kissed her again. "Such sweet sorcery."

She smiled up at him. The warmth in his eyes heated her more than the fire of the pyre that had been meant for her. "We just won't tell the king."

"Nay. We won't." He leaned down and nipped at the lobe of her ear. " 'Tis a different sort of burning I have in mind for my wife."